Select praise for S

D1012365

"Morgan expertly avoids cliché and easy [...]
believable portrait of a family relearning how to love each other. Readers
will be delighted."
                    —*Publishers Weekly*, starred review, on *One More for Christmas*

"Morgan's latest Christmas tale will delight readers and give them the
perfect excuse to snuggle up for a few hours with a cup of hot cocoa."
                                        —*Booklist* on *The Christmas Escape*

"A journey of love and festive cheer."
                                        —*Woman's World* on *The Christmas Escape*

"Morgan's gently humorous aesthetic will leave readers feeling optimistic
and satisfied."   —*Publishers Weekly* on *A Wedding in December*

"Her lovingly created characters come to life, the [dialogue]
rings true, and readers will fly through the pages and then wish
for more."   —*Library Journal*, starred review, on *How to Keep a Secret*

"Packed full of love, loss, heartbreak, and hope, this may just be Morgan's
best book yet."   —*Booklist* on *One Summer in Paris*

"Warm, funny and often insightful, *The Summer Seekers* is a satisfying dose
of escapism with plenty of heart."   —*Shelf Awareness*

"The perfect gift for readers who relish heartwarming tales of sisters and
love."   —*Booklist* on *The Christmas Sisters*

"The ultimate road-trippin' beach read and just what we all need after the
long lockdown."   —*Booklist*, starred review, on *The Summer Seekers*

Also by Sarah Morgan

Beach House Summer
The Christmas Escape
The Summer Seekers
One More for Christmas
Family for Beginners
A Wedding in December
One Summer in Paris
The Christmas Sisters
How to Keep a Secret

For additional books by Sarah Morgan,
visit her website, www.sarahmorgan.com.

SARAH MORGAN

Snowed In *for* Christmas

If you purchased this book without a cover you should be aware
that this book is stolen property. It was reported as "unsold and
destroyed" to the publisher, and neither the author nor the
publisher has received any payment for this "stripped book."

Recycling programs
for this product may
not exist in your area.

ISBN-13: 978-1-335-63094-0

Snowed In for Christmas

Copyright © 2022 by Sarah Morgan

All rights reserved. No part of this book may be used or reproduced in
any manner whatsoever without written permission except in the case of
brief quotations embodied in critical articles and reviews.

This is a work of fiction. Names, characters, places and incidents are either
the product of the author's imagination or are used fictitiously. Any resemblance
to actual persons, living or dead, businesses, companies, events or locales is
entirely coincidental.

For questions and comments about the quality of this book, please contact us
at CustomerService@Harlequin.com.

HQN
22 Adelaide St. West, 41st Floor
Toronto, Ontario M5H 4E3, Canada
www.Harlequin.com

Printed in U.S.A.

To my family, for all the wonderful Christmases.

Snowed In

for

Christmas

1

Lucy Clarke pushed her way through the revolving glass doors and sprinted to the reception desk, stripping off her coat and scarf as she ran. She was late for the most important meeting of her life.

"There you are! I've been calling you. I'll take that—" Rhea, the receptionist, rose from her chair and grabbed the coat from her. "Wow. You look stunning. You're the only person I know who can look good in a Christmas sweater. Where did you find that one?"

"My grandmother knitted it. She said the sparkly yarn was a nightmare to work with. Feels weird wearing it today of all days, but Arnie insisted that we look festive so here I am, bringing the sparkle. They've started?" She'd hoped she might just make it, but the desks around her were all empty.

"Yes. Get in there."

Lucy replaced her running shoes with suede boots, hopping around as she pulled them on. Her fingers were so cold she fumbled. "Sorry. Forgot my gloves." She thrust her bag toward Rhea, who stowed it under the desk.

"What was it? Trains not running?"

"Signal failure. I walked."

"You *walked*? You couldn't have grabbed a cab?"

"Everyone else had the same idea so there wasn't one to be had." She dropped her scarf on Rhea's desk. "How is the mood?"

"Dismally lacking in festive joy given that we are all waiting to lose our jobs. Even the Christmas sweaters aren't raising a smile, and there are some truly terrible ones. Ellis from Accounts is wearing what looks like a woolly Christmas tree and it's making him itch. I've given him an antihistamine."

"We are not going to lose our jobs."

"You don't know that," Rhea said. "We've lost two big accounts in the last month. Not our fault, I know, but the end result is the same."

"So we need to replace them."

"I admire your optimism, but I don't want to raise my hopes and then have them crash around me. I love my job. Companies always say *we're a family* and it's usually a load of rubbish, but this one really does feel like a family. But it's not as if you really need to worry. You're brilliant at what you do. You'll get another job easily."

She didn't want another job. She wanted this job.

She thought about the fun they all had in the office. The laughter. Late-night pizza when they were preparing a pitch. Friday fizz when they had something to celebrate. The camaraderie and the friendship. She knew she'd never forget the support her colleagues had given her during what had undoubtedly been the worst couple of years of her life.

And then there was Arnie himself. She owed him everything. He'd given her back all the confidence that had been sucked from her in her first job, and he'd been there for her at her lowest moment. She'd worked for Arnie for six years and she still learned something new from him every day. She had a feeling she always would, because the company was small and nimble and everyone was encouraged to contribute, whatever their level of seniority. That wouldn't happen if she moved to one of the major players.

"Do I look okay?"

Rhea reached out and smoothed a strand of hair out of Lucy's eyes. "You look calmer than the rest of us. We're all in a state of panic. Maya has just bought her first flat. Ted's wife is expecting their first baby any day."

"Stop! If you keep reminding me of the stakes I'll be waving goodbye to calm." Lucy pressed her hands to her burning cheeks. "I ran the last mile. Tell me honestly, does my face look like a tomato?"

"It has a seasonal tint."

"You mean green like holly, or red like Santa?"

"Get in there——" Rhea gave her a push and Lucy sprinted toward the meeting room.

She could see all of them gathered around the table, Arnie standing at the head wearing the same red sweater he always wore when he wanted to be festive.

Arnie, who had set up this company over thirty years ago. Arnie, who had left his family's Christmas celebrations to be by her side in the hospital when her grandmother had died two years earlier.

Lucy pushed open the door and thirty heads turned toward her.

"Sorry I'm late."

"Don't worry. We've only just started." Arnie's smile was warm, but she could see the dark shadows under his eyes. The situation was hard for all of them, but particularly him. The unexpected blow to their bottom line meant he had difficult decisions to make. The thought of it was obviously giving him sleepless nights.

She'd seen him working until midnight at his desk, staring at numbers as if willpower alone could change them. It was no wonder he was tired.

She sat down in an empty seat and tried to ignore the horrible burn of anxiety.

"It's a Christmas campaign," Arnie returned to the subject they'd been discussing before she'd interrupted. "Think festive sparkle, think Christmas trees, think snow. We want photographs of log fires, luxurious throws, candles, mugs of hot chocolate heaped with marshmallows. And fairy lights. Fairy lights everywhere. The images need to be so festive and appealing that people who think they hate Christmas suddenly fall in love with Christmas. Most of all they need to feel that their Christmas will not be complete unless they buy themselves and everyone they know, a—" Arnie looked blank. "What is the product called again?"

Lucy's gaze slid to the box on the table. "The Fingersnug, Arnie."

"Fingersnug. Right." Arnie dragged his hand through his hair, leaving it standing upright. It was one of his many endearing habits. "The person who advised them on product name should rethink his job, but that's not our problem. Our problem is how to make it *the* must-have product for Christmas, despite the name and the lack of time to build a heavyweight campaign. And we're going to do that with social media. It's instant. It's impactful. Show people looking warm and cosy. Has anyone tried the damn thing? Lucy, as you were the last one in through the door and you always forget to wear gloves, you can take one for the team and thank me later."

Lucy dutifully slipped her hand inside the Fingersnug and activated it.

They all watched her expectantly.

Arnie spread his hands. "Anything? Are you feeling a warm glow? Is this life-changing?"

She felt depressed and a little sick, but neither of those things had anything to do with the Fingersnug. "I think it takes a minute to warm up, Arnie."

Ted looked puzzled. "It's basically a glove."

"Maybe—" Arnie planted his hands on the table and leaned forward "—but running shoes are running shoes until *we* persuade the public that this particular pair will change their lives. There are few original products out there, only original campaigns."

The comment was so Arnie. He was a relentless optimist.

Lucy felt the lump in her throat grow. Arnie had so many big things to deal with, but the client was still his priority. Even a client as small as this one.

"It's warming up," she said. "It may even cure my frostbite."

Arnie grabbed one from the box. "It would be the perfect stocking filler. I can see it now, keeping hands warm on frosty winter nights. Does it come in small sizes? Can kids use it? Is it safe? We don't want to damage a child."

"Children can use it, and it comes in different sizes." Lucy felt her fingers grow steadily warmer. "This might be the first time in my life I've had warm hands. It might be my new favorite thing."

"We need photographs that appeal to kids, or more specifically parents of kids. All those activities parents do at Christmas. Ice skating, reindeer—the client specifically mentioned reindeer," he floundered and glanced around for inspiration, "doing what? I have no idea. Where does one even find a reindeer, apart from on the front of Alison's sweater, obviously? And what do you do when you find one? Maybe someone could ride it. Yes! I love that idea." One of the reasons Arnie was such a legend in the creative agency world was because he let nothing get in the way of his imagination. Sometimes that approach led to spectacular success, but other times…

There was an exchange of glances. A few people shifted in their chairs and sneaked glances at Lucy.

She looked straight at him. "I think using reindeer is an inspired idea, Arnie. Gives us the potential for some great creative shots. Maybe a child clutching a stack of prettily wrapped parcels next to a reindeer, capture that look of wonder on their face, patch of snow, warm fingers—" she let her mind drift "—aspirational Christmas photos. Make it relatable."

"You don't think someone should ride it?"

She didn't hesitate. "No, Arnie, I don't."

"Why not? Santa does it."

"Santa is a special case. And he's generally in the sleigh." Were they seriously having this conversation?

There was a moment of tense silence and then Arnie laughed and the tension in the room eased.

"Right. Well…" Arnie waved a hand dismissively. "Get creative. Whatever you think will add that extra festive touch, you're to do it, Lucy. I won't tell you to impress me, because you always do."

"You want me to take on the account?" Lucy glanced round the room. There were twenty-nine other people in the meeting. "Maybe someone else should—"

"No. I want you on this. Getting influencers on board at this late stage is going to be next to impossible, and you're the one who makes the impossible happen." He rubbed his chest and Lucy felt a flash of concern.

"Are you feeling all right, Arnie?"

"Not brilliant. I had dinner with one of our competitors last night, Martin Cooper, CEO of Fitzwilliam Cooper. He was boasting about having too much business to handle, which was enough to give me indigestion. Or maybe it was the lamb. It was very spicy and I'm not good with spicy food." He stopped rubbing his chest and scowled. "Do you know he had the gall to ask if I could give him your contact list, Lucy? I told him it would do him no good, because it's your relationship with those contacts that adds the magic. The whole thing works because of you. You have a way of persuading people to do things they don't want to do, and definitely don't have time for."

Lucy chose not to mention the fact that a recruiter from Fitzwilliam Cooper had approached her twice in the last month about a job.

She thought it wise to change the subject. "Finding a reindeer in the middle of London might be—"

"There are reindeer in Finland and Norway, but we don't have the time or the budget for that. Wait—" Arnie lifted a hand. "Scotland! There are reindeer in Scotland. I read about it recently. I'm going to ask Rhea to track down that article and send it to you. Scotland. Perfect. I love this job. Don't you all love this job?"

Everyone grinned nervously because almost without exception they *did* love the job and were all wondering how much longer they'd be doing it.

Lucy was focused on the more immediate problem. How was she supposed to fit a trip to Scotland into her schedule?

"It's only two weeks until Christmas, Arnie."

"And you know what I always say. Nothing—" He put his hand to his ear and waited.

"Focuses the mind like a deadline," they all chorused and

he beamed like a conductor whose orchestra had just given a virtuoso performance.

"Exactly. You'll handle it, Lucy, I know you will. You're the one who always swoops in and saves the day and you're always great with everything Christmas." Arnie waved a hand as if he'd just gifted her something special. "The job is yours. Pick your team."

Lucy managed a weak smile. His enthusiasm and warmth swept you along. You couldn't say no to him, even if you wanted to.

And what would she say, anyway?

Christmas isn't really my thing anymore. No, she couldn't say that. She'd leaned on them hard at the beginning, when the agony of grief had been raw and sharp. But time had passed, and she couldn't keep being a misery, no matter how tough she found this time of year. She needed to pull herself together, but she hadn't yet figured out how to do that. There were days when she felt as if she hadn't moved forward at all.

But her priority right now was the company, which meant she would have to go to Scotland. Unless she could find reindeer closer to home. The zoo? Maybe she could persuade the client to switch the reindeer for a llama. Alpaca? Large sheep? Her mind wandered and then someone's phone pinged.

Ted jumped to his feet in a panic, sending papers flying. He checked his phone and turned pale. "This is it! It's coming. The baby I mean. The baby is coming. My baby. Our baby. I have to go to the hospital. Right now." He dropped his phone on the floor, bent to retrieve it and banged his head on the table.

Lucy winced. "Ouch. Ted—"

"I'm fine!" He rubbed his forehead and gave a goofy smile. "I'm going to be a dad."

Maya grinned. "We got that part, Ted. Way to go."

"Sophie needs me. I—" Ted dropped his phone again but this time Alison was the one who bent and retrieved it.

"Breathe, Ted."

"Yes. Good advice. Breathe. We've done lots of practice. I mean obviously it's Sophie who is meant to be doing that part, but no reason why I can't do it, too." Ted pushed his glasses back up his nose and cast an apologetic look at Arnie. "I'm—"

"Go." Arnie waved him toward the door. "And keep us updated."

Ted looked torn. "But this is an important meeting, and—"

"Family first." Arnie's voice was rough. "Go and be with Sophie. Call us when you have news."

Ted rushed out of the room, then rushed back in a moment later to collect the coat he'd forgotten, and back again a moment after that because he'd left his laptop bag.

"Also," he said, pausing by the door, breathless, "I have a train set arriving here today. Can someone take the delivery?"

Maya raised her perfectly sculpted eyebrows. "A train set?"

"Yes. It's a Christmas present for my baby." His voice cracked and Arnie walked round the table and put his hand on Ted's shoulder.

"A train set is a great choice. We'll take the delivery. Now go. Ask Rhea to call you a cab. You need to get to the hospital as fast as possible."

"Yes. Thank you." Ted sped out of the room, knocking into the doorframe on his way out.

Maya winced. "Can they give him a sedative or something? And is a cab really going to be quicker than taking the train?"

"It's going to be quicker than Ted getting flustered and lost," Arnie said. "At least the cab will deliver him to the door, hopefully in one piece and with all his belongings still about his person."

"A train set?" Ryan, the intern, grinned. "He does know that a baby can't play with a train set, doesn't he?"

"I suspect it will be Ted playing with the train set," Arnie said. "Now, exciting though this is, we should return to business. Where were we? Fingersnug. Lucy? Are you on it?"

"I'm on it, Arnie." She'd find a way to show it at its most appealing. She'd put together a last-minute Christmas campaign. She'd find a reindeer from somewhere. She'd pull in favors from her contacts, content creators with high profiles and engaged followings who she'd worked with before. She'd find a way to handle it all and try not to think about the fact that her job was occasionally ridiculous.

Arnie cleared his throat and Lucy glanced at him.

It was obvious from the look on Arnie's face that they'd reached that point in the meeting everyone had been dreading.

"Now for the tough stuff. You all know we lost two big accounts last month. Not our fault. One company is downsizing because they've lost so much business lately, and the other is trying to cut costs and decided to go with someone cheaper. I tried telling him that you get what you pay for, but he wasn't listening. It's a significant blow," he said. "I'm not going to pretend otherwise."

"Just give us the bad news, Arnie. Have you made a decision about who you're going to let go?" Maya, always direct, was the one to voice what they were all wondering.

"I don't want to let anyone go." He let out a long breath. "And not just because you're a fun bunch of people when you're not being annoying."

They all tried to grin.

"Thanks, Arnie."

"And the truth is that to win accounts, we need good people. To staff accounts, we need good people. But I also need to be able to pay those people and unless we bring in a significant piece of business soon, we're in trouble." He rested his hands on the table and was silent for a moment. "I've never lied to you and I'm not going to start now. This is the most challenging time we have faced since I started the company thirty years ago, but all is not lost. I have a few new business leads, and I'm going to be following those up personally. And there's something else we're going to try—speculative, but worth a shot. It's major. If we could land that, then we'd be fine."

But what if they weren't fine?

Lucy thought about Ted and his new baby. She thought about Maya and her new flat and how scared she'd been taking on the responsibility of a mortgage. She thought about herself, about how much she loved this job and how badly she needed to keep doing it. In the early days after she'd lost her grandmother, work had given her a reason to get out of bed in the morning. Her job was her source of security, both financial and emotional.

It was the most important thing in her life.

She felt her chest grow tight.

She couldn't handle more change. More loss.

She gazed through the glass of the meeting room, forcing herself to breathe steadily. From her vantage point twenty floors up she had an aerial view of London. She could see the dome of St. Paul's Cathedral and the River Thames winding its way under Tower Bridge. Three red London buses nosed their way through traffic, and people scurried along, heads down looking at their phones, always in a hurry.

A lump formed in her throat.

If she had to leave the company, would it mean moving?

She didn't want to move. She'd been raised here, by her grandmother, who had loved everything about London and had been keen to share its joys and its history with her grand-daughter.

Do you see this, Lucy? Pudding Lane, where the Great Fire of London started in 1666.

They'd visited the Tower of London, Lucy's favorite place. They'd strolled through the parks hand in hand, picnicked on damp grass, fed ducks, rowed a boat on the Serpentine. Her annual Christmas treat had been a visit to the Royal Opera House to watch a performance of *The Nutcracker.* Every street and every landmark, famous and not so famous, were tangled up with memories of her grandmother.

She loved London. She belonged here. Sometimes it felt as if the city had wrapped its arms around her, as her grandmother had in those early days after her parents had died.

This time of year was particularly tough. It was impossible not to think about her grandmother at Christmas. Impossible not to wish for one more day with her, walking through the city looking at the sparkling window displays, and then sipping hot chocolate in a warm café. They'd talked about everything. There wasn't a single thing Lucy had held back from her grandmother, and she desperately missed that. She missed being able to talk freely, without worrying that she was a burden.

Unconditional love. Love that could be depended on. That was what she missed, but that gift had been ripped away from her, leaving her feeling cold, exposed and alone.

She sat, made miserable by memories, and then caught sight of Arnie's face and felt guilty for being selfish and thinking about herself when he was going through hell. He was worrying about everyone's futures.

They had to win a big account, they *had* to.

Arnie was still talking. "Let's start by looking at the positive. We are harnessing the power of social media and changing the way brands reach their customers. We are experts in influencer marketing. We are changing consumer habits—"

Lucy made a few notes on the pad in front of her.

In less than a minute she had a list of about ten people to call who might be able to help her with the Fingersnug. People she'd built a relationship with. People who would be only too happy to do her a favor, knowing that they'd be able to reclaim it in the future.

"We are raising our profile. And on that note, a special shout-out to Lucy, our cover girl." Arnie gestured to the latest edition of the glossy marketing magazine stacked on the table. "*The Face of Modern Marketing*. Looking good, Lucy. Great interview. Great publicity for the company. If any of you still haven't read it then you should. Lucy, we're proud of you and for the rest of you—let's have more of this. Let's get ourselves noticed."

There was a chorus of "Go Lucy," and a few claps.

Lucy gave a self-conscious smile and glanced at the cover. She barely recognized her own image. She'd spent an hour in hair and makeup before the photoshoot and had felt completely unlike herself. On the other hand, feeling unlike herself hadn't been a bad thing. The Lucy in the picture looked as if she had her life together. The Lucy in the picture didn't stand in front of the bathroom mirror in the morning hyperventilating, worrying that her control was going to shatter and she was going to lose it in public. She didn't stand there feeling as if her emotions were a ticking time bomb, ready to explode without warning. Anxiety had plagued her since she'd lost her grandmother. She felt as if she was on the edge, navigating life with no safety net.

And now it was almost Christmas, and if ever there was a time designed to emphasize the lack of family, it was now. The worst thing was that she'd always *adored* Christmas. It had been her absolute favorite time of the year until that horrible Christmas two years before when she'd spent Christmas Eve and Christmas Day in a vigil by her grandmother's hospital bed. Now Christmas wasn't tinsel and fir trees and wrapping up warm to listen to carol singers. It was beeping machines, and doctors with serious faces, and her grandmother's frail, bruised hand in hers. *Massive stroke*, they'd said, but she'd hung on until December 31, before finally leaving Lucy to face the new year, and all the years ahead, without the person she loved most. The person who had taken on the role of both parent and grandparent. The one person who knew her and loved her unconditionally.

The previous year she'd forced herself to celebrate Christmas, although maybe *celebrate* was the wrong word. She bought herself a tree, and she decorated it with all the ornaments she and her grandmother had collected over the years. *I'm doing this, Gran. You'd be proud of me.* But it had been hard work, the emotional equivalent of running a marathon uphill in bare feet. Christmas had always been a magical time, but now the magic was gone, and she didn't know how to get it back. The truth was she was dreading it, and given the choice she would have canceled Christmas.

Panic rose, digging its claws into her skin.

"This is the point where I'm going to challenge you all," Arnie said. "Do I believe in miracles? Maybe I do, because I have my eye on one of the biggest prizes of all. One piece of new business in particular that would solve all our problems. The biggest fish in the pond. Any guesses?" He glanced around expectantly. "Think sportswear brands. Think fitness and gyms."

And now she had a whole new reason to panic.

Not sports. Anything but that.

She was intimidated by gyms and she had no reason to

wear sportswear. Her exercise regime involved racing round London meeting clients and influencers, and scoping out new cool places to include in their visual campaigns.

Wishing Ted was here because it was right up his street, Lucy scrolled through the big brands in her mind, discarding the ones she knew were already locked into other agencies.

One stood out.

"Are you talking about Miller Active? The CEO is Ross Miller."

"You know him?"

"Only by reputation. His family own Glen Shortbread." Her grandmother had described it as *comfort in a tin* and it had been her favorite treat at Christmas.

"Is Glen Shortbread the one in the pretty tin?" Maya chewed the end of her pen. "The one that changes every year? Last year was snowy mountains and a loch? I love it. Delicious. I buy it for my mum every year. Just looking at it makes me feel Christmassy."

"That's the one." Lucy still had three of the empty tins in her apartment, even though she didn't have room for them. She couldn't bear to throw them away, so she used them as storage. Two were full of old photographs, and the third held the letters her grandmother had written to her during her first year of college when she'd been homesick and tempted to give it up.

"Same Miller, different business." Arnie rubbed his chest again. "Son Ross went a different route."

"Rebel Ross," Lucy murmured and saw Arnie glance at her with a question in his eyes. "I read an article—last year, I think. That was the title. 'Rebel Ross.' All about how he was the first generation not to go into the family business. He wanted to strike out on his own. The implication was that he and his father were like two stags fighting over their territory, although given the way Miller Active has grown I'm assuming he has proved himself by now. There was a lot about the family. Grandmother—can't remember her name. Jane, maybe? No, it was Jean. His father is Douglas, still at the helm of Glen Shortbread. His mother is Glenda, she's been involved with the business from time to time, although I'm not sure she still is. There are three children—Ross, obviously. He's the eldest. Then Alice, who is a doctor, and Clemmie, who—I don't know what she does."

Maya was staring. "How do you remember all that?"

"I have a good memory for useless facts." She wasn't going to tell them the truth. That the article had stuck in her mind because she'd had serious family envy.

There had been photographs of the family estate in the Scottish Highlands, showing ancient trees and herds of deer and their baronial home, Miller Lodge, with its gardens sloping down to a deep loch. There had been glossy photos of the whole family gathered around a roaring log fire, their world-famous shortbread piled on an antique plate on a table in front of them. Who had been in that photo? She couldn't remember. She'd been too busy gazing at their big, perfect family and envying their perfect life. They'd all been smiling. Even the dogs had looked contented. The message was that no matter what happened in life they had each other, and their gorgeous home. After she'd salivated over the picture, she'd ripped out those pages and thrown them away because no good ever came from wanting what you couldn't have. Now she wished she'd kept them. It would have been a good place to start with her research.

"I'm impressed." Arnie seemed cheered by her response. "Background is important, we all know that. Context. Where does a client come from? What does he need? These are the questions we ask ourselves. They're the questions you're going to be asking yourselves when you come up with ideas for a campaign. That's the challenge. I'm hearing a rumor that Ross Miller has reached out to a few agencies. He wants to shake things up."

"He's invited us to pitch?"

"Not exactly." Arnie shuffled some papers. "But he would, if he knew how good we were. We need to grab his attention. We need to find a way to do that. We need to be the ones to give him what he needs."

Lucy thought back to that article. It seemed to her that Ross Miller already had everything he needed.

"Doesn't Miller Active use Fitzwilliam Cooper?"

"Yes, but their last campaign was uninspired. That's just my opinion, obviously, but that doesn't mean I'm not right. Miller Active has a strong customer base, but seem unable to expand beyond that. They're going to be shopping around in the New Year. They need us. And it's our job—" Arnie waved a hand at the team seated around the table "—to persuade them of that fact. Over the next few weeks, I want you to come up with some ideas that will blow them away. Then we need to find a way to get those ideas in front of Ross Miller. It will be our number one priority for the New Year."

"This is one for Ted," Lucy said. "He lives at the gym."

Maya leaned back in her chair. "He's not going to be going to the gym for a while or Sophie will kill him."

"We have to assume that Ted is out of the picture, but we can handle this without him."

"I love their yoga pants, if that helps," Maya said. "They're the only ones that don't move when you do downward dog. But somehow I don't think I can build a whole campaign out of that."

"We'll figure it out." Arnie gathered up his files and his laptop. "The timing is good. Everyone thinks about fitness in January, right? We've all stuffed ourselves over the festive period. Turkey. Multiple family meals."

If only…

Lucy kept her expression neutral. "It's true that there is a focus on health and fitness in January."

"All we have to do is find a unique angle, and that's what we're good at."

Maybe. But a sports client? Why did it have to be a sports client?

If gym membership was what it was going to take to save Arnie's company, she was doomed.

Unless…

An idea exploded into her head out of nowhere. Maybe the perfect idea.

She opened her mouth and closed it again. Maybe it wasn't a perfect idea. She needed to think about it, work it through in her head. But still…

She was definitely onto something.

Ross Miller hadn't built a successful business in a competitive space by being predictable. When he'd started out there was no way he could outspend the big brands, so he'd chosen to outsmart them and that approach had seen his business grow faster than all predictions.

Arnie was right. Whatever they came up with, had to be creative and the idea bubbling in her brain was certainly a little different.

People started to file out of the meeting room, except for Arnie, who was checking his phone.

Lucy stood up and headed to the coffee machine. She poured two cups and took one to him. Now that she was close, she could see that his face was pale. "Have you taken something for that indigestion? Maybe I shouldn't give you this coffee."

"Give me the coffee. The indigestion will pass, I'm sure." He took the coffee and caught her eye. "What?"

"I'm worried about you."

"Why? I'm fine. Never better."

It was tough, Lucy thought, keeping up an act. No one knew that better than she did.

"Everyone has gone. It's just you and me. You can be honest."

His shoulders sagged. "There's no fooling you, is there? I'm worried, that's true. But all we can do is our best. I'm going to reach out to a few more contacts this afternoon. It will be all right, I'm sure it will. Next year will be better. It has to be better."

"About Ross Miller—"

"Don't worry. I know sport isn't your thing," Arnie said. "It was just an idea. Grasping at straws. Even if we came up with an idea that was a game changer, Ross Miller is a tough cookie. I doubt he's going to give us a meeting or agree to hear our pitch. He has always used the big names. We're not on his approved agency list."

"Then we need to get ourselves on that list."

She was not going to give up. And she wasn't going to let him give up, either.

"We can do this, Arnie."

"That's the spirit." He managed a smile. "You're not to worry. If the worst happens, I can make some calls and you'll be in another job before the day is out."

"I don't want another job."

"I know." He put the coffee down untouched. "You and I go back a long way, Lucy. And frankly that makes me feel worse. We have so many loyal and wonderful people in this company and I've let you down. We should have spread our net wider. We relied on a few big accounts, instead of taking on multiple small ones. It has left us vulnerable, and that's on me."

It was typical of Arnie to take responsibility. Typical of him to blame himself and not others.

"You're not responsible for the economy and world events, Arnie. You're brilliant."

"Not so brilliant." He gave a tired smile. "Anyway, enough of that. How are you doing, Lucy? I know this is a difficult enough time of year for you without all these additional worries."

"I'm doing fine, thanks." Now she was the one putting on an act, but that was fine. The last thing he needed was to listen to her problems on top of everything else. "You've been working too hard. Maybe you should go home."

"Too much to do." He rubbed his hand across his chest again. "I need to make some calls. Start putting together some ideas ready for January."

"Right." But if major agencies were going to be pitching to Miller Active in the New Year, they needed to get in front of Ross Miller before that. He was known to be a workaholic. Surely he wasn't going to waste time partying around the Christmas tree?

She left the room and when she glanced back she saw Arnie slumped in a chair at the head of the long empty table, his head in his hands.

Feeling sick for him, she headed to the watercooler. She was going to do whatever she could to fix this, and not only because this job was the one thing in her life that was good and stable.

Maya was leaning against the wall, swallowing down an entire cup of water. "Sorry." She stood to one side when she saw Lucy. "Fear makes me thirsty. I'm pretending this is gin. What are we going to do?"

"We're going to go after new accounts, starting with Miller Active. What we're not going to do is panic." At least not outwardly. She was keeping all her panic carefully locked inside.

"If you're serious about Miller Active then you should be in a panic. Do you have any idea who you're dealing with? Ross Miller has a black belt in three different martial arts. He can ski. He's a killer in the boxing ring. He sailed across the Atlantic. He has muscles in all the right places."

"When have you ever seen his muscles?"

"In photos." Maya put her cup down. "He did some fitness challenge for charity last summer—trust me, I would have handed over my credit card happily."

"You have nothing but debt on your credit card. And what does any of this have to do with pitching?"

"I love you to bits, but your exercise program is couch to kitchen. Is there any chance I can turn you into an exercise fanatic before January so we can increase your credibility? Or give you any credibility at all?"

"I don't need to be an exercise fanatic."

Maya frowned. "Why? This is a fitness account. Sportswear. The brief is to expand their customer base. No offense, Lucy, but do you even own yoga pants?"

"No. But in this case it's going to work to my advantage." Lucy helped herself to water. "Think about it. Ross Miller wants new customers. What is the profile of a new customer? Not someone like Ted, who is already a convert. It's people like me, who would never go near a gym. What would it take to make me buy a pair of sexy workout leggings and show up for a morning weights session?"

"I honestly can't answer that," Maya said. "Knowing you, I'm guessing it would take something major."

"The Miller account is major."

"Lucy, I'm your biggest admirer but be realistic. The major

agencies are pitching. This is the big time. How would you begin to compete?"

"By being smarter than they are, and by getting ahead of them."

"But it's Christmas."

"Exactly. It's the perfect time to work."

"For you, maybe, but not for most people. And probably not for Ross Miller." Maya hesitated. "Look, about Christmas—I've already told you, you can come and spend it with Jenny and me. It's our first Christmas in the new place. Jenny's mother is joining us, and her brother. Not her dad because he still can't bear seeing the two of us together and I don't want to spend Christmas with a knot in my stomach."

"I'm sorry."

"Don't be. I've never been happier, that's the truth, and if some family tension is the price I have to pay then I'll gladly pay it. And we'd love to have you."

"It's a kind offer and I appreciate it, but no thanks." She knew Christmas would be rough. She didn't want to inflict her misery on anyone else, and pretending to be fine when you weren't fine became exhausting after a while. Her Christmas gift to herself would be to give herself permission to feel horrible.

Maya sighed. "Lucy—"

"I'm fine, honestly. I'm going to be busy with work." She didn't mention her conversation with Arnie. If the team knew how worried he was, they'd worry even more than they already were. What was the point of ruining everyone's Christmas? It would be better for the team to return from their holidays well rested and optimistic. "I'm going to come up with a plan to get us in front of Ross Miller."

"I can't bear to think of you on your own and working over Christmas."

"I'm thrilled to be working. It will make the whole thing so much easier."

This would be her second Christmas alone. Third, if you counted the one she'd spent with her grandmother in hospital although Arnie had been by her side for that one. She'd survived the others. She'd survive this one. Work would be just the distraction she needed.

"Lucy—"

"Christmas is just one day, Maya. This year I'm going to be too busy even to notice it." She'd been dreading Christmas, but at least now she had a purpose. "I'm going to find out everything there is to know about the Miller family and Ross Miller in particular, and I'm going to secure a meeting with him before the other agencies have even swallowed their first helping of turkey. And then we are going to knock him dead with our brilliance."

"I'm assuming you don't mean that literally." Maya didn't look convinced. "The competition are big players. They're motivated."

Lucy thought about Arnie, sitting with his head in his hands. She thought about Ted and his new baby. About Maya spending her first Christmas in her new flat. She thought about her own situation. "I'm one step further on than motivated. I'm desperate." Desperate for Arnie. Desperate for her colleagues. Desperate for herself.

"That's all very well," Maya said, "but how are you going to get yourself in front of Ross Miller?"

"That's something I'm—" Lucy stopped as she heard Rhea shout her name. She turned. "What?"

"Come quickly!" Rhea was breathless and pale. "Arnie has collapsed. The paramedics are on their way. Oh, Lucy, this is terrible."

2

Glenda

"She's bringing him home!" Glenda burst into the kitchen. Was this the best news she'd had all year? Very possibly. "Did you see the email?"

"I'm eating breakfast. I never check my emails when I'm eating breakfast. It's bad for the digestion." Douglas put his spoon down. "Who are we talking about?"

"Alice! Alice has invited Nico to spend Christmas with us." And already Glenda's mind was racing ahead. "I'm excited."

"You're excited to have another mouth to feed?"

"I'm excited because our workaholic daughter is finally in a relationship. And all the signs are that it's serious. She has never brought anyone home before. Do you know what this means? At last there is something in her life other than work. *Someone*. I've been so worried about the lack of balance in her life. This is significant, Douglas." She knew she worried far too much about her children, but she couldn't help it. And she knew Alice. Her eldest daughter was single-minded in her relentless pursuit of perfection. She'd been the same as a child. The mere thought of failure had made her study into the night until Glenda had been forced to intervene.

"Workaholic?" He frowned. "You say it as if it's a failing, but there's nothing wrong with hard work."

"There is when it's to the exclusion of everything else. Balance, that's what a person needs. But I don't blame Alice for the way she is. Ross is the same. It's in their DNA." She gave him a pointed look, although she had to admit that since his heart scare a year earlier he'd slowed down a lot. He'd lost weight and started exercising. It would have been good if he'd also reduced his working hours, but she knew that was asking too much.

"You're blaming me? Clemmie is mine, too, so how do you explain that?"

"She takes after me." Glenda gave him a smile. "I'll put them in the Loch Room. I've been planning a makeover for that room for a while. Do you think Fergus could help me turn it around in a week?"

Douglas grunted. "The boy is a carpenter, not cupid. And he is busy finishing off his own house, and also our stable block."

"This takes precedence over your stable block. And he may be a carpenter, but he can turn his hand to anything practical, you know that." She picked up her phone and typed a message to Fergus. "I'm sure he'll help. We're practically family. He and Clemmie were inseparable growing up."

"That was years ago. They're adults now. And what's wrong with Alice's bedroom, anyway?"

"Her bedroom isn't big enough for two. They're going to want privacy. Space to spend time alone together." Glenda sent the message and put her phone down. "And it's not as romantic as the Loch Room. I want their stay to be perfect. Why didn't I do something about it in the summer?" She was cross with herself for not pushing ahead with something she'd been meaning to do for ages. "This is a special occasion. We need something grander. I can't wait to meet Alice's boyfriend. What do you think he's like?"

"Tolerant," Douglas said, "if he's with our Alice."

She ignored that. "He's a heart surgeon. I never know what to say to surgeons. I hope he isn't arrogant. Remember when I talked to that one about my eyes when I was having all those problems? He made me feel about six years old. So patronizing! I hope Nico isn't intimidating. What if he doesn't like us? Or the lodge?" She glanced around, trying to imagine how a stranger might see her much loved home. Why was it that when you lived in a place the imperfections melted into the background? There were scratches on the kitchen table, and a small dent in the wall, a legacy from that time Ross had once ridden his bike indoors. It was a home that was loved, and lived in. The place had nurtured her family and she would no more criticize its appearance than she would her own face. A wrinkle? A silvery hair? It was all part of life. Or so she'd always thought. Now she wasn't so sure. She wanted it to look its best. They redecorated from time to time, but there were always more important demands on the family's time and finances. The house was big, old and drafty and swallowed money as if it were permanently thirsty. "Will he mind chaos do you think?"

"If he's dating Alice I doubt it. That girl doesn't know the meaning of the word *tidy*."

"She's thirty, Douglas. A woman. A doctor. Responsible for lives." And she was proud of her for pursuing her dreams. Alice had always wanted to be a doctor. As a child she'd operated on dolls and run clinics for her siblings. Glenda had lost count of the times she'd had to unwrap bandages from Clemmie's limbs. And like everything else in Alice's life, once she set a goal for herself she didn't deviate. She focused on what she needed to do to achieve that goal, and she did it whatever the cost.

It was so different from her own experience. She'd married Douglas when she was eighteen and had started working for Glen Shortbread right away. It hadn't entered anyone's heads, not even hers, that she might do something different. It was a family business and she was family. She'd chosen to stop working after the children were born, a decision she'd never regretted.

Douglas peered at her over the top of his glasses. "Maybe she is a doctor, but she's family, which means I can speak the truth. And the truth is that I hope when she's seeing patients she is more organized than she was at home, or her patients don't stand a hope."

"I'm sure she is, although I do know what you mean." It was sometimes hard to see your child as an adult. Hard to imagine their Alice making life-and-death decisions. She had a clear vision of her daughter with braces and pigtails. But the one thing she'd always shown was fierce determination. *I can do this myself. Don't help me.*

"It will alter the dynamic, having a stranger here. Are you sure you don't mind?"

"He's not a stranger to Alice and hopefully he won't be a stranger to us for long, either. It will be fun. I love Christmas and the fact that one of our children is finally in a serious relationship is the icing on the cake. Which reminds me—" she grabbed a pen and a scrap of paper from the messy pile at the end of the table and started scribbling notes for herself "—I still need to ice the cake. And I'll need to order a bigger turkey."

Douglas watched her. "How serious do you think this is? Do I need to put on my stern father act? Ask him his intentions?"

"You do not. You are not going to do anything embarrassing. No getting out the baby photos. No telling Nico about that time Alice fell off the stage during the school play, or how she fought with her brother." She glanced up from the list she was making. "For once in your life you are going to behave yourself, Douglas Fraser Miller."

"Where's the fun in that?" He paused. "And I feel obliged to point out that it was *you* who caused chaos two Christmases ago when you reminded Alice that when you were her age you'd already had two children, and that you were always available to help with babysitting."

"That wasn't my finest moment." Glenda cringed at the memory. "She stormed out, do you remember?"

"I do because I was the one who had to fix the painting that fell off the wall when she slammed the door."

"It was your fault. You poured me a gin and tonic that was more gin than tonic."

"It was Christmas."

"And I ended up saying things that normally I just think. Like how much I would love to have grandchildren." Remembering made her want to rewind the clock. "I cannot *believe* I said that aloud. This Christmas I'm not going to touch a drop."

"That will be boring." Douglas was studying her. "Are we talking wedding-serious, do you think?"

"I don't know, and I'm not going to ask. I've learned that lesson." But that didn't mean she didn't care, of course, because what parent didn't want to see their child settled with their own family, whatever shape or form that took. She put her pen down. "Times change, don't they? These days people don't need a piece of paper to say they're committed."

"If you're committed you're committed. Why not formalize it?"

"They might argue that if you're committed, you don't need to formalize it. If we're putting them in the Loch view room, I'll need to buy new bedding. The place can be chilly in winter." She made a note for herself and noticed she'd already filled more than half the paper. "And I'm going to cover the cushions on the window seat. I bought the fabric last year and never got round to it. And I have new towels for the bathroom."

"You're not running a five-star hotel, Glenda. Why can't they just take us as they find us?"

"Because they're not random callers. They're family. I want them to love being home."

"Home is about family, not a fluffy bath towel." His tone was rough. "And what are you hoping for? That one of our children will decide that misty mountains and the still waters of the loch are more appealing than those crowded, noisy London streets? You're trying to tempt them to stay for good?"

He knew her so well.

"Are you telling me you wouldn't be delighted if that happened, too?"

"I would. But it isn't going to happen. The three of them have made their choice, even our Clemmie, who was always such a home bird."

And of all her children, she worried most about Clemmie. "Remember that sleepover when I had to fetch her at two in the morning because they were all watching horror movies and she was scared out of her wits? I was surprised when she chose to go to London."

"The others are in London."

"That's different. Alice wanted to be in a London teaching hospital. Ross needed to be in the city, too. That all makes sense. But Clemmie? She could have been a nanny anywhere. Why London? It doesn't seem like her, somehow." She'd often wondered what had triggered that decision. Keeping up with her siblings? That was something she'd always done. Or maybe something else. Glenda had her own thoughts about that, but she kept them to herself. "I always thought she'd be the one to stay close to home. Why are you scowling?"

"Because you're reminding me that we're a family business. Six generations," Douglas said. "So why is it that none of my offspring want to work in this business?"

"Because times change. They needed to make their own choices. Make their own mark on the world."

"I know all that," he grumbled. "Doesn't mean I can't sometimes be upset about it. It's not as if Ross isn't interested in business. He is. Just not mine."

She was sad for him because she knew how much he would have loved to have Ross working alongside him. And she would have liked that, too, because then maybe Douglas wouldn't have worked so hard.

"Ross is happy. That's what matters. And his choice of business makes sense. You know how interested Ross has always been in sport and fitness. All those climbing courses he went on as a child. Sailing lessons. Any excuse to get out there and do something active, and Ross grabs it with both hands."

Douglas glanced at her. "And gives you sleepless nights worrying."

"Maybe, but that's my problem not his." Glenda pushed the bowl of fresh fruit salad toward her husband. "Now finish your oats and stop pretending to be fierce or I'll call Dr. Hammond and he will lecture you about your blood pressure."

Douglas picked up his spoon without enthusiasm. "What does he know about anything?"

"He knows a great deal. As do you. You're a clever man. If you stopped scowling, you'd be handsome." She stood up and walked around the table. "Please tell me you're not going to do this again, Douglas."

"Do what?"

She wrapped her arms round him and kissed him. "Ruin Christmas with your passive-aggressive comments."

"I've never ruined Christmas. It's my favorite time of year. The whole family together. And I'm never passive-aggressive. I'm direct. I say it how it is." He rubbed her hand gently and Glenda sighed.

"No. You say it how you *wish* it was. Not the same thing." It was hard for him, she knew that. But it was also hard for Ross. And hard for her because she was always in the middle. The peacekeeper. "You make him feel guilty, Douglas, but he's doing what he loves." She straightened. "You lived your life, and now you have to let him live his."

"Why are you putting it in the past tense?" He poked at the contents of his bowl. "I'm still living my life, and I intend to keep on living it. That's why I'm chewing oats and fruit and not sinking my teeth into bacon and black pudding."

"I know." She placed a bowl of yogurt next to him and saw him shudder. "And I know how much this business means to you, but Ross's business means a lot to him, too. He's made such a success of it, but have you ever told him that?"

Douglas picked apple out of his bowl. "Too much praise makes a man complacent. Imagine what he could do for this place if he put all that energy and expertise behind Glen Shortbread. I'd be able to retire."

She sat down next to him. "You'd hate to retire, but I do wish you would reduce your hours."

"How am I supposed to do that? The business needs me. And we're not going to talk about that now. Why is there chopped apple in this fruit salad? I hate chopped apple."

His smile was a little more strained than usual. Another person might not have noticed but she'd known him since he was ten years old and she knew every expression.

"Is the business in trouble?" Over the years they'd shared the good and the bad. Since she'd stepped away from the business, she only knew what he shared with her.

He gave up on his fruit and reached for his coffee. The one cup a day he allowed himself. "No. But things are changing. The way we run the business is changing." He took a sip of coffee. "The days of personal contact are gone. Now it's all social media and influencers—what am I supposed to do with that? Wear a kilt and dance around a plate of shortbread? I'm out of step, that's the truth."

"Nonsense. You've embraced all the latest technology."

"But it's not natural for me. Not like it is for Clemmie and Alice. Their phones are an extension of them."

"That's why you employ a range of people, plenty of them social media savvy."

"I know, but there's probably more we should be doing. Do you know what they call me? Dinosaur Douglas. I suppose I should be grateful it's not Dino Doug." He gave a laugh and finished his coffee. "I'm getting too old for this, Glenda."

"Not true." It was awful to see her usually confident husband doubting himself. She covered his hand with hers.

"It is true. If my son was in the business this would be the point where I'd be stepping back. You're right, I should be reducing my hours. I should be spending more time with you. Taking you on a world cruise."

"Do I look like someone who would be interested in a world cruise? Don't you know me at all?"

He gave a tired smile. "It would be nice to have the option."

Paris, she thought. If she could go anywhere, it would be Paris.

"You should talk to Ross," she said. "Ask his advice. He's made a great success of his business. He might have ideas about how you could structure the management team so you can cut your hours."

"If I raise it, he'll think I'm putting pressure on him. Trying to make him feel guilty. Enough of that. Talking of business, that magazine is still pestering me for photographs."

"Oh." Glenda sat up. "That's good. All publicity welcome."

"Maybe. They want the whole family together. Granny. Kids. Dogs."

Hunter, their black Labrador, rose from his position on the floor by Douglas's chair and wagged his tail. Douglas reached down to stroke his head. "Fancy being a film star, boy? We'd have to cover up your shady past."

Hunter pressed his nose into his hand.

Glenda remembered the day she'd brought him back from the rescue center, skinny and unloved. The whole family had been mourning the loss of Bess, their golden retriever, who had been a loyal and constant companion for twelve years. Douglas had scolded Glenda for bringing another dog into the house before they were ready, and then fallen in love with Hunter about a minute later. They'd been inseparable since. Hunter accompanied Douglas wherever he went, whether it was a hike in the hills or to the office. The only person who loved Hunter more than Douglas was Clemmie.

"When is the deadline for this article?"

"The article is written. It's just photos. I told them the children wouldn't be home until Christmas, but they were fine with that." He scratched Hunter behind the ears. "Think they'll do it?"

Glenda wasn't at all sure. The children hated being involved in those family photoshoots. "You can always ask."

"I'll ask Clemmie. She never says no, and she will talk the others into it."

"Perhaps if you explain that we need the publicity—"

"I'm not telling them that." He glanced at her and read her mind. "Not because I'm being stubborn. They'd worry, and I don't want them to worry."

"Douglas—" She broke off as the kitchen door opened and her mother-in-law walked in. Jean Miller—Nanna Jean to the whole family—was eighty-six but looked ten years younger.

Douglas stood up in a gesture of old-fashioned courtesy and waved a hand at the empty space laid at the table. "Come and join us. Are you willing and able to be part of a family photograph?"

Nanna Jean patted her hair. "Providing I'm cast in the role of glamorous granny." She took a long hard look at her son. "Why the serious face, Douglas?"

"This is the only face I own. If it looks serious then it's because your daughter-in-law is trying to make me eat chopped apple. Grounds for divorce if you ask me." Douglas pushed the plate with the offending apple away from him.

Jean took it. "Lucky for all of us, and your marriage, chopped apple is my favorite. Now I'll ask you again—what's wrong?"

"Nothing's wrong, Nanna Jean." Glenda poured her mother-in-law a cup of coffee. She knew Douglas wouldn't want to worry his mother. When his father had died suddenly two decades earlier, they'd both agreed that his mother should move in with them. Douglas had converted three rooms of the old lodge into separate accommodation so that Nanna

Jean could be near them, but still maintain her independence. It was an arrangement that had worked well for everyone. "We were just talking about Christmas. And the children."

Douglas gave a grunt. "Not children. Ross is thirty-two."

"At thirty-two I'd been married for twelve years." Jean shook her head. "Perhaps, this year, he'll bring someone home with him. I'd like to see him with someone. It isn't good to be alone. And I'd like great-grandchildren before I'm too old and creaky to play with them. I've written to Santa and asked him."

"For great-grandchildren?"

"The little ones at school were all making their lists—they ask for a lot these days by the way—anyway, I had to think of something and at my age I have everything I need, apart from new hips of course, but I wasn't sure that Santa's gifts come with installation. I've been damaged by all those occasions when we opened gifts only to find there were no batteries, so I opted for something simpler."

Jean always made her smile. After handing over the business to Douglas, her mother-in-law had trained as a teacher and taught for years at the local primary school. Although she'd retired decades before, she was still a welcome guest at school celebrations, particularly at Christmas. "You asked Santa for great-grandchildren?"

"I was helping out on the day they wrote their letters. They wanted to know what I wanted from Santa. What was I supposed to say? There is no Santa? It's not my place to kill a child's dreams." She spread butter on a slice of toast. "I had to think of something. My letter is winging its way to the North Pole as we speak. So that's all sorted." She bit into her toast and Douglas shook his head.

"I hate to kill *your* dreams, but I'm pretty sure Santa won't be bringing you a great-grandchild anytime soon."

"Why not? Health and safety? Everything is rules now. He's probably not allowed to carry an infant on a sleigh without a helmet, a seat belt and a passport." Jean spooned sugar into her coffee and caught Glenda's eye. "Don't lecture me."

"Did I say a word?"

"You didn't need to. I'm eighty-six. If I want to add sugar to my coffee, I'll add it. And don't pretend you wouldn't love a grandchild."

Glenda wasn't going there. And she didn't want anyone else to go there, either. "We have to keep thoughts like that to ourselves." She poured herself a coffee. "And Ross isn't bringing anyone home, but Alice is."

"Alice?" Nanna Jean brightened. "It's the first time she's ever done that, so it must be serious."

"I made the same observation," Douglas said, "but we're not allowed to comment on it, Nanna Jean."

"Well why ever not? It's the most exciting thing that has happened around here for a long time!"

"We mustn't look excited. We have to pretend it's completely normal for Alice to bring a man home to meet us."

Nanna Jean gave an impish smile. "Do you want me to call him by a different name and apologize for getting all her boyfriends mixed up? I could look vague and forgetful and call him Stan? It might wake him up, thinking he's one of many. Maybe he'll propose."

Glenda felt a flicker of anxiety about Christmas. "You're not to interfere, Nanna Jean."

"Why not? I'm old. People make allowances when you're old."

"I just want you to behave normally," Glenda said. "If that's at all possible."

"Normal is overrated. We believe in individuality," Douglas said. "And when it comes to boyfriends, we don't know what normal is because she's never brought anyone home before. He must be special. He's a heart surgeon, Nanna Jean."

"Hearing that makes my own heart flutter. I'm already in love with the idea of him." His mother finished her toast. "And look at it this way, if he breaks her heart then at least he'll know how to fix it."

"Stop, both of you." Glenda didn't know whether to laugh or cry. "I don't want to put pressure on them. We need to keep it low-key."

Douglas raised his eyebrows. "Which is why you're planning to redecorate the Loch Room?"

"Ha! Good plan." Nanna Jean took a sip of coffee. "I've been telling you to do it for ages. It used to be the master bedroom. The honeymoon suite. I remember talking to your grandmother about it, Douglas. That bed has seen more action than—"

"Enough!" Glenda was in despair.

"Don't be a prude, Glenda. Next you'll be telling me you're giving them separate bedrooms."

"I'm not." She paused. "Do you think I should?"

"I do not. I think you should do everything you can to nurture intimacy. Maybe light a fire. A fire is always nice. Fanning the flames, so to speak. When did we last light a fire in that room? Would we all die of smoke inhalation? We might need to clean the chimney. There was a dead bird in mine a few years ago and the smell of that did not induce feelings of lust I can tell you."

"I'll make a call and get the chimneys swept." A real fire was one of her mother-in-law's better ideas. Glenda added a note to her pad.

"Another good plan. We don't mind them setting fire to the sheets, but preferably not to the room. What else is romantic? Candles in the bathroom."

"Which bit of 'low-key' don't you understand?" Glenda was starting to panic. "You two are going to ruin everything if you're not careful. None of us is going to mention marriage. Or babies. Or grandchildren. Especially not grandchildren."

"Like you did, you mean?" Nanna Jean gave her a look and Glenda felt herself blush.

"I did include myself in that warning, and we've already talked about that incident. I won't be drinking this Christmas. I'm going to watch every word I say."

"It's a family Christmas. Everyone expects the occasional meltdown. It's half the fun."

"It is not fun! And the stakes are higher this year, with Nico coming. We need to behave."

Douglas gave a grunt. "What are we allowed to talk about? The weather? They're forecasting heavy snow, so that would be interesting."

"You can ask about their lives. Show an interest."

"I'm interested." Jean took a sip of coffee. "I'm interested in why not one of them has settled down. Ross has made a success of his company, why can't he make a success of a relationship? It's time he had a family."

"Please don't say that to him," Glenda said. "You're as bad as Douglas."

"Bad? It's not bad to want the people you love to be happy."

"People have different ideas about what will make them happy. And Ross *is* happy. He loves his work."

"But as you're always telling me, work is only part of a life," Douglas said. "Not a whole life. Balance. Family. If they don't have children, who are we going to leave this place to when we die?"

"Keep eating your fruit and veg," Glenda said, "and hopefully you won't die anytime soon."

"I'd love to be a great-grandmother." Nanna Jean stared

dreamily into space. "And I'd love to go to a wedding. I've already chosen my hat. I always looked good in hats. Maybe there will be an announcement this Christmas."

"An announcement?"

"Alice has been with Nico for nine months. And bringing him home is a big deal. And he has agreed! Meeting the family at any time is stressful, but at Christmas? Playing charades with your future in-laws?"

Glenda resisted the temptation to let her head thump onto the table. "Nanna Jean—"

"What? We like the sound of Nico, don't we? We think he might be the one. And he must earn a decent living which means that between them they'd be able to afford a cleaning service which is good because Lord knows I love our Alice, but that girl is no housekeeper."

"I said the same thing myself." Douglas looked smug and Glenda wondered whether they were being intentionally frustrating.

"Why should she do the cleaning? If they're both working full-time they should share all the domestic responsibilities."

"Of course they should. But would she? I've always thought it was interesting that Alice is such a competitive person, and a perfectionist, but neither of those traits motivate her to clean a bath after she has used it," Nanna Jean said. "She used to pay Clemmie to do it for her, do you remember? And it was a terrible rate. I used to tell Clemmie she should ask for minimum wage at least, but she has never been the assertive type. She's a people pleaser."

Glenda was saved from responding by the appearance of Fergus. His shoulders almost filled the doorway.

"Oh, Fergus—" She stood up. "Thank you for coming. I know how busy you are."

His smile was warm. "I have a few minutes before I do the school run and I saw your message."

Glenda noticed the child hiding behind his legs. "Iona! What a treat to see you. Have you written your letter to Santa yet?"

Iona nodded and pressed closer to Fergus, who scooped her up easily.

"Tell Glenda and Nanna Jean what you asked for."

Glenda felt a lump in her throat. He was always there for the child. Always protective.

When Iona's mother—Fergus's older sister, Laura—had died, Fergus had taken the child without hesitation.

Life was so unfair.

It still felt strange to her seeing the boy as a man. And he was a good man. Not many would have done what he'd done. He didn't deserve what life had thrown at him, but he'd stepped up and he was doing everything he could to be the best father possible.

Iona clung to his neck. "I want snow for Christmas. So I can build a big snowman."

Glenda felt a pang of sympathy for Fergus. Not only was he expected to parent, but he was now expected to control the weather.

"Snow!" Nanna Jean beamed. "I'm sure Santa will do everything he can."

Iona gave a shy nod and Fergus shifted her onto his other arm.

"What can I do for you all?"

"It's exciting," Nanna Jean said. "We have an extra guest for Christmas."

"It's true." Douglas rolled his eyes. "Although why we have to redecorate the house because our daughter is finally in a romantic relationship, I have no idea."

Fergus went very still. "Clemmie is getting married?"

"No, not Clemmie. Alice," Douglas said. "And no one said anything about marriage. Do *not* mention marriage, Fergus, or you and I will be spending Christmas in the cow shed."

Glenda was watching Fergus. Was she the only one who noticed the color in his cheeks when Clemmie's name was mentioned?

They'd been so close as children, but then they'd seemed to lose touch.

Glenda had always wondered if something other than friendship might kindle between Fergus and Clemmie, but it hadn't so she'd obviously been wrong about that.

None of my business, she reminded herself.

"I want to make some changes to the Loch Room."

"For Alice. Right." Fergus nodded, his expression unreadable. "Why don't I come back after I've dropped Iona at school and we can talk about it?"

"Sounds good."

"We need the room to look romantic, Fergus." Nanna Jean winked at Fergus, who sent a bemused glance toward Glenda.

"I'm not sure I know exactly what—"

"Ignore Nanna Jean. I just want to freshen the place up, that's all."

"Nonsense. Your brief is to create a love nest, Fergus." Nanna Jean was her usual irrepressible self and Glenda felt a rush of panic. One thoughtless joke could wreck everything.

Maybe she should warn Alice. If her daughter was truly serious about Nico, maybe it was too soon to expose him to the Miller family. What if Douglas or his mother opened their mouths and ruined everything?

She loved this time of year. She looked forward to it for months in advance, but even she had to admit that the gathering wasn't without its stresses. And this year, to add to the usual tension between Douglas and Ross, there was the fact that Alice was bringing someone home! A special someone. And if the family put a foot wrong, Alice would never forgive them.

For the first time in her life, Glenda wondered if she might actually be dreading Christmas.

3

"What do you mean they want to do a feature on our perfect family? Since when have we been a perfect family?" Alice Miller wriggled out of her stained scrubs and turned on the shower. She'd been working for twelve hours straight and she was shattered, physically and emotionally. "What exactly do they want? Not another one of those photoshoots where we all sit round the tree smiling in front of a plate of shortbread?" It all seemed so far removed from the day she'd just had. Real life, up close, unfiltered and ugly. No shortbread and definitely no smiles. Emergency Medicine was not for the fainthearted. She closed her eyes. Occasionally there was such a thing as too much reality.

"It's not that much to ask, Alice." Her sister's soft, smoky voice floated from the phone.

"Right now it is. I've just finished my busiest shift ever and I'm meeting Nico in half an hour for dinner. I was late last time, and I cannot be late this time. I have to go. I need time to make myself look human."

"Mum and Dad want us to do it. It would mean a lot to them."

"You mean Mum wants us to do it. I'm sure Dad couldn't care less." She squinted at herself in the mirror. She looked awful. Washed-out. Exhausted.

"You'll be home anyway, so why not?"

Alice rummaged in her bag for makeup. "Because it isn't really how I want to spend my precious Christmas break." She rested the phone on top of the hand basin and switched it to speaker. "When is the photographer coming?" She removed the clip from her hair and briefly massaged her scalp. She didn't have time to wash it, so a quick spritz of dry shampoo was going to have to do.

"The day after we arrive I think."

"Fine. We can talk about it then."

"And Ross wants to have our usual sibling meetup on Saturday. His apartment. Seven o'clock."

"Ah, the annual pre-Christmas Parent Strategy Meeting. Yes, of course." That particular gathering was essential. It was the time they agreed what they would, and wouldn't, be telling their parents about their lives. The words *whatever you do, don't mention this*, usually punctuated the conversation.

"They're waiting for us to announce that Ross is getting married and his wife is having triplets, and that you're finally marrying Nico."

"I don't know which one of those statements makes me laugh most." Alice put the clip back in her hair and turned on the shower. Steam gathered, misting the room. "Ross hasn't been on a date in months to the best of my knowledge and I'm married to my job, although right now I'm contemplating divorce. And why are you off the hook? We all know their only hope of grandchildren lies with you. You're the maternal one. You need to hurry up and meet someone, Clemmie, to take the attention away from us. How's that guy you were seeing—" She tried to remember the name of her sister's last boyfriend but her brain was too tired.

"I ended it five months ago. I did tell you."

"Yes, you did. Sorry. Time you got back out there, Clem. We're all relying on you. Do your filial duty. Look, I've got to go. I'll see you at Ross's on Saturday."

She ended the call, showered quickly without getting her hair wet and then wriggled into the black dress she'd brought to work with her.

She did what she could with her hair, twisted it into what she hoped would pass as a glamorous updo, swiftly applied makeup and slid her feet into her shoes.

On her way out of the hospital she messaged Nico. On my way. Order wine. Urgent.

She arrived at the restaurant out of breath and paused for a moment before pushing open the door and stepping into the warmth. The cozy, family-run Italian restaurant was their favorite place to eat. She wasn't a sentimental person, but it was where she and Nico had come on their first date, and it felt special to her.

Now it was decorated for Christmas, with twists of holly and mistletoe on every table and fairy lights strung along the windows. Candles flickered on every table and there, in their usual table by the window, was Nico.

Her heart bumped a little harder, as it always did when she saw him.

He looked cool, calm and handsome and she was envious because he never seemed to feel the pressure the way she did. It helped that he was a man, of course. Nico was a cardiac surgeon and was as focused on his career as she was on hers.

The difference was that he'd never had a patient ask when they were going to see the doctor, or assume he was a medical secretary or a nurse. He didn't have to work twice as hard to prove himself.

She headed straight to the table and sat down opposite him.

"Hi there, I'm sorry to bother you but I need a doctor and someone said you might be able to help."

He put the menu down. "You have a medical emergency?"

"I do."

"Describe your symptoms."

"Heart racing, sweaty, breathless—oh wait…" she paused as a waiter arrived with two large glasses of wine "…here's the cure right here. Thank you, Doctor." She raised her glass and he smiled.

"You're welcome. Easiest consultation I've ever done. You're obviously easily satisfied."

She fluttered her lashes and tried not to laugh. "I wouldn't say that."

"You wouldn't?"

"No. Of course it could be your skill and bedside manner."

"I charge for both." He named a figure and she raised her eyebrows.

"That much for a two-minute consultation? Your fees are high."

"They have to be. My girlfriend is demanding and expensive."

She almost choked on her wine. "Maybe you should rethink your relationship."

"Funny you should say that, because I came to the same conclusion myself." He took a sip of his own wine and put his glass down slowly.

The atmosphere shifted.

She felt a moment of disquiet. Rethinking their relationship? What exactly did he mean by that? Was he breaking up with her? She'd been working stupidly long hours lately because they were under such pressure in the hospital, but unlike the previous men she'd dated, Nico had never complained about her work. He was equally, if not more, committed to his own career.

Maybe it wasn't work. Maybe all this was because she'd invited him home with her for Christmas. Maybe she'd freaked him out. Nico had avoided serious commitment up until this point in his life, as had she, and suddenly she'd plunged their relationship into new territory. *Meet the family.* How could she recover it?

"In what way have you been rethinking our relationship?" She tried to sound casual and he gestured to the menu.

"Let's order. They have a Christmas menu, but I'm assuming you want the fish?"

He thought she could eat after saying something like that? He was just going to leave those words hanging there?

She glanced at the menu without interest. It hadn't occurred to her that his choice of venue might be significant. They'd come here on their first date. Had he booked the place because tonight was going to be their last?

"Fish is great. And a green salad." Hopefully she could force that down past the knot in her stomach.

The waiter took their order and Alice stared across the table at him, trying to read his expression.

"What's going on, Nico?"

He paused. "Are you happy, Alice?" He was the sort of person who chose his words carefully, so she knew it wasn't a random question.

"Of course I'm happy." She stopped. Was that the wrong thing to say? If he was about to break up with her then maybe she should have been more guarded. But she'd never had to watch her words around Nico. They'd never played games, and she didn't want to start now. "Are you saying you're not happy?"

"No. I'm not saying that."

The waiter stepped forward to top up their wine.

Alice wanted to tell him to go away, but she ground her teeth and waited until he'd refilled her glass and left them alone.

"Nico?" Maybe this was about something else. Something more immediate. "Did you have a bad day?"

"No. My day was good. Yours?"

She thought about the crush in the waiting area, people with everything from cut fingers to major injuries. Too many patients, not enough staff. The challenge of not knowing what was coming through the door next was one of the things she loved about emergency medicine, but the pressure was more intense than it had ever been in the entire time she'd worked in the emergency department.

"It was—interesting."

Their food arrived at that point and she immediately pushed her plate across to Nico, who smiled and boned her fish with slick, swift precision. She could have done it herself (although Ross always said that her attempts to bone a fish left it looking as if it had been caught in a propeller), but she liked watching him do it. She'd never seen him operate, but now she thought she might like to.

He pushed the plate back to her. "Tell me about your day."

He'd obviously decided not to say whatever it was he was thinking of saying and that was fine with her. If he was breaking up with her then she'd rather he didn't do it in their special restaurant. She'd had a long day. She was exhausted. She didn't want to lose control of her emotions in a public place. So instead of questioning him further, she told him about the woman who had been wearing headphones and had stepped into the road without seeing an approaching cyclist, and the toddler who had tried to ride the dog and fallen onto the concrete path.

He updated her on his research and mentioned that he'd been invited to speak at a conference in Prague the following summer.

He traveled a lot. In the past few months he'd been to Singapore, New York and Zurich.

She understood his passion for his work, because she was exactly the same.

"Sorry I was late. Clemmie called as I was getting ready to come here. I didn't want to just cut her off." Guilt stabbed at her because she knew she'd had the conversation without really listening.

"Is Clemmie okay?" He always asked after her family, which she found touching.

And now she felt guilty because she didn't actually know if Clemmie was okay. She hadn't asked. The conversation had been one of logistics. Will you pose for this magazine photo? Tick. Are we meeting at Ross's on Saturday? Tick.

Alice didn't share intimate details of her life and didn't expect others to.

"She wanted to warn me that our parents have agreed to be featured in a magazine. They want a family photograph."

"Eat shortbread and you, too, could have a family like this?"

She managed a smile. "Something like that. Eat shortbread and then have a cardiac surgeon sort out your arteries later."

"That may not be the best strapline. Stick to medicine. Your marketing skills are lacking."

"I know." Thinking about the family business gave her a pang.

He watched her. "What?"

She shrugged. "I always feel guilty when we do these family photos. Glen Shortbread is our heritage, and not one of the three of us works in the business. Not that I'd be any use. Apart from my obvious lack of marketing skills, I'd eat all the product. And Clemmie would hate it. She has only ever wanted to work with children. So that heaps all the pressure on Ross. I know he feels bad about it."

"You can't live the life your parents want you to live. You have to follow your own passions." Nico sat back in his chair. "I'm looking forward to meeting your family."

Presumably that meant he was still planning to join her, which in turn meant that it wasn't the prospect of a Miller family Christmas that had rattled him. Although that could be because he was ignorant as to what that really meant. Charades. Silly hats. Nanna Jean telling embarrassing stories. Alice loved her family, but she didn't entirely trust them not to say something embarrassing. She cringed at the thought of what Nico might make of it all. She'd never taken anyone home before. What had possessed her to do it this time? If Nico wasn't having second thoughts before he arrived, he probably would by the time he left.

"Do you want dessert?"

"No." His gaze held hers for a long moment. "Let's have coffee at home."

"Fine. Mine or yours?" They'd kept both apartments, even though they spent most nights together.

"Mine." He paid for their meal and she pulled on her coat as she walked to the door.

"Shall we grab a cab?"

"Let's walk."

Something was definitely wrong. "Are you okay? You seem tense."

"I'm fine." He took her hand and they crossed the road and headed for the river.

Maybe it was work. They didn't always share the details because both of them preferred to switch off when they were away from the hospital, but that didn't mean that some cases didn't stay with them.

"I love London at night." She watched as the lights from the buildings danced across the surface of the water. Walking around the historic parts of London was one of their favorite things to do. If they booked tickets to a play or the ballet, inevitably they ended up canceling because one or both of them had to work. The last time they'd met friends for dinner Nico had been called away halfway through the main course. They were unreliable guests and therefore it was often simpler to spend their time together.

She realized he wasn't responding and glanced at him. "Nico?" Her heart skittered. "Okay. Enough. I can't stand this. Are you breaking up with me? Because if you want to break up with me, then just do it. I'm not good with suspense."

"What?" He stopped walking. "Why would you say that? Why would you assume I want to end our relationship?"

Because she wasn't easy to be with. Because that was what had always happened before. *I'm sorry Alice, but...*

"Because you've been behaving oddly all night, and you said you'd been rethinking our relationship—"

"That's true. I have been thinking about it, but not because I want to break up. Far from it."

"Oh." Intense relief was followed by a rush of warmth. "Well—good."

"Good?"

"Yes. I don't want to break up." Should she tell him how anxious she'd been? No. She didn't want to put pressure on him. She was tiptoeing, careful not to put any weight on their relationship in case it cracked. She'd invited him home for Christmas. That was enough.

He put his hands on her shoulders and turned her to face him. "Why don't you want to break up, Alice?"

"What sort of a question is that?" What was she supposed to say? Why was he looking at her like that? "Because I—" *I love you.* No. She couldn't say that. That was *way* too much. He'd run for the hills. "I like you. You're good company. You have excellent taste in food and wine, you are good at crossword puzzles and filleting fish, you're a brilliant pianist, and you always seem to be able to find a parking space. Also, I'd hate to be without a good heart surgeon. You never know."

His smile was brief, his gaze intense. "Everyone should have their own heart surgeon."

"Exactly."

He cupped her face with his hands, his gaze fixed on hers. "Alice—"

"What? Nico, *what?* You're behaving really weirdly." She was conscious of people passing them. Some turned their heads, curious about the couple standing still, staring at each other and not at the glittering skyline. "Are you sick or something? Did something happen at work?"

"Yes, in a way it did."

"Well, then, why don't you—Nico?" She gaped as he dropped to one knee. "What are you doing? There's frost on the ground. You'll—"

"Marry me, Alice." His voice was unsteady. "I want us to get married."

"I— *What?*" She caught the eye of a couple walking past. The girl was grinning.

"Happy Christmas!"

Alice didn't respond. The world around her swam. Her head spun. "Are you proposing?"

"Is there another way to interpret the words *Marry me*? Also, why else would a guy kneel on a filthy London street?" He held out a box. "For you."

Her heart was hammering. "What is it?"

"It's a horse. I know you love horses." He sighed and stood up. "This whole one knee thing isn't working for me. Orthopedic surgeons must get a lot of business from proposals. It's a ring, Alice. What do you think it is?"

A ring? He'd bought her a *ring*?

"I don't know. This is all so unexpected. I—" She opened the box and a diamond winked and gleamed under the streetlamp. "Oh—"

"'Oh' in a good way, or 'oh' in a bad way?"

"It's—beautiful." She stared at the diamond, captivated by the sparkle. "I—you—you're really asking me to marry me? I didn't expect this."

"Good. I hate to be predictable." He waited. "I confess this isn't going exactly how I hoped it would go."

And that was her fault. She was meant to squeal, fling her arms round him and say yes, yes, *yes*.

Only a few moments before she'd been panicking that he'd been breaking up with her, and now here she was panicking that he was offering her forever.

This was the fairy tale, but she'd never liked fairy tales. Occasionally growing up she'd read them to Clemmie, but her sister had been unimpressed by Alice's version of the stories. *The princess doesn't punch the prince, Alice, and she doesn't cook the frog in garlic butter.*

She didn't have particularly traditional views, did she? The whole concept of "happy-ever-after" made her roll her eyes. Was anyone naive enough to believe in that? Her work had taught her that the goal should be to enjoy the moment because no one knew what lay around the corner. But here was Nico promising her forever and asking her to make the same promise to him.

She wouldn't make a good wife.

"It's a bit sudden, that's all."

"We've been dating for nine months, and we virtually moved in together after our second date."

"I know. But we've never even said——" She swallowed. This was awful.

"Said what? That I love you? I'm saying it now. I love you, Alice. And you love me." He cupped her face in his hands and kissed her gently. "You *know* I love you."

Did she know that? She wasn't good at reading people's emotions. Except for fear and anxiety maybe, which she saw all the time in her work. Those were pretty obvious.

"This all feels fast. We're going from naught to sixty in four seconds. I feel as if we've missed out on a few stages."

He smiled down at her. "Maybe we have but when you know, you know."

Was that true? Relationships weren't that simple, were they? "I don't have much experience with long-term relationships, you know that. I wouldn't say I'm good at them." Which was why she'd had long periods in her life when she hadn't dated anyone. Every time a relationship ended, she felt like a failure.

How did she know for sure that with Nico it would be different?

What if there came a point where she couldn't meet his expectations?

Nico turned up the collar of her coat to keep out the cold. "Why are you so surprised by this? It's been clear for a while that what we have is special."

"But you didn't say anything. And—" She frowned. "How do you know I love you?"

"You invited me home for Christmas."

"Well you don't have family in this country, and I thought you might like a proper cooked dinner, and—"

"How many men have you invited home for Christmas, Alice?"

She'd never invited a man home at all, let alone for the festive season. "Not many." She almost said *none*, but that would have been far too revealing. She was good at many things, but not at sustaining a romantic relationship.

"I know you're cautious," he said. "I know you think things through before making a decision. I know you've been hurt in the past. We both have, which is probably why we've both been slow to say those three little words. They feel heavy, don't they?" His voice was soft and he stroked her cheek with the backs of his fingers. "And they should, because they're serious words and I'm not using them lightly. I love you, Alice. I want to be with you, always. Make a life with you." He paused and took a breath. "I'll try this again—will you marry me?"

She was shaking. "I love you, too." She said the words for the first time, and meant them. But marriage? There were so many ways she could fail at that. And so many things to consider. Practical things. Things that would probably make him run in the opposite direction. "I—can I think about it?"

He breathed in sharply. "You need to *think* about it?"

"Yes. And you should think about it, too. Nico, I'm flattered. Pleased, even. But this is *huge*. Marriage is different from dating. Marriage is about expectations, and shared goals, and—" Where had all the oxygen in the air gone? She couldn't catch her breath. Maybe it was the diamond ring in her hand. She thrust it back at him. "There's so much to talk about—your career, my career—"

"This is about us, not our jobs. Our careers have no impact on our decision to be together." He stared down at the ring she'd pressed into his hand as if he didn't quite know what to do with it. "You think I'm going to expect you to give up your career? You know me better than that, Alice, or at least I hope you do. I'm not going to expect you to change a single thing about yourself. I love you, exactly the way you are."

"But you don't know exactly who I am. You only know what you've seen when we've been dating."

"You have some dubious habits I don't know about?"

"No! Yes. Maybe." They were standing in a busy street, people strolling past on their way back from office Christmas celebrations. It wasn't the place to have the most important conversation of their relationship, possibly of her life. "What if you get tired because of my working patterns?"

"I won't. You're committed to your patients and to making a difference. That's one of the many things I love about you."

But there were other things she hadn't shared with him. Things they'd never touched on.

"I just—I need some time, Nico. To get used to the idea."

"Of marriage?"

"To begin with, the fact that you love me."

"I can't believe that comes as a shock. Why do you think I wanted to come home with you for Christmas?"

Her heart was pounding. "I assumed you wanted to try my family's shortbread."

He smiled. "You're funny. You always make me laugh. All right, this is what we're going to do. I'm going to put this ring back in my pocket, we are going to practice saying 'I love you' until you get used to the idea and then, when the time feels right, I'm going to propose again. Unless you decide to propose to me in the meantime." He put the ring carefully back into the box and slid it into his pocket. "How does that sound?"

It sounded reasonable. More than reasonable. But she knew it wouldn't be as simple as that.

There were serious discussions to be had. But first she needed to get her thoughts straight.

"It sounds good. Just promise me you won't mention your proposal to my family."

"Why not?" He gave her a curious look. "I've already met Ross and Clemmie. We get on fine and they must know we're serious."

"What I share with my siblings and what I share with my parents are two very different things."

Nico was an only child, independent and very self-contained, so maybe he didn't understand that.

"You don't think your parents will approve?"

They would more than approve.

She knew her family would love him, particularly her mother and Nanna Jean. If they suspected he'd proposed and she hadn't immediately said yes, she'd never hear the end of it. They'd probably arrange a wedding before she'd eaten her last mouthful of turkey.

"I don't want the pressure, that's all."

She could already imagine what Christmas would be like. The hopeful looks. The questions. She couldn't deal with it. And that was without them knowing that Nico had proposed. She needed to be careful, or they'd guess that something was going on. She needed to distract them. She needed to find a way to divert attention from herself, and for that she'd enlist the help of her siblings.

They were a team after all.

4

Clemmie

"Time you were in bed, Georgie." Clemmie scooped the little girl out of the bath, giggling as she was showered with water. "You're slippery."

"I love you, Clem." She wound her chubby arms round Clemmie's neck and gave her a wet kiss.

"Oh—that's nice. Good thing I can't get any wetter." She screwed up her face, loving every minute. She loved Georgie. She loved the way her hair curled, the way she smiled, the way her little arms gripped tightly when she hugged.

Was this her favorite age? Four years old? Maybe. At four, children were old enough to ensure entertaining conversation, but young enough that life still seemed simple. No friendship issues. No playground bullying. But she loved babies, too. Every age came with its charms and horrors. It amazed her that a small, helpless baby could turn into a fully functioning adult.

"Clementine?" A voice floated up the stairs and Clemmie sighed.

Most turned into fully functioning adults. Some were just adults.

She wrapped Georgie in a towel. "Sounds as if your mummy is home early." *Goodbye carefully nurtured routine. Goodbye calm, quiet child all warm, sleepy and ready for bed.*

Georgie pressed her face close. "Why are you doing that funny thing with your eyes?"

"What funny thing?"

"They go up. Like this." Georgie rolled her eyes and Clemmie didn't know whether to laugh or panic. She needed to be more careful.

"I had something in my eye. Probably water."

"Clementine!" The voice came again, more desperate this time.

Georgie clung to her. "Will you still read my story?"

"I don't know. That depends on whether your mummy wants to read it."

"I don't want her to read it. She doesn't do the voices like you do. And she's always looking at her phone in case there's a mergency."

"Emergency." She rubbed the child dry and then reached for the pajamas she'd been warming.

"Don't leave, Clemmie." Georgie pushed her arms and head into the pajamas and emerged flushed.

Clemmie felt a rush of guilt. "I have to leave. I'm going out tonight."

"On a date?"

Fat chance. Clemmie reached for her toothbrush. "No. I'm meeting my brother and sister."

"I'd like a baby brother but Mummy and Daddy are too busy to make one."

The door opened. "Georgie! Mummy's home." Karen Kingston stood in the doorway, immaculate in a white silk shirt under a dark fitted suit. She'd come straight from a meeting, which no doubt she'd dominated, but here, in her child's bathroom, she looked oddly uncertain and insecure.

Clemmie was conscious of her damp T-shirt and jeans. "Hi, Karen. You're home early."

"I'm having a small group of colleagues over for dinner. The caterers will be here in ten minutes to start setting up."

Karen worked for a leading investment bank in securities. Clemmie had no idea what she actually did, but it required leaving the house at five in the morning, often not returning until after nine at night and being on the phone for the hours in between. What she did was important apparently although what was defined as *important* was, in Clemmie's opinion, a matter for debate. Society had strange priorities.

Not for anything would she have swapped places with Karen, but being the younger sister of two of the most competitive people on the planet, she understood more about ambition and drive than most.

"We have some exciting news, don't we, Georgie?"

"Exciting?" Karen sneaked a quick look at her phone. "What news?"

"Today, Georgie dressed herself with no help at all."

Georgie beamed with pride, and Karen gave a bright smile. "That's—great. Clever Georgie! Er…she couldn't do that before?"

"Undressing, yes. Dressing is much harder. And Georgie even managed to do a couple of buttons." She gave the little girl a hug and a kiss and Karen clapped her hands.

"Fantastic. Well done, Georgie. And you, Clementine, for teaching her. I need Georgie to wear something adorable tonight. That striped dress would be nice."

Clemmie frowned. "She's ready for bed, Karen."

"I thought that tonight she could stay up later as a treat."

"You were finding it difficult when she woke in the night, and we've been very careful with her routine and—"

"I'm worried I don't see enough of her." Karen checked her phone quickly. "I thought she could stay up late tonight and have fun."

Clemmie was torn between exasperation and sympathy. Karen was in a difficult position, she knew that, constantly torn between her work commitments and her desire to be a good mother.

And it wasn't her place to argue. "Of course. I understand. I'm sure Georgie will enjoy staying up later." She wasn't sure at all, but she knew it was the right thing to say.

"Do you think so?" Karen looked uncertain. "Would you like to have some grown-up fun with Mummy tonight, Georgie?"

Georgie pressed closer to Clemmie. "I want Clemmie to read to me."

"Of course she's going to read to you. Clemmie can stay with you when my guests arrive." Her gaze lingered on Clemmie's jeans and damp T-shirt. "Do you have a smart dress, Clemmie?"

Clemmie stood up. "I can't stay tonight, I'm afraid. It's my night off, Karen. I have plans."

"Could you rearrange? I'll pay you, of course." Karen was unfailingly generous, but money wasn't the issue here.

"No, I can't rearrange. I'm meeting my brother and sister and trying to find a time when Ross and Alice aren't working is impossible." Tonight was their annual pre-Christmas gathering and she had no intention of missing it.

"Oh, well that's—" Karen broke off. Frowned. "Did you say Ross?"

"Yes."

"Your brother is Ross Miller? *The* Ross Miller?"

"Er—I don't know. That depends on which Ross Miller you're thinking about."

"Miller Active? Gyms? Sportswear?"

"Yes, that's him."

"I buy his yoga pants. They're perfect." Karen gave a self-conscious laugh. "That sounds odd, doesn't it? But they're the only ones I've tried that don't slip when you do downward dog. Your brother. I had no idea." She stared at her, reassessing, no doubt wondering how Clemmie with her sturdy thighs, curvy frame and total lack of ambition could possibly be related to Ross. "And your sister? Does she work in the business, too?"

"No. She's a doctor. Emergency medicine."

"Ah—she's the one you called when Georgie banged her head on the living room table."

"That's right." Clemmie could see Karen's mind working and knew she was trying to work out how the übersuccessful Miller family had managed to produce someone like Clemmie. It didn't worry her. She was used to it. Ross had powered his way through school, top in every subject. Alice had followed. They were both brilliant at everything, whether academic or sport. The Miller children were something of a legend locally.

And then came Clemmie. According to her mother, she'd barely bothered to talk until she was three because her brother and sister had done it for her. She'd been slow to read because she'd trailed around after them, wanting to join in whatever game they were playing. At school her concentration had been terrible because she'd spent most of her time in the classroom staring out the window and dreaming.

Unlike her siblings, she'd struggled to pass exams, mostly

because she wasn't particularly interested. The thing that did interest her was children. Growing up, she'd liked nothing more than being asked to look after the children of her parents' friends, or people who lived in the village.

She'd been in such demand as a babysitter that Ross had told her she should raise her prices. Alice told her she should specialize and offer a service to parents whose children were generally too difficult to be left with adults less skilled than Clemmie.

Clemmie didn't find children difficult. She found them interesting and was fascinated by how early their personalities were formed.

Ross went to a leading university and Alice went to a leading medical school, so perhaps it was inevitable that when Clemmie chose to train as a nanny, she did it at a leading institution which now meant her services were in demand across the world. But Clemmie wasn't interested in status. Clemmie did her job because it was fun and rewarding. While other people were commuting and toiling in an office, she spent her time in the park or splashing paint onto paper. And she was pretty sure there was no sense of achievement greater than teaching a child to read.

She'd chosen to settle in London, partly because that was where her siblings had chosen to live, and partly because—

She killed the thought before it could even develop in her brain. She wasn't going there.

She wasn't going to think about *him*. It was one of the rules she'd set herself and she stuck by it as rigidly as she could, even though it had been hard.

Alice and Ross had left their home in the Scottish Highlands without a backward glance. Clemmie had looked backward so many times it was a wonder she hadn't developed neck ache. She missed Scotland. She missed the mountains and the loch. She missed stepping out of her front door and breathing in a crisp winter air. She missed the smell of woodsmoke and the vast space. She missed her family. Her parents, Nanna Jean and their black lab, Hunter.

A lump formed in her throat at the thought of Hunter. She kept wanting to scoop him up and bring him here but she couldn't have a dog in London. And, anyway, her dad would miss him too much.

Thinking about her dad didn't help her emotions.

The truth was she was homesick. She'd been homesick since she'd arrived in London and it hadn't got any easier. She couldn't wait until Christmas.

She would have liked to see more of her siblings, but they were always so busy.

Still, she was incredibly proud of them both. She'd even go so far as to say they were close. But they were very different. Same upbringing, entirely different personalities and view of the world. It was fascinating. She'd studied the "nature versus nurture" debate at college and firmly believed that nature played a bigger part.

"I have to leave in half an hour, Karen." She kept her voice firm and saw Georgie's lip wobble.

"Want you to stay and read."

"Clemmie will be back in the morning," Karen said. "And in the meantime you're going to have a special evening with Mummy and Daddy."

Georgie was so tired after their active day that she could barely keep her eyes open.

The evening was promising to be memorable for all the wrong reasons.

"Could you dress her before you leave? She hates it when I try and pull something over her head." Karen glanced around her, taking in the tidy bathroom with the neatly stored toys.

"You're a wonder, Clementine. I'm so lucky that there are people like you in the world, happy to spend their days picking up wet towels and reading the same story over and over again. Brett always says you're our biggest asset. If you change your mind about leaving in January—"

"I'm not going to change my mind." Clemmie hung the wet towel over the heated rail. She imagined herself being added to a balance sheet under "assets." Did she depreciate over time? How much would be deducted for wear and tear?

Clemmie changed a grumpy and confused Georgie out of her pajamas and into a dress.

"I hate this dress." She wriggled and squirmed. "It's itchy."

The child was far too tired to socialize. If Karen and Brett were hoping to show her off, it was probably going to backfire.

But she wouldn't be here to see it.

She had to constantly remind herself that Georgie wasn't her child, and some decisions weren't hers to make.

"I need to get ready now." She kissed Georgie and handed her over to her mother. She felt a pang. There were aspects of the job she wouldn't miss, but she was definitely going to miss Georgie. "Have fun tonight."

Forcing herself to ignore Georgie's squirming protests and crestfallen expression, she retreated upstairs to the suite of rooms that were hers alone.

Half an hour later, after a quick shower and change of clothes, she stepped out of the large town house into the freezing air. The Kingstons' home was in Chelsea, just steps away from the river. The Albert Bridge lay ahead of her, lights sparkling in the darkness. Whatever the time of year, it always made her think of Christmas. Was it the prettiest bridge in London? In her opinion, most definitely. She could see it from her bedroom on the top floor of the house, which surely had one of the most enviable views in London. If she had to live in a city, then she was glad she lived here.

When she'd taken the job it had been exactly what she'd needed, even though she'd missed home badly. But now?

Now things were about to change. She'd given Karen plenty of notice so that she had time to find a new nanny for Georgie. But she was leaving, and nothing was going to change that.

She had other plans. Exciting plans.

She snuggled deeper inside her scarf and walked toward the pier. The bitterly cold wind sneaked inside her coat. Ross had offered to send a car for her, but she'd refused and opted instead to take the riverboat along the Thames to London Bridge.

It gave her time to think about the decision she'd made.

And it was a big one.

She was pretty sure her family's reaction wasn't going to be positive, which was why she hadn't yet told them. That discussion was better had face-to-face, but she knew that her parents and Nanna Jean would be dismayed by her plans and she didn't want to spend Christmas in an atmosphere of tension. She didn't know how her siblings would react, but neither Ross nor Alice were slow to express an opinion on anything and everything, and even though they were all now adults they still tended to treat Clemmie as someone who needed guidance and protection for her own good.

Nerves fluttered as she anticipated the conversations that were coming her way. She was a people pleaser and didn't enjoy difficult conversations. And this particular conversation was going to be difficult.

They thought they knew her. They were in for a shock.

Once on the boat, the other passengers chose to huddle indoors whilst Clemmie stayed on the deck, her chin tucked inside her scarf, gazing at the buildings that crowded the riverbank. She thought about all the people scurrying around inside those glass buildings, living their own lives. She'd grown up in a place where everyone's lives intersected, where a community was a tangled web of people and tradition. She missed that.

She arrived at Ross's apartment to find Alice already there, talking to someone on her phone. Her hair was twisted into a messy bun. She'd teamed black ski pants with a black roll neck sweater that made her look slimmer than ever. She glanced up when Clemmie walked in, waggled her fingers by way of greeting and went back to the conversation.

Ross was wearing a smart shirt over jeans and smiled when he saw Clemmie's raised eyebrows.

"Working from home." He proffered the explanation as he slipped a stack of papers into a slim black case. "Conference calls all afternoon. They could only see my top half."

"But what if there's a fire and you suddenly stand up?"

"That's why I pulled on the jeans." He put the case down and hugged her. "How are you doing?"

"I'm—" His greeting was so warm that she almost told him, right there and then, but stopped herself. *Not the right time.* "I'm great, thank you. You?"

"Good. Busy."

"Of course." She'd never known her brother to be anything else. He was like their father. Constantly on the go. Alice was the same. "I'm looking forward to Christmas."

"Of course you are." He took her coat from her. "Christmas always was your favorite time of year. I remember you begging Dad to put the tree up in November."

"It's never too early to have a Christmas tree." She followed him into the living area of his apartment and paused. She'd been here on so many occasions and still the view from his glass-walled apartment took her breath away. In one direction you could see Canary Wharf, the Docklands and Greenwich, and in the other Tower Bridge and the famous dome of St. Paul's Cathedral. It was a spectacular view, but still...

She leaned her head against the glass, missing mountains and trees, and then realized he was talking to her. "Sorry?" She turned. "I missed what you said."

"I asked if you finished your Christmas shopping."

"I finished ages ago. You know me." She studied his face. "Don't tell me—you haven't started yet and you'd like to share my presents."

"We may reach that point, but there are still a few days to go so I might manage to pull it together."

She looked around her. "Where's your tree?"

"I'm not bothering this year. Making a big fuss about Christmas just adds to the to-do list. I suppose I could have paid someone to find me a tree and decorate it, and then take it down after but I'm always staring at a screen anyway, so what's the point?"

"What?" She was horrified. "Ross! You are *not* going to turn into one of those people who think it's all too much trouble."

"It *is* too much trouble. And I'm not even going to be here for Christmas. We're going to Scotland—"

"What if you date someone who loves Christmas?" She found an angle that might work for him. "You'll bring her back here and once she sees your stark, unseasonal apartment she will dump you."

"Or maybe she'll find my presence so sparkly she doesn't notice the absence of a tree."

"I don't understand you." Clemmie shook her head in despair and glanced across the room to Alice, who was still focused on her phone. "Who is she talking to?"

"Someone at work."

She hated to think that her brother's life was filled with nothing but work. Alice's, too.

"You two need to think about something other than work."

"Now you're sounding like Mum and Nanna Jean. And I do think about something other than work. I think about sport."

"That's work!"

"Not always. I spent two weeks in the Himalayas this summer."

"Testing out your new range of high-performance jackets."

"That was the excuse." He smiled. "I've just signed for another marathon."

"Fine, fine." Each to his own, Clemmie thought. "Are you looking forward to going home for Christmas?"

"Of course." Ross reached for an open bottle of wine. "Except for the part where Dad makes me feel guilty for not joining the family business, and Nanna Jean and Mum have a glass of wine too many and then expect me to tell them everything about my love life."

"Last year it wasn't wine. It was gin," Clemmie said. "It was a gift from the McLeans." She remembered Alice stomping out of the dining room. "Is there something to tell about your love life? Because Mum isn't the only one who can ask embarrassing questions. Your little sister is pretty good at it, too. Tell all!"

She thought it would be good for Ross if he met someone. At least then he might think about something other than work. She didn't like to think of her brother alone. She ignored the little voice in her head that reminded her that she was alone, too.

Better alone than with the wrong person.

"There's nothing to tell. I haven't dated anyone for a while.

I've been busy. And I know that won't be seen as a reasonable excuse, so I'm relying on you and Alice to take the heat off me." He poured wine into a glass. "Please tell me you have a doting new boyfriend and that you've set a wedding date, Clem."

"No." She kept her voice light. "No boyfriend. No wedding."

"Not dating, either? What a disappointment we all are. Let's hope Alice is going to compensate." He handed her a glass and Clemmie hesitated.

"Give that one to Alice. Do you have anything nonalcoholic?"

"Yes. Grab whatever you want from the fridge." He waved a hand toward the kitchen area of his spacious apartment. "Are you okay? Did you have a heavy night last night or something?"

"No. Just a long day. Bit of a headache."

"Headache?" Alice ended the call and slid her phone into her pocket. "How long have you had it? Describe the pain. Is it constant? Does it come and go? Let me examine you. The doctor is in the house."

Ross muttered something that sounded suspiciously like *Lord help us*, and Clemmie shook her head.

"It's just a headache, Alice."

"That's for me to decide."

Ross sent her an impatient look. "What are you going to do? Send her for an MRI? Are you this reassuring with your patients, Dr. Doom? *I'm pretty sure that your presenting symptoms are serious*," he did a fair imitation of Alice, "*but just to be sure there is no boring and simple explanation we're going to subject you to every test available to inflict maximum anxiety.*"

"You're not funny."

"I'm hilarious. And it's scarier having you around than

searching your symptoms on the internet." Ross handed her the wine he'd poured for Clemmie. "You're not at work now. Switch off, I beg you, for all our sakes."

"I'm being caring! If Clemmie has a headache then I want to—"

"Fine, I don't have a headache!" Clemmie interrupted, mildly exasperated even though their bickering was all too familiar. Alice and Ross had spent half their childhood locked in verbal combat. They'd fought about who was going to sit in the front of the car, who was going to choose the music that was played, who had the extra helping of apple pie, what they watched on TV. It was like background noise most of the time, but occasionally it felt like too much. "If you must know, I'm on a health drive."

Alice looked astonished. "You?"

"Yes, me. I've given up alcohol."

"In that case I'm definitely sending you for a whole raft of tests. The words *Clemmie* and *health drive* don't go together."

"Ignore her." A buzzer sounded and Ross glanced at his sisters. "That will be the food. I ordered Thai. Is that okay?" He strode toward the door without waiting for an answer, spoke into an intercom, and a moment later several bags of food arrived.

Clemmie fetched plates while Alice grabbed one of the bags from him.

"What if I didn't feel like Thai?"

"Then you would have had the choice of going hungry, or going home." Ross set three bags down on the kitchen island, pushing aside a stack of magazines and newspapers.

"How are you, Alice?" Clemmie spread out the plates. "No more drama at work? No more drunk patients punching you on a Saturday night?"

"So far, no. And don't, whatever you do, mention that incident in front of our parents." Alice glanced at Ross. "Are you going to heat the food up?"

"No. I'm hungry, and it's already hot enough. And if you're about to give me a list of bacteria that could potentially be growing in it, then don't." He smiled at Clemmie. "I'm curious. What sort of health drive? You've taken up exercise? Obviously I have a professional interest. I can kit you out with whatever you need."

"You're trying to sell your products to your own sister?" Alice grabbed one of the bags. "You have no shame."

He ignored her. "I ordered your favorite prawn dish, Alice. Clem, there's chicken."

Alice ripped the top from the carton closest to her and peered down at it. "This isn't chicken."

"I never said it was the chicken. You just grabbed it."

"Did you order chicken for me?"

"Prawns. I ordered you prawns! That one's mine. You don't eat cashews. And it's true that I have no shame." Ross leaned across and took the carton from her. "But in this case, I happen to be interested. Exercise and fitness is my thing."

They opened pots, served themselves, swapped, tasted.

Clemmie quietly helped herself to a drink from his fridge. They were talking about her and yet they'd forgotten her. She'd learned over the years that if she let them get on with it, eventually they'd stop sniping at each other and remember she existed.

Alice tipped half the prawns onto her plate. "What does this health drive of yours involve? Are you exercising?"

"Not exactly." Clemmie helped herself to a small portion of chicken. Now she had their full attention, she wasn't sure she wanted it. "But I do about a million steps a day running after Georgie. Yesterday we went to an indoor gym for under fives, so I guess you could say I went to the gym. It takes a ton of calories to wade through a ball pool."

Ross added rice and broccoli to his plate. "That's not a health drive. That's masochism."

"Not to me."

He looked mystified. "You really do love it, don't you?"

"Yes." She should tell them. She should tell them right now about the decision she'd made.

But the words wouldn't leave her mouth and instead she helped herself to broccoli, too, and pushed the container toward Alice.

"Georgie is interesting. There is nothing quite like the worldview of a four-year-old. She's at that age where she questions everything and says it like it is. It's hilarious and adorable."

Alice was staring at her. There was an odd look on her face.

Clemmie put her fork down. "What's wrong?"

"Nothing at all." Alice speared another prawn. "Those kids you look after are lucky to have you, Clem. You should have a hundred children of your own. We need to work harder on finding you a man."

"I wish you'd stop saying that. I don't want a man, and I don't want a hundred children." But one would be good, she thought. One would be perfect.

"You haven't dated anyone since—" Alice paused and glanced at Ross.

"Liam." His mouth tightened. "Let's not talk about Liam."

Clemmie couldn't blame him for thinking that way. He was the one who had driven halfway across London in the pouring rain at two in the morning without hesitation or question after she'd called him sobbing.

And she hadn't forgotten it.

It didn't matter how different they were, she always knew she could count on her big brother.

"It wasn't the best breakup ever. My fault. He said I broke his heart."

"Relationships end. It's a fact of life. That's no excuse for anger," Ross said. "You had a narrow escape."

Clemmie didn't disagree, although she hadn't broken up with Liam because of his temper. Until that night she hadn't even known he had a temper.

She'd broken up with him because he wasn't who she wanted him to be. And she'd learned something that night.

She'd learned that she was better on her own than with the wrong person. And that there was no point drifting through life hoping things might happen. She had to do what she could to make them happen.

"Don't mention Liam to Mum and Dad, will you? He's a banned subject."

"I'd be happy if his name was never mentioned again, but you shouldn't let him put you off men," Ross said. "Do you want some dating advice?"

"From *you*?" Alice reached across and spooned some of his rice onto her plate. "You don't know a single thing about dating."

"On the contrary, I'm a very experienced dater. And stop eating my food."

"*Our* food." She popped rice into her mouth. "We're family. What's yours is mine."

He pulled his plate farther away from her. "This reminds me of all those weekend breakfasts when you stole my bacon."

"I love bacon. And you, Ross Miller—" she pointed at him with her fork "—are a serial dater. You go on two dates and then move on. Which means you haven't found anyone that you connect with, which also means presumably that you're picking the wrong people which means you actually know *nothing* about dating."

"And you're suddenly an expert? Just because you've been with Nico for a record nine months? Finally you meet a guy who can tolerate you and now you know everything?"

"Tolerate?" Alice narrowed her eyes. "He does more than tolerate me. He loves me."

Ross yawned. "Because he doesn't know you the way we do."

"Stop it, you two." Clemmie tried to block it out. Bickering was a pastime for them, like doing a crossword puzzle. They thrived on it. The lively exchange of words energized them.

"Sorry," Alice said. "We don't mean it. I love you, Ross. You're the best big brother any woman could have. I hope all your dreams come true this Christmas."

Ross grinned. "Are you going to leave my bacon alone? Because that would be a start."

"I'll think about it." Alice helped herself to Clem's chicken. "So how's it all going in your tycoon world, Ross? I read an article about you last week. Apparently, you're an investor favorite."

"Business is good, thanks, but it's time to shake things up a little. We're going to start looking for a new creative agency in the New Year," Ross said. "We need to broaden our audience. But that's between us. Not to be discussed in front of Dad, obviously."

"We know that. You don't have to spell it out." And it upset Clemmie that there was tension between them. "I wish the two of you could talk about it. I'm sure Dad would be interested in what you're doing."

"He wouldn't, believe me. Not unless the conversation ended with me announcing I was selling the business and coming to work for him. Six generations running the business," Ross said, stabbing a piece of chicken, "and then I drop the ball."

Clemmie felt sorry for her brother because it was true the pressure was all on him. "I wish you didn't feel so guilty about that."

Ross gave a half smile. "So do I. Now, let's change the subject. Alice, you should have brought Nico tonight."

"He's in Paris at a conference this weekend—leave my food alone." She snatched her plate away. "And, anyway, this is sibling time."

Ross grinned. "Probably Nico's last chance for peace and quiet before he joins you for Christmas."

Alice narrowed her eyes. "I'll have you know he can't wait to join me for Christmas." She poked at her food. Her cheeks were pink. "He proposed to me."

There was a stunned silence.

"No way." Ross stared at her and Alice put her fork down.

"What's that supposed to mean? Why are you looking at me like that?"

"I'm just trying to figure out why anyone would want to marry you."

"Shut up, Ross. Alice, that's wonderful." Clemmie gave her sister a hug. It hadn't occurred to her that of the three of them Alice would be the first to settle down. "I'm so happy for you, truly. Congratulations. Mum and Dad are going to be thrilled."

"You can't tell Mum and Dad! Promise me. Not a word." Alice took a big gulp of wine and Clemmie glanced at Ross.

He shrugged. "Don't look at me. Nothing she does ever makes sense to me. But the list of things we can't tell our parents is growing. It might be safer to make a list of the things we *can* talk about. How about the weather? Is that safe?"

"But why wouldn't you tell them?" Clemmie was confused. "You said he proposed, and—"

"I haven't said yes. I'm still thinking about it."

"He proposed, and you said you'd *think* about it?" Ross shook his head and emptied the last of the rice onto his plate. "This is why I'm never proposing. You put it all out there, make yourself vulnerable and then get your face slapped. Who needs that?"

"I did not slap anyone's face."

"I bet it feels that way to Nico."

Alice looked stricken. "It does not. And it's perfectly fine to say I want to think about it. Life isn't a romantic movie. Marriage is a serious life choice. It requires proper thought."

"I know," Ross said. "Why do you think I'm single?"

"You're single because no one can tolerate you for a week, let alone the rest of your life."

"Stop it!" Clemmie returned to her food and picked up her fork. "Did he give you a ring?"

"Yes. But don't ask to see it." Alice swallowed. "I gave it back."

"You didn't like it?"

"It was stunning. Gorgeous."

Ross shook his head. "That's why Nico isn't here tonight. He isn't in Paris, he's in therapy."

Clemmie ignored her brother. Couldn't he see that this was *huge*? "Don't you love him, Alice?" She felt a pang of sympathy for Nico. One-sided love had to be one of the worst things in the world.

"Yes, I love him." Her sister didn't hesitate. "I love him so much it hurts."

"And you believe he loves you?"

"I know he does."

Clemmie felt a twinge of envy. "Then what's the problem?" In this busy, complicated world it was so hard for two people to find each other and fall in love. Surely if that happened, you'd grab the chance without hesitation?

"It's not a *problem* exactly." But there was a troubled look in Alice's eyes that Clemmie couldn't ever remember seeing before.

If people asked, she would have said that she and her sister were close, but the truth was that although there was plenty of love between them, Alice rarely confided in her. Alice didn't seem to confide in anyone. She'd never been good at opening up. Clemmie had often wondered whether that was because her sister refused to admit her fears and vulnerabilities.

She would have left the subject alone, but Ross wasn't so sensitive.

"Then why didn't you say yes?"

"Relationships are complicated and—I love my work. Not all the time, obviously. Sometimes I hate it, but even when I'm hating it, and I'm too busy and stressed, and we're understaffed, and it feels as if the whole world is sitting in the waiting room and the system is buckling and straining under the pressure, I'd still rather be doing what I do than anything else. It means something to me."

"Still not seeing the problem." Ross picked up his glass and sat back. "What's your work got to do with anything?"

Clemmie sent him a warning look but he wasn't paying attention to her. His gaze was fixed on Alice, who was looking more and more uncomfortable.

"I'm not sure I'd be very good at being a wife, that's all."

"What's that supposed to mean? We're not in the nineteenth century. Are you saying Nico is expecting you to give up work, swap scrubs for an apron and prepare his meals?"

"He's not expecting that. At least—" Alice had given up

on her food "—I don't think he is. We haven't talked about the details so I don't really know what he expects."

That didn't sound right to Clemmie. "You haven't talked?"

"No. And—marriage changes things, doesn't it?"

"Why are you asking us? Here." Ross topped up her glass. "Maybe wine will give you clarity."

Clemmie focused on her sister. "What exactly are you afraid will change, Alice?"

"Life." Alice stared at her glass. "*My* life. Dating is fine, but marriage—marriage comes with expectations. What if once we're married it turns out that he wants things I don't want. Things I'd be no good at?"

"Like what?"

"I don't know—" Alice gave a shrug. "Family. Kids. Nico probably wants all that."

"And you don't?"

Alice played with the stem of her glass and avoided eye contact. "I don't know. Until Nico proposed I hadn't thought much about it. But no." Finally she looked at them. "I don't think I want children."

"Right." It seemed Ross had finally understood that his sister was upset and conflicted. "It's okay not to want kids, Alice. It's not compulsory."

"But people expect it, don't they? If I tell Mum and Dad we're going to get married we all know that the first thing they'll be thinking is *grandchildren*."

"Maybe. But that's just a type of conditioning. And what they think doesn't matter, Ally." Ross reverted to his childhood name for her. "The only thing that matters is what you want."

"And what Nico wants."

"Sure. But do you know for sure he wants kids?"

"I don't know anything. We've barely spoken since the

night he proposed. He's been working. I've been working."
Alice lifted her gaze, miserable. "I suppose I've also been
avoiding him because I didn't want to ask the question. He's
half-Italian and Italians are all about family, aren't they?"

"That's a sweeping generalization. And isn't Italy's birth
rate falling?" Clemmie cleared the empty cartons into a bag.
Her own emotions were churning around inside her. "But
that's irrelevant. You can't think about society's expectations,
or his family's expectations. You have to do what's right for
you."

"Easy enough for you to say. You're the traditional type.
You're not the one who is going to be judged."

She was definitely going to be judged, Clemmie thought,
but she didn't want to dwell on that right now.

"All I'm saying is that you're making a lot of assumptions,
Alice. You need to talk to him."

"I know, but what if I bring it up and he says '*I want ten
children* and I expect you to give up your job to look after
them.' Then our relationship is probably over, and I can't
bear for it to be over. I really do love him. He's smart, and
funny, and kind, and interesting and also no one fillets a fish
like he does—"

Ross raised an eyebrow. "Fillets a fish?"

Alice waved a hand. "It's probably being a surgeon. He's
good with knives and you know I can't stand bones in my
fish—"

"Right. Fillets a fish. Well you're obviously a perfect
match—" Ross reached across the table, gave her hand a
squeeze. "Have the conversation, Alice. Nico loves you. If
he didn't love you he wouldn't have proposed."

"Don't be nice to me. It scares me when you're nice." She
sniffed. "And not wanting kids is huge."

"Kids aren't everything," Ross said. "What if you both desperately wanted kids but then couldn't have them for some reason? Would you break up? I hope not. Life is full of obstacles, Alice, you know that better than anyone. What you need is someone who will work through all those obstacles with you."

"There speaks a man who is an island and works through everything himself."

"Hey, I'm willing to welcome the right woman onto my island in the right circumstances." Ross flashed a smile and Clemmie stood up and cleared the plates.

"So what happens next with you and Nico?"

"We've agreed to let it lie for a while and discuss it again. But now I'm nervous about the holidays. We've been giving each other some space, but there won't be any space at Christmas. And you know what Nanna Jean is like. She'll love Nico and before you know it she will be poking and prodding and finding out his intentions. Chances are he'll tell her, because she looks at you in that way—"

"We know the way."

"Exactly. Everything spills out. And they'll be shocked that I haven't immediately said yes. And probably disappointed in me." Alice glanced at them both, pleading. "I need your help. Anytime the topic turns to my relationship with Nico, distract them."

"Don't look at me." Ross stood up. "I love you, but not enough to turn the heat onto myself at Christmas. Anyway, I'm not dating anyone."

"Pretend you are." Alice stood up and helped herself to a glass of water. "You could invent some high-flying power-hungry executive who is always working and tell them you invited her for Christmas but sadly she couldn't make it on account of being high-flying and power-hungry."

"A fictitious girlfriend?" Ross thought about it. "That's not the worst idea in the world."

Clemmie rolled her eyes. "Trust me, it's the worst idea in the world."

"I'm not so sure. It sounds like low-maintenance dating to me. I don't know why I haven't thought of it before." Ross was laughing. "Does this fictitious girlfriend have a name? How about Victoria."

"No." Alice set her glass on the table. "You need a softer name."

"I thought you said she was a high-flying power-hungry executive. If she was given a 'soft name,' whatever that is, then she would have changed it."

"No. Because she isn't insecure. This woman is comfortable in her own skin. She knows who she is. She doesn't need her name to work hard for her because she's already proven herself."

"I like the sound of her," Ross said. "But she still needs a name."

"Alison? No. Too like Alice. It would be a nightmare at family gatherings."

Ross raised an eyebrow. "You do realize this is fictitious, so she won't actually *be* at a family gathering?"

"Rosemary." Alice looked at Clemmie. "What do you think?"

"I think you've both drunk too much wine."

"We need inspiration." Alice grabbed a magazine from the top of the pile. "*The Face of Modern Marketing.* Meet Lucy. There you go, Ross. Lucy." She tossed the magazine over to her brother. "Lucy is a good name. Friendly, approachable but a killer at her job."

"Lucy." Ross glanced briefly at the cover. "Fine. Lucy it

is. I'm dating Lucy, but she's the face of modern marketing so we barely get to see each other. Sounds perfect."

Seriously?

"You're not actually going to do this, are you?" Clemmie loaded plates into the dishwasher. "You can't make up a girlfriend, Ross."

"Why not? I'm only using it as a way to stop the conversation. It will be a throwaway comment, although I have to say I might be falling in love with fictitious Lucy." He looked at Alice. "I don't suppose you have a number for her as well as a name?"

"She wouldn't take your call," Alice said, "because you are exactly the type of alpha male she avoids. Killer Lucy is far too sensible and sure of herself to date a man like you."

"I am not an alpha male. I'm a modern man with evolved views."

"Your level of self-delusion is unbelievable."

And just like that they were off again.

Clemmie focused on clearing up.

The irony was that all she had to do was confess her current plans to her family and she'd have their full attention.

But she had no intention of doing that. Not before Christmas. Like her siblings, she wanted a peaceful happy time and telling them what she had in mind would kill all hope of that.

5

Lucy

"Are you sure this is a good idea?" Maya helped Lucy pack boxes of the Fingersnug into a bag. "Isn't there a risk that turning up at his house in Scotland makes you look like a stalker?"

"I can see why you might be concerned about that and I'm not going to say it didn't cross my mind, but no. Firstly because I'm in Scotland anyway, doing a photoshoot for the Fingersnug along with reindeer and several influencers, and secondly because this is what Zoe told me to do. I'm simply following her advice. And it's not as if I haven't tried every other route first." Maybe she was overstepping a little, but sometimes you had to take a risk to get ahead.

Ever since Arnie's health scare she'd been working flat out to put together ideas for Miller Active. She was excited about her plan and desperate to get her proposal in front of Ross Miller before the competition snagged his attention. She was willing to take the chance that the whole thing could explode in her face. What was the worst that could happen? He'd slam the door on her, which wouldn't be pleasant but at least she'd be able to limp home knowing that she'd done everything she could to help Arnie and protect people's jobs.

"Who is Zoe?"

"Ross Miller's personal assistant. She's great. She's organized, and she knows everything. We went to that new wine bar near the river last night, and—"

"You went to a wine bar with Ross Miller's assistant?"

"Yes." Lucy tucked some of the festive "props" she'd bought into the bag. "We've been talking every day for the past week, and we've become friendly."

Maya shook her head in disbelief. "How do you do it? If someone stands still for long enough, you befriend them."

"It wasn't hard. I like her. I took my proposal over to the office and we got chatting. Turns out she's from Scotland, too, and she knows Ross from school."

"And he gave her a job?"

"Why not? She's brilliant. And who knows, maybe she threatened to reveal all his secrets if he didn't employ her." Lucy added two boxes of fairy lights to the bag. "They're obviously good friends. Sounds as if they have one of those fun relationships full of banter where she scolds him, and he pretends to do as he's told. Can you pass me the snow globe?"

Maya handed it to her. "Good friends? Or very good friends."

"Not romantic. According to Zoe, Ross isn't involved with anyone. He occasionally dates, but women tend to get frustrated by his focus on work. He actually forgot about his last date, left her sitting in a restaurant." She forced the snow globe into the bulging bag. Maybe it had been optimistic of her to think she could manage with the one bag.

"Not the king of romance, then," Maya said. "Does Ross know that his assistant is revealing his entire personal life to strangers?"

"I'm not a stranger. I've seen her four times this week."

Maya rolled her eyes. "And no doubt by Friday you'll be godmother to her children."

"She doesn't have children, although she would like to. She's dating William, but he's currently living in Edinburgh and she misses him horribly. William, it seems, is very slow to make a commitment so Zoe is thinking of proposing herself. We talked through a few strategies." Lucy tried to close the bag and failed. "A little help, please?"

Maya pushed the sides of the bag together. "No offense, but since when did you become the expert on marriage proposals?"

"I know a lot about the theory." Finally, Lucy managed to close the bag. "You don't have to travel the world to teach geography. I'm creative, that's my job. I know how to make an impact. Also, I pay attention to what people want and need. That's the basis of successful selling and, in the end, that's what we're doing. All the time. Every day. I'm going to be selling the idea of me to Ross."

"So where does William fit into this?"

"William works in risk assurance so it's understandable that he won't be given to impulse. He needs a little something to nudge him past that caution barrier. Fortunately Ross Miller closes the office for a week over Christmas, which means Zoe can go home, too." Lucy lifted the bag. "This weighs a ton. Nothing else is fitting in there."

"He closes the office?"

"Yes. He goes home to Scotland to spend time with his family."

"That's nice."

"It is. I like it when people appreciate family." Lucy lowered the bag back to the floor. "I feel as if I've forgotten something. What else do I need?"

"A whole lot of good luck and the bound copies of your proposal. You wanted two, is that right?" Maya handed them to her. "You haven't discussed this with Arnie, have you?"

"No. He is supposed to be resting. No stress. You know what he's like. If I even mention this, he'll want to be involved." She knew she'd never forget the sight of Arnie being taken away in an ambulance. For a horrible moment she'd thought she might lose another person she loved, but fortunately it hadn't turned out to be as serious as they'd feared.

Arnie had been discharged with medication and a lecture on lifestyle.

He was keeping in touch with the office, but Lucy had given everyone strict instructions not to contact him.

The office felt strange without him there. Even the Christmas tree and the decorations couldn't make up for his absence. But if he rested now, hopefully he'd be well enough to come back to work in January.

In the meantime she was holding the fort.

Maya gestured to the proposals in Lucy's hand. "Good work, by the way. Clever. I think Ross Miller will be impressed."

"Let's hope so." She grabbed some Christmas wrapping. "Did you see the photo Ted sent round? The baby is gorgeous."

"They're not getting any sleep."

"I know. Ted says he watches the baby half the night to check she's still breathing." Lucy knelt on the floor, cut the wrapping paper and measured a length of ribbon.

"Ribbon?" Maya frowned. "You're not seriously gift wrapping the proposal?"

"Why not? It's Christmas." She wrapped the document carefully. "Even the most hard-hearted businessman can't help but respond to wrapping paper covered in cheerful robins, surely?"

"That's why you're wrapping it? To fill his hardened heart with festive joy?"

"No." Lucy tied the ribbon and secured the label she'd handwritten in careful script. "I'm wrapping it in case something happens and I'm not able to deliver it to him personally. It's Christmas, and they have a big family gathering every year."

"Zoe again?"

"No. I read about it in that magazine feature I mentioned." She'd pored over every page, envious of the oversize Christmas trees, the lush garlands adorning fireplaces and the curved banister. "If I hand them a boring-looking proposal the chances are they're going to forget about it. Who wants to read a boring document at Christmas? If I wrap it, then there is a good chance that at some point over the festive season it's going to be opened."

"Possibly by one very disappointed kid who is immediately going to throw a tantrum before tossing it out of the window."

"No young children in the family, according to my research." She tucked the wrapped parcel carefully into her laptop bag, along with the spare unwrapped proposal.

"Please tell me you're not dressing as Santa when you drop it off."

"I wasn't planning to—" Lucy rocked back on her heels "—but now you're making me think."

"Well don't think. You've done enough thinking." Maya rested her hip on the desk and folded her arms. "So why didn't he go into the family business?"

"Ross? I have no idea, and it's not relevant. I am not there to interfere with family politics. I am simply going to ring the doorbell and hand over my gift. Merry Christmas. That's it."

"You should have put a copy of that marketing magazine in with the proposal. Cover girl Lucy."

Lucy stood up and put the unused wrapping paper back on her desk. "That's one of those awards that we are all super proud of, but no one else in the world has ever heard of."

"But you're the face of modern marketing. He might be impressed."

"Or not." Lucy glanced at her phone. "I have an hour before my train leaves."

"The sleeper. I've always thought that sounds romantic. Traveling on a train through the darkness, clickety-clack, clickety-clack."

"There is nothing romantic about having a carriage to myself."

"Maybe it will be like one of those spy movies," Maya said, "where the bad guy is lurking, waiting to throw you out of the window."

"And for that comforting thought, I thank you."

"You should have taken some days for yourself while you're up there. Have a mini break."

Lucy couldn't think of anything worse. "I've already booked my return journey the following night. All organized. It's a flying visit."

Even if she had the money for it, she didn't want to spend time in a hotel on her own at Christmas. How miserable would *that* be?

No, she'd spend the day taking creative photos of the Fingersnug with the reindeer herd as her backdrop, and then she'd deliver her proposal to Ross Miller on her way back to catch the train.

As far as she could see, there was nothing that could go wrong.

6

Glenda

Glenda loved Christmas. Ever since she was a little girl she'd loved this time of year, and that sentiment hadn't changed when she'd had a family of her own. Did she overdo it? Were there too many branches of holly, ivy and mistletoe festooning the rooms of the old lodge? Maybe, but really where was the harm in it? Christmas and everything associated with the season was the warm bright beacon of cheer in the long, dark winter. She loved the way Christmas filled the house, not just the decorations and the greenery but the anticipation and then the people. The place felt warmer somehow. Even though she knew it was ridiculous, it sometimes felt as if the house itself shared her feelings. It was as if for a few weeks every year it shook off the creaks and leaks and got ready to welcome the family inside its sturdy walls. Doors were flung open on rooms that often went unused for the rest of the year, fires were lit, dark corners gleamed with candles and lights.

She loved the scents, the build of anticipation, the way excitement throbbed through the house. She enjoyed the food preparation—the weighing, the chopping, the frying, the stirring—and the finished products, slow simmered casseroles dense with flavor, puddings rich with fruit and spice. She filled the freezer with carefully labeled containers *venison casserole for ten* and planned big celebratory meals around the table where everyone stayed up too late and drank too much. Her version of hot chocolate was legendary, freshly grated chocolate melted into hot milk and served in sturdy red mugs topped with generous swirls of thick cream.

Most of all she loved decorating the trees that Douglas and Fergus hauled back from the forest. She enjoyed it even when Nanna Jean was in one of her fussier moods. Like now, when every decoration Glenda hung turned out to be the wrong one in the wrong place.

"Right a bit," Nanna Jean said, squinting up at the tree. She was clutching a large box of decorations that Glenda had unearthed from the attic a few days earlier. "No, not there—further up—wait, that looks terrible. It's too close to the other one. Try lower down."

Glenda turned and felt the chair wobble. She looked at her mother-in-law. This, too, was part of the Christmas routine. "Would you prefer to do it yourself?"

"And land myself in hospital with a broken hip? Miss the first Christmas our Alice brings a man home? I don't think so. I'm not doing anything that might mean I miss the fun here. I even delayed my morning walk because there was a large patch of ice outside the front door. I hope all that snow they're forecasting doesn't arrive before they do, or they might not get here. It's a long drive and that last section, all those twisty narrow roads, isn't fun in winter."

It was something that was worrying Glenda, too. They were predicting the storm of the century, which didn't bode well. One of the newspapers had named it Storm Scrooge, a weather event ready to ruin Christmas for everyone.

From her perch on the chair, she glanced through the tall windows to the wild landscape outside. The light was flat, the skies heavy and ominous. There was already a layer of snow on the tops of the mountains that rose up behind the lodge, and the trees were dusted with it.

"The forecast could be wrong. Let's hope so." But she couldn't deny that the ground had been icy when she'd taken Hunter out earlier that morning.

"It always used to snow at this time of year. Maybe we'll all be snowed in. That would be fun." Nanna Jean gave a mischievous look. "We could rope Alice and her young man together with tinsel and ask as many questions as we like. There would be no escape for them. And don't give me that disapproving look—I know you're thinking the same things I am. You're just doing better at hiding it."

"That's probably true." Glenda laughed and turned back to the tree. She was bursting with questions but was determined not to ask any of them. She had to trust her children to make good decisions. That was what you did when you were a parent. You wanted to hug your children close, but you had to let them go and then you had to watch them fly and not yell, *Be careful*. And if you sometimes lay awake at night worrying about them, then you had to keep it to yourself. Just because you thought things, didn't mean you had to say those thoughts aloud, did it? Not that Nanna Jean had ever subscribed to that ethos.

Glenda pulled herself together. The children were coming

home, not leaving, and she wasn't going to waste a moment of their time together feeling sad.

"We need to finish this before they arrive. There has to be a decorated tree when they walk through that door." And this one was a beauty, with a sturdy trunk and bushy branches with spiky needles that smelled divine. Having a Christmas tree in the house always lifted her spirits and this year they had several. She was determined to make the house as festive as possible and had been working flat out since Alice had announced that she was bringing a guest.

The rooms had been cleaned and decorated with festive touches. The beds were made and adorned with extra cushions and thick, warm throws. She'd put books on nightstands, fresh soap in bathrooms, and she'd dusted, polished and vacuumed until her limbs ached and she'd fallen into her own bed, exhausted. This tree was the last thing on her list of things to do.

"Where do you want this?" She lifted up a pretty silver decoration that had belonged to Jean's mother.

"That decoration is older than I am. I thought it was going to meet an untimely end last year thanks to Hunter's over-enthusiastic tail. Hang it high this year. Up a bit—and left—perfect." Nanna Jean handed her another decoration. "You're a good girl."

"I'm sixty-two, Nanna Jean."

"I've known you since your first day of school when you refused to be parted from your teddy bear. You'll always be that girl to me."

"Thank you for that embarrassing memory."

"You're hanging that too close to the other one—move it to the right…" And so it continued, but Glenda secretly enjoyed it. Their arguments over decorations were another part of the festive routine.

"Is that it?" Finally, Glenda scrambled off the chair and took the box from Jean. "All that is left is the star Clemmie made at school." She lifted it out and felt her chest grow a little tight. Occasionally Douglas suggested that they have a massive clear out, but there were some things Glenda couldn't bear to part with.

"Oh, it's a *star*. I've always wondered." Nanna Jean caught her eye. "Sorry, but it looks like a UFO."

Laughter helped. It did look like a UFO, but she loved it anyway. "Perfection is overrated."

"I tell myself that daily when I look in the mirror."

"I made this with her when she had chicken pox."

"I remember. You were trying to stop her scratching so you kept thinking up things for her to do with her hands. You were a good mother, Glenda. Still are. Those children are lucky to have you. I hope they know that." Nanna Jean, who was neither demonstrative nor particularly sentimental, patted her on the arm. The words and the gesture made Glenda uneasy.

"Is everything all right, Nanna Jean?"

"You mean apart from my wrinkles and my arthritis? Never better." Nanna Jean studied the tree. "Douglas left early this morning. I heard his car."

"Yes." Glenda adjusted a pretty jeweled star that was dangling precariously close to the end of the branch. "They had issues with a delivery so in the end he decided to do it himself."

"He's driving a van?"

"No." Glenda tweaked some of the decorations hanging on the lower branches. "This is a small order for a gift shop near Inverness. Scottish specialties, that sort of thing. They've been customers of ours for two generations and Douglas didn't want to let them down."

"You're talking about the McLeod family. I can't believe he's driving the stock there himself." Nanna Jean sat down suddenly on the nearest chair and Glenda forgot the tree, the decorations and Clemmie's UFO, and hurried across to her mother-in-law.

"Are you feeling unwell?"

"No. I'm being a silly old woman."

Glenda recognized the tone. Brisk. No-nonsense. The tone of someone struggling hard to hold back emotion.

"Nanna Jean?" She spoke gently this time. "Tell me what's wrong."

"I feel guilty, that's all. Guilty." Nanna Jean took a breath. "It's a burden, I know it is, and I'm the one who gave him that burden."

"You mean the business? It's not a burden, Jean—" this was one of those rare occasions when using her given name seemed appropriate "—it's been a gift. Douglas loves the business. He has lived and breathed it since he was a boy."

"I know. I remember him six years old going to work with his father."

"Exactly. He loved it. And he worked in all parts of the business. He even worked in the shop one Christmas."

"And ate more than he sold." Jean gave a sniff. "But he never had a choice, did he? I never gave him the choice. I never once said, *Do you want this?* I never once asked him, *Is there something you'd rather do instead?* You've let your children choose their own paths, and they've all chosen something else. It never occurred to me that Douglas would do anything but join the family business. I never even asked him if he wanted to."

Glenda felt a flicker of unease. Her mother-in-law had always been strong and fierce. This show of introspection and self-doubt was unlike her.

"Where is this coming from, Nanna Jean? If there was something he would rather have done, he would have said so."

"We both know that isn't true. He's a good son. He was a good son to his father, taking over the business. He's a good son to me." Nanna Jean rummaged in her pockets for a tissue. "Because of him you have your old mother-in-law rattling round in your home. What woman needs that?"

"I do." Glenda felt her throat grow thick. "I need that. And this is your home. *Our* home. We love having you here, Nanna Jean."

Jean blew her nose hard. "Probably because I make you feel young and sprightly."

"That's what it is." At least she was making an attempt at a joke. That was a good sign. "Also, when you're not in command of Christmas tree decorating, you're great company. This house feels far too big and empty since the children left and it's not as if we're all on top of each other. We have all this space—" Too much space, she often thought, but there was nothing to be done about that. There was no way any of them would contemplate selling the lodge, and they needed every bit of that space when the children came home.

"When the children were here, I felt as if I was a help."

"You were a help. You still are a help. But you don't have to earn your keep, Jean." Glenda took her hand, feeling the fragility of the fingers under hers. "You're the best mother any man could have, and the best mother-in-law if it comes to that. Why are you thinking like this now?"

"Because I saw his face at breakfast the other day. He's struggling. It's too much for him. But he can't slow down because the responsibility is all his. He was hoping to share it with the children, but they didn't want it. So now he's left holding the weight of it with no one to help. He should be retiring. At least, slowing down. Passing it on. Instead he is working harder than ever and I know you're worried, too, so don't pretend it's nothing."

How could she? Jean had peeled the lid off her own carefully contained worry. Anxiety sank its teeth into her. She couldn't do this now! She had a houseful of people about to descend on her. She didn't have time for a worry attack. She was concerned about Douglas, but this wasn't the time to try and solve a problem that seemed unsolvable.

But it was so unlike Nanna Jean to express concern, that she couldn't ignore it. "I am worried, but not because I think Douglas doesn't want to do this. He loves it. It's true that things need to change and he needs to hand over some of the responsibility so that he can reduce his hours, but it's for him to decide when the time is right to do that. Douglas loves the business. He loves it as much as you do."

"Or maybe he never felt he had a choice but to love it."

Was that true? No, definitely not. Or maybe it was. The business had always been part of their lives and they'd never considered an alternative. "It's never a good idea to try and guess what people are thinking. You should talk to him about it. I think I know what he'll say."

"I don't want to talk about it, in case I hear something I don't want to hear. I'd rather put my head in the sand. I'm sorry. Ignore me. I'm old and creaky and I was having a weak moment." Nanna Jean stuffed the tissue back in her pocket, patted Glenda's hand and stood up. "Enough of this. There's work to be done. I haven't finished nagging you yet. You really think I'm the best mother-in-law?"

"Well you're the only one I've ever had," Glenda said, "but I can't think of a version I'd prefer."

"Douglas is lucky to have you."

"I tell him so daily."

Nanna Jean straightened her shoulders and stared at the

tree. "Apart from the UFO, that's done. You and Fergus have transformed the Loch Room. What else do we need to do before they arrive?"

"Nothing. I've already lit the fire in the bedroom. The trees are decorated, there's shortbread in the oven…" she checked her watch "…due out in five minutes. Which means, I think, that we should put the kettle on."

Nanna Jean nodded. "It looks beautiful, Glenda. Like a fairy-tale house. Exactly as I remember it being when I was a girl."

"Good." Glenda gave her a quick hug. "Now let's head to the kitchen. It would be embarrassing if we burned the shortbread."

"We could always open a tin of our own, although I suppose eating the stock doesn't do much for profits." Nanna Jean glanced toward the door. "Do you think Hunter will bark when they arrive?"

"Probably. Not much passes him by."

They headed to the kitchen, which was filled with the delicious scents of home-baked shortbread.

Glenda removed the tray from the oven while Nanna Jean made the tea.

The shortbread was cooling on a rack in the middle of the table when Hunter dutifully barked.

Nanna Jean looked up. "That must be them! Let's go to the living room. We can watch from there."

"Watch?"

"Yes. You can tell a lot about a relationship by watching a couple when they don't know they're being watched."

"Nanna Jean, I am not spying on my children through a crack in the curtains, and neither are you."

"Who said anything about a crack in the curtains? I intend to stand in the middle of the window in full view. And if they see me, I'll wave. They won't think they're being spied on. They'll think I'm an old woman who shouldn't be risking pneumonia standing on the front doorstep in a howling wind in the middle of winter. One of the advantages of aging is that people often excuse odd behavior." Nanna Jean walked briskly toward the living room, and Glenda hesitated for a moment and then followed.

How should she handle this?

"Please don't be embarrassing."

"I do not intend to be embarrassing. 'Scatty old lady' is the role I'm playing today." The insecurities of less than an hour ago seemed to have vanished. Glenda wasn't sure whether to be concerned or relieved. Still, it was probably good for both of them to be distracted.

She stood by the window and saw a sleek black sports car pull up outside the lodge.

"Look at that car. Good thing the worst of the winter isn't on us yet because there is no way that would make its way safely over our rutted roads. Sexy car, though. Now I want to see the man."

"Nanna Jean—"

"What? This is the most exciting thing that has happened in my life for a long time, so I intend to enjoy every moment. I hope he's tall," Nanna Jean said. "I love a tall man. And he'd be able to put the UFO on top of the tree."

"Clemmie is with them. Please don't call it a UFO. I should—"

"Don't go out yet." Nanna Jean grabbed her arm. "Give them a minute. Goodness that car must be uncomfortable in the back. Lucky our Clemmie isn't that tall. Still, she must be twisted like a pretzel. Let me see them first—oh." She craned her neck. "Look at that. He's as handsome as his car. Dark hair. I used to love a man with dark hair, although of course as you grow older your standards change. Now I love a man with any hair."

"Nanna Jean—"

"Don't use that tone with me. There's no age limit to fantasies. Oh, look at that—" Jean nudged her "—he's walking round to open the car door for her—"

"I can see that."

"—but she's Alice, so she's jumped out without waiting. I suppose such an old-fashioned gesture will offend her feminist sensibilities, but I've never understood why one should be offended by good manners."

Glenda saw Alice step out of the car. Her heart lurched. Alice. So fierce and focused. And so intensely vulnerable. She felt an ache in her chest. Was she the only one who saw that side of her daughter? Was she the only one who understand how much she feared failure? Whether it was learning to walk, or passing her exams, Alice never gave up until she'd succeeded.

Nanna Jean leaned closer to the window. "She's thinner."

Was that true?

"Whatever you say, do *not* mention her weight. Or her hair. Or anything personal."

"I'm going to talk about the weather for the entire time they're here. I've been practicing in my room. I'm confident I can have a ten-minute conversation about storm clouds without looking at my notes."

Glenda paused. "Do you really think she's thinner?"

"Yes. And that's with her coat on."

Concern crept through her. Alice *did* look thinner. Was she working too hard, or was it something else?

She wasn't going to ask, because asking was a sure way of ensuring that Alice left the room with a *Don't fuss, Mum* and very possibly a slammed door.

She'd have to hold the worry inside, but she was used to that. Worry never went away, no matter how old your children were. It was her problem to deal with.

"Do you think it's work?" Glenda knew that the hours were long and the work hard and stressful, even though Alice generally spared them the details.

"Maybe. Or maybe it's being in love," Nanna Jean said. "I couldn't eat a thing when I was first in love."

"Really?"

"No, not really. I'm just trying to make you feel better."

Glenda saw Alice and Nico exchange a glance—*what did that mean exactly?*—and then her view was blocked by Nico's wide shoulders and Clemmie stepped into view, hair curling wildly around her face. She wore colorful leggings, heavy boots and an oversize sweater that she'd knitted herself. Nanna Jean had taught her to knit during the long winter evenings when both Alice and Ross had left home and Clemmie was the only one left. They'd sat together on the sofa closest to the fire, Clemmie's lip caught between her teeth as she concentrated.

Clemmie had spent half her life trying to keep pace with her brother and sister and finally given up the race.

I'm never going to be like them, she'd told Glenda one day on the drive home from school.

You don't want to be like them, Glenda had replied. *You don't need to be. You just need to be you.*

She'd been careful to treat her children as individuals because that was how she saw them. She'd never made comparisons, but that hadn't stopped Clemmie making them herself. Occasionally a teacher would casually comment that she was *nothing like her siblings*, a remark that meant Clemmie would walk around with red eyes for days, her confidence crushed.

Glenda had been careful to nurture her interests, but it

had taken a while for Clemmie to accept that her talents lay elsewhere.

"Right, enough of this, I'm going to give them a warm welcome." She headed out of the room, cast a last satisfied glance at the Christmas tree and opened the door.

Alice as usual had one small suitcase, and Clemmie had so much luggage it looked as if she was moving home. Glenda smiled. The luggage summed up her girls. One traveled light through life, no baggage and no commitments, the other surrounded herself with things of comfort.

The man with them scooped up two of the bags in one hand, tucked an elaborately wrapped box under his arm and Glenda reminded herself that this time, it seemed, Alice had made a commitment.

Hunter bounded past Glenda before she could grab his collar, barking with excitement when he saw Clemmie.

"Hunter." She dropped her bag and bent to hug the dog, which wasn't easy because his tail was wagging so hard his whole body was a moving target. "I've missed you." Daughter and dog were tangled up for a moment and then Hunter turned his attention toward Nico, who crouched down and rubbed the dog's fur.

"Well look at that," Nanna Jean said from behind her. "A man who likes dogs. Marry him right away, I say."

"Please *don't* say," Glenda begged. "Don't say anything at all."

"Mum!" Clemmie sped forward and enveloped Glenda in a tight hug.

"It's good to have you home. We've missed you. I've missed you." Her heart flew. Happiness seeped into her, lifting her mood. She wanted to hold on to this moment, where the long lazy, cozy days together still lay ahead. She knew the time would pass far too quickly. She wished so often that they lived closer so that visits could be frequent and casual, but she knew she was lucky that they still wanted to come home.

For now she simply enjoyed the hug. Clemmie had always been the hugger in the family. She'd hugged Glenda when she'd picked her up from school, right up until the day she'd left, unlike Alice, who had hung out with her friends and sauntered to the car at the last minute, *Don't ever hug me in front of my friends, Mum.* Clemmie never rationed affection.

"How was the journey?"

"Great when Nico was driving." Clemmie stepped back and picked up her bags. "Not so good when Alice took over."

Alice unwrapped her scarf. "Are you criticizing my driving? Because I took an advanced driving course recently and the instructor said I was the best he'd ever taught."

"You're a very competent driver," Clemmie said. "But you're always stressed. You yell at fellow road users. Was that part of your course?"

"If you're talking about the cyclist we passed who wasn't wearing a helmet, then I had reason. If you'd ever had to tell someone that their relative had died because of a massive head injury that quite possibly could have been avoided had they been wearing a helmet, then you'd be stressed, too."

Clemmie pulled a face. "People aren't perfect, Alice."

"Well if he'd come off his bike he would have been a long way from perfect, I can tell you that for nothing."

"Too much detail, Alice."

"All I'm saying is that there are enough ways to accidentally kill yourself without being wantonly careless. And if you'd seen firsthand the injuries that can occur when—"

"Enough!" Clemmie covered her ears. "You are not to talk about blood, or anything related to blood."

"You're so weird. How on earth do you manage when the kids you look after fall over? Hi, Mum." Alice stepped forward and hugged Glenda. It was a more restrained hug, and briefer, than her sister's but that was Alice.

"I call you when Georgie falls over," Clemmie was saying but Glenda wasn't paying full attention because Nico held out his hand.

"Mrs. Miller. I'm Nico. It's good of you to invite me. *Grazie*." His smile was warm, his voice deep, and Glenda looked into those dark eyes and thought, *Oh, Alice.*

She gasped as Nanna Jean gave her a less-than-discreet prod in the ribs. "Call me Glenda, please. Come on in. You must be exhausted and starving." Was she chattering? She was so determined not to say the wrong thing and embarrass Alice that her normal grasp of social situations seemed to have abandoned her. She had no idea what to say.

"We stayed overnight with friends in Cumbria so it hasn't been too bad." Alice walked into the house, closely followed by Clemmie.

"Nanna Jean!" There was a further round of hugs and introductions, and it was another five minutes before they were seated in the kitchen.

Alice sat opposite Nico rather than next to him.

"The roads were busy," she said brightly. "I suppose everyone is driving up north for Christmas. They probably left early because of the storm bearing down on us. Fortunately the weather was reasonable for our journey."

"Good." Glenda couldn't remember a time when Alice had given a thought to the weather, let alone expanded on it with such enthusiasm.

Was she finding it awkward bringing someone home for the first time? Was she worried that her family might embarrass her? Glenda would have liked to have reassured her, but with Nanna Jean virtually vibrating with curiosity next to her she knew it was entirely possible that they *would* embarrass her.

How was she going to get everyone to relax?

Perhaps she should have given them some time to unwind first. "Are you sure you're fine having tea before you unpack? I could take you to your rooms first if you prefer."

"You're not running a hotel, Mum." Alice picked up a piece of warm, sugary shortbread. "And I think I know where my own bedroom is."

"You're not in your bedroom," Glenda said. "I've put you in the Loch Room."

"The Loch Room?" Alice put the shortbread down on her plate without touching it. "Why?"

"Because it's the most romantic room in the house," Nanna Jean said. "Apart from your parents' room, obviously, but they're not going to give that up even for an occasion as momentous as this one."

"You are celebrating a special occasion?" Nico leaned forward, curious. "What occasion?"

Nanna Jean beamed at him. "Well the first time Alice brings—"

"More tea, Nanna Jean?" Glenda sploshed tea into her mother-in-law's already overflowing cup and struggled desperately to recover the situation. "What Nanna Jean was about to say was that the first time Alice brings herself home in a while is a cause for celebration." Was that even vaguely grammatical? Could you "bring yourself" home? No, probably not, but at least she'd managed to interrupt Nanna Jean before she could finish her sentence and hopefully Nico would put her warbled explanation down to nerves. "And we love having her here. We should visit London more often I suppose, but it's not exactly round the corner and what with this old house demanding attention, and the business and—anyway, what Nanna Jean was trying to say was that it's always an occasion when the children come home."

Nanna Jean blinked. "Actually that wasn't exactly what I was—"

"We were talking about the Loch Room!" Glenda interrupted again. The knot in her stomach grew tighter and tighter. At this rate Christmas was going to be exhausting. "I've put you both in there because we've had a bit of a problem with damp in your bedroom, Alice. Such a nuisance, but you know what these old houses are like. Anyway, I thought the Loch Room would be better. It's a beautiful room."

Why was Alice looking so appalled? Surely she would have appreciated the extra space? And it was unlike her to be sentimental. Was she really that attached to her old bedroom?

"I like my bedroom," Alice said. "I like it more than the Loch Room. Honestly, Mum, I'd rather—"

"Wait until you see the place. It's been redecorated especially for you," Nanna Jean said. "Fergus has been over here every day working himself into a sweat."

"Fergus?" Clemmie dropped her shortbread. "He's been here?"

"He's here all the time, or it seems that way. He's helping your father convert the stable block into offices."

Alice wasn't interested in Fergus's schedule. "Clemmie can sleep in the Loch Room. Or Ross."

"You're probably worried about the cobwebs and dust bunnies," Nanna Jean said, "but you needn't be. You won't recognize the place. We've renamed it the Royal Suite because if royalty ever visit that's where they'll be staying."

"Wait—" Alice frowned. "You redecorated for *me*?"

"Of course not." Glenda was starting to sweat. This conversation wasn't going the way she'd hoped it would. She hadn't expected Alice to be so prickly and defensive. "Nanna Jean is teasing. You know I've been meaning to do it for years, but it never seems to be the priority. And then when I saw the damp patch in your room I thought, *This is a sign, just do it, Glenda.*"

"I don't mind damp," Alice said. "My place in London is—"

"Don't tell me, or I'll be worrying about the health of your lungs. You are not sleeping in a damp room here, Alice. The Loch Room is all ready for you, and it's looking beautiful. You're going to love it."

Alice's expression suggested there was no hope of that. "You shouldn't have made a fuss, Mum."

She'd thought Alice would be delighted to be staying in the larger room with the better view. She'd thought it would be romantic.

She seemed to have done something wrong, and she didn't understand what.

"It was no bother at all. Just a few hours here and there. Nanna Jean is exaggerating."

"I never exaggerate, and don't let Fergus hear you say that. The boy was here day and night for the best part of two weeks," Nanna Jean muttered. "No fuss whatsoever."

"It's bigger than your room," Glenda said quickly. "And it's Christmas. You always have so much luggage at Christmas. You'll have more space to spread out there. Oh, Clemmie, I can't believe you're using that old mug of yours. You've had it since you were twelve." She had no idea what was bothering Alice but the best way to deal with it was probably to change the subject.

"This is my Christmas mug. I love it. So—how is Fergus?" Clemmie was already on her second piece of shortbread. She'd swapped her shoes for a pair of thick, warm slipper socks that Ross had given her a few winters earlier because he was fed up with her complaining about having cold feet.

"Fergus is grand," Nanna Jean said. "He's raising that little girl as if she was his own. He's a great father. Somehow still manages to do the work of ten people. And little Iona helps him at weekends. He's bought her a tool kit, can you believe that? He's a good lad. And he's single."

Glenda tensed but Clemmie just rolled her eyes.

"I'm sure that between you and Fergus's mother, that situation will soon be fixed. Is he still staying with his parents while he finishes the work on his house? I might drop by and say hello."

"He moved out six months ago. He finally finished the renovations. Although how he found the time between helping us out here and all the work he does for his father, I've no idea. He's a worker, that boy."

"Don't let him hear you call him a boy." Glenda relaxed a little. The conversation had shifted onto safer ground and she didn't have to watch her words with her youngest daughter the way she did with Alice. There was nothing complicated about Clemmie. She was open, easy to understand and never kept secrets.

Clemmie picked up the pot and topped up her tea. "Where's Dad?"

"He had to go into work today, but he's looking forward to seeing you at dinner."

Clemmie put the pot down. "He usually takes the day off when we come home. Is everything okay?"

"You're not six years old, Clem." Alice rolled her eyes. "You don't need your dad waiting at the front door for you."

Glenda welcomed the gentle bickering. It felt normal, and any conversation that wasn't forced was fine with her. Also, any conversation that wasn't focused on Alice's romance.

"I'm worried, that's all," Clemmie said. "He shouldn't be working this hard."

"It's Christmas. Busy time of year. And not being able to

delegate is exactly like Dad." Alice finished her shortbread and looked at her mother. "That's it, isn't it? Nothing's wrong?"

Interesting, Glenda thought, how both children viewed the same problem in different ways. Clemmie was concerned about the long hours, whereas Alice saw them as entirely normal.

How honest should she be? Was a parent's job to shield or to share? It was something she'd pondered often, particularly lately, and still wasn't clear on the answer. If she told them the truth, that it was time for their father to slow down, Ross would feel guilty. She didn't want him to feel guilty. She wanted all three of her children to live the lives they wanted to live. And she definitely didn't want to discuss this now.

"He's fine. Busy, as Alice says. Nico, have more shortbread. I've made a venison casserole for supper, I hope that's all right. Alice said there was nothing you didn't eat."

"That's correct." Nico smiled. "And Alice has told me you're an excellent cook."

Oh pressure, Glenda thought. She'd better not burn anything. "We'll eat at seven thirty because I'm not sure what time Douglas will be home and I'm sure you'll want time to freshen up and change."

"Change?" Alice finished her tea. "Since when did we change for dinner?"

Glenda flushed. "Well it's Christmas, and we have a guest, and—"

"Nico just wants us to behave normally," Alice said, and Nanna Jean muttered something that sounded like, *He's come to the wrong house for that.*

"Of course he does." Glenda put her cup down. This was ridiculous. She was so nervous of saying the wrong thing that the entire encounter felt unnatural and her shoulders were starting to ache with the tension. "I hope you'll make yourself at home, Nico. If there's anything at all you need, just let me know."

"You're very kind."

"So you're a heart surgeon, Nico. How did you meet our Alice?" Nanna Jean leaned forward and now it was Alice who was tense.

Nico, however, seemed entirely relaxed. "We met at work. I was called down to see a patient, and there was Alice. She was—"

"They don't want to hear about that. Clem hates medical talk." Alice cut across at him. "What time is Ross arriving? Will he be here in time for dinner?"

Glenda took a long, hard look at her daughter.

Was she the only one who thought Alice was behaving strangely? She was tense to the point of rudeness. "He called earlier to say that he'd been unexpectedly delayed so he won't be arriving until tomorrow."

"Delayed? You're kidding!" Alice looked appalled. "It's Christmas and there's a storm coming."

"I expect he's busy," Glenda said, but that didn't cut any slack with Alice. Other people were allowed to be busy, but apparently not her brother.

But Alice looked truly unsettled by the news that Ross wouldn't be arriving tonight. "He should try working in the emergency department on a Saturday night, then he'd know busy."

"It's not a competition, Alice." Clemmie stood up and put her mug in the dishwasher. "Can I do anything to help prepare dinner, Mum?"

Glenda was wondering why Ross's absence would bother Alice so much.

"Thank you, but I can manage. You're home now, you can relax. Go and unpack, and then I'm sure Hunter would appreciate a walk." The dog hadn't left Clemmie's side since she'd arrived.

"A walk can wait. I don't want you working too hard. That isn't fair." Clemmie picked up a cloth and wiped down the side. "I can peel vegetables."

"The help would be appreciated, but take a little time to settle in first. Anything else to bring in from the car?"

"No. It's all in the house." Alice stood up, even though she'd barely finished her tea. "We'll take the luggage and unpack."

Clemmie frowned. "We just sat down, Alice, and—"

"I want to unpack. I don't want you accidentally coming across your Christmas presents."

"You remembered to buy presents this year?" Clemmie's face dimpled into a smile. "That's progress."

"One year," Alice muttered. "One year I didn't buy presents. And in fact I *did* buy them, but I was late for the train and left them all at home. But have I ever been allowed to forget it?"

"You go and unpack," Nanna Jean said, "and we will take good care of Nico."

A look of alarm crossed Alice's face. "He's coming, too," she said, beckoning to him, "I need him to lift my suitcase."

Alice had never needed anyone to lift her suitcase in her life, but Glenda said nothing.

The two of them left the room and Nanna Jean cleared her throat.

"Well," she said, "that was more painful than my arthritis on a cold day. What on *earth* is wrong with our Alice?"

7

Alice

She should never have invited Nico home with her for Christmas. At the time it had seemed like a good idea, but that had been before he'd proposed. She loved his company. She loved *him*. But right now she felt nothing but pressure. Bringing him here was a gesture loaded with meaning, at least to her family, and added still more pressure on her. If it hadn't been for her mother's timely interruption, Nanna Jean would have announced to the world that this was the first time Alice had brought a man home and what sort of message would that have sent? Firstly, that Alice was so bad at relationships that no one had ever stuck by her for long enough to meet her family, and secondly, that this relationship must be serious. And it *was* serious, of course, but she still had to figure out exactly where she wanted it to go. She didn't need the extra pressure of making big decisions under the scrutiny of her well-meaning family.

It made it worse that Ross had been delayed. There was no one to take the heat off her.

She sent him a quick text:

Where are you? You'd better show up soon.

There was a knot in her stomach and she could feel the tension in her muscles. Coming home wasn't meant to feel like this. She wasn't supposed to feel defensive and on edge. Of course there was sometimes a little tension while everyone settled back in to being together, and while they carefully managed not to ask about her love life, but generally she slotted back into the family as if she'd never left, like pieces of a jigsaw, all with their own place. But not this time. This time things felt different and the reason for that was the man following her up the stairs.

Ever since that awkward night when he had proposed, they'd both been so busy at work that they'd barely spent time together. She knew they had to have The Conversation, as she'd taken to calling it in her mind, and the longer they waited the harder it was. It grew and grew, this thing between them, the words hovering unsaid, until she could barely see past the obstacle. It was there in every exchange and conversation. It was in her mind the whole time.

Maybe it was in his mind, too, but she didn't know because he hadn't mentioned it and she was too afraid to ask.

She knew she needed to talk to him about it, but she couldn't do that because she still didn't know what she wanted.

She wanted the relationship, absolutely. But did she want marriage? Marriage was different. Marriage came with expectations. What if she couldn't meet those expectations? What if she wasn't good at it? Tackling something she wasn't good at was a quick route to misery.

Was it normal to feel this mixed up? She had no idea. Presumably not. She tried to think of a single movie where the heroine said, "Er, can I think about it?" in response to a proposal.

Since that night she'd stared at babies in prams, and babies who were brought into the hospital and she'd tried to imagine how she'd feel if the child was hers. She was nothing like Clemmie, who clearly found children interesting and loved being around them. She didn't have maternal feelings. She was pretty sure she didn't want a child of her own, although a part of her was nervous that she might change her mind at some point when it was too late.

Either way, she'd told herself that this week away from work would be the perfect time to think carefully about what she wanted and have the conversation, but now she was realizing she'd been wrong about that. Having her family around didn't give her space, it gave her more pressure.

That brief, awkward cup of tea around the kitchen table had been all she'd needed to confirm it. She hadn't been able to relax even for a second, nervous about what her family might say to Nico. She'd barely made it through one cup of tea before making a run for it. How was she going to get through a whole week? She'd have an ulcer by the end of it.

And now, to add to the discomfort of the whole experience, she wouldn't even be sleeping in her own bedroom.

Resigned to her fate, Alice pushed open the door and stopped dead. Nico, right behind her, was forced to put his hands on her shoulders to steady himself.

"What's wrong?"

What was *wrong*? This room, that was what was wrong.

She almost glanced over her shoulder to check she was in the right place, because this looked nothing like the room she remembered. The "Loch Room," as they called it, had always shown signs of wear and tear, but that was no longer the case. It had been transformed from tired to country-style elegance.

The frayed and faded fabric on the window seat had been replaced by dark green velvet and was now piled with soft cushions. The four-poster bed remained but instead of the old quilt, it was draped with luxurious throws. A fire flickered in the fireplace.

Nico put the bags down. "It's like a five-star hotel."

"Yes." She was pretty sure that the "damp" in her bedroom had played no part whatsoever in their decision to give her and Nico this room, but she didn't want to reveal the extent to which the place had been transformed in case he questioned it. *She* was questioning it. The room hadn't been touched for years. Why now? Surely they hadn't done this simply because she'd brought a man home?

But maybe they had. There were fresh flowers on the table by the window, and fruit in a bowl. The rug on the floor was one she hadn't seen before.

The room encouraged the occupants to curl up and enjoy a conversation in front of the fire, or sit on the window seat among soft cushions and admire the view together. The space felt intimate and there was no way, *no way*, she would be able to avoid having the conversation she'd been postponing.

"The view is spectacular." Nico walked to the window. "I had no idea you lived in such a beautiful place. It's incredible, Alice."

"You like it?"

He turned. "You don't?"

She shrugged. "I have mixed feelings. Growing up I hated the fact that we lived so far from civilization. If I wanted to go to a party, Dad had to drive me and pick me up. We're only a ten-minute drive from the village, but if it snows you can forget it. That little bridge we crossed? It becomes impassable. We've been snowed in here a few times over the years. They do clear the snow eventually, but we're the last village at the end of the valley so it takes a while."

"Sounds romantic." He smiled, and her heart kicked against her chest.

When he looked at her that way she found it difficult to focus. She found everything about the situation difficult. She was used to feeling competent and sure of herself, but right now she didn't have a clue.

He hadn't mentioned his proposal since that night.

Had he changed his mind?

"Nico—"

"Alice." He strolled across to her. "It's been a busy couple of weeks. It's good to be here. Good to spend some time together and finally have a chance to talk."

Talk? Did he mean now? She wasn't ready.

"We should go outdoors! We've been cooped up in the car for too long. I should show you around. You can't walk all the way round the loch at this time of year because the waterfall is in full flood, but we can get halfway round and it's gorgeous. We might see deer."

"First you need to relax." He put his hands on her shoulders. "Tell me what's wrong."

"Wrong? Nothing is wrong. Why would you think that?"

"Because you're behaving strangely. You haven't seen your family for a while and yet you couldn't wait to get away from them. And you're tense and jumpy. I've never seen you like this."

She didn't know whether to be pleased or perturbed that he knew her so well. "My family can be embarrassing, that's all."

He gave a half smile. "Everyone's family can be embarrassing, Alice."

"But mine can be *really* embarrassing."

He sighed. "If I promise not to hold you responsible for anything your family do or say during the duration of our visit, will you relax?"

"Okay." It was a lie. She wasn't relaxed, and the reason for that had nothing to do with her family but it was easier to blame them than acknowledge the fact that all her problems really lay inside, not outside. She swallowed. "How do you feel about that walk?"

He watched her for a moment and then let his hands drop from her shoulders. "Sure. Let's walk. I'd like that."

And now she realized that perhaps he was thinking that a walk together would be the perfect time to have the talk they'd both been avoiding.

"We could invite Clemmie."

"Clemmie has already spent about fourteen hours in a car with us. I should think she needs a break." He paused. "And it would be nice to have some time alone with you."

She was out of excuses.

"Right. Why don't you unpack and I'll pop downstairs and see if I can find my old boots and some extra clothing. I packed in a hurry, forgetting how cold it can be up here. I'll meet you back downstairs when you're ready."

She headed back downstairs to the kitchen where her mother, Nanna Jean and Clemmie were gathered. Clemmie and Nanna Jean were peeling vegetables at one end of the table and her mother was rolling out pastry.

They stopped talking when she walked in, which made her wonder if she was the focus of their conversation.

She was becoming paranoid.

"Everything all right?" Her mother sprinkled more flour onto the table. "Do you love the room?"

"Of course she loves the room." Nanna Jean picked up a

parsnip from the small pile in front of her. "How can she not love the room? Do you know how much you'd be paying to stay in a room like that if this was a hotel?"

"It's looking beautiful, don't you think?"

Alice felt guilty and exasperated at the same time.

What was she supposed to say? *Yes, it looks like the honeymoon suite, and by the way that kind of vibe is the last thing I need right now.*

"It's great. Thank you."

"Sit down for a moment." Her mother put the rolling pin down and wiped her hands on her apron. "Is everything okay, sweetheart?"

No, it most definitely wasn't.

"It's fine," she said. "Couldn't be better. I won't sit down, I'm taking Nico for a walk to the loch." And much as she'd been dreading that, she dreaded it less than sitting down for a possible interrogation. "Just need to grab my boots and a scarf."

"I'll fetch them for you." Her mother removed her apron and headed to the "boot room" as they all called the little room that lay between the kitchen and the back door. It was stuffed with coats, hats, boots and snow gear in various sizes that had accumulated over the years. Visitors could almost always find something to fit them. Clemmie's old sledge was still there, ready to be jammed against the door on windy nights to stop it rattling.

"I can do this, Mum. I didn't mean to disturb you."

"Disturb me? How can you possibly be disturbing me? Having you home is the best thing. I know how hard you work, and you must let me spoil you a little bit. I'm making your favorite pie for dessert. Apple and blackberry. We had a good crop of both this year. The freezer is bursting with them."

Alice felt a pressure in her throat and chest.

"Yum. I can't wait."

"I want you to relax while you're here, if you can even remember how to do that." Her mother handed her a scarf and several layers. Then she reached up and touched Alice's cheek. "You look tired. I can imagine how hard you've been working. I've been reading about how busy the hospitals are. It must be exhausting."

It was exhausting, and she *was* tired, but for once she couldn't blame work. She was exercising her brain so hard, trying to find an answer to Nico's question, trying to figure out what it was that she wanted, that she was struggling to sleep.

Rest would be good, but there wasn't much hope of that. She could have relaxed more if she'd come on her own. But it was too late to change that now.

Her mother put her boots by the door. "You'll want to wrap up. It's bitterly cold out there. I think we really could have snow for Christmas. Too much snow, probably. Does Nico need anything? He can borrow something of Ross's. They're about the same build I think."

"He has everything he needs. His family come from the mountains in Italy and he grew up skiing and doing all the outdoor stuff. He has plenty of gear and, unlike me, he remembered to pack it." Alice pulled on the layers but left the boots by the back door. She'd put those on at the last minute.

She walked back into the kitchen and for a moment all she wanted to do was sit at the kitchen table and let Nanna Jean and her mother make a fuss of her.

The impulse freaked her out a little. Since when had she needed to be fussed over? She hated being fussed over.

"Nico is lovely." Her mother sat back down at the table and

picked up her tea. "Such a charmer. We were pleased when you said you were bringing him home to meet us."

Alice was immediately cured of her desire to linger and be fussed over. She wanted to get away before the questions started. Questions she couldn't answer. This was exactly the scenario she'd been dreading, but at least Nico wasn't in the room to hear it.

Nanna Jean looked animated. "He's very handsome. And he has good manners. I like that in a man. You've chosen well, Alice."

"Well, I haven't exactly—I mean this isn't—" Backed into a corner, she gave Clemmie a desperate look.

Clemmie pulled a face, indicating that Alice was just going to have to accept a small amount of parental interest.

"We're pleased you felt you could invite him," her mother said. "Your dad is looking forward to meeting him."

"It's not a big deal, Mum." *He asked me to marry him.*

"You bringing someone home? It's a very big deal. I thought the day would never come." Nanna Jean carefully peeled a parsnip and handed it to Clemmie to slice into batons. "The two of you must be very serious."

"We're just dating, Nanna Jean. We don't even see that much of each other because we're both working so hard."

"Well I can see he has strong feelings. I saw the way he looked at you." Nanna Jean picked up another parsnip and gave Alice a knowing look. "Before you know it, that boy will be proposing."

Alice froze.

Clemmie dropped the parsnip she was holding.

"Ross," she said in a loud voice, and both Glenda and Nanna Jean turned to look at her, startled.

"Ross? What about Ross?"

"I—" Clemmie sent her sister a wild look. "It's just occurred to me that you probably don't know his big news. He's never good at talking about himself, is he?"

"Big news?" Their mother looked baffled. "What big news?"

Clemmie was looking at Alice. "Why don't you tell them, Alice?"

"Er—no. You should definitely do it." Given that she had no idea what her sister was about to say, it was the only answer she could give.

Clemmie stabbed the knife into a parsnip. "Maybe we should let Ross tell them himself."

She'd successfully redirected the spotlight of familial attention from Alice to herself and Alice felt a flash of gratitude. It made her feel less alone to know that her sister had just stepped in front of her to protect her.

But now that Clemmie had successfully diverted everyone's attention, she had to deliver.

Nanna Jean handed her the last parsnip. "Don't tease us. Tell us about Ross."

"I should probably let him—"

"Clementine!"

"He's dating," Clemmie blurted out, and Alice thought, *Oh crap, did she really just say that?*

Although she was relieved to no longer be the focus of attention, that wasn't the route she would have taken. She didn't know whether to laugh or cover her eyes.

Ross was going to kill them.

"Dating?" Nanna Jean's eyes lit up. "Did you hear that, Glenda? Our boy is dating!"

"I heard."

"But why hasn't he mentioned it? Why wouldn't he tell us something like that?"

Alice saw panic in Clemmie's eyes. "Probably because he

didn't want a fuss," she said. "It's very early days. They've not known each other for long."

"But it's serious enough for you two to know about it." Glenda raised her hands. "No, you're right. I'm not going to ask you to gossip about your brother. If he wants to tell us, then I'm sure he'll tell us."

"But if he doesn't tell us, then we're going to ask," Nanna Jean said and Glenda sighed.

"We're not going to ask."

"I am. I'm too old to wait around to be told things. At least tell us her name."

There was a tense awkward silence.

Clemmie was obviously wishing she'd never opened her mouth. "I really shouldn't have—"

"What harm is there in telling us her name?"

Clemmie floundered. "Well um, she—I—" Suddenly her eyes gleamed. "Lucy. Her name is Lucy, and she works in marketing and I believe she's very, very good at her job. I've only seen her once, but she has very shiny dark hair and a nice smile."

Alice covered her mouth with her hand to stop herself from laughing.

Seriously? Had her sister seriously just said that?

"Lucy." Nanna Jean said the name a few times and then nodded. "That's a pretty name. I like it. And it goes well with Miller. Lucy Miller."

If the table hadn't been covered in flour, Alice would have thumped her head down on it.

"You're not to say anything, Nanna Jean," Clemmie said quickly. "Promise me you will not mention Lucy unless Ross mentions her first. Not even after a glass of fizz."

"I'm not responsible for anything I say after a glass of fizz."

Which meant that she was definitely going to say something.

Alice could already predict what lay ahead.

Ross was definitely going to kill them.

8

Clemmie

Clemmie hauled her bags up to her bedroom at the top of the house, wishing she hadn't eaten so much shortbread. Her stomach churned, although she wasn't sure whether that was down to the ingestion of too much sugar or the guilt that had followed her impulsive declaration that Ross had a girl-friend. In trying to save one sibling, she'd condemned the other to a Christmas of fevered parental speculation, but what else could she have done? Alice had been a bag of nerves on the journey from London to Scotland. Clemmie had almost wished she hadn't known about the proposal. It had made her feel awkward around Nico, who was thoughtful and consid-erate but also mildly bemused. He clearly didn't understand what was going on, which presumably meant Alice still hadn't had the conversation she needed to have. And Clemmie had some sympathy with that. After all, there was an important conversation she had never had, wasn't there?

Given that Alice and Nico's relationship was at such a delicate stage, Clemmie hadn't been sure it would withstand parental pressure. Ross was far more capable of handling their mother and Nanna Jean than Alice, which was why she'd stepped in to protect her sister.

But now she needed to find a way of unraveling the tangle she'd just created.

Pushing open the door she walked into her bedroom and instantly felt better. There was her bed, with its patchwork bedcover that she and Nanna Jean had sewn together over long winter evenings when she'd been the last of the Miller children to be living at home. They'd used pieces of fabric from old clothes—there was the blue-and-green-spotted cotton that had originally been a dress that Alice had worn to a school play, and a white patch that had been Ross's tennis shorts. She sat down and stroked her hand over the midnight blue velvet patch that had once been a dress that Nanna Jean had made her for Christmas when she was nine. Feeling its silky softness under her fingers she was transported right back there, to the excitement of Christmas Eve, the scent and sparkle of the Christmas tree her father had brought in from the forest, and the anticipation of the day to come. Her bedcover was as much a family history as the photographs balanced on her overcrowded bookshelves.

She glanced around and felt a pang. Wherever she went, she took plenty of personal items with her, but she'd never managed to re-create the feeling that came from being in this room.

Her brief moment of sentimentality was interrupted by Alice, who thrust open the door without warning. Alice never remembered to knock, although if Clemmie did the same to her she'd never let her forget it.

"I came to thank you." She closed the door behind her. "You are officially my favorite sister."

"Unless there's something Mum and Dad have been keeping from us, I'm your only sister."

"I'm serious." Alice was uncharacteristically hesitant. "That was a very kind thing to do and I'm grateful. It was a horrible moment and if you hadn't stepped in—"

"Come and sit down." Clemmie patted the bed. "Are you okay?"

"Not really." It said a lot about how stressed she was that Alice was willing to admit it. It was unlike her to show vulnerability. "It was a mistake to bring Nico."

"Do you really think that?"

"Yes. It's not his fault. It's me. All me. I'm just not ready for the inquisition. Things were already complicated, and now they're even more complicated and I can't focus on what I want when I'm constantly on alert. I really thought they were about to ask me a direct question, and there wasn't even a bottle of gin on the table. What's it going to be like when they've opened the Christmas fizz?"

"Don't worry about that now. I'm sure it will all calm down."

"I hope so. At least you've given them something else to think about." Alice finally smiled. "Their faces! Sorry I was slow to respond. I couldn't believe you'd actually said that." She sat down on the bed amidst Clemmie's old soft toys and big pillows.

It was Clemmie's turn to feel stressed.

"You looked so panicked I said the first thing that came into my head." But it had been stupid, she could see that now. Clemmie wished she'd used a different source of distraction. She already had enough to think about this Christmas, and now this. "Do you think I should call Ross and confess?"

"Warn him that you've just introduced his imaginary girl-friend to the family? No. Because there's a chance he'll make an excuse and not show up at all and there is no way I'm being the only one under the spotlight. Thanks, Clem. You're the best."

"I'm not sure Ross is going to agree with you."

"He's big and tough. He'll handle it. And he'll forgive you."

"That's what I was telling myself, but now I'm not so sure."

"Chances are they won't mention it, so I'm sure the subject is over and done." Alice grabbed an old, threadbare bunny with pink ears. "I can't believe you still have this."

"You gave it to me when I was eight."

"I know. That's why I can't believe you still have it. I don't think I own a single thing from when I was eight. Mum has some of my paintings but they're awful, and I wish she'd throw them away. Why on earth she wants to keep my embarrassing multicoloured splodges, I have no idea."

"She doesn't keep them because they're brilliant," Clemmie said. "She keeps them because you did them and they're a nice memory."

"Not for me. For me they're a hideous reminder of how generally bad I was at art. Why didn't she keep my science exam paper or something instead?" Alice stroked the bunny's ears absently. "Your room looks exactly the way it did when we were growing up."

"I like it this way. I'd hate it if they changed it." Clemmie glanced at the fairy lights strung around her room. She remembered their father hanging them for her to cheer her up after she'd failed two exams. *There's more to life than exams, Clem.*

Home, Clemmie thought, was the best place in the world. No matter how many posh and stupidly enormous houses she lived in as part of her job, the lodge was still her home. She loved every familiar brick of the place, loved the windows, the views. And she never loved it more than at Christmas, when the whole place sparkled, and the massive tree in the hallway made the place smell like the forest that stretched up from the shores of the loch. When she was little she'd snuggle behind the tree with her book and the family dog—because there was always a family dog—and she'd breathe it in and wish that she could freeze time because Christmas, with the lights and the scents and her family altogether, was her favorite time of year.

She lay back on her bed. "It feels good to be here. Do you hate not being in your room for Christmas?"

Alice shrugged. "No. I'm not sentimental about my bedroom."

"I'd hate not to sleep in my own room. It feels like home. You don't feel that way?"

Alice frowned. "London is home to me. It's where my life is. I love it. Don't you?"

No, she didn't love it.

Clemmie sat up and looked at her sister. Her big sister, who was obviously so conflicted and confused at the moment.

They rarely shared moments like this—moments of emotional honesty—but that episode in the kitchen seemed to have lowered the barriers Alice kept around her and drawn them closer.

Maybe this was the time to tell Alice what was going on with her. What she'd decided.

No. She wasn't going to mention it yet. Alice probably wouldn't understand the decision Clemmie had made and Clemmie wasn't ready to defend herself. And, anyway, Alice was too stressed right now to be able to focus on anything but her own issues.

"London is fine. But if you're not that attached to your

room, why were you so upset that Mum put you in the Loch Room?"

"That had nothing to do with nostalgia. Have you seen what they've done to the place?"

"The Loch Room? No. Obviously not. I arrived when you did."

"It would definitely qualify for Most Romantic Room in the Highlands," Alice said. "It's like a love nest or something. A snuggly Christmas hideaway. Fire. Candles. Soft throws on the bed."

"And that's a bad thing?" Sometimes she struggled to understand her sister but that didn't mean she wasn't prepared to try.

"I don't know. It feels contrived and a bit awkward. It's probably part of a family conspiracy to romance the two of us into an announcement. I'm surprised they didn't put a sign on the door—Propose Here." Alice chewed the edge of her nail as she'd done whenever she was stressed as a teenager.

"Forget them. This is about you. I gather you haven't had the conversation with Nico yet."

Alice let her hand drop and tugged at the rabbit's ears instead. "I'm waiting for the right moment."

Clemmie removed her precious rabbit from her sister's fraught groping. "Hopefully you will have the space and privacy to talk while you're here."

"Are you kidding? Privacy? What's that?" Alice snorted. "Didn't you hear Nanna Jean? *In no time he'll be proposing.* And how about last Christmas? When I was given a list of all the people in my year at school who are now settled down and producing babies every month?"

Clemmie grinned. "That was Dad's fault. His hand slipped when he was pouring the gin. And to be fair they're only doing it because they love you and want you to be happy."

"But what if the things that would make them happy, wouldn't make me happy?" Alice sighed and sat up. "Never mind. Thanks to you, they'll hopefully be speculating about Ross now."

Clemmie groaned. "Thanks for reminding me. Are you sure I shouldn't text him a warning?" She had a feeling Ross wasn't going to be amused. He wasn't going to want to spend his Christmas fending off questions about a fictitious girl-friend.

"Do not text him," Alice said. "Stop worrying about it."

"I feel a crisis coming on."

"Don't be dramatic." Alice yawned. "It's all fine."

"It's not fine! I told Mum and Nanna Jean that Ross is dating."

"I know. And I love you for it." Alice hesitated and then leaned across and hugged her. "You saved me. I'm so grateful."

When had her sister last hugged her? She couldn't remember. It was almost worth what was coming to have this unusual moment of bonding. Alice let her go and picked up an ancient kangaroo that had been Clemmie's favorite toy growing up.

"What if they mention it?"

"What's the worst that can happen? They'll mention that they know about Lucy. Ross will make some noncommittal comment in public, and then threaten us in private. I will take full responsibility. You protected me and I'll protect you. And that will be the end of it."

"Do you think so?"

"Of course." Alice put the kangaroo down and sat up. "Even if Nanna Jean does mention it, Ross will just say we made a mistake—or maybe he'll play along and say it's not going well. He can break up with her and that will be the end of it."

"Break up with her? At Christmas? That's awful."

"It isn't awful! She doesn't exist, Clemmie!" Alice sounded exasperated. "This isn't a real relationship. Lucy isn't real." She stopped. "Well she is real, but fortunately she doesn't know she's temporarily joined our family. She will never know what a narrow escape she had."

Clemmie imagined her mother and Nanna Jean downstairs in the kitchen speculating on the relationship.

She felt for her sister.

She stood up and started to unpack her bags. Being home usually made all her problems fall away, but not this time. She was standing on the edge of a new life. The decision she'd made felt exciting, but also scary and fragile and somehow momentous. She was terrified of telling people, because she didn't want to handle their emotions, and she knew there would be plenty of emotions, so she was carrying around this secret but having a secret didn't feel natural. She'd always been open and honest with her parents, who had proved themselves to be calm and tolerant in every situation. But she knew that this time she was going to worry them or, worse, disappoint them. And how would Ross and Alice react?

Clemmie opened her bags and started stuffing her clothes into her drawers. Her bedroom was the same as it had always been. Her mother had offered to update it, but Clemmie loved it precisely because it hadn't changed. Her walls were still covered in photographs of horses, and her bookshelves were still crammed with all her favorite books, some of them from childhood. She rarely read them now, but she liked the fact that they were there, sharing the room with her like old friends. She had her own tiny bathroom which she loved, even if the pipes did sometimes make weird noises in the night. Better that than sharing with Alice, who left wet towels and empty shampoo bottles littering the place. Tidiness wasn't her sister's forte.

Alice slid off the bed. "I'd better get back to Nico. I don't want to risk him being alone with Nanna Jean."

"He seemed to like her."

"That's not the part that's worrying me." Alice walked to the door. "Thanks again. When Ross marries Lucy I'll be sure to thank you in my sister-of-the-groom speech."

Clemmie wasn't in the mood for being teased. "As you were the reason I did it in the first place, you can explain it to him."

"He'll probably laugh."

"I hope you're right."

"Of course I'm right." Alice opened the door. "This is a fictitious relationship. What could possibly go wrong?"

9

Lucy

Lucy pushed open the door of the old post office that was now no longer a post office but a thriving café that served homemade cakes and frothy coffees alongside locally painted cards and jewelery.

She stepped into a warm fug of cinnamon-scented air. The place smelled like Christmas.

She glanced around her, enchanted.

Here she was in a small village she'd never heard of, far to the north of Scotland where, if the locals were correct, instead of buying a stamp she'd be able to buy a slice of the best, most chocolaty chocolate brownie around.

She hoped they were right, because after navigating tiny winding roads that were no more than tracks in places, she'd earned a sugary treat.

The place was charming and, thankfully, well heated. Her fingers were freezing, her toes were freezing, and she was as grateful for the warmth as she was the delicious smell of coffee, chocolate and winter spices.

There was a small Christmas tree in the corner of the room, and each wooden table had its own festive centerpiece—a flickering candle nestled in a circle of greenery fresh from the forest that surrounded them.

She waited to feel festive and excited about Christmas, but nothing happened. It was as if that part of her had died along with her grandmother.

"Hi there. Welcome." The girl creating magic with the elaborate coffee machine behind the counter was wearing a cheerful red sweater and a matching red hat set at a jaunty angle.

Lucy scanned the temptations behind the glass and settled on the brownie, which looked as good as its reputation suggested. She hoped desperately that the coffee was strong. She was exhausted.

She'd taken the sleeper train from London to Scotland the day before. Despite the name, she'd had no sleep at all and had been surviving on adrenaline and coffee ever since. Her head was ever so slightly fuzzy and she was uneasily aware that she was a bit hyper and that her caffeine-fueled high was going to plunge into a low at any moment. Hopefully she wouldn't fall asleep with her head in her chocolate brownie.

But it had been a successful day.

She'd located a small herd of reindeer who had proved to be remarkably photogenic and, more importantly, well-behaved. She'd spent the day with a couple of influencers who had taken a range of creative and suitably Christmassy shots of the Fingersnug. One of them had brought her two young children. Both of them had been captivated by the presence of reindeer although they'd been slightly less captivated by the Fingersnug. But they'd taken photos, had fun, and Lucy was confident that the client was going to be thrilled with the results. Arnie, too, who insisted on checking his emails even though he was still supposed to be resting.

Before leaving the office she'd shipped the Fingersnug to a small carefully selected number of her contacts and they were already posting content so festive and eye-catching that she might have been tempted to buy a Fingersnug herself if it hadn't been for the fact that she had ten in her bag unused.

All in all it was a job well done, and now she needed another injection of coffee before finding Ross Miller's home. According to her research it was close to here, which meant she should have time to deliver her proposal and then head to the station in time to catch the sleeper train back to London. By her calculations she would just about beat the storm.

The idea of returning home didn't thrill her anywhere near as much as she would have thought. Her empty flat awaited her. She'd put her tree up, but hadn't yet had the energy or motivation to decorate it.

She gave the girl behind the counter her order and then sat down at a vacant table, put her overnight bag and her laptop on the empty chair next to her and gingerly removed her coat. Within moments of stepping off the train she'd discovered that her coat was woefully inadequate for the weather this far north and she'd been freezing all day. All the standing around hadn't helped.

The two women seated at the table next to her were sharing a pot of tea. One of them smiled at her.

"You look cold."

"Big storm on its way," her friend said. "We're going to have snow for Christmas."

Lucy smiled back, trying to remember the last time a stranger had greeted her in a café.

"I'm going home tonight, sadly, so I won't be here to see it."

And now she was wondering if maybe she should have taken Maya's advice and stayed up in Scotland for a few days.

The woman stirred her tea. "Are you on holiday, dear?"

"No, I've been working. I'm from London." That confession earned her a sympathetic look.

"You poor thing," the woman said. "Still, someone has to live there I suppose."

Lucy smothered a smile. Should she confess that she liked London very much? No, maybe not. And right now she was enjoying being here, in this cozy not-a-post-office, surrounded by people who had big smiles and seemed to know each other.

The girl in the red hat delivered possibly the prettiest-looking coffee Lucy had ever been given, decorated with a cocoa snowflake.

"That's gorgeous."

"Hannah went to art school," the woman at the table said. "You could put every coffee she makes in a gallery. Her mother keeps telling her she's wasted working in a café, but I can't imagine anything better than producing food and drink that can make a person's day."

Lucy was inclined to agree. She dug her fork into the deliciously gooey chocolate brownie and took a mouthful. It was delicious. If she could find a way to transport an entire tray of them back to the office she'd undoubtedly be the most popular person in the company.

She glanced at her companions. "Do you live near here?"

"Down the road. Next to the little nursery." The woman gestured with her head and Lucy put her fork down.

"Do you happen to know the Miller family? I have the address right here—" She rummaged through her bag and pulled out the file where she'd scribbled the address. "I have to deliver something to Ross Miller and his assistant gave me the address. Only I don't want to get lost and miss my train."

The woman exchanged glances with her friend. "We wouldn't normally give directions—privacy, you know—but as you already have his address I can't see the problem." She took a pen and a notepad out of her bag. "It's not clear on the map, so this will help you. You're driving?"

"Yes. Driving."

"Because it's possible to walk across the fields. It's a more direct route."

Lucy imagined herself falling into a ditch and arriving spattered in mud. "Definitely driving."

"In that case go straight down the road from here and you'll see the church and next to it the community hall—" she drew it on the paper "—turn right there, drive for a couple of minutes and then you'll see the nursery. My house is the one with the blue door right next to it. I'd invite you in for tea, but you won't be able to eat a thing after your brownie." She drew another picture. "Turn left at the nursery, and keep going. Past the primary school and The Stag's Head until you see a sign saying No Through Road." She tore the page out and handed it to Lucy.

"There's also a sign saying No Trespassing," her friend added. "That's where you turn."

"I turn where it says No Through Road and No Trespassing?" Lucy wasn't sure she wanted to drive down a road that seemed to be discouraging that particular activity.

"That's right. It ends at the Miller property. Be careful. The road is a bit bumpy. And be careful as you cross the bridge. It's very narrow."

The road, as it turned out, was more than a bit bumpy. On one side of the car was forest, the trees clustered together thickly, on the other the road fell away steeply to a tumbling, frothy river below. In places there was a small guardrail, and in others there was nothing at all.

Lucy gripped the wheel and gritted her teeth to stop them rattling in her head. Hopefully she wasn't going to remove the undercarriage of her rental car or, worse, crash and tumble down to a watery death in the river below. She had a vague impression that her surroundings were very picturesque but she didn't dare take her eyes off the road for long enough to appreciate them. To make matters worse the weak winter sun was fading and a few flakes of the promised snow danced and swirled in her line of vision.

If she hadn't been concentrating so hard on not dying, she might have smiled. Snow. Real snow. They'd had snow in London the previous winter but it had been slushy and wet and had turned gray depressingly quickly.

She tried not to think about the fact that she was going to have to drive back down this road very shortly. In the dark. And, very possibly, with snow on the ground. She gave a hysterical laugh. At least if she crashed, she'd have ten Fingersnugs to keep hypothermia at bay.

She slowed down as she approached a bend in the road, crept cautiously around it and there was the house. Miller Lodge.

What was it like having a house named after the family? What happened if one day they had to sell it? Would the new occupants have to pay extra for the name?

Envy dug its claws into her. *Lucy Lodge*.

In her dreams.

She parked in front of the house, next to a flashy sports car that seemed somehow to have survived the challenges of the single-track road. She switched off the engine and sat for a moment. Right now, all she wanted to do was sleep. She wanted it even more than she wanted Ross Miller's business.

But that was the exhausted part of her talking. The part that was running on fumes. The part that was drained from pretending to be fine when she wasn't fine. The part that was dreading returning to London to spend Christmas alone.

The other part of her was urging her to get out of the car and do what she'd come here to do.

Make or break. Do or die.

Right on cue her phone pinged and there was a message from Ted, complete with a photo of baby Violet.

Lucy sent a series of heart emojis back to him.

It was the motivation she needed to push through for a bit longer.

She had to make one more supreme effort to be cheerful and enthusiastic and then she could sleep all the way home.

She slapped her cheeks to put some color into them, grabbed the wrapped "gift" she'd been carrying around all day and opened the car door.

The cold punched the air from her lungs and she muttered a few words that would have guaranteed a frown and a telling off from her grandmother had she still been alive.

She wrapped her coat more tightly around her body and walked briskly toward the house. Lights glowed in the windows and a festive wreath adorned the front door.

Hopefully Ross Miller wouldn't scowl or yell at her or think she was a weird stalker.

She pressed the bell, heard furious barking followed by voices and then the door opened and a woman stood there. Lucy guessed her to be around the same age her grandmother would have been.

"Hi there—" She felt self-conscious. Perhaps they didn't have many visitors. This place wasn't exactly on the beaten track. "This is going to sound strange, but I happened to be in the area and I wondered if I could see Ross for just five

minutes. It's Christmas, and I feel terribly guilty for disturbing you, but—"

"You're looking for Ross?" The woman's face brightened
and she gave a mischievous smile. "Are you Lucy by any
chance?"

"I—" Lucy stared at her. How could she possibly know
that? Presumably from Zoe, Ross's assistant. As well as con-
tacting Ross, she must have called ahead and warned the
family that Lucy might be dropping off her business proposal
for Ross. It made sense, and in a way it was a relief to be expected. "Yes, I'm Lucy."

"Lucy! It's wonderful to see you." The woman pressed a
hand to her chest and her smile widened. "I am delighted
you're here. Glenda!" She called to someone behind her and
another woman, presumably Ross's mother, joined her in the
doorway. "Glenda, you will *never* guess who is at the door!
It's Lucy. She's here for Ross."

"Lucy? Oh my goodness, this *is* exciting. Ross hasn't arrived yet, but that doesn't matter at *all.* It will be a treat to
have a little time alone with you before he arrives. We are so
happy you're here!" Glenda opened the door wide.

Lucy was pleasantly surprised. She hadn't expected such
a warm welcome, given that she was simply dropping off a
business proposal. She'd been braced to have to beg them to
take it.

Behind Glenda she caught a glimpse of a huge galleried
hallway with an enormous Christmas tree taking up half the
space. It was a perfect tree, in a perfect house, and for a moment she thought about her last Christmas with her grandmother when they'd found a tree that was much too big for
the room. Every time they walked into the kitchen they'd
been poked in the ribs by branches.

Ross Miller, she thought, *is a lucky man.*

"I didn't mean to disturb you, and I probably shouldn't—"

"Of course you should. I know we haven't met before, but we've heard about you."

"You have?" It *had* to be Zoe who had mentioned her. No one else knew she was coming here, apart from Maya. "Ross isn't expecting me. He doesn't know—"

"It's a surprise? Oh, we love a surprise, don't we, Glenda? We won't say a *word*. Come in. Have you come all the way from London? Obviously we don't know much about you, but I presume you live in London, as that's where Ross is."

"Yes. I traveled up overnight on the sleeper, but I've been working all day and—"

"Say no more. You must be exhausted. And probably freezing because you city folks always underestimate the windchill up here in the mountains. You need a sit down. A hot cup of tea and something sweet and you'll soon be feeling better. The kettle is hot. Come in!"

She should probably say no, she really should, but she *was* exhausted and these people were so friendly, the house looked like a Christmas grotto and Ross wasn't here anyway, so would it really do any harm to go inside and warm up just for five minutes?

"I have something to give him. That's why I'm here." She held out the present and they waved her in.

"If you came all this way to surprise him with your gift then you should give it to him in person."

Gift? "Well it isn't exactly—"

"I'm Ross's grandmother. Call me Nanna Jean, everyone does. And this is Glenda, his mother, but I expect he has told you all about us," said the woman with the white hair, hustling her inside where a large black Labrador proceeded to nudge her legs and hands with his damp nose, quivering with excitement.

Lucy bent to stroke him. She adored Labradors. *One day*, she thought. One day she was going to have a dog, and then she'd be guaranteed a warm enthusiastic greeting every day. "Ross hasn't told me about you, because we've never actually—"

"Talked about family? Of course you haven't. It probably didn't feel appropriate. Are you all right with dogs, dear? This is Hunter. He's very friendly."

"He's beautiful." If she could take the dog home with her, she would have done it. "And that has to be the most gorgeous Christmas tree I've ever seen."

"Do you love Christmas? Then you're going to fit right in. We love Christmas trees, and we're lucky enough to be surrounded by them. We have one in every room. I always think that if a Christmas tree doesn't make a person smile, nothing will. Now come into the kitchen and warm up. I hope you love shortbread."

"It's my favorite." Lucy gave Hunter a final stroke and stood up. "My grandmother bought a tin of your festive specials every year. It was our Christmas tradition. We collected the tins. I still have them. I use them to store photos and things."

"Did you hear that, Glenda? And people say our tins are old-fashioned. I don't think so, and here's the evidence. We must send Lucy with a few of our special tins for her grandmother. You'll have to tell us which ones she doesn't have."

"Oh, there's no need—I mean—" *Crap.* Lucy felt her bottled-up emotion push hard against the edges of her control, trying to find a way out. "She passed away. Two years ago." *Hold it in, Lucy. Hold it in. Breathe. In and out. In and out.*

"Oh no." Nanna Jean put a hand on her arm. "I'm sorry to hear that, dear. That must be very hard for the family."

Family?

"Well…yes." She wasn't going to go there. She wasn't going

to confess that it was just her. She didn't want to think about that side of her life and she doubted they wanted to think about it, either. They didn't need her problems darkening their bright, happy Christmas. "It's fine. I mean, it's not fine, obviously. I still get sad, and I miss her terribly. We were very close. But I was lucky to have her, and she raised me to be strong and independent and to keep going when things are tough, so—that's what I'm doing and I'm fine." She needed to stop talking. Right now, but it was obviously too late because she saw Nanna Jean exchange glances with Glenda.

"Tea," Glenda said firmly. "You need tea, dear."

"Good plan. But not in the kitchen," Nanna Jean said. "Lucy loves Christmas trees, so let's have tea in the living room because the one in there is a beauty and she is, after all, a very special guest."

Lucy was pondering why she should be a special guest—maybe they didn't see that many people this far away from the village?—when Nanna Jean guided her into a large living room with windows on three sides. There was indeed another large Christmas tree, this one decorated with a host of intriguing decorations that had obviously been passed down through the family. A log fire blazed in the hearth and a cat lay stretched out and contented on the rug.

"That's the most relaxed cat I've ever seen."

"That's Poker. So called because we could never read his expression or figure out his mood. He's fourteen. All he wants to do is sleep, bless him."

Lucy sympathized with Poker. Right now all she wanted to do was sleep, too.

"Can you believe it's snowing? Sit down, dear. Make yourself comfortable." Nanna Jean plumped up a cushion and patted the sofa. "It looks as if it really will be a white Christmas."

"Maybe." But she wouldn't be here to see it. She'd be back

in London in her decidedly nonfestive home. It was almost as if the apartment sensed her indifference and so couldn't be bothered to make an effort to be warm and welcoming.

Gloom settled on her.

She wished she hadn't come here. Now, whatever she did over Christmas, it would be impossible not to think about the Miller family, with their beautiful house, their log fire, their wonderful dog and very relaxed cat and, best of all, each other.

She sat down and sank into the most comfortable sofa she'd ever encountered. Bliss. She wanted to close her eyes and sleep for a week. Her eyes drifted shut and she dug her fingers in her leg to wake herself up. It would have been better if they'd invited her into the kitchen. Easier to concentrate and stay alert while seated on a hard kitchen chair but here in front of the warmth of the fire with the effects of caffeine wearing off, she could barely stay awake.

Tea was served, along with warm, buttery shortbread, and Lucy was starting to think that she should probably leave if she was going to get to the train on time when her phone pinged.

With an apologetic glance at her hosts, she fished her phone out of her bag. "I should probably get this—"

"Of course! It might be Ross."

Why would it be Ross?

It wasn't Ross. "Oh no. My train is canceled." Seriously? Frustration with the railways and general exhaustion overtook her. Now what? A sob built inside her throat, but this was technically a business meeting and she was still trying to behave like a professional, despite being surrounded by so much festivity, so she swallowed it back and gave a resigned shrug. "Just my luck. No more trains running until tomorrow. I should go."

"Go?" Nanna Jean frowned. "But Ross will be here any minute. Why would you leave?"

"Because I need to find somewhere to stay tonight."

"Well you'll stay *here*, of course. We have plenty of empty rooms and we won't take no for an answer, will we, Glenda?"

"We most certainly won't. In fact we insist. What would Ross think of us if we turned you out on a night like this?"

Wouldn't he think it was exactly the right thing to do given that she was a stranger?

It wasn't as if she even worked for him.

"I think—" Lucy's attempt to interject was interrupted by voices and then a woman and man appeared in the doorway. They weren't looking at each other and Lucy had the strangest feeling they'd just had a fight of some sort. She could *feel* the tension. The man's mouth was tight, as if he was trying not to say something he'd regret, and the woman's cheeks were flushed, as if she'd just said something she definitely did regret.

"Alice! And Nico. Come in," Glenda said. "Join us for tea. You'll never guess who is here? It's Lucy."

"Who? Wait—did you say *Lucy*?" The woman—Alice— unzipped her padded coat, stared at her mother and then at Lucy. Her mouth fell open a little way. Confusion flashed across her face followed by a swift rush of color. But before she could say anything another woman appeared. She had a mass of curly hair, a big smile, and Hunter leaped from his place in front of the fire and treated her like a long-lost friend.

"Did someone say something about Lucy?"

"Clemmie, she's here—" Alice shot her an intense look and Lucy was sure that look meant something although she had no idea what.

It seemed Clemmie had no idea what, either, although that

might have been because her face was buried in the dog's fur as she hugged him. "Who is here?"

"Lucy."

"You're not even remotely funny." She stood up, saw Lucy and then suddenly went still. "Lucy. *Lucy?* Oh my—" Her voice was oddly squeaky and Lucy shifted uncomfortably.

What was going on? There had to be a reason they'd both said her name twice. And why were they looking at each other? What was she missing?

"You're probably wondering why I'm here—"

"Of course they're not," Glenda said. "They're delighted you're here. I'm not clear whether you've actually met—I'm assuming from your expressions that you haven't. This is Alice, my eldest daughter." Glenda gestured. "She's a doctor in London, and this is Nico her—friend—" the hesitation and brief glance she sent Alice suggested Nico's status was yet to be clarified "—and Clemmie. She works as a nanny. I've no idea why all three of my children chose to flee the nest and live in the south, but I'm glad they're home."

Lucy marveled at the friendly and detailed introduction given that she was just here to drop off her proposal to Ross. She saw Alice and Clemmie exchange a look, this time loaded with meaning and a trace of panic, and she thought how nice it would be to be part of a family where people could communicate just by looking at one another because they knew each other so well.

She, however, had no idea what that look meant and it made her horribly conscious that she was the outsider here, and that she was intruding on this lovely family's special time together at Christmas. They were probably waiting for her to leave so that they could play Christmas games, or wrap presents, or maybe sing carols around the piano she'd seen through the open door of one of the rooms.

Envy pierced through her.

She wanted to slide inside their family and stay there. She wanted to snuggle in front of the fire with Hunter the Labrador, and Poker the relaxed cat, and never move again. But she forced herself to stand up. "Thank you for tea. I really should be going."

"You're not going anywhere." Nanna Jean spoke so firmly Lucy wondered if her reluctance was visible.

"But—"

"You only just arrived. And Ross isn't here yet."

They were waiting for Ross to complete their family gathering and here she was, the outsider. It would be inappropriate to stay.

"I don't have to see him in person. If you could just give him the wrapped parcel—" She was so tired that for a moment she couldn't remember where she'd left it. The effects of the caffeine were wearing off and the warmth from the fire was making her soporific. Was she really in a fit state to drive again tonight? Maybe she'd just bump her way along the road until she was out of sight of the house and then sleep in the car. "It's on the table in the hallway, by the huge tree." She grabbed her coat and her bag. "I've intruded on your family gathering for long enough."

"But you *are* family," Nanna Jean said. "You're Ross's girlfriend. So put your coat down and stop this nonsense about leaving."

"Girlfriend?" Apparently it was possible to be sleepy one minute and wide-awake the next. "Ross's girlfriend? Me? Why would you—"

"I can explain!" Clemmie cleared her throat and everyone turned to look at her.

Glenda frowned. "Explain what?"

"It's my fault. Well, partly my fault. Alice isn't blameless.

In fact I think she was the one who first came up with the idea—or maybe it was Ross—I can't remember—" Clemmie closed her eyes briefly and took a deep breath. "Mum, Nanna Jean, there's something Alice and I should—"

"Hello? Where is everyone?" A deep male voice loaded with humor came from the hallway, followed by the sound of footsteps. "The prodigal son returns and there's not even a dog to welcome me? What sort of Christmas gathering is this?"

Hunter barked furiously and bounded toward the voice.

Glenda's face lit up like the Christmas tree and so did Nanna Jean's.

"Ross! Perfect timing," she said as a man appeared in the doorway. "Do *we* have a surprise for *you*! All your Christmases have come at once. It's going to knock you off your feet."

"It was one hell of a journey, so that's not going to take much." He was tall, with tired eyes and a shadowed jaw that suggested shaving had been low on his list of priorities for the past day or two. He hugged his mother, kissed his grandmother on the cheek and told her with a cheeky grin that she didn't look a day over ninety-six.

Lucy grinned, too, because she used to say the same thing to her own grandmother.

Snow dusted his dark hair and her first thought was that she hadn't made a list for Santa, but if she had, this man with the laughing eyes and the killer smile would be right at the top of it.

Except that this was Ross Miller and she was actually in his house at Christmas, which wasn't at all what she'd intended when she'd arrived here.

He kept his arm wrapped lightly around his grandmother's shoulders. "So…where's this surprise that is going to knock me off my feet?"

"What are you talking about? She's standing right there!"

Nanna Jean extended an arm toward Lucy, as if she was introducing an act in the circus and she remembered that, for a reason she had yet to figure out, his family seemed to think she was his girlfriend.

Lucy gulped. This wasn't at all how she'd envisaged this scenario unfolding when she'd planned it and she was about to apologize and make a rapid exit when he smiled at her quizzically.

"Hi there. I'm Ross. I don't think we've met, although you do look familiar. Are you local?" He gave her a long look, as if he was trying to work out where he'd seen her before. "I'm going to have to beg you to excuse my terrible memory."

"I'm Lucy, and—"

"What do you mean you haven't met?" Nanna Jean was astounded. "Are you trying to pretend you don't know your own girlfriend, Ross?"

"My...?" The question died on his lips along with the smile. He breathed deeply. "Wait. Did you say your name was Lucy?" He looked at her, looked a little harder and then slowly turned his head and shifted his gaze onto his sisters. "What the—"

The youngest, Clemmie, flattened herself against the doorframe. "Ross—"

"If you'll excuse me, I need to—" Alice started to slide from the room but quick as a whip her brother clamped his hand over her arm.

"Stay right where you are. You're not going anywhere."

Everyone was silent. Even the dog was silent. The relaxed cat flicked its tail.

Clemmie swallowed. "Ross—"

"Girlfriend?" His voice was silky smooth as he addressed his sisters, who didn't seem in any way reassured by his moderate tone.

"We can explain," Clemmie muttered, and he gave what seemed, on the surface, to be a pleasant smile.

"I wish you would."

Lucy wished that, too. Was she the only one who had no idea what was going on here?

A glance at Nanna Jean and Glenda suggested they were equally confused.

"The thing is—" Clemmie squirmed "—you're probably not going to believe us—"

"Try me," he offered, and Lucy felt she should probably leave, except that she had no idea what was going on and given that she seemed to be playing a central part in this mystery she should probably stay and find out the ending.

"It's my fault," Alice said finally. "Nanna Jean and Mum started asking awkward questions about my relationship with Nico and it was all horribly uncomfortable, so Clemmie jumped in. She was trying to help."

Ross raised an eyebrow expectantly. "By...?"

"By telling them that you had a girlfriend. Lucy. It was supposed to be a distraction. Your love life is always a more interesting topic than mine, but obviously that was supposed to be the end of it. We didn't expect *actual* Lucy to show up here."

Actual Lucy?

Lucy felt as if the whole thing was somehow her fault, although she had no idea why.

None of this made any sense to her, although judging from the lethal gleam in Ross's eyes it did mean something to him.

"I didn't mean to say it," Clemmie said. "It just sort of fell out of my mouth."

Lucy cleared her throat. "Am I 'actual Lucy' in this scenario?"

But no one was paying her any attention.

"Do you see what you've done?" Glenda glared at Nanna

Jean. "This is your fault. You were the one who said they must be serious."

"Did I?" Nanna Jean plucked fluff from the sleeve of her sweater. "I don't remember, and I can't be blamed for that. You can't reach almost ninety and remember every word that's said. Sometimes I get confused."

Nico was frowning at Alice. "You don't think our relationship is serious?"

"That wasn't what I said." She turned scarlet. "Can we do this later?"

"Yes, do it later." Ross spoke through his teeth. "So if I'm understanding this correctly, you told them I was dating Lucy, and then by some strange coincidence we have yet to understand, actual Lucy turns up here at the house."

Actual Lucy tried again. "If I could just—"

"I mean, what are the chances?" Clemmie gave a helpless shrug and Glenda looked confused.

"Wait—" She glanced at her son. "Are you saying that you're *not* dating Lucy? That you really haven't met her before this moment?"

Lucy sighed. Hadn't she already told them that? Didn't any of them listen? The whole family was obviously batshit crazy. And still none of them were paying any attention to her.

"I am *not dating Ross*." She spoke in a loud, clear voice and everyone turned to look at her. "This is the first time I've laid eyes on Ross—nice to meet you by the way—" she nodded to him "—and I'm here because I work for a leading creative agency in London." Whether or not they were "leading" depended on how you looked at it, but she was banking on the fact that her employment credentials were the last thing on Ross's mind right now.

"The face of modern marketing," Alice murmured and Lucy gaped.

How could she possibly know about that?

"Well, yes. I had some ideas for Miller Active, for a campaign, and—"

"Wait. You're saying you're here in a professional capacity? You want to talk about work, so you thought you'd turn up at my house?" The outrage Ross had directed toward his sisters, was now directed at her. "Whatever happened to making an appointment through the conventional route?"

"I tried. Numerous times. I was told you wouldn't be back in the office until the New Year. You're not an easy man to get hold of, Mr. Miller."

"And that is the truth," Clemmie said. "You're always in a meeting and your phone is always going to voice mail. It's infuriating. You need to sort that out, Ross. What if we need you in an emergency?"

Ross wasn't listening. All his attention was now focused on Lucy. "You couldn't get hold of me, so you thought you'd invite yourself for Christmas?"

"I didn't invite myself anywhere. I was up in Scotland filming for another client and as I was so close to your home, Zoe suggested I drop the proposal off in person."

"Zoe? You know my assistant?"

"Yes. She said she'd clear it with you."

His gaze didn't shift from hers. "She didn't."

"Well that's not my fault. And it's not really hers, either. She has been a little distracted because of William. And who can blame her?"

He blinked. "William? What does he have to do with this?"

"If you don't know, then it's not my place to tell you. I won't reveal the intricacies of another person's romantic relationship, but you have to understand that I thought she had contacted you, and I had no reason to doubt that because when I arrived at the door your family seemed to know who I was. They behaved as if they were expecting me."

"We weren't exactly expecting you," Nanna Jean said, "but Clemmie had already told us you were dating Ross so we assumed that this was one of those lovely surprises that life sometimes delivers."

Life hadn't delivered that many lovely surprises lately, just bad ones, but to say so would be self-pitying and if she was going to do a "poor me" act, she'd do it when she was alone.

"I do not understand the dating Ross part," she said. "But given that this whole thing has obviously been a giant confusion and mistake, it's probably best if I leave now and let you sort it out among yourselves. Thank you for the tea, and I hope you all have a very happy Christmas."

No one was listening.

Clemmie was blaming Alice, who was blaming Nanna Jean for putting her on the spot, and Ross was asking why it was that his love life was of so much interest anyway, and Nanna Jean was saying that it wasn't her fault that she wanted the people she loved to be happy, nor was it a crime, and Glenda was trying to soothe everyone, and it was obvious they'd forgotten about her.

Lucy stood apart and alone.

How would it feel to be part of that family? How would it feel to be questioned, and argued with, and interrupted by people who had known you your whole life and loved you? To know that you were spending Christmas in this beautiful house, surrounded by family?

Unconditional love.

The noise and the connection between them simply accentuated her own loneliness.

She stood, self-conscious, and then stepped over Hunter and walked out of the cozy living room, past the glittering tree and the stack of neatly wrapped presents waiting for eager hands to rip apart the festive packaging.

It felt rude to leave without saying goodbye, but they probably wouldn't even notice she'd gone. And although the family had been wonderfully welcoming, Ross Miller himself had been far from pleased to see her. And she didn't blame him.

Feeling strangely empty and detached, she opened the front door. The freezing air smacked her hard and she gasped and snuggled deeper into her less-than-adequate coat. She'd prioritized style over substance but now she was rethinking that decision.

In the time she'd been in the house, the weather had taken a dramatic turn for the worse.

In front of her was nothing but swirling white. She could barely see her car even though it was parked just a few steps away.

Great. A white Christmas. That was the dream, wasn't it? And it might have been her dream had it not been for the timing.

Visibility was close to zero and she had to drive back down that bumpy narrow track in the dark, and over that rickety bridge without sliding off the road, and in the unlikely event she survived that challenge she'd have to find a place to stay for the night.

Merry Christmas, Lucy.

10

Glenda

"How is it my fault," Alice was saying, "I didn't ask Clemmie to mention Lucy's name."

"You traitor! I was trying to help you!" Stressed by the family discord, Clemmie dropped to her knees to make a fuss of Hunter while Glenda contemplated the unsteadying fact that this entire situation was her fault.

She still didn't fully understand the details—why they'd chosen "Lucy" to be Ross's fictitious girlfriend, or how someone called Lucy had arrived on their doorstep—but there was one thing she did understand.

Clemmie had stepped in to protect her sister. From her. From Nanna Jean.

The fact that they felt the need to cover for each other, horrified her.

She could forgive Nanna Jean—grandparents played a different role—but as their mother, she'd always made it clear that she loved them, no matter what. That they could talk to her about anything. And she'd believed that. But they clearly didn't. Acknowledging that was bruising, but worse was acknowledging the fact that she was a source of stress to them, not comfort.

She should have been the one to shield Alice from questions she didn't want to answer when Nanna Jean overstepped, not Clemmie. She should have protected her child.

"This is all my fault. I'm a terrible mother." She said it to no one in particular, and it was Nanna Jean who patted her on the shoulder.

"Nonsense. You're a wonderful mother. You care. What's terrible about that?" Nanna Jean sniffed. "I'm the one with the big mouth, but I'm not apologizing for who I am. I'm old. When you're old, you don't want to waste time playing games. You want to make the most of every moment. If one of my grandchildren is dating someone then I want to know so I can get excited. I may have danced my last tango, but there's no reason why my imagination can't still have fun."

Ross sighed. "I'm not dating anyone."

"And that's part of the problem." Nanna Jean waggled her finger. "If you were, then you wouldn't have felt the need to invent a girlfriend, and I wouldn't have been so excited, and we wouldn't have inadvertently entangled a poor innocent stranger in our family issues."

Glenda wondered if there was a way of banishing Nanna Jean to the kitchen. "But why not just tell the truth?"

"Because we know how much you want to see us all settled," Clemmie said, "so we joked that he should invent a girlfriend to keep you happy."

"*You* joked," Ross said. "It was banter. It wasn't supposed to be reality. And that's the last time I give Alice unfettered access to my wine fridge."

To keep *her* happy? It was true that she wanted to see them in a relationship, but that was because she was thinking about their happiness, not hers. Couldn't they see that?

What else were they hiding from her?

Nanna Jean shook her head. "You have a fridge just for wine? Why does wine get special treatment?"

Glenda felt terrible. She tried hard, so hard, to be the best mother possible and support her children in all their endeavors and yet when they were together they were discussing ways to deflect her questions about their romantic life. Which meant she clearly wasn't doing anywhere near as well as she thought she was. Was that why Alice had been behaving so strangely? Because she'd been worried about possible interference?

"I'm sorry you feel you have to do that."

"Mum!" It was Clemmie who noticed how upset she was. Clemmie who put her arms round her and gave her a hug. "It's okay! Not a big deal. It's just that when someone asks you if you're dating, and you're not, it can get a bit awkward. Feel a bit pressured, you know?"

She'd put pressure on her children.

She was never going to ask them a single relationship question ever again.

And somehow she had to make it clear that they could talk to her about anything.

But there were still elements of the current situation that she didn't understand. "Why Lucy? Was that a coincidence?"

"In a way. Lucy was profiled in a trade magazine that just happened to be sitting in my kitchen when the girls came for supper. Her picture was on the cover," Ross said. "They were looking for a name for my imaginary girlfriend and her name happened to be right there. Lucy."

"Lucy is delightful," Nanna Jean said. "A perfect girlfriend. And you were rude."

Unlike Glenda, Nanna Jean continued undaunted.

"She is *not* my girlfriend." Ross spoke through his teeth, "For the final time, I don't have a girlfriend."

"Of course you don't! If that's the way you behave then that fact won't surprise anyone." Nanna Jean gave a sniff of disapproval. "No wonder your girlfriends are imaginary."

Alice gave a snort of laughter and even Ross was smiling as he rubbed his fingers across his forehead.

"Nanna Jean—"

"Don't use that cajoling voice. It won't work. I like Lucy, and you owe her an apology."

"I like Lucy, too," Clemmie said, her arm still tucked firmly through Glenda's.

Ross let his hand drop. "She showed up at my house to discuss business. At Christmas. Who goes to a person's house to discuss a business deal?"

"Someone who is driven and ambitious. Not that we know anyone else like that…" Clemmie gave her siblings a pointed look and Alice rolled her eyes.

"Don't look at me. None of this is my fault. Can you really tango, Nanna Jean? Who taught you? I don't think I've heard that story."

"Everyone has their secrets." Nanna Jean brushed fluff from her skirt. "If you must know, his name was Gilberto."

Glenda couldn't believe the direction of the conversation. Were all families like theirs?

Clemmie was curious. "You still remember him?"

"Of course. Why wouldn't I remember him? He was a real boyfriend. I had several real boyfriends. I never felt the need to make one up."

Ross clenched his jaw. "I haven't been home in six months," he said. "Is there any chance we could talk about something other than my deficient love life?"

Yes, Glenda thought. *Please let's talk about something else.*
The whole conversation was making her uncomfortable.

"We are talking about something else." Alice folded her arms. "We're finding out how Nanna Jean learned to tango."

"He was Argentinian. We had an exciting time together. I knew how to make the most of life." Nanna Jean gave her grandson a pointed look. "I learned a lot from him."

"Enough of this," Glenda interrupted before Nanna Jean revealed some detail that none of them would be able to forget. "Where *is* Lucy?"

"She was here a moment ago." Nanna Jean looked toward the tree, as if expecting to see Lucy tucked conveniently beneath its branches. "Alice? Did you see her go?"

"No. I was too busy defending myself from attack."

"Clemmie?"

"No." Clemmie looked over her shoulder. "Maybe she's using the bathroom."

"She's not using the bathroom. She's walking toward her car. Slowly and carefully." Nico was standing by the window, apart from the family. "The snow is coming down hard and it looks lethal out there. How did so much snow fall so quickly?"

Alice went to stand next to him, but he didn't look at her.

Glenda looked at the space between the two of them and remembered Nico's question.

You don't think we're serious?

No. She wasn't going to get involved. Whatever happened, happened. It wasn't her business.

But she couldn't help wondering what exactly he and Alice had talked about on their walk.

"She left?" Alice pressed closer to the window. "But she didn't even say goodbye."

Glenda felt a sense of shame. Since when had they treated a guest with such a lack of respect?

"Maybe she did say goodbye, but we were too busy talking to hear her."

"I blame Ross," Nanna Jean said, "for not giving her the traditional, warm Miller welcome."

"Once again, it's all my fault. She's a stranger." Ross jabbed his fingers into his hair, exasperated. "What exactly were you expecting me to do? Propose?" But he joined Nico at the window. "What is she wearing on her feet? Are those boots with heels? Who wears boots with heels here? She's dressed for shopping on the King's Road."

"She didn't expect to be staying." Clemmie joined the crowd by the window. "Her boots are great. And I love her coat. I'd love to go shopping on the King's Road with her. She has great taste. And she's pretty. Do you think I could wear my hair like that?"

Glenda sighed. "Is it appropriate for you all to be standing in the window watching?"

No one took any notice.

"What does it matter how she looks?" Alice scowled. "Why does society always judge women on age and looks?"

"I was admiring her coat, that's all. Since when is it a crime to admire a coat?" Clemmie looked wounded. "Why must you make a political point out of everything?"

"I'm not. All I'm saying is that she's obviously great at her job, but that isn't what you commented on."

"I don't know anything about her job. I'm not interested in her job. I'm interested in her coat." Seeing her sister's blank look, Clemmie rolled her eyes. "Forget it."

Glenda was confused. "How do you know she's good at her job. What exactly *is* her job? She said something about working for an agency, but I have no idea what that means."

"Can we focus on what matters here?" Ross interrupted.

"The weather is grim and getting worse by the minute. What are her plans? Where is she going now?"

"Who knows?" Alice shrugged. "Back to the train? Home to London? Probably to her *actual* boyfriend who, if she's lucky, doesn't have a weird family."

The words made Glenda catch her breath. Was their family weird? She'd always thought they were rather wonderful. Close-knit and supportive. But maybe she'd got that part wrong. Her children didn't want her support. They wanted her to back off.

"Her train was canceled. She had a text, moments before you arrived." Glenda shelved her analysis of family and thought about Lucy. "I don't like the idea of her driving in this weather. You're right, Ross. It isn't safe. She doesn't know the roads, she's exhausted from her day and we've added to her stress by exposing her to our family squabbles and problems—"

"Problems?" Nanna Jean frowned. "We don't have problems—"

"No problems?" Alice rolled her eyes. "Believe me, we could keep a psychiatrist busy for at least a year."

"That's enough, Alice. Watch your tone with your grandmother." Just because she wasn't going to ask about the details of their lives didn't mean she couldn't call out rudeness. "And it's true that we were all arguing and blaming each other for the confusion—"

"Well that's just being a family," Nanna Jean said. "It's not a clinical diagnosis."

With a growl of frustration, Ross strode out of the room and Glenda called after him. "Where are you going?"

"To make sure she makes it to her car safely. And from there to the end of the valley. I'll take my car and follow her as far as the main road."

"That's my boy," Nanna Jean said. "He's kind, really, despite the way he spoke to Lucy. And he's being protective toward her now, which is a very good sign. What?" She straightened slightly as everyone turned to look at her. "I like Lucy. I think she'd do very nicely for Ross. Wouldn't that be a good story? What started as fiction, ends up as fact."

"You've known her for an hour, Nanna Jean," Clemmie said and Nanna Jean shrugged.

"It takes me less than a minute to figure out a person."

Alice gave her a look of disbelief. "You don't know anything about her. She could be married."

"She wasn't wearing a ring."

"So? That doesn't mean she isn't in a serious relationship."

"If there's no ring, then there is everything to play for."

"I cannot believe you just said that, Nanna Jean."

"I hope he reaches her before she drives away." Glenda had a feeling that Ross's proposal had less to do with protecting Lucy, and more to do with protecting himself. Had he used this as an excuse to escape from them? Or was she now overthinking everything? She joined Nico and Clemmie at the window. "Oh no! She's slipped. And it looks bad—"

"How bad?" Alice nudged Clemmie to one side so that she could see properly. "Should I go and examine her?"

"No. You should stay right where you are. Ross is helping her." Nanna Jean sounded almost smug. "This couldn't be better."

Alice, incredulous, turned to look at her grandmother. "I have a feeling Lucy might disagree. She fell. Badly, by the looks of it because she's still on the ground and given that it's covered in a layer of snow I'm guessing that's not a choice."

"I think it's called a 'meet cute.'"

"Nanna Jean!" Clemmie gave a snort of laughter. "Where did you learn that? Gilberto the tango dancer?"

"No. Someone different. I was young once, you know. Also, I read romance."

"I don't read romance," Alice said, "but I hardly think frostbite and fractures qualify as a 'meet cute.' And how is this situation romantic? They don't know each other, Nanna Jean."

"They do now." Nanna Jean's face was so close to the window that the glass started to mist. "He's helping her up—oh, she's slipped again, but he's caught her and he's holding her steady—so now she knows he's strong, capable and he isn't going to let a woman fall flat on her face. Look at that! She's clutching the front of his coat and their faces are *so close*. He should kiss her, right now. This is like watching a romantic movie with the sound turned off. The snow is falling and he just saved her and—*kiss her, Ross!*"

"Nanna Jean!" Alice was appalled. "That is so many levels of inappropriate I don't know where to start."

Nanna Jean didn't appear to hear her. "Clemmie is right, she *is* a pretty girl. All that beautiful dark hair. And she has the bluest eyes and very long eyelashes. Did you notice that? What's wrong?" She stared at Alice, whose mouth was still hanging open after her last statement. "I haven't seen you with your mouth open that wide since I fed you as a toddler, and you were such a fussy eater that didn't happen often."

Glenda sighed. "Nanna Jean, please don't tease Alice."

"I wasn't teasing. I was making a statement. You're upset because I think Lucy has nice hair? Is that on the ever growing list of things I absolutely mustn't say in public?" Nanna Jean shook her head and turned back to the window. "I'm a product of a different century. If I want to admire Lucy's hair, I'll admire her hair. That magazine you talked about obviously thought she was pretty or they wouldn't have put her on the cover."

Alice looked as if she might explode. "They put her on the cover because she's brilliant at her job."

"Brains and beauty. Perfect." Nanna Jean craned her neck to see properly. "Why isn't she just coming back inside? Oh no—she's shaking her head and trying to get into her car. She seems upset."

"I'm not surprised," Clemmie muttered, "she probably thinks we're very strange. Except for Hunter." She grinned as Hunter heard his name and barked on cue. "You're strange, too, don't worry."

Glenda's concern grew as she watched the scene unfolding beyond the window. "She can't put her foot down. He's trying to reason with her."

"Enough of this." Alice spun away from the window. "If she can't weight bear then it's time for medical intervention. Clemmie, you can help me."

Glenda wondered why she'd asked her sister for help rather than her boyfriend who was, after all, medically qualified.

"I'm not good in emergency medical situations. I panic and vomit," Clemmie said. "Nico would be better."

"Nico is a heart surgeon." Alice hesitated by the door. "Actually, maybe you could come with me, Nico. You and Ross can carry her to the living room and I'll examine her there."

"Ross doesn't need your help," Nanna Jean's voice was dreamy. "He just scooped her up as if she weighed nothing. Would you look at that? It's like one of those old romantic movies."

Alice, who never watched movies and whose reading was restricted to medical texts and serious nonfiction, frowned. "What?"

"Never mind." Clemmie pushed past her toward the door. "We have been the most terrible hosts ever, and now poor

Lucy is hurt so could we *please* put our family issues aside and make her feel welcome?"

"Family issues?" Nanna Jean looked at Glenda. "What family issues?"

Glenda was in despair. She'd planned the perfect Christmas, and it was rapidly falling apart. Ross hadn't even been home long enough to take off his coat, and already the tension was pulsing in the air.

But Clemmie was right. The priority right now was Lucy.

"That poor girl. Let's give her some space." Her practical side took over. Her family, as she well knew, could be overwhelming. "Nanna Jean and I will go to the kitchen and finish preparing dinner. Clemmie, why don't you help?"

Nanna Jean didn't budge. "I thought I'd stay here in case—"

"You're peeling potatoes." Glenda put her hand on her mother-in-law's back and was about to propel her toward the kitchen when Ross walked through the door carrying Lucy.

Glenda could see right away that she was in pain. Her face was pinched, and she was clenching her jaw.

"Oh, Lucy, you poor thing. What a thing to happen, and at Christmas, too."

"She's hurt her ankle badly. Alice—" Ross deferred to his sister "—what do you want me to do?"

"Put her on the sofa." Alice was all brisk efficiency. "Lucy, you poor thing. Do not worry. I will take a look at you and see what needs to be done."

"I'm so sorry." Lucy's face was pale. "There was a patch of ice and my feet just went from under me, but I'm sure it's okay. It will settle down. I really should be leaving. I'm disturbing your family Christmas."

"You're not going anywhere right now." Ross laid her gently on the sofa and Alice took over.

"I want to take your boot off, Lucy, so that I can examine you properly. Clemmie? Can you help?"

"I can do it." Lucy leaned forward and tried to unzip her boots but the movement had her wincing in agony.

"We'll do it together," Clemmie said and Alice frowned.

"You might need to get scissors. It looks as if we're going to have to cut these off. And her tights."

"No way. It would be a crime to damage these boots, and those sparkly tights are cute, too. We can do this." Clemmie gently slid the zip down and together they eased the boot from Lucy's injured foot, followed by her tights.

Already her ankle was starting to swell and Glenda saw Lucy grit her teeth and dig her fingers hard into the cushions of the sofa.

"Oh, that's bad. How can it be so bruised already?" Clemmie covered her mouth with her hand and her sister gave her a none-too-gentle push and turned back to Lucy.

"Tell me exactly what happened." Alice touched her fingers gently to the side of Lucy's foot.

"There was ice. I wasn't expecting that. My foot went from under me and I heard a crack."

"And you can't put weight on it?"

"She tried," Ross said. "She was in a lot of pain."

Alice was silent for a moment, pressing with her fingers, asking, "Does this hurt?" and "Can you feel this?" And after a few moments she rocked back on her heels and pulled a face.

"I'm sorry to say this, but I think you've broken it." Her voice was both calm and kind. "But we can sort this out, so don't worry."

Ross frowned. "It could be a sprain."

"Excuse me—" Alice gave her brother a look "—which one of us is the doctor?"

"All I'm telling you is—"

"Unless you went to medical school without telling me, I don't need you to tell me anything. If we need an unqualified opinion, we'll use a search engine. I don't tell you how to sell workout gear."

Still concerned for Lucy, Glenda was relieved and reassured that Alice was with them. There was no doubt she knew what she was doing.

Watching her daughter in action, she felt a rush of pride. She could imagine Alice working in the emergency department, calm and confident, helping people.

Alice glanced at Lucy's ankle. "I think it's broken, but the only way to tell for sure is to do an X-ray. Maybe an MRI. I'll call the hospital and talk to them."

"No." Lucy tried to sit up. "I have to get back to London. If it's no better by tomorrow, I'll see a doctor. I've already taken up enough of your time."

"Well given that it was our drive that tried to half kill you, I think you need to stop worrying about that side of things." Alice stood up. "Also if my brother was more accessible and you could have made an appointment in the normal way, then you wouldn't have had to make this detour to give him the benefit of your brilliant ideas. So indirectly this is his fault."

"Of course it is," Ross said. "Everything is my fault."

Alice pulled out her phone. "I'll make a call to the emergency department, and then we'll drive you over there."

Glenda glanced toward the window. "The snow is coming down heavily."

"I'll drive. My car is fine in the snow, and it's a way of atoning for my many sins." Ross hadn't even taken off his coat. "I'll bring the car to the door so we don't have a repeat experience." He left the room and Lucy tried to move herself.

"There's no need for any of this. I could call a cab."

"There is only one cab in the village, and the driver needs

to be given at least two days' notice. This isn't London." Alice gave her shoulder a squeeze. "Don't worry. I'm going to stay with you the whole time."

"I can't ask you to do that. It's Christmas and you've only just arrived home. I'm sure you're desperate to catch up. Spend time as a family. You'll have things to talk about—"

"Plenty of time for that." Alice disappeared for a few minutes and they could hear her talking on the phone, her voice crisp and professional. When she returned, she was smiling. "You're in luck. They're not busy for once. Presumably people are staying home because of the storm, so hopefully we won't have a long wait. We might even be back in time for dinner."

Lucy looked increasingly distressed. "I can't possibly stay for dinner."

Glenda looked at the snow swirling outdoors. No one should be driving in this weather. She wouldn't be able to relax until they were all home, Douglas included.

And even if Ross, Alice and Lucy made it safely to the hospital and back, what happened after that? If this carried on, Lucy would be here for a lot longer than dinner.

Despair washed over her. So much for her dreams of a cozy family Christmas. So much for spending quality time with her children. So far they seemed to be doing everything they could to avoid being alone with her, and now they had a stranger in their midst.

But none of this was Lucy's fault.

"Let's take this a step at a time."

Nanna Jean gave her a look. "It was taking one step at a time that got her in this mess. Jump right in, I say. It's safer."

"All right, let's do this." Lucy clenched her teeth and tried to move but Alice stopped her.

"I don't want to risk you doing more damage. Ross will carry you."

Glenda saw Lucy's cheeks turn pink and wondered if Ross had noticed. And then she remembered that she was no longer asking herself that sort of question.

If her children were adult enough to run a company, and save lives, they were adult enough to handle their own romantic relationships.

"Put your arms round my neck," he said, and Lucy hesitated for a moment and then did as he'd instructed. He lifted her easily and headed toward the door.

Alice followed.

"Sorry to desert you." She gave Nico an apologetic smile on the way past. "Hopefully we won't be long."

Was she sorry? Glenda had a feeling Alice was grateful for this interlude that gave her time away. Was that because of the family, or Nico?

She glanced at her daughter's boyfriend, but his face revealed nothing.

Something was definitely wrong, but now she wasn't going to feel comfortable asking.

She felt the familiar tug of anxiety. Whenever people complained about the challenges of being a parent to a toddler she had to bite her lip to stop herself saying *wait until they're adults*.

You wanted to help, but at the same time you knew they probably didn't want your help. You wanted to show them that you were available, but you didn't want to intrude on their privacy. She felt like Lucy, walking on icy ground, trying not to slip and break something.

There was a blast of cold air when they opened the door, and then they were gone.

Glenda stood for a moment, staring at the closed door. Then she pulled herself together.

"Nico." She sent him a look of apology. "My daughter

seems to have deserted you. I hope you'll join us in the kitchen for a snack."

"You're very kind, but I need to call my family and this seems like a good time." With a brief smile, he headed toward the stairs and Glenda wondered what on earth was going on in her daughter's head.

Reminding herself that you could never see inside another person's relationship, she headed to the kitchen with Nanna Jean.

"Douglas will be home soon." Nanna Jean started to lay the table. "And I, for one, will be glad when he walks through that door. I don't like my family being out and about in this weather."

"He'll be fine. He has good tires on that car and he's been driving these roads since he was a teenager." Glenda was more concerned about the fact that Douglas was going to walk through the door to discover his family had descended into chaos once more. Last night there had been no Ross, and tonight there would be no Ross or Alice. Or maybe there would be Ross, Alice and a stranger.

"We should be making up a bed." Nanna Jean's thoughts were clearly moving in the same direction. "Whatever happens at the hospital, that girl won't be going anywhere tonight."

"I was thinking the same, but—" she sighed "—do you really think that's a possibility?"

"Definitely. The girl can barely walk without help. Even if Alice is wrong and her poor ankle isn't broken, and I doubt our girl is wrong because even though she can't clean a bath she was top of her year in medical school, Lucy won't be able to drive anywhere. And the train is canceled."

Glenda sifted through options in her head. "I suppose there might be a train tomorrow, but even if Ross drove her to the station, how would she manage at the other end? Poor Lucy. This is awful."

Nanna Jean lifted plates from the cupboard. "Why is it awful?"

"Because it's Christmas and she'll want to get home."

"Maybe."

"Why maybe?"

"I don't know. I thought she looked a bit sad, that's all, when she talked about her grandmother." Nanna Jean started laying the table. "You heard her."

"All the more reason for her to be back with her family." Glenda noticed that she laid an extra place. "Lucy might not be able to join us at the table."

"If that's the case, then Ross can take her dinner to her on a tray." Nanna Jean found a tray and laid it carefully. "There. We are now ready for all eventualities."

Glenda studied her mother-in-law. "Are you matchmaking? Because I don't think that's a good idea. Look what has happened so far. It was because of us that Clemmie told a lie."

"She was protecting her sister. Didn't it make you feel warm inside to see it? That's a sister's role."

"But she wouldn't have had to lie if you'd just done what we agreed and left the subject of their private life alone."

"I didn't agree. I said I'd try. I failed. Unlike Alice, I've learned to embrace failure."

Glenda coated the parsnips in maple syrup. "You could try a little harder."

"I'm old."

Glenda gave the tray a shake. "Stop saying that."

"Why? It's true. And you can't blame me for enjoying a little romance when I find it."

"If Alice is right, Lucy very possibly has a broken ankle." Exasperated, Glenda slid the parsnips into the oven with more force than was necessary. "Even you cannot possibly find that situation romantic."

"Let's see, shall we?" Nanna Jean stood back to admire the table. "That's done. So now we should go and make up the spare room. I do love Christmas."

11

Alice

Alice walked back through the emergency department to the trolley where Lucy was waiting with Ross.

She was uncomfortably aware that she didn't *have* to be here. That Lucy would be perfectly well cared for without her presence, and that one person to drive her and offer support—Ross—would have been enough. But she'd desperately wanted to get out of the house.

Things were tense, thanks to Nico's assumption that she had told her family they weren't serious. That wasn't what had happened at all, but even before that misunderstanding, things hadn't been great.

Even their walk had been a disaster.

What is wrong, Alice? Tell me what you're thinking.

And she'd intended to. She'd thought it would be as good a time as any to talk properly, without fear of interruption. But then she'd realized that if it all went wrong—if Nico wanted

something different—then they'd be in the invidious position of having to spend Christmas together under the curious
gaze of her family. Her family, who were waiting for her to
announce her engagement and already planning for grandchildren. How would that work?

"Alice?" Ross's voice cut through her thoughts and she
pulled herself back to the present.

Lucy. She was here because of Lucy.

She still couldn't quite believe that Lucy had shown up at
their house—*what were the chances?*—and now they had an
added complication because Alice knew, even if her family
didn't, that Lucy was unlikely to be traveling anywhere for
a few days.

Poor Lucy. It was Christmas and she was stranded far from
her home and family. No wonder she'd looked so upset and
been so desperate to leave.

"You're frowning," Lucy said, watching her closely. "Does
that mean it's bad news? Will I have to have surgery?"

"Am I frowning?" Alice tried to stop thinking about her
own complicated life, and focus on Lucy. "No, it's not bad
news. The doctor is on her way to talk to you and then we
can get you out of here."

"Good. Because the snow is getting heavier so unless we
want to spend Christmas here, we should be getting back."
Ross watched as staff moved swiftly around them. "I don't
know how you can stand working in a place like this."

"What's wrong with it?" Alice observed her brother's discomfort with interest. These surroundings were so familiar
and comfortable to her she'd lost her ability to see it from the
point of view of a patient or visitor.

"Everything is wrong with it. The smell. The noises. The
injured people. The constant wail of sirens."

"This place is peaceful compared to the hospital I work at

in London. You're soft, that's your problem. That's what happens when you work in a glass office with free cappuccino on tap." She rolled up the sleeves of her sweater and focused on Lucy. "How are you feeling? How is the pain?"

"It's okay." Lucy's strained expression contradicted her words. "Is it broken?"

Alice hesitated, conscious of professional courtesy. "I should let the doctor who examined you—"

"You're a doctor," Ross said, "and you examined her. So why don't you tell us. I'm not good with suspense and I'm sure Lucy isn't, either."

Alice was about to argue with him, when a young female doctor appeared.

"Lucy. Sorry you've had to wait. We've been looking at your X-rays. You have a lateral malleolus tip avulsion fracture—"

Oh, for goodness' sake, Alice thought. Why didn't the woman use language that the patient might have a chance of understanding? Nothing irritated her more than watching doctors explain a situation in words that left the patient none the wiser. How was that reassuring?

Predictably, Lucy slumped. "I have no idea what that is, but I'm guessing it's not going to be on the average person's Christmas list?"

"The only word I understood was *fracture*." Ross frowned. "So it *is* broken?"

"It means that Lucy has fractured a bone on the outside of her ankle," Alice said. "But it's in an area that usually heals well. She won't require surgery, and the pain and swelling will settle down over the next few weeks." Her clear explanation earned her a grateful smile from both her brother and Lucy.

"That's right," the doctor confirmed. "Most avulsion fractures heal well without surgical intervention."

"It could be worse," Alice added. "It's generally treated like a soft tissue injury."

Lucy looked slightly dazed. "How long do you think it will take to heal?"

"Around six weeks, although you may have some discomfort for longer than that. I have a leaflet of instructions for you, but obviously you have your own personal expert on hand which will make things easier." The doctor smiled briefly at Alice and then turned back to her patient. "For the next few days you need to rest that foot. Elevate the ankle and ice the swelling." She gave detailed instructions and Lucy looked more and more distressed.

"A few days? But it's Christmas."

"Well you won't be rocking around the Christmas tree if that's what you were hoping, but I'm sure there are plenty of ways in which you can still celebrate and enjoy the festive season."

"No, you don't understand—" Lucy shifted in an attempt to get comfortable. "I live in London. I need to get home."

"Ah. Well not for a few days. You need to give the swelling a chance to go down, and then you'll need to use crutches."

Lucy was quiet on the journey home, although whether that was because she was in pain, weighing up her options, or simply allowing Ross silence so that he could concentrate on negotiating the worsening snowstorm without distraction, Alice wasn't sure.

As they crossed the bridge Lucy gripped the seat, her knuckles white. Alice didn't blame her. She was probably hoping she'd make it back to London with nothing worse than a broken ankle.

But Ross had driven these roads in all weathers since he was a teenager and he arrived back at the house without mishap and pulled up right next to the front door. The driveway had lost all definition, snow blurring the edges and landing in a sheet of lethal white on the windscreen.

"Stay there," Ross instructed and opened the door. The snow swirled into the car and Alice made her exit as fast as possible, just as the door opened and a soft, golden light welcomed them into the warmth.

"Thank goodness." Her mother stood there, with Nanna Jean and Clemmie hovering behind. "We were worried sick. Come into the warmth."

"Put your arms around my neck." Ross bent to scoop up Lucy, who this time didn't argue.

Alice retrieved the crutches and locked the car.

"Why are you locking the car?" Nanna Jean ushered her inside. "You're not in London now."

"Force of habit I suppose." Alice brushed the snow from her hair and took off her coat.

"You must be frozen, all three of you. Did you have a long wait at the hospital?"

"Considering everything, no." Alice unwrapped her scarf from her neck and hung it with her coat. She saw her mother step forward to help Lucy.

"Look at you, so pale. You poor thing. Ross, take Lucy into the living room. There's a fire blazing and you'll soon warm up."

"I can walk—"

"Not tonight." Alice took over. "For the first couple of days you need to rest that ankle."

"I can use crutches."

"Plenty of time to do that tomorrow. The least Ross can do is carry you, particularly as you wouldn't even be in this mess if he ran a decent appointment system or occasionally picked up his phone."

Alice saw her brother draw breath, but to his credit he didn't argue.

Instead he carried Lucy through to the living room and laid her on the sofa.

Glenda immediately fussed over her. "There. We'll soon have you more comfortable. Alice, you need to tell us exactly what Lucy can and can't do so we can help her." She popped cushions behind Lucy. "I'm going to bring you supper on a tray because it's too awkward for you to sit at the table and the more careful we are with that ankle of yours, the sooner we can get you back to your family for Christmas."

Her mother was a born nurturer, Alice thought. She was made of flesh, bone and kindness.

Lucy obviously thought the same thing.

"Thank you." Her voice sounded strange, slightly thickened, and Alice looked a little closer and saw that her eyes were shiny.

"Are you in pain, Lucy?"

"What? Oh no, I'm fine." She gave a bright smile and Nanna Jean tucked a soft blanket over her legs.

"Of course you're not fine. How could you be after the day you've had? You were already tired, and then your train was canceled and then there was the whole mix-up, and your fall, and the hospital," she tutted, "it's all too much I'm sure, but you'll feel better after a good hot meal."

Alice grinned. Her family thought a meal fixed everything. If only.

Clemmie walked into the room. "Hunter and I have made up a room for you, Lucy. It's warm and cozy and right next door to Ross—" She stopped as everyone turned to stare at her. "What? I just meant that if she falls out of bed or something. Or can't manage the stairs…" Her voice trailed off.

"It's kind of you, but I really can't stay." Lucy sounded distressed. "I have to get back to London as soon as possible. It's Christmas. I need to be at home."

Alice tried to imagine herself in Lucy's position, incapacitated in the middle of nowhere with a bunch of strangers. Nightmare.

But she didn't believe in lying to a patient or giving false hope. "You can't go anywhere tonight. If it stops snowing Dad and Ross will try and clear the road over the bridge tomorrow. But I'm sure you're worried about your family, and they're worried about you, so you should contact them. Do you have your phone? You can borrow mine."

"Good thinking, Alice. Lucy, you should definitely call them." Glenda popped a glass of water on the table next to Lucy. "I know I'd be worried sick if it was one of my girls who was stranded. Tell them you're safe here."

"Reassure them that we're not mass murderers," Clemmie said, and Nanna Jean gave her a look.

"Do not tell them that."

"You'll stay the night," Glenda said, "and we will take another look at the weather tomorrow."

"I found your bag. You left it in the car." Clemmie popped it next to her and Lucy hesitated and then pulled out her phone.

She stared at it for a moment, as if she didn't know what to do.

"You don't want to worry them?" Nanna Jean patted her on the shoulder. "Trust me, they'd much rather know you were safe."

"We'll give you privacy, Lucy." Glenda ushered them all out of the room, except for Alice.

"Are you sure you're all right?" She sat down on the sofa next to Lucy, who tried to smile.

"Yes. Well, no. Not really. I feel terrible, encroaching on your hospitality like this."

"Don't. There is nothing my mother and Nanna Jean love more than a house full of people to fuss over. Is it too much for you?"

"Too much?" Lucy's eyes were shiny. "Are you kidding? They're wonderful. You are so lucky to have a family like that. People who care so much about you. But I'm sure you already know that."

Did she know that?

The love of her family was something she took for granted and occasionally found intrusive. But just for a moment she imagined how it might be if her mother wasn't interested in her life, romantic or otherwise. If her mother didn't give her a huge hug the moment she walked through the door. If her mother wasn't there at all.

Alice felt uncomfortable.

She knew her mother was blaming herself for this situation but if anyone was to blame it was her, Alice.

She should have found the courage to tell Nico the truth of how she was feeling right at the beginning. She should have used the same courage to tell her family. Instead she'd hidden behind a lie. Worse, she'd hidden behind a lie her sister had told to protect her.

She had no problem with being accountable in her work. Why couldn't she do the same in her personal life?

The answer was because she didn't have the same confidence in her personal life. She was good at her job. She wasn't good at relationships, or so she'd always thought.

She smiled and stood up. "Don't worry about any of it. Just focus on healing. I'll give you some peace so that you can ring your own family."

She walked out of the room and closed the door quietly behind her.

She headed to the kitchen where the whole family had gathered.

Clemmie was scraping cake mixture into baking tins.

Alice looked at her sister. "Why did you have to make the point that her room was next to Ross's?"

"I thought she might find it reassuring." Clemmie put another blob of mixture into the tin.

"He's a stranger, Clem!" Alice was exasperated. There was no doubt that her sister had inherited Nanna Jean's romantic streak. "Why would she find it reassuring?"

"I don't know. I just thought she might." Clemmie scraped the bowl clean. "I was trying to be hospitable."

"I think what Lucy needs now is some time alone to explain things to her family," Glenda said. "Supper will be ready in half an hour. Lucy can have hers on a tray. Alice, do you want to tell Nico we'll be eating soon?"

Her insides lurched. She was going to have the conversation that she should have had weeks ago.

"Do you know where he is?"

"We haven't seen him since you left to take Lucy to the hospital." Nanna Jean exchanged a look with Glenda. "We did ask him to join us, but he said something about making some calls."

"Which is fine," Glenda said quickly. "No one is obliged to be sociable. I know how busy you all are. I want you to be able to relax and do what you want to do while you're home."

Alice wanted that, too. Unfortunately, by inviting Nico she'd all but guaranteed that relaxation was unlikely.

She stood in the hallway while they all vanished into the kitchen, but instead of closing the door her mother hesitated and came back to her.

"Is everything all right, Alice?"

"Of course. Why wouldn't it be?"

"You seem a little tense, that's all."

Why was it that her mother always just knew?

"I'm tired. It's been a busy time."

"Of course." Her mother gave her arm a squeeze. "As long as that's all it is. I'm not interfering, but I just want you to know you can talk to me. About anything."

The temptation to blurt it all out and tell her mother everything was almost overwhelming, but she stopped herself. She wasn't a child anymore. She shouldn't need her mother to give her a hug and a cookie. She was an adult. She dealt with life and death on a daily basis. She should be able to handle the matter of her love life without the help of her mother.

"Thanks, Mum." It was difficult to talk through the lump in her throat. "I'm fine. I'll go and find Nico. Tell him we're back and that dinner is nearly ready."

Feeling nervous, Alice took the stairs to the Loch Room and found Nico repacking the bag he'd only recently unpacked.

Her stomach fell away and she closed the door firmly behind her. "What are you doing?"

"What does it look like I'm doing?" He sounded tired. "I'm leaving."

"Leaving?" Of all the things she'd expected him to say, that hadn't been on the list. Even while her heart was thudding her brain was noticing how neat and orderly his packing was. Everything rolled or folded, tucked into the bag to make maximum use of the space. Why couldn't she be like that? "Why would you leave?"

He straightened. "Because this isn't working."

"What isn't?"

"Me being here." He paused and looked at her. "Us. We're not working."

"What are you talking about?" Panic gripped her. She hadn't anticipated this. He was going to walk out? Without so much as a conversation? She ignored the little voice inside her reminding her that she was the one who had ignored or removed all opportunities for conversation.

"I don't know what's happened to our relationship, Alice. We used to have fun and enjoy each other's company. When I wasn't working, you were the one I wanted to spend time with but these last few weeks…" He let out a breath. "I don't know what's wrong, but you're not yourself and you're not telling me why and I'm tired of asking and getting nowhere. This is stressful for both of us, and it isn't fair on your family for us to be sorting out our relationship issues over Christmas, so I'm going back to London and we'll talk when you're back."

"No!" The strength of her feelings were a shock. She'd been wishing she hadn't invited him to join them for Christmas, but now that he was intending to leave she realized how badly she wanted him to stay. "You can't do that. Please don't go."

"Why?" His gaze was fixed on her face. "Give me one good reason why I should stay."

There were multiple reasons, but right now she was exhausted. If she tried to explain it, she was bound to mess it up. "Because I don't want you to."

"Really? Because that's not what I'm sensing. You have been behaving oddly since we left London. Since before that. We don't talk—"

"I've been talking."

"Polite conversation, and since when did we do that? We talk about real things, or we used to. But I swear you've made enough observations about the weather since we drove up here to last a lifetime. You're stressed. You don't want to be alone with me. Anytime your family try and ask us anything personal, you cut them off—"

"I find it intrusive. Their questions feel like pressure." Her head was threatening to explode.

"They're showing an interest, Alice." He sounded tired. "They care. They love you. I understand that. What I don't understand is why you feel our relationship is something that should be hidden from them. We're not teenagers. We don't have to sneak around. I couldn't work out why you wouldn't simply tell them the truth about us, and then I realized that maybe the reason you're afraid to tell them how you feel is because you don't feel the same way I do."

"That isn't true." She was conscious that any moment her mother would be calling them for supper, and that the timing couldn't have been worse. "Nico—"

He turned away. "Forget it, Alice. If I'm not here, then you can answer your family's questions about our relationship honestly, without having to factor in my feelings. Tell them whatever you like. Tell them whatever you feel because I, for one, have no idea what that is." He zipped the bag and she winced because the gesture had a finality to it. "When you're back in London, give me a call if you want to."

If she wanted to?

"No! Wait." She hurried across to him and grabbed his arm. "This is my fault. All my fault. I know it is."

"It's not about apportioning blame—"

"You want to know what's wrong with our relationship? You proposed—" the words fell out of her mouth "—and it changed everything. I wasn't expecting it, I wasn't ready for it and—"

"And you weren't happy about it." His mouth was tight. "I'm aware."

"You are?"

He sighed. "The clue was in the fact that you didn't say yes. And since then I don't think we've had a conversation that involved anything other than the practical. *What time will you be home? Will you pick up food?*" He gently removed her hand from his arm and picked up his coat and bag. "I misjudged the situation and for that you'll have to forgive me, but I've never actually proposed before. That was my first time."

And probably his last, she thought miserably.

"You probably think I'm ungrateful—"

"Ungrateful?" He frowned. "I wasn't doing you a favor by proposing, Alice. I was telling you I loved you. That I wanted to spend the rest of my life with you."

The lump in her throat grew bigger. "I know. And I'm sorry. I'm sorry I messed everything up. I love you, too."

"Do you?"

She felt an ache in her chest. Didn't he know? "Yes, I do. But I don't blame you for questioning that. There are things we need to talk about, I know that. I was waiting for the right time, but that time never seems to come."

He put the bag back down on the floor. "So talk. Right now."

Now? Her heart raced. No way.

"We're eating soon, and I don't want to rush this. Tomorrow we'll take a walk, or find somewhere quiet where we won't be disturbed which isn't easy in this house."

"I won't be here tomorrow."

"I'm sorry I've made you feel as if you should leave, but you can't leave, Nico. Even if you want to, you can't."

"Why? Give me one reason."

Oh, the irony.

"Apart from the fact I don't want you to go, there's the weather." She gave a humorless laugh. "I hardly dare mention it after everything you just said, but haven't you read about Storm Scrooge? That's what the local media are calling it. Storms are a pretty big deal up here. We only just made it back from the hospital. Lucy can't leave, either, at least not tonight. When did you last look out of the window? It's a blizzard out there. Visibility is zero, and the ground is icy. You wouldn't even make it to the main road. So awkward though it may be, we're all stuck here."

12

Lucy

Was there ever a more perfect room?
Lucy gazed at the twinkling lights on the tree, and then at the fireplace where flames licked and danced around carefully stacked logs. Three Christmas stockings hung from the mantelpiece. *Ross, Alice, Clemmie.*

She felt a pang. Of course they had stockings. They were the sort of family who loved Christmas and paid attention to every detail. And they loved each other. Everything she'd seen had made her sure of that, even the arguments. In fact, the friction between them had confirmed it. The way they'd challenged each other showed that they weren't afraid to express themselves freely. Their love was deep. They were truly connected. There was no way Santa would miss calling at this house.

She stared at those stockings, thinking of her own Christmas stocking currently tucked away at the bottom of the box her grandmother had used to store Christmas decorations.

That was the one tradition she'd let slide. She couldn't see the point of hanging it up.

She shifted her gaze away from those stockings to the huge glass windows. They faced the mountains but right now all she could see was swirling snow against darkness.

What would it feel like to come down here on Christmas morning? To be able to curl up on that rug in front of the fire and open those presents. To tease each other, and just enjoy being together. What would it be like to know this was your home?

Stop it, Lucy!

She wasn't part of the Miller family. This wasn't her home, that wasn't her Christmas tree, and those weren't her presents. None of this was hers and she shouldn't even be here. There was no point in settling in. No point in savoring the atmosphere.

She was an outsider, and the sooner she went back to her own life the better for everyone.

She shifted her position on the sofa. Thanks to her ankle it was impossible to get comfortable. She was in pain but bigger than the ache in her foot was the sense of frustration.

She'd spent hours working on a proposal that she was convinced would impress even the not-easily-impressed Ross Miller and now, thanks to a cascade of bad luck, he thought she was an annoying stalker who had ruined the first day of his hard-earned Christmas break. In the hospital he'd been polite and considerate, but underneath the impeccable manners she'd sensed a certain exasperation. And she didn't blame him for that.

Who wanted to spend the first hours of their holiday in a hospital? Not her, and presumably not him, either.

Why had she ever thought that coming here in person was a good idea? If she'd thought her life was a mess before, that was nothing compared to now.

She'd blown it. She'd blown it for Arnie, she'd blown it for Ted, for Rhea, for all of them.

From her comfortable nest on the sofa, she could hear the conversation drifting in from the kitchen, along with the clatter of plates and the occasional burst of laughter.

"Does Lucy like parsnips?"

"Of course she likes parsnips. Everyone likes parsnips. Could someone get the roast potatoes out of the oven?"

"That's not true, Nanna Jean. Not everyone likes parsnips."

"If she doesn't like parsnips then it's because she's never tasted mine."

"I haven't even met Lucy yet." A deep male voice, presumably belonging to Douglas Miller.

"We should offer her wine. Alice? Can she drink with a broken ankle?"

"I can't see how a broken ankle will impede her ability to lift a glass."

"Don't pour too much, we don't want her to fall and break the other ankle."

"Give her more—if she's staying with us, she's going to need it."

"Don't give Clemmie wine, she's not drinking."

"Not drinking?"

"I'm on a health drive."

"At Christmas? That's ridiculous."

"There's nothing ridiculous about a health drive."

"How all-encompassing is this health drive? Does it mean I can eat your bacon?"

Lucy leaned her head back against the cushions and smiled. Did they know how lucky they were? They reminded her of a sports team, passing the ball from one person to the next, knowing each other so well that their movements were instinctive.

Maybe the storm would be so terrible and last so long that she'd have no choice but to stay for Christmas.

Unsettled, she sat up. Had she really just thought that? No. That wasn't going to happen. It wouldn't be fair on anyone. And although Glenda and Nanna Jean were warm and welcoming, and so was Clemmie, Ross Miller definitely hadn't been welcoming. She could just imagine his face if he woke up on Christmas morning to find her here.

He already saw her as an intruder, and any hope she might have had that he'd invite them to pitch for his business had vanished.

Lucy picked up her phone to message Maya, and then put it down again. What was she going to say? *I've blown it, sorry. Blame Storm Scrooge.*

No. There would be plenty of time to worry her colleagues after Christmas.

Glenda walked into the room carrying a tray and Lucy put her phone down.

"This is mortifying. I am truly sorry to put you to so much trouble."

"It's no trouble. It's delightful to have a guest. Douglas is home and I'm going to introduce you once we've all eaten. There's nothing worse than cold food." Glenda put the tray on the table next to her.

"He must be wondering how he ended up with a stranger in his house at Christmas."

"He's not wondering that at all. There's nothing we love more than a house full of people."

Lucy gestured to her phone. "I was just seeing if there was anyone who could come and get me."

"In this storm? I hope they had the sense to say no."

"They did. I need to find another way. Tomorrow I'm going to track down a taxi." There must be someone willing to do it if she made it worth their while. She'd worry about the cost later.

"Let's see what the weather brings." Glenda moved the glass closer to her. "I've poured you a small glass of wine, but there's water, too, if you'd prefer that."

"Wine is perfect. And the food looks amazing. It all smells delicious."

"I wish you could join us at the table, but Alice insists you keep that leg elevated for this evening at least." Glenda handed her a napkin. "I'm glad you managed to speak to your family. This must be very stressful for you, but we'll get you home to them for Christmas. We will find a way."

Home for Christmas to her empty apartment. Great. Wasn't *that* something to look forward to?

Should she confess that she had no family? No, because then Glenda and Nanna Jean would invite her to stay, because they were the kindest people she'd ever met.

And she'd have a tough time doing the right thing and saying no.

"Thank you, Glenda. I appreciate that."

"I'm going to leave the door open, and you call if you need anything. We'll all join you in here for dessert and coffee. Nanna Jean made one of her crumbles. You won't have tasted anything better." She paused to put another log on the fire, patted Hunter and then returned to the kitchen.

Lucy ate every last scrap of her meal, including the parsnips, and was just putting her plate on the side table when Ross walked into the room.

At some point between arriving back from the hospital and eating dinner he'd showered and changed and now he was wearing a pair of dark jeans and a soft ribbed sweater.

There was something about him that made her jumpy.

Unlike the rest of his family, who seemed to freely exhibit their emotions complete with subtitles, Ross Miller revealed nothing, which was probably the reason he was so successful in business.

She could imagine him in a boardroom, cool and calm while everyone around him grew more and more flustered.

She was flustered now, trapped as she was with her leg in a boot wearing the same clothes she'd been wearing all day, with the addition of a pair of wool socks on loan from Clemmie. It was hardly the way she'd choose to present herself to a prospective client.

But she no longer had to worry about that, did she? Thanks to a little bit of bad luck and a whole lot of snow, Ross Miller was never going to be a client.

She'd have to confess her impulsive mistake to Arnie, who would be understanding and not blame her at all, which would make her feel a thousand times worse. For the rest of her life she'd suffer agonies of embarrassment every time Ross Miller's name was mentioned.

"Mind if I join you?" He had a glass of wine in one hand and the bottle in the other. "Top up?"

"I'd better not." It was going to be hard enough walking around with a boot and crutches, without adding alcohol to the challenge. This whole situation was unspeakably awkward. She felt intimidated and reminded herself that this man was kind to his grandmother so he had to have a human streak. "I'm sorry about this. I can't apologize enough."

He put the bottle down on the table. "For what?"

Where to start? The list was growing. "For thinking that coming here to deliver my proposal in person was a good idea. It seemed like a good idea at the time because I was in the area, but I see now why you would think it was inappropriate. All I can say in my defense is that I never intended to set foot inside your house. I was going to hand it over and leave, but then there was a misunderstanding and your family—"

"That part you don't have to explain. If apologies are needed then I should be apologizing to you for my family."

"Don't. They're possibly the nicest bunch of people I've ever met." .

"I'm relieved you still think that, given everything that has happened." He sat in the chair opposite her. "And having assumed that you were my girlfriend, no doubt they dragged you inside to feed you tea and cake."

"Yes. And I probably should have refused, but I'd had a long day and your family made it hard to say no and your Christmas tree looked spectacular and I thought to myself, *Why not treat yourself to a little festive moment, Lucy.* Also, there was your dog."

"My dog?"

"Hunter."

His gaze was steady. "I know who my dog is. I was questioning his role in your decision to join my family for tea."

"I love dogs. Particularly Labradors. They're generally affectionate and nonjudgmental and I don't often get the opportunity to enjoy a full-on waggy-tailed dog moment."

For a second she thought she saw him smile, but then it was gone and she was left doubting herself.

"I owe you another apology." He sat in one of the chairs facing her. "Turns out you were right. Zoe did indeed leave numerous messages on my phone informing me that you'd be dropping something off. I had a busy day yesterday and somehow I missed them."

At least he was capable of admitting when he was wrong.

"And then today ended with a trip to the emergency department with me." She pulled a face. "It hasn't been a great

trip home for you so far, has it? You began by fielding relationship questions, and then spent the next few hours in
hospital."

He smiled. "It's been eventful, that's for sure."

"Also, I've eaten your food."

"That part isn't true. One thing you'll soon discover about
my mother and grandmother is that they always over cater."
He paused. "How are you feeling?"

"Honestly? Embarrassed. If I could crawl under a rock and
hide, I would."

"I was asking about your ankle, not your emotional state."

"Oh." Well done, Lucy, for oversharing. "It's not too bad
as long as I don't move, thank you for asking."

"Now let's talk about your emotional state. Why do you
want to hide?"

Wasn't it obvious?

She leaned back against the cushions. "Have you ever had
what seemed like a really good idea and then with hindsight
you realize it was monumentally stupid?"

"Hasn't everyone?" He stretched out his legs. "Do you
want to tell me about it?"

"Which part exactly?"

"Start with how you ended up knocking on my door a
few days before Christmas. I have members of my team who
I would describe as dedicated, but I'm not sure I have anyone who would be prepared to go to the lengths you did to
deliver something speculative."

"I've explained that—"

"You couldn't get hold of me in London. That part I understand." He drank some wine and then rested the glass on
the arm of the chair. "What I don't understand is why this
couldn't wait until January? Why does it matter so much to
you?"

She could lie, but what was the point of that?

She never lied to clients, and although he wasn't a client and probably never would be thanks to all the unfortunate circumstances leading up to this meeting, he deserved the same respect.

"The short version is that I know that in January you are inviting agencies to pitch for your business. Once that happens it will be impossible for a boutique agency like ours to get your attention. I wanted to show you our ideas first, in the hope that you might allow us to pitch, too."

He was silent for a moment. "And the long version?"

"Why do you want the long version?"

"Have you looked outside lately?" He glanced toward the window, where snowflakes still swirled furiously. "It's not as if we'll be going anywhere for the foreseeable future."

There was something about the coziness of the house, the warming effects of the wine and the way he was looking at her that made her decide to tell the truth.

Why not? She had already blown all chances of him seeing her as an impressive professional.

"It matters to me for a combination of reasons," she said. "Mostly it's because I love my job."

"So you're competitive—"

"Yes, but not just that." She paused. How far back should she go? "Arnie, who runs the agency, gave me a job when I was at a pretty low point. I'd been working for another agency and my boss was a horrible bully. Passive-aggressive. Critical. She shredded everyone's nerves and also their confidence. I worked for her for three years, and every day of those three years was miserable. Nothing I, or anyone else, did was right."

"So why didn't you leave?"

It was a question she'd asked herself repeatedly.

"She eroded my belief in myself. Made me feel as if I was

unemployable. Who else would want me? When people did summon up the courage to leave, she'd give them a bad reference."

"She sounds like a real peach." He watched her. "Go on."

"A friend of mine had gone to work at A Creative. That's the name of the company. The *A* is for Arnie."

"I know." He tilted his head. "I've heard of the company."

He had? Well maybe that was a good sign.

"They were a fast-growing agency, and my friend was loving it there. She was the one who persuaded Arnie to interview me. If she hadn't done that, I'd probably still be working for that woman. My confidence was rock bottom. I didn't feel I had anything to offer anyone."

"But Arnie gave you the job, so you obviously impressed him."

"I didn't. Far from it." The embarrassment was as acute now as it had been on the day. "I was so nervous I totally fluffed the interview. I messed up every answer. I stumbled. My mind was blank. I couldn't sell myself because my boss had made me believe there was nothing to sell. I knew that there was no way he'd give me the job—honestly, *I* wouldn't have given me the job—and I was beating myself up about it as I left the building, trying to convince myself that it didn't matter, that the job wouldn't have been that great anyway—all the usual excuses you make to try and be okay about something."

"And then?"

"I'd reached the street when Arnie caught up with me." Thinking about that moment reminded her of the reason she was here. *She'd do anything for Arnie.* "He asked me to join him for a coffee at the café next door, and I agreed although I had no idea why he would want to waste even one more second of his time in my company. And he basically gave me a second chance at an interview, in a more relaxed setting."

"You obviously didn't mess the interview up as badly as you thought."

"But that's just it. I did. And that's one of the many amazing things about Arnie. He doesn't expect you to be perfect. He knows people are human, and that they can mess up. And when they do, instead of firing them he gives them a second chance and support."

Ross topped up his wineglass. "He sounds like a prince among men."

Was he being sarcastic? She couldn't tell.

"He is, but he also sets the company culture. That kind of approach trickles top down. I'd gone from working in a culture where everyone was afraid, defensive and jumpy, to one where everyone was open, supportive and collaborative. People were eager to try things because they knew that if something didn't work there would be a postmortem, but no blame. Every week we sit down as a team and talk through what we think has worked well and what we'd do differently. It makes everyone want to do better. Do you know what it's like to work in a company where you don't constantly feel you have to watch your back?" She felt herself blush. "Sorry. I forgot for a moment that you run your own company. Although you're the boss, so you probably don't have to ever watch your back."

He toyed with his wineglass. "I understand your loyalty to your company and this all sounds great in theory, but sometimes companies need to make tough decisions. Is Arnie's relaxed approach one of the reasons your company is struggling?"

"No." She immediately leaped to defend Arnie and then realized what he'd said. "What makes you think we're struggling?"

"You lost two of your major clients recently."

"How do you know that?"

"It's my business to know as much as possible." He reached down and stroked Hunter, who had settled comfortably at his feet. "I haven't seen your accounts, of course, but two big losses like that have to hurt."

"They do hurt." There didn't seem to be any point in lying about that.

"So Arnie is facing some difficult staffing decisions over the festive season and from what you've just told me, I'm assuming that would be particularly hard for him."

She thought about Arnie, sitting with his head in his hands. Arnie being rushed to hospital. "Yes."

"Job losses?"

"I hope not." She thought about Ted and baby Violet and her insides lurched. "Arnie is doing everything he can not to make anyone redundant."

"Which presumably means he is trying hard to replace those lost accounts and bring in new business as soon as possible. Hence your presence in my home at Christmas. Was that his idea?"

She bristled. "You think Arnie asked me to come here and break my ankle in order to have more time with you? I love him, but my loyalty falls short of being prepared to damage myself physically on his behalf. And no, he didn't send me. He doesn't even know I'm here."

His eyes narrowed. "You love him?"

"As a friend. A colleague. A mentor. He's brilliant and I owe him so much. We all do. Not only because he allowed me to escape from a job I hated, but also because he was so supportive when—" She stopped.

"When?"

She really shouldn't talk about it. Normally she wouldn't

have done, but they'd already crossed the line from professional to personal so what did it matter?

"Two years ago, my grandmother died. She was in hospital over Christmas and…it was tough. It was really tough." She wished she hadn't started this conversation, and no doubt he was feeling the same way. She expected him to change the subject, but he didn't.

"I can imagine how hard that must have been. The two of you were close?"

"As close as two people can be. She raised me after my parents died. She was my family." And now she'd told him that much, she didn't see a reason to stop. "It's scary, being on your own, watching someone fade. You want desperately to hang on to them, but at the same time you know you're being selfish and thinking about yourself and not them."

"You were on your own in the hospital? You had no one with you?"

"Arnie." She fiddled with the edge of her sweater. "It was Christmas, and he has his own family, but he came to the hospital and sat with me for hours at a time. He came every single day." He'd brought her sandwiches she couldn't eat, and flasks of hot chocolate that she couldn't drink. "No matter how many times I told him he didn't need to be there, that I was okay, he kept showing up. I'll never forget that."

Ross was silent for a long time. "I guess he knew that he did need to be there, and that you weren't okay."

She swallowed. "I guess he did."

They shared a long look that made her feel as if he saw every single thing she was hiding. Knew every single thing she wasn't saying.

But how could he? In her desperate need for connection, she was imagining things.

"You said you were up in Scotland for another account," he said. "Which one is it?"

"The Fingersnug."

"Excuse me?"

"It's called the Fingersnug, and I'm in Scotland because the client wanted reindeer."

"Who doesn't? It is Christmas after all." There was a smile in his eyes and some of her tension melted away. She didn't blame him for being suspicious of her motives for being here, and at least he had a sense of humor.

Why wasn't he dating anyone? Why was a man like him inventing fake girlfriends? He was so gorgeous she would have thought they were lining up.

He glanced at her. "Do you have one with you?"

"A reindeer? Sadly no. A Fingersnug? Yes." She reached for her bag, delved inside and handed him one.

He turned it over, examined it, and then slid his hand into it. "It's basically a glove that heats up."

"Exactly."

"But it might be perfect for early morning runs when there is snow on the ground." He pulled it off. "Can I borrow it? I'd like to try it out."

She could hardly refuse, could she? "Keep it. It's the least I can do given that I'm currently treating your place like a hotel. I have more in my bag. One for each family member."

He smiled. "That's my Christmas shopping sorted."

"You seriously intend to go for a run? In this?"

"I run in all weathers."

"Right. Me, too."

He put the Fingersnug down. "Really?"

"No, not really. I can't run to save my life. I get calf ache and rib ache and brain ache, and I honestly don't understand why people would ever do it voluntarily unless they were being chased by a lion."

"And yet you think you're the right person to handle what is essentially a sportswear account?"

She took a deep breath. "Yes, I do. I think I'm exactly the right person. And if you read the proposal I prepared, you'll see why."

"I haven't seen it. What happened to it?"

"I gave it to your mother. It's A4 sized, wrapped in pretty paper covered in robins. And red ribbon."

He stared at her. "You *wrapped* the proposal?"

"I assumed I'd be leaving it here. I didn't expect to see you in person, and I thought a boring proposal might get lost in the chaos and excitement of Christmas, so—"

"So you made it look like a gift. I'm not sure if that's genius, or cruel."

Lucy winced. "Can we go with genius?"

"Tell me what's in it."

"Now?"

"Why not?"

Because she wasn't feeling at her most professional, lying on his sofa. But this might be the only opportunity she'd get, so she'd take it.

"Obviously Miller Active is a very successful company, and I started by thinking about what you need."

He stretched out his legs. "And what do I need?"

"Your market is—" She broke off as Glenda walked into the room, closely followed by everyone else.

"This is where you're hiding, Ross! You've finished your meal, Lucy? Clemmie, take Lucy's plate so that there's room on her table for dessert."

Lucy wasn't sure whether to be relieved or frustrated that

they'd been interrupted before she could get into the details of her pitch with Ross.

She took the bowl that Glenda gave her. "Thank you. Although having eaten all this, I'm not going to be able to move from the sofa."

"We don't want you to move from the sofa," Alice said, "and if overfeeding you is a way to make sure you rest your ankle then it works for me." She sat down on one of the armchairs and Nico perched on the arm next to her.

Whatever tension had been between them earlier, appeared to have vanished at least for the moment.

Nanna Jean handed a bowl to Ross. "Ross and Lucy were talking," she said with a total lack of subtlety. "Perhaps we should go back into the kitchen and allow them some privacy?"

"No need." Ross took the bowl from her. "We were talking about work. It can wait."

"Work? You've been alone with Lucy for twenty minutes and all you've talked about is work?" Nanna Jean opened her mouth and then caught Glenda's eyes and closed it again. "I'm not saying anything."

"A rare occurrence." Douglas stepped forward and introduced himself before settling himself in the chair closest to the fire. "I understand that you work in marketing, Lucy?"

"Yes. I work for an agency and we do a bit of everything, but mostly I focus on the social media side. Short-form video, and I work with influencers."

Nanna Jean frowned. "What did she say? She works with influenza? That doesn't sound safe."

"Influencers," Glenda articulated carefully. "*Influencers*, Nanna Jean."

"Well no wonder I didn't quite get the word. I don't know what that is. And there's no need to shout. I'm not deaf."

"Influencers." Douglas stirred his coffee. "So you use other people to spread the word about a brand."

"Exactly."

He took a sip of coffee. "What would you do for Glen Shortbread?"

"Douglas Miller, she is not here to offer you free advice." Glenda handed him a coffee. "Ignore him, Lucy."

"Well she's trapped here with nothing else to do," Douglas said, "so I don't see the harm in her giving her opinion on a few things."

Lucy put her spoon down. "If you tell me what you're already doing, I'd be happy to talk through some ideas with you."

"Advice?" Ross frowned. "What do you need advice on, Dad? Is there a problem with the business?"

"No there isn't. Everything is fine," Glenda said. "Eat your dessert, Ross. It's delicious."

Ross was watching his father. "Dad?"

"Your mother is right. You should eat more dessert."

Lucy remembered the article she'd read. Rebel Ross. Clearly there was tension between the two men.

Ross glanced at his sisters and Lucy saw Clemmie give a brief shake of her head.

"Right." Ross's voice was rough. "We'll talk about this another time."

"We will not be talking about it at all." Glenda looked stressed. "We've all had more than enough drama for one day, what with poor Lucy's ankle and this terrible storm. It's Christmas. Problems get left at the door at Christmas. Did you bring the champagne, Alice?"

"Yes, but we've already had wine. We seem to be cramming the entire season's alcohol consumption into one evening. Why are we having champagne?"

"Because having you all home together is reason to celebrate. Douglas…" Glenda handed the bottle to him and he popped the cork and Hunter jumped and pressed closer to Clemmie.

The champagne was poured and the next moment Lucy was holding a glass in her hand.

She'd never eaten so much in her life. It was a good job she had an excuse not to move from the sofa.

At least she wasn't going to have to cook for the rest of the Christmas period.

"To family." Glenda raised her glass and everyone chorused "To family," and then they suddenly realized that their toast didn't include Lucy, and Nanna Jean raised her glass again.

"To *Lucy's* family, who no doubt are very worried about her and looking forward to having her home soon."

Everyone raised their glasses again. "To Lucy's family."

Lucy swallowed and tried to smile. "Thank you."

"Do you have brothers, Lucy? Sisters?"

How was she supposed to answer that? It was all very well being evasive, but she couldn't ignore a direct question.

"I don't—" this was hideously awkward "—I don't actually have family."

"No family at all?" It was Clemmie who spoke.

"No. My parents died when I was little. My grandmother raised me, and she died two years ago, around Christmas." If she'd felt exposed and vulnerable before, she felt doubly so now.

She could feel Ross's gaze on her.

They were supposed to be celebrating, and instead they were standing there feeling guilty for being unintentionally insensitive, and sorry for her.

She never should have said anything.

Well done, Lucy. She'd succeeded in killing the Christmas atmosphere.

"Oh, Lucy." Glenda sat down on the sofa next to her. "We had no idea. And we've been so tactless."

"You weren't tactless at all. You weren't to know. And it's fine. I have lots of good friends in my life. And friends can be like family."

"Well that's the theory," Nanna Jean said, "but it's not exactly the—"

"Of course they can." Glenda gave Lucy's leg a gentle squeeze. "A good friend is worth everything, and I'm sure you have wonderful friends."

If she'd thought the situation was awkward before, it was even more awkward now.

"I wouldn't have mentioned it, but—"

"But we made it impossible not to." Ross stood up, grabbed the champagne bottle and topped up her glass. "Lucy obviously doesn't want to talk about this. Time to change the subject."

She was relieved by his intervention, and grateful.

There was another brief silence while everyone frantically searched for a suitable alternative topic.

Alice spoke first. "Clemmie should tell us all about her fitness drive. How's it going, Clem?"

"Actually, I don't want to talk about that, either. Not right now." Clemmie shot her sister a warning look that Alice missed because she was holding out her glass to Ross.

"What's wrong with telling everyone you're trying to get fitter? That's nothing to feel awkward about. You should be proud. And you ought to use Ross's expertise while you're here. He could be your personal trainer. We can all cheer you on."

Lucy relaxed, relieved that the attention had moved away from her.

Clemmie, however, looked far from relieved to be the focus of that attention. "I don't want to talk about it."

"If you want my opinion, I'd say that Christmas is the wrong time to start a fitness drive," Nanna Jean said. "January would be better. At least then you can enjoy my Christmas cake and a glass of champagne without feeling guilty."

"A glass of champagne probably contains less alcohol than Nanna Jean's cake," Alice said, "so you might as well enjoy a glass, Clem."

"No thanks. I'm not drinking." Her voice rose a little and Lucy wondered why it was that none of them seemed to have noticed Clemmie's increasing stress.

"If Clemmie doesn't want to drink, then that's fine." Glenda clearly had noticed. "I made a delicious ginger fizz for the nondrinkers."

"That's full of sugar," Alice said, "so not exactly healthy, either. Are you sure you're okay, Clem? You love champagne."

"Normally I do, yes."

"Then why wouldn't you want to drink it at Christmas?"

"Because I'm going to have a baby!" The words exploded out of Clemmie like the cork from the champagne bottle and with that one sentence she finally managed to silence her family.

13

Clemmie

Clemmie trudged through the deep snow, her vision partially obscured by her fur-lined hood that kept falling over her eyes.

Her head ached from crying and lack of sleep.

Next to her, Hunter heaved himself valiantly through deep drifts, determined to stay as close to her side as possible.

Guilt engulfed her. "Sorry." Clemmie bent to brush snow from his body. "I shouldn't have brought you out in this, but I wanted nonjudgmental company and you're the only one that fits that description."

What she'd really wanted to do was head to the kitchen, make herself a hot cup of tea and sit quietly warming her feet on the range cooker. But she knew that if she'd stayed in the house then someone would have wanted to continue the conversation that had ended so abruptly the evening before. Which was why this morning, instead of relaxing, she'd grabbed every layer she could find and headed out into the bitter cold. A record amount of snow had fallen overnight, but for now it seemed to have stopped. Parts of the country had lost power, but fortunately they were still fine in the lodge.

And Clemmie wasn't thinking about the snowstorm, because she was dealing with a storm of her own.

Why had she blurted it out like that? She should have told them her plans in a quiet, one-on-one conversation, but she hadn't been able to find the right moment. And the right moment, whatever that looked like, didn't always come, did it? Sometimes you could wait so long for the right moment that you never said anything at all, which was the reason Alice still hadn't talked to Nico. At least Clemmie had said what she wanted to say, even if the response wasn't what she'd hoped for.

Remembering the look of shock on her mother's face made her want to cry again.

And then there were her words.

But, Clemmie, why would you do this? Are you sure?

Yes, she was sure, but having to defend her decision hadn't been easy. She hated conflict and confrontation and it was clear they all thought her decision was a terrible one. Except for Nanna Jean. Nanna Jean hadn't seemed shocked or upset but her reaction had been overshadowed by everyone else's.

Was it really that terrible? Maybe her plan wasn't exactly traditional, but it wasn't as if she hadn't thought it through carefully.

She'd felt excited, but now she just felt alone. She'd done the brave thing and said what needed to be said but doing so hadn't made her feel proud. It had made her feel terrible.

She badly wanted to rewind the clock, but that wasn't an option so instead she hugged Hunter. "I want to be a dog. Your life is so much simpler than mine."

Hunter wagged his tail and licked her face.

"At least you still love me. You're probably the only one who does." She kept her arms round him and glanced around. The mountains and the forest were cloaked in white. "Are you okay? You like snow, don't you? We won't go far."

It had finally stopped snowing an hour earlier, but the sky was still dark and heavy with the promise of more snow to come.

The air was freezing, but at least it would keep her awake.

She hadn't slept at all, and she'd locked her bedroom door for the first time in her life. At one point she'd heard Alice tapping quietly, urging her to open it so that they could talk, but she'd pretended to be asleep.

She didn't want Alice telling her why she was making a mistake. She didn't want to talk to anyone.

She was so preoccupied with hugging the dog that it took her a moment to realize someone was calling her.

"Clemmie! Clem!"

She looked up and saw a male figure in outdoor gear plodding toward her through the deep snow. Ross? No. The man coming toward her had a stockier build than Ross, and also he was coming from the direction of the village, not the house.

She stood up and Hunter immediately shot away from her and bounded toward the man, snow flying, tail wagging. Which meant he was someone familiar.

Finally he drew close enough for Clemmie to recognize him, too.

Fergus.

She groaned and resisted the temptation to plant her face in the snow. Why now? He was about the last person she wanted to see, especially looking like this. She had red eyes and bed hair because she'd rushed out of the house without even thinking about her appearance. And why would she? How could she have predicted that she might bump into Fergus?

Because the universe obviously hated her.

"Clem? This is a surprise." He pulled her into a hug and she stood for a moment, relieved to find she no longer wanted to cry. That had to be a good sign.

"Hi, Fergus."

He released her. "What are you doing out here on your own? Are you okay?"

"I'm fine. Just grabbing an early walk. Wasn't expecting to bump into you—anyone—out here."

"I was coming over to see if you were all okay. I thought if I timed it with breakfast I might earn myself one of your mother's famous bacon sandwiches."

"Why wouldn't we be okay? Not that it isn't great to see you. It always is." Although she would have preferred it if she'd had more notice, and if it hadn't been this morning.

"Your bridge is impassable." He bent to pat Hunter. "You didn't know?"

"No. But I left before anyone else was awake."

His gaze was searching. "Was there a reason for that?"

"Just enjoying the snow and the scenery."

He glanced at the mountains. "It's stunning, isn't it? Are you ready to go back to the house? We can go together. You can put in a good word for me and maybe your mother will give me extra bacon."

"You go ahead. I'm going to walk for a bit longer." Maybe her eyes weren't as red as she'd assumed they were. Or maybe he was blaming it on the freezing weather. "Perhaps I'll see you later."

She started to trudge away from him, but he caught her arm.

"Wait. You still haven't seen my house, have you? I invited

you last Christmas, but you were busy and, anyway, the place was only half-finished."

"Sorry. The whole thing was a whirlwind." And last Christmas she'd been dating Liam, and very confused about the whole thing. "Mum says you've made progress."

"Almost done. Why don't you come and see for yourself?"

"Now? I thought you were going to my house?"

"I was, but there's no hurry. Particularly if you're saying that no one is awake. Why don't we go back to mine for breakfast? I can show off the work I've done."

She couldn't think of a reason to say no. And maybe she shouldn't look for one. Maybe she should do this. It was another thing she'd been putting off, so she might as well get it over with. Maybe she'd feel better about this bit of personal growth than she did about the other.

"All right. Where's Iona?"

"She stayed with my parents last night. I had to work late. I've been making custom bookshelves for a client. It's a surprise for her husband, and I can only go into the house when he is out. All very cloak-and-dagger." He walked alongside her, his boots leaving deep prints in the thick snow. "So how is London?"

"London is London. I'm planning on moving back here, actually. Early in the New Year." She said it casually, as if totally upending her life was a natural thing to do and he nodded.

"Right."

"You don't seem surprised."

"That you're coming home? No. I was more surprised when you said you were moving to London in the first place. I couldn't quite figure out why."

Some people were incredibly slow-witted.

Clemmie tugged her feet out of the deep snow. None of

that mattered now. That was in the past and she'd designed herself a different future.

"London was exciting. It was good to be close to Ross and Alice. And I learned a lot. It was busy."

"I knew you were busy. I hardly ever heard from you."

"Yes. Sorry about that." She thought of the willpower it had taken not to reply to his emails instantly, and not to email him daily to share all the small things that were happening in her life as she once had. She thought of all the long emails she'd typed and then forced herself to delete because the way to get over someone wasn't to be in constant contact.

"Remember when we used to email and message each other all the time, even when we were seeing each other regularly?"

The fact that he'd been thinking the same thing was unsettling. "That seems like a long time ago."

"Yes." He glanced at her. "Does it feel good to be back?"

"Oh yes. It's always good to be home."

They trudged side by side through the deep snow until finally the trail opened up and they could see the village. Smoke curled upward from chimneys, and roofs were covered in snow. There was the spire of the church, so familiar, and the Christmas tree that always took pride of place on the village green. She remembered being eight years old and standing around it with the rest of the children in her class, huddled in warm coats and woolly hats, singing carols off-key.

He grinned at her. "Remember the time the sheep escaped from the pen?"

"I do." They shared so many memories. "I can't look at that tree and not remember it."

"Greg Mason left the gate open. They still sing, the kids," he said, pausing to scoop up snow, "but they don't use live animals."

"Probably best. Are you going to throw that at me?"

"I was considering it."

"Well don't. My aim was always better than yours."

"But I've had more practice. You don't have proper snow in London." But instead of throwing the snow, he pressed it to the shoulder of the snowman that someone had built next to the tree.

The cottages that bordered the green were adorned with lights, as were the hedges and trees.

It was charming, and Christmassy and she realized just how much she'd missed this place.

She shouldn't have stayed away so long. She should have pulled herself together before now.

"It's like something out of a children's picture book. I don't remember it looking like this before."

"It didn't." He knocked the snow from his gloves. "The village committee decided that it would be fun if everyone put up some sort of outdoor lights."

"And everyone agreed?"

"Yes." He glanced at her. "I was surprised, too. I expected at least a few to refuse, but they approached the idea with collective enthusiasm. And then they needed volunteers to help those who couldn't put the lights up themselves."

"And I'm guessing that was you."

"It was. But you'd be surprised how many sweet treats you can earn by stringing lights around an old lady's door."

It made her smile. "You remind me of Hunter."

"We have many traits in common. Remember when you used to give me the chocolate from your lunch box?"

"Of course I remember. You think I give my chocolate to anyone?" This was good. This was better than good. She was managing to joke and tease and sound entirely normal. "Your friends used to tease you for hanging out with me."

"I've never much cared what other people thought about my actions."

If only she was the same.

Clemmie thought back to her family's reaction to her ill-timed announcement the night before and the slightly sick feeling returned.

"Any tips on not caring gratefully received."

He gave her a curious look. "Is someone judging you, Clem?"

She shouldn't have said anything, but fortunately for her a woman walking her dog approached.

"Morning, Fergus. It's a cold one."

"Morning, Anna. Morning, Rufus."

Rufus was busy sniffing and tail wagging with Hunter.

"Clemmie." Anna smiled. "Good to see you home, pet. And together with Fergus. Now, isn't that a happy sight. There was a time when we never saw one of you without the other. Still, times change as Ray is always reminding me. And talking of Ray—" She touched Fergus's arm. "He loves the bookcase you made us. Best Christmas surprise ever. Thank you."

"You're very welcome. You didn't manage to keep it a secret until Christmas Day, then?"

"No. The house is small, and his curiosity large. He wanted to know why he wasn't allowed in that room. But it didn't matter. His reaction couldn't have been better." She bent to stroke Hunter. "How are you, you gorgeous thing?"

Anna had worked in the library for the whole of Clemmie's childhood and knew everyone.

There would be gossip, Clemmie knew that. In a village the size of this one, there was always gossip.

But if she followed through with her plan she was going to have to get used to that. And maybe it would be worth the gossip to be able to slide back into this community and find her place. She'd missed that. There was something warming about going for a walk and meeting people you'd known since you were a child.

As Anna walked away, Clemmie turned to Fergus.

"You built her a library?"

"It was her retirement gift to Ray."

"Great gift."

"I hope so."

They trudged across the village green, leaving footprints in the snow. A row of cottages faced the green, their roofs hidden under a layer of white, gardens crusted with snow. The air was filled with the smell of woodsmoke.

She breathed in. "Can you believe we're going to have a white Christmas?"

"I know. Iona is beside herself with excitement. I'm just hoping we don't lose power." He pushed open the gate of one of the cottages. The door was painted a cheerful shade of green and lights twinkled from the windows.

"I can't believe you've never actually seen this place." He dug in his pocket for the key and opened the door.

"There always seems to be so little time whenever I'm home." She toed off her boots and left them by the front door. She eyed the beautiful hardwood floor, no doubt laid by Fergus. "What about Hunter?"

"He's fine. He can't do more damage than a six-year-old." He took her coat and she followed him through the house to the kitchen.

"Oh, Fergus!" She glanced up at the glass atrium that rose above her and then out through more glass to the small garden. There was an apple tree, and a bird table, and a bench that was obviously Fergus's handiwork. Heat seeped from the floor to her socks, warming her freezing feet. "You built this?"

"Yes. The moment I saw the cottage I knew there was a lot I could do with it. There was barely room for one person in the kitchen, but I figured we didn't need all the garden when we're surrounded by hills." He gazed outside for a moment. "It's been a major job. Taken longer than I hoped. My parents were forced to endure my company for a lot longer than originally planned, but I wanted to get it right. It seemed important to get it right."

And of course he would have got it right.

She stood next to him, feeling emotional again. He'd built the perfect home for himself and his sister's child. It was so Fergus. He was the same, and yet not the same. Familiar, and yet unfamiliar. There was a maturity that hadn't been there before. A seriousness layered under his easy nature. A seriousness that had come from family tragedy. "I'm sure they loved having you. And Iona."

"They did. My mother spoils her." He turned his head and studied her for a moment. "You look cold. Coffee? No, wait—how about hot chocolate? That's always comforting."

"That would be perfect." But did she look as if she needed comforting?

"It's Iona's favorite, so I'm an expert at making it. I'm also great at homemade pizza." He grabbed two mugs from one of the cabinets and, because he had his back to her, she allowed herself a moment to enjoy the way his sweater hugged the width of his shoulders. Why not? She was human, wasn't she?

"What else did you have to do apart from the kitchen?"

"The windows were rotten, so I replaced those. I tore out the bathroom and started again. But the biggest job was the attic. I converted it into a bedroom for Iona. She finally moved in there a month ago. She loves looking at the sky and the stars, so I've put in big windows. I've bought her a telescope for Christmas, so she can see more."

"A telescope? That's brilliant."

"She wrote to Santa and asked for snow for Christmas. Gave me a few sleepless nights. Fortunately, he delivered." He glanced out of the window. "In fact he might have over delivered."

She was sure that if he could have produced snow with his bare hands, he would have done it for his niece.

And now she was fascinated. "Can I take a look at the rest of the house?"

"I'll show you round after we've had a drink. You need warming up. Your lips were turning blue when I saw you in the snow with Hunter."

She watched as he moved around the kitchen, pulling chocolate from another cupboard and milk from the fridge.

Because watching him unsettled her, she turned her head and focused on the kitchen island instead. It was messy, covered in half-made Christmas cards, piles of crayons, glue, squares of fabric and a few hair ribbons.

He intercepted her look as he waited for the milk to heat. "We both overslept. It was a bit of a rush this morning and Iona wanted her hair plaited. Usually I set the alarm ten minutes earlier if I know it's a plait day."

"You plait hair?" She glanced at his fingers, long and strong and covered in cuts and grazes from working with wood. They were the hands of a craftsman, not a hairdresser.

He intercepted her gaze. "I'm the first to admit I'm better at working with wood than a girl's hair, but I'm getting better. Angela gave me a private lesson. I was all fingers and thumbs, but I got there in the end."

She was still dealing with the image of Fergus plaiting hair when the name finally registered. "Angela? Do you mean Angela Sutton?"

"The same. She owns the salon in the village. She took

pity on me and came around one evening. Iona and I made her our legendary homemade pizza, and Angela taught me to plait hair."

"That was nice of her." It would have been an adorable image if it weren't for the fact that Angela Sutton had always been a heartbreaker. There was nothing adorable about the thought of her with Fergus.

Was she a regular in his home for homemade pizza?

She killed the thought instantly. It was none of her business.

He waved a hand toward the mess. "If I'd known you were coming, I would have tidied up. We were making Christmas cards. It's Iona's favorite thing to do at the moment but we've run out of people to send them to. I don't suppose you'd like two or three—or maybe ten? We did two designs this year. A penguin and a reindeer." He lifted the milk from the heat. "I'm not even going to ask what you're thinking."

"I'm thinking this looks like a happy home and that the child who lives here is a lucky girl."

He glanced at her. "Really?" His gaze lingered. "Thank you for that."

She tried to imagine any of the other men she'd met in her life doing what he had done. "It must have been tough."

"You can't possibly imagine." He poured chocolate into mugs. "Or maybe you can. You're a child expert after all. I still feel like a novice."

"You must miss Laura."

"Every day. It's worse for my parents though. Thank goodness for Iona. She has been their whole focus, which is good on many levels. They make it possible for me to do my job. They pick her up from school three nights a week and have her overnight on a Friday. It's an arrangement that works. Gives everybody structure." He added cream and marshmallows.

"Did you really just put marshmallows on my chocolate?"

"Sorry. Force of habit. Iona's favorite." He put the mugs on the countertop and sat down next to her.

His knee jutted forward, almost touching hers. She couldn't shift back without attracting attention so she stayed where she was, paralyzed by his close proximity, the need in her so acute that she almost couldn't draw breath.

Maybe she wasn't doing as well as she'd thought.

She was twenty-seven years old, and she'd loved Fergus Maclennon for at least twenty-three of those years.

She'd tried everything. Moving to the other end of the country. Not seeing him. Dating other people. When she'd met Liam, she'd thought for a short time that maybe she could make it work. He'd made her laugh. He was decent, or so she'd thought. He liked kids. In fact the only thing wrong with him was that he wasn't Fergus. The night he told her he loved her was the night she'd realized that no relationship was ever going to work for her and that it wasn't fair for anyone to be her second choice. It was annoying, frustrating, that she couldn't move on but that was the way it was so she had to learn to live with it. And she thought she had.

She'd broken up with Liam that night and that had been a turning point for her.

Since then she hadn't dated. What was the point? It wasn't fair on anyone. No man wanted to be second best and that was all they would ever be.

There had been a moment, one tiny precious moment in the pub five years earlier, where she'd thought that maybe her feelings were reciprocated. It had been crowded, a large group of hikers jostling each other to reach the bar. Clemmie had been pushed hard into Fergus, but instead of pushing her away he'd pulled her closer, holding her against him, sheltering her from the press of people. And she'd stood, unable to move and feeling grateful for the excuse not to because it was the closest she'd been to Fergus and given the choice she would have stayed like that forever. She'd felt his thigh against hers. Hardness and heat. His hand on her back. Warmth and promise. And she'd closed her eyes and pretended, just for a moment, that this was about more than just crowd management. She'd looked up at him and met his gaze and been sure, absolutely sure, that he was feeling something, too.

But then the crowd had dispersed, and the moment passed. She'd had no reason not to step away and he hadn't given her one.

Neither of them had ever mentioned it and the next thing she knew Fergus was dating Tina Watts, who had been the year above Clemmie at school and always seemed to be smiling. Then Laura had died, he'd taken charge of Iona, and Tina Watts seemed to vanish from the scene.

Occasionally, Clemmie thought about that moment. About how close she'd come to telling him how she felt. How close she'd come to making a total and utter fool of herself. She was relieved now that she hadn't. It was all very well deciding to be braver, thinking that you should have the difficult conversations, but what happened when those conversations didn't have the outcome you wanted? Take the night before. She'd done it, and now she wished she hadn't. But she'd get over that because her family had to be told sometime. But Fergus? That was different. He didn't need to know how she felt. The risk was too great. If she'd said something all those years ago she probably wouldn't be sitting here now. And she was glad to be sitting here now. It was the closest to truly content that she'd felt for a long time.

"So, enough catching up," he said, taking a mouthful of hot chocolate. "Are you going to tell me what's wrong?"

"I'm sitting in the warm with hot chocolate. What could possibly be wrong?"

He put his mug down. "I'm talking about the reason you were on your own in the snow this morning. With red eyes."

Of course he'd noticed. He knew her. And that made everything more painful.

"It was the wind and the cold."

"Mmm. We've always been able to tell each other everything."

Not everything.

And not for a long time. They'd been close, until she'd decided she just couldn't handle being close but not being with him.

He was the reason she'd moved to London. But now she was moving back.

If she was living here, she was going to see Fergus. She *wanted* to be able to see him.

A few hours in his company had taught her that. She could handle her emotions, and she'd rather have his friendship than nothing at all. Friendship was good. Friendships often lasted longer than romantic relationships.

Why not talk to him?

Her decision was going to be common knowledge soon enough if everything went according to plan.

"I had some drama at home. It's been a bit of a strange Christmas so far." She told him about Lucy, about her breaking her ankle, about Alice trying to divert parental attention. "And then…" she paused "… I told them about me. And I didn't intend to. Not right at that moment, with everyone gathered together. I intended to tell Mum and Dad quietly on their own, but they couldn't understand why I wasn't drinking and I just blurted it out. I told them that I was going to have a baby." She saw something flicker in his eyes.

"A baby?"

"You're shocked. Don't worry, my family reacted pretty much the same way."

"You're pregnant?" His voice sounded strange. "I—well—congratulations, Clem. You'll be an amazing mother, no doubt about that."

"I'm not pregnant. I never said I was pregnant. Not yet."

"But—"

"I said I'm going to have a baby. And I am. That's what I want. More than anything. It's my dream." Not her whole dream, but part of her dream. The part she could hopefully control. The part she could pursue.

Fergus pushed his mug to one side, leaving his drink unfinished. "How long have you been seeing each other?"

"Excuse me?"

"You and the baby's father. I didn't know you were in a relationship. Your mother must have forgotten to mention it."

"I'm not in a relationship." There didn't seem to be a way to explain that didn't create surprise, so she just stated the facts. "I've never met the baby's father, and I never will."

He was silent for a moment. "I'm confused."

"Donor sperm." She said it quickly. "I'm going to use donor sperm. I've found a clinic—reputable. I have an appointment in January. Do you have to look so shocked? You look exactly the way my mother looked." But having been through this once, it didn't seem so bad this time. Or maybe it was just that she'd always found Fergus easy to talk to. "I know it's a little unconventional, but not massively so. And what is so wrong with it? You could argue that a baby should have two loving parents, but there are plenty of instances where that doesn't happen. There are plenty of couples who have a baby and turn out to be terrible parents. I know I'll be a great mum, so why shouldn't I be one? I don't need a partner for that." She would have liked one. She would have liked to be with *him*, but she wasn't going to waste any more of her life wanting something she couldn't have. She'd thought about it long and hard and she knew she was doing the right thing. "Look at you. You're raising Iona alone and you're doing a great job. Children need love and stability, and that comes in different forms."

He said nothing and she felt emotion build inside her. He had to be thinking *something*, surely?

"I shouldn't have told you. Sorry." She stood up, vision blurred. She'd never felt more alone in her life. "Thanks for the chocolate. I'll let myself out."

"Wait—slow down." He grabbed her hand. "Sit down, Clem."

"I really don't—"

"You think I'm judging you, but I'm not. I agree that you will make a wonderful mother. The very best." He let go of her hand. "I suppose I'm a little surprised that you've decided to go it alone. I assumed you would have met someone special by now. Fallen in love."

She'd hoped for that, too, but it turned out that you couldn't fall in love when you were already in love.

"Life doesn't always turn out the way you plan, does it?"

"And don't I know it." He looked at her for a long moment. "Finish telling me the story. Once your family calmed down, what happened then?"

"They didn't calm down. My dad didn't understand at all and kept asking Alice questions." And to be fair her sister had answered them calmly, and without judgment.

"And your mother?"

That was the part she'd been trying not to think about. "She was shocked, and then disappointed. And worried. She said, *Oh, Clemmie,* in a voice I've never heard her use before.

And then she cried. I actually made my mother cry." Thinking about it brought all the emotion rushing to the surface again. "It was hideous. There has never been a single thing in my life I haven't been able to talk to my mother about, but this—she looked shattered. She kept saying, *But, Clem, on your own? And—like that? It's so—*" She broke off as he pulled her into a tight hug. "What are you doing?"

"Giving you the hug you badly need."

She knew she should pull away. But instead she leaned her head against his chest and allowed herself to stay there. Just for a moment, that was all. As friends.

"I've ruined Christmas."

"You haven't ruined anything." His arms tightened around her. "They were surprised, Clem, that's all. I remember when Laura told our parents she was pregnant with Iona, they were pretty shocked. I was there because Laura was so nervous about telling them she wanted moral support. The guy she'd been seeing wanted nothing to do with it, and our parents were really worried about how Laura would cope as a single mother. Laura was upset because she thought she'd disappointed them, but really it was just that everyone was anxious. Everyone needed some time to digest it and deal with it. I'm sure it's the same with your parents."

She lifted her head to look at him. "Do you really think that?"

"Yes, I do. They'll come around, Clem. And they'll be there for you, just as mine were there for Laura. And now for Iona."

"I hope you're right. I'm not so sure. And right now I can't even face going back home." And because being with him like this was too comfortable, too right, and just too damn hard, she forced herself to ease away. Perhaps she shouldn't have told him. Her confession had created an intimacy that made the whole situation more difficult.

Perhaps he felt it, too, because he let go of her reluctantly. "Stay awhile. Come and see the rest of the house and you can tell me all about what's been happening in your life while we look around."

They'd seen so little of each other over the past few years, and that was her fault, of course. Her choice. It had been part of her "get over Fergus" program. But now she could see that everything she'd done had been for nothing.

She loved him with every bone in her body and that was never going to change.

She was never going to fall out of love with him, so she just had to learn to live with it.

"This is our living room." He pushed open a door and she poked her head around, admiring the pretty tree with the presents stacked underneath.

"You have a piano?"

"Laura played. I thought she'd want Iona to learn. I've been taking lessons so that I can help her. I think my skills at that are about the same level as my hairdressing."

"You've been taking piano lessons?"

"You're finding it difficult to imagine. I can understand that. I'm not a natural musician, but fortunately Mrs. Killmartin is the patient type and she loves Iona, so we rub along well enough." He smiled. "Not sure whether it will work out. Iona seems more interested in climbing. I took her a few times in the summer. She's a natural. And that's more in line with my skill set."

Clemmie felt a lump lodge in her throat. He hadn't only taken on his sister's child, he'd tried to do what his sister would have wanted. That thoughtfulness was one of the many reasons she loved him. "You're a good dad."

"Wait until you hear me play the piano. You might want to rethink that assessment." He closed the living room door. "Where are you going to live? If—when—you get pregnant?"

"I'm going to move up here. Property is so much cheaper. And I'll find a childcare job that allows me to bring my own child to work."

"Your mum and Nanna Jean will want to help, trust me on that. They used to love me bringing Iona over when she was a toddler. They still enjoy it." He led her upstairs and showed her the bedrooms and then up another flight of stairs to the attic.

"Oh, Fergus…" The moment she stepped into the room, she could see how much thought had gone into it. The bed was on a shelf, positioned under one of the skylights and surrounded by fairy lights. There was a cozy seating area piled with cushions and soft toys, and surrounded by shelves stacked with books. Next to the books were several framed photographs of Laura. In one she was smiling into the camera, her hair messy from the wind. In the other she was holding the baby—Iona—and Clemmie had never seen so much love on anyone's face before. Next to it was a photograph of Iona with her grandparents and Fergus.

He followed her gaze. "I wanted her to constantly be reminded that she has lots of people who love her in her life."

She swallowed. "It's perfect. The whole room is perfect."

"She helped me design it."

"And the telescope is going under this skylight?" She gazed up through the glass, trying to imagine it at night. "It's a great idea."

"She likes looking at the sky." He paused. "She thinks her mother is up there, among the stars. I thought a telescope might bring it all closer for her."

Her heart ached. Her eyes filled. "Damn it, Fergus—"

she almost choked on the words "—you're going to make me cry again."

"Don't. It's all good. It's been hard, obviously, but she's doing okay. We're doing okay. She's a great kid, and I'm lucky." He put his hand on her shoulder and pointed. "If you look out of the skylight from her bed, you can see my parents' house. She likes knowing she can signal Grandma in the middle of the night. The chances of my mother being awake to see it are slim to none, but that doesn't matter."

Iona was doing okay because of her family. Her grandparents. Fergus.

Clemmie thought about how much her mother would love grandchildren.

"I think I've messed up my mother's dream."

He pushed his hands into his pockets and leaned against the wall. "You have to live your life, Clem, exactly the way you want to live it. A parent's job is to accept that."

She turned to look at him. "Do you believe that?"

"Of course. This is your life, Clemmie. They should respect your decisions, even if they're not the decisions they would have made for you. And they will, I'm sure. They're probably just anxious for you. You're still their child, even though you're an adult. My mother tried to explain it to me once, when I couldn't understand why she would be anxious about me." He gave a rueful smile. "Your child is always your child, no matter how old they are. You want the best for them. You want life to be kind to them, even though you know that's unlikely. And because it's unlikely and bad things happen, you want to know they have good people around them and that they're supported. That's why your mother reacted the way she did. Because she loves you and she is worried about you. It's true that plenty of people end up raising kids in a single-parent family, and also that families come in all shapes and sizes, but she is concerned because she thinks you'll be doing this alone. But you won't be."

"I won't?"

"Not if you come back here." He eased away from the wall. "They say it takes a village—and you have a village. And if you decide you don't want to take the baby to work with you, there's a great nursery in the village."

"That's true." The nursery in the village. Why hadn't she thought of that? In January she'd contact them and see if they might have a job.

"And you'll have plenty of emergency babysitters, and that's not even counting your own family. I'm sure there is nothing Iona would love more than having a baby to fuss over. She keeps asking for a little sister for Christmas, which is a little awkward in the circumstances."

Her heart bumped a little harder. She imagined him, head to head with Angela over homemade pizza. "You're not seeing anyone?"

"Nothing serious."

The sense of joy those words gave her made her realize she hadn't made anywhere near as much progress as she'd first thought.

But his words had cheered her. It had been unrealistic of her not to expect her mother to be shocked. It was hardly an everyday decision she was making, was it? And Fergus was right. She needed to talk to her mother. She needed to explain just how much she wanted a baby, and how sure she was that she was doing the right thing.

Thinking about her mother made her check the time. "I should go." Although no one had been awake when she'd left the house so they weren't likely to be worried.

"So is this Lucy staying with you?"

"Looks that way, although she still seems keen to try and get back to London."

"She might not have much choice." Fergus closed the door of the attic room. "It's going to take a day or two to clear the snow and fix that bridge."

"And longer than that to fix her ankle, so if you want my opinion I don't think Lucy is going anywhere. She seems nice. Hunter likes her, so she'll probably fit in well. I just hope Nanna Jean doesn't do any embarrassing matchmaking." She followed Fergus back downstairs. "Thanks for the hot chocolate and the tour. And for listening."

"Anytime." He grabbed her coat, and also his own.

"You're going out again?"

"I thought I'd come with you."

"Why?"

"Because you're dreading seeing your family, and those first few moments will be easier if I'm there."

Her entire body turned warm. "You'd do that?"

"Of course. That's what friends are for."

Friends.

She smiled. "Thanks. I appreciate that. And if you're lucky, you might get bacon."

"I'm counting on it."

She slid into her coat and he reached forward and zipped it for her.

It made her smile. "Marshmallows on my hot chocolate and now you're zipping my coat? Are you going to plait my hair next?"

He stood back, hands raised in apology. "Sorry. Reflex action. I'm so used to zipping up coats, I forget some people can do it themselves."

"You can help me with my scarf if you like. I always struggle with that."

Now he was the one grinning and he took her scarf from her and wound it around, the movement bringing him close.

Too close.

The attraction was overwhelming. She stood there, fighting it. Fighting temptation. It was impossible, she knew that, but his face was right there, so close that she could see the dark grainy stubble that shadowed his jaw. All she had to do was lift herself onto her toes and she'd be able to kiss him. She'd thought about it so many times. Awake. Asleep. Eyes open. Eyes closed. She'd kissed Fergus so many times in her imagination she was sure she knew how it would feel.

He turned his head slowly and looked at her and Clemmie stopped breathing.

In that brief moment there was a sense of connection that felt as right as not being with him felt wrong.

She stepped back.

No. She wasn't going to do this again. She'd done it too many times before. Wondered. Hoped. Asked herself whether maybe he had feelings he wasn't expressing. Tortured herself with delicious fantasies that ended up dying like all the rest.

This morning had reminded her just what a good friend he was. And she wanted that friendship. She imagined bringing the baby over and introducing him or her to Iona. Imagined evenings where she and Fergus shared a bottle of wine and relaxed together over his famous homemade pizza.

Friendship was good. She'd settle for friendship.

It wasn't everything, but who had everything?

She was going to build a good life for herself, and it would be enough.

14

Glenda

"Have you seen Clemmie? I can't find her anywhere."
It was probably the first time in her life she'd used
those words. When Clemmie was a child, Glenda had always
known where she was, mostly because she never strayed far.
If she'd been asked to describe her youngest daughter in one
word, she would have said *easy*. She was her most straightforward child. Clemmie never had tantrums or moods and
she never surprised Glenda, mostly because they talked about
everything. They talked on the school run, they talked while
they made shortbread together or walked Hunter. Clemmie
made sense of life, and her problems, by talking them through.
Glenda had always enjoyed the fact that Clemmie found it easy
to talk to her. For that reason she would have said that she was
closer to Clemmie than the others, but it turned out she was
wrong about that. She'd been wrong about so many things.

Douglas was absorbed in the business section of the newspaper. "Have you tried her room?"

"Of course I've tried her room. She's not there. I've asked Ross and Alice. They haven't seen her, either. I even checked Lucy's room, but she hasn't seen her."

"Lucy has her own room now?" Douglas lowered the newspaper. "Did I miss something? Is she moving in? What a Christmas this is turning out to be."

"I had no idea Clemmie was going to suddenly say something like that. I wasn't prepared. I handled it badly. And now she's gone."

"She won't have gone far. Maybe she's in the living room. You know how much she loves sitting by the tree." Douglas turned to the sports pages but Glenda tugged the paper away from him. How could he be so calm?

"The living room was the first place I looked. I'm telling you, Douglas, she's not in the house."

Douglas glanced toward the window. "There's a foot of new snow out there. Of course she's in the house. Where else would she be?"

"That's what I'm trying to figure out." Glenda gave up trying to elicit support. *Men.* She closed her eyes for a moment and tried to imagine what she would do if she were Clemmie. "She loves walking in the mountains."

"She's not going to be walking in the mountains today. It would be lethal out there. Give the girl space, Glenda. She'll turn up when she's ready." Douglas reached for the newspaper but Glenda moved it out of reach.

"Aren't you at all concerned?"

"She's upset," he said. "She needs space."

"But when Clemmie is upset she doesn't want space. She wants someone to talk to. That's who she is. But who would she be talking to? Why is she doing this alone? She's a very special person. Why can't she find someone?"

"Why are you asking me?"

"Because you're her— Oh never mind. This is all my fault." Glenda sank onto the nearest chair just as Nanna Jean walked into the room.

"What's all your fault? What are you taking the blame for now?"

"Poor Clemmie. I feel terrible. I didn't react the way I should have done. I was so *shocked*." And she was still shocked, but partly because she was dealing with the realization that her most straightforward child was, in fact, her most complicated.

She was starting to think she didn't know her children at all.

"Well of course you were shocked," Douglas said. "It's not every day you discover your daughter is intending to have a baby by herself, with no outside help."

"She has some outside help," Nanna Jean said. "Just not the conventional sort of help. I don't know why you're all in such a twist about it. The world is full of single mothers. I, for one, am pleased to see our Clemmie finally going after what she wants regardless of what anyone else thinks." She headed to the kettle and made a fresh pot of tea.

"I'm aware that the world is full of single mothers, but usually there's a man involved somewhere, even if he doesn't hang around," Douglas said.

"There is a man. She just isn't going to meet him, that's all."

"You're an expert now?"

"It so happens I am." Nanna Jean gave a sniff. "I did some research and I now know all about donor sperm. I borrowed Ross's laptop and looked it up."

Douglas choked on his tea. "What exactly did you look up?"

"I've told you. Donated sperm." Nanna Jean poured milk into her favorite cup. "I had a few false starts and all sorts of surprising images came up on the screen, but I got there in the end. I do hope no one checks Ross's search history. He might have some explaining to do. I couldn't remember how to close the page so I just opened new ones over the top. I didn't want to lose something important."

Glenda didn't know whether to laugh or cry. "Did you discover anything interesting?"

"I was checking out this clinic that she intends to use. I want to make sure they're not taking advantage of our girl. They do appear to be reputable, but I intend to discuss it with Alice."

"Discuss what with Alice?" Alice entered the room, yawning.

"Sperm."

"Excuse me?"

"Don't look so shocked. You're a doctor."

"I'm also someone who woke up less than ten minutes ago. This is heavy for the first conversation of the day." Alice ignored the teapot and headed for the coffee machine while Nanna Jean spread butter on a thick slice of toast.

"Does she have to use a clinic?" Douglas frowned. "Can't she meet someone who would provide sperm the conventional way?"

"I think that's called a relationship, Dad." Alice filled her mug to the brim. "Where is Clemmie?"

"None of us knows." Glenda felt sick with panic. She'd always believed that no matter what choices her children made, she'd support them unconditionally. She was ashamed of the way she'd reacted and she desperately wanted to rewind the clock.

This wasn't about her, but she'd somehow made it about her.

Yes, she had questions, the biggest of which was why Clemmie, of all people, would want to have a baby on her own. But it was Clemmie's decision. And she deserved to have her decisions accepted without having to give an explanation.

The door flew open and Ross strode in. "Who has been messing with my laptop? I opened it to check my emails and I was confronted by pornographic images."

"That's your grandmother." Glenda stood up. "Tea?"

"Tea? I need something stronger than tea. What the—" Ross stopped himself. "Never mind. Am I allowed to ask exactly what you were looking up? I'd like to know what I'm likely to be charged with when the law comes knocking on the door."

"I was researching donor sperm." Nanna Jean was calm. "But I may have taken a few wrong turns."

"No kidding. When the police turn up to confiscate my laptop I expect you to give a full confession."

"No one will be turning up for the next few days. There's far too much snow on the ground. Also, the 'police' is Roy MacLean, and given that I taught three of his children I don't think he'll be arresting me in a hurry. And can I say that you're all very prudish. I'm shocked at all of you. You need to move with the times."

Ross followed his sister's example and helped himself to a brimming mug of hot coffee. "Where is Clemmie?"

"That's what we're trying to discover." Douglas looked at Alice and Ross. "Did you two know about this?"

"No," Ross said.

"No." Alice pulled bacon out of the fridge and laid the rashers carefully in the frying pan.

"She didn't talk to you?" That made Glenda feel a hundred times worse. "Then who has she talked to? Poor Clemmie. This is a huge decision. Probably the biggest decision she's ever made in her life and she's done it all alone. Why didn't she talk to us?"

"Probably because she was afraid of how we'd react." Alice watched as the bacon started to sizzle. "And it turns out she had reason. If this was an exam, I think we failed."

Ross frowned. "That's not true——"

"It is true." Alice flipped the strands of bacon over. "Did any one of us say, *That's great Clemmie? Good decision? You will be an amazing mother. How can we help?* No. Dad choked on his drink. Mum cried, and I——well I didn't say the right thing, either. Thanks to society's expectations, we had her pushed into a box labeled 'mother,' and we assumed that came with marriage. But the expectations of those around you can be really tough to live with when that's not the route you want to take. If you ask me she was brave. Really brave." Her voice rose and Glenda looked closely at her daughter.

"Brave for deciding to have a child on her own?"

Why was Alice so upset? Presumably because she felt she'd let Clemmie down, too.

"No." Alice transferred the bacon to a plate. "Well, yes, I guess that's brave, too, but I really meant that she was brave for standing up for what she wanted and ignoring convention."

Glenda hadn't thought about what it must have taken for Clemmie to tell them, but Alice was right, of course.

"I didn't exactly cry——"

"You cried. You asked her if she was sure, which is code for 'you're making a mistake.' I didn't say anything at all, which is as good as saying nothing. So no——" Alice waved the fork in the air "——I don't think any of us exactly covered ourselves in glory, except for Nanna Jean."

"All I said was that I asked for a great-grandchild for Christmas," Nanna Jean said. "And you can always rely on Santa."

Glenda couldn't raise a smile, although she was grateful

that at least one person in the room hadn't reacted as if the world had ended.

"You didn't pass judgment," Alice said. "And you didn't ask her if she was sure. You just accepted what she told you. Which makes you the only hero of this story."

Nanna Jean sighed. "The difference between us is that I'm old enough to know I'm not perfect. You all still want to be perfect and then you waste time beating yourselves up when you're not. You're human. You're going to make mistakes. You're going to say the wrong thing. The important thing is to acknowledge when that happens and put it right. Talk about it."

I'd love to talk about it, Glenda thought. She wanted to put it right.

But how could she when she didn't even know where Clemmie was?

Emotion threatened to engulf her, but this time she fought to control it. In the event that Clemmie suddenly appeared, a loss of control could so easily be misconstrued, and she didn't want to risk making things worse than they already were.

"You're right, Nanna Jean. And of course we're going to support whatever decision she has made." But she hated the thought of warm, affectionate Clemmie navigating life alone. She'd always known that Clemmie wanted children, but she'd assumed that when that time came there would be a supportive partner in the wings. She couldn't help worrying about the practicalities. A baby on her own? How would she take care of it? "Does she intend to stay in London, do you think?"

"We don't know. None of us knows anything," Alice said. "We should ask her. Then we can figure out how we can help."

"We can't ask her," Nanna Jean said. "We don't know where she is."

"Did you try calling?"

"Yes. Her phone is in the living room. She must have left it there last night when she walked out. Extraordinary, isn't it? Usually you can't get a young person to lift their heads from their phones and then when you actually want to contact them, they have it switched off."

Douglas folded his newspaper. "Maybe she has gone for a walk."

"In the snow?" Ross frowned. "Is her coat still hanging up?"

Why hadn't she thought to check that? Glenda walked to the boot room. *Please let there be some simple explanation.*

But there was no sign of Clemmie's coat. Or her boots. Or any of the other clothes she used to wrap up warm when she was home.

"Her stuff is gone. She's gone out in this. I can't believe it. Ross, you have to go after her."

To be fair he was on his feet in an instant. "Do you know which direction she would have walked in?"

"No." If she'd been worried before she was doubly so now. "The snow is deep. Surely she wouldn't have gone up the mountain trail?"

"Wherever she's gone, she has Hunter with her. I see paw prints." Alice was staring through the kitchen window. "Hunter won't let anything happen to Clemmie."

Hunter. Glenda felt relief weaken her limbs. "Yes. That's true. Why didn't I think of that sooner? I didn't even notice that Hunter had gone."

Douglas stood up, too. "Let's take a walk, Ross."

"Good plan." Ross already had his coat on. "Before I go, has anyone seen Lucy this morning?"

"She's still in her room I think," Alice said. "She's probably had enough Miller family drama. We ought to find a way to

help her get back to London. Or maybe she has already escaped through the window."

"We will not be helping her go back to London. That
would be the wrong thing to do." Nanna Jean spoke firmly.
"That girl doesn't have family of her own. She's lonely. And
you want to send her back to a cold, empty home?"

Douglas pulled his coat on. "How do you know her home
is cold?"

"I was thinking more about the emotional temperature,
rather than the physical one."

"You don't know she's lonely," Alice said. "That's a huge
assumption. Many people are happy on their own. Some
people find families stressful, particularly at Christmas. Not
that I'm saying that's me…" She saw everyone looking at her
and backtracked quickly. "But I think it would be wrong to
assume Lucy won't be happy to go home. She obviously has
lots of friends."

"Friends are good," Nanna Jean said, "but they're not
family. Didn't you see her expression when she thought we
weren't looking? I'm telling you that girl is lonely."

"You cannot possibly know that."

"And you're a doctor? It's not rocket science, Alice. She
lost her grandmother at Christmas. Her only family member.
And we toasted her family."

Had they got a single thing right the evening before?

Glenda wished she could rewind the clock. "You're probably right, Nanna Jean, and of course Lucy is welcome to
stay, but can we keep the focus on Clemmie until we know
she's safe? Ross, will you call me the moment you find her?
It hasn't snowed yet today so you might even be able to follow her footprints."

Ross paused in the doorway, his back to them. "I'm not
going to need to call you."

"But—"

"She's here. And Fergus is with her."

"Fergus? She's with Fergus? Oh thank goodness—" *She'd had someone to talk to.* "All of you, out of the kitchen right now."

"Out?" Douglas looked startled and so did Nanna Jean.

"Out? Why?"

"She needs privacy."

"Why? You think she's going to make a baby with Fergus?" Nanna Jean was peering through the door. "Not that I'd object. He's a lovely boy and a great deal more appealing than anything I saw on Ross's laptop, I can tell you that. But I'm not sure the kitchen is—"

"*Out!* Now. Can you imagine her walking into this big family gathering? How daunting would that be."

"If she wants daunting, she should see what's currently on my computer." Ross hung his coat back up. "If you ever intend to borrow my laptop again, will you let me know, Nanna Jean? I'll put parental controls on it."

Did anyone have a more maddening family?

Glenda ushered them all toward the door. "Go, go, *go!*"

"But I haven't eaten my bacon." Alice was looking longingly at the plate. "The only time I allow myself bacon is when I come home. Can't I at least—"

"No. Go, all of you. Douglas, you can stay if you want to."

"I don't want to. I'd rather digest my breakfast in peace if that's all right. And I might even have a chance to read a page of my paper without having it snatched out of my hand." He picked up his mug and his paper. "I'll leave this situation in your capable hands. I'll be in the living room if anyone needs me."

Capable? She'd never felt less capable in her life.

As the door closed behind the rest of her family she noticed that her palms were sweaty, and her heart was pounding.

How was she going to apologize to Clemmie with Fergus there? How was she going to make this right?

It had never been more important that she say the right thing.

On impulse she added fresh bacon to the pan and grabbed some eggs and mushrooms from the fridge.

She heard the door open, closed her eyes briefly and then turned with a smile. "There you are. We—I was worried about you."

"I took Hunter for a walk." Clemmie shrugged off her coat and gave her a wary look and that look almost broke her because when had her youngest daughter ever looked at her that way? When had there ever been a topic they couldn't talk about?

"I'm sure he loved that. He's always had fun in the snow. And I see you met up with Fergus." The effort to behave normally was half killing her. "How's it looking out there?"

"Snow's pretty deep." Fergus pulled off his hat, leaving sections of his hair standing upright. "The bridge is impassable. Did you know?"

"No." It meant that none of them would be leaving anytime soon, but that was the last thing on her mind right now. "You must be starving having been out in the cold. How about some breakfast?"

"That would be appreciated." Fergus sat down and after a moment's hesitation Clemmie did the same.

Glenda felt so awful she wanted to fix everything immediately, and she had to remind herself that this wasn't about her. She wasn't the priority here.

And maybe Clemmie didn't want to discuss it in front of Fergus.

"How's Iona, Fergus? Excited about Christmas I'm sure."

"She is." He took the tea she handed him with a nod of thanks. "She was staying with my parents last night. They took her to the Christmas market yesterday, and to see the Christmas lights. Managed it before the storm set in."

"I'm sure she loved that." She didn't know whether to be grateful that Fergus was here or frustrated that she couldn't use this opportunity to talk to her daughter.

Had Clemmie told him? She had no idea. There had been a time when Fergus and Clemmie had been so close that she'd wondered if maybe they might even—

But no. That hadn't happened. And she had to stop thinking about what might have been, and focus on what was.

All she wanted was for her children to be happy, and if having a baby by herself was what was going to make Clemmie happy (was it?—it still seemed like such an un-Clemmie decision to Glenda) then that was all that mattered.

She flipped the bacon, only half listening as Fergus described the problems he was having with Iona.

"She used to be great about bedtime, but lately she just doesn't want to go. She makes bedtime last as long as possible. *Read another story, Daddy*, so I read another story because I'm a sucker and before we know it another hour has passed. One night I even fell asleep on the bed before she did. I'm worried I'm doing something wrong."

Welcome to parenthood, Glenda thought as she tipped bacon onto plates, the hardest job in the world. If you were awarded pass or fail, she'd definitely be failing.

And now she was turning into Alice, who didn't want to do anything unless she could be top. Perfect.

Maybe Nanna Jean was right. Maybe she should accept that she was occasionally going to get things wrong.

She added mushrooms and tomatoes to the plates and put them on the table. "I'm sure you're doing a great job, Fergus."

"I'm not so sure." He picked up his knife and fork. "Any tips, Clem?"

"On sleeping? Has her routine changed? Has something happened lately that could have unsettled her? Something at school? Thanks, Mum." Clemmie took the plate from Glenda. "This looks delicious. Who were you cooking it for?"

"You." Glenda sent a silent apology to Alice. "Toast to go with that?"

Fergus nodded as he chewed and Glenda cut two thick slices from the loaf she'd baked the day before.

"I don't think anything has happened," he said. "You think I ought to talk to her teacher?"

"It wouldn't hurt. And you could also talk to her. Does she have a special friend? Could it be a friend problem?"

Fergus put his fork down. "She's six."

"It might not be that. But it's worth considering." Clemmie made a few other suggestions and Glenda listened, and realized she hadn't seen this side of Clemmie before. Clemmie the childcare professional.

Clemmie added ketchup to her plate. "Where's everyone else, Mum?"

"I don't know. Your dad was last seen reading the paper in the living room. Ross was doing something on his laptop," *removing your grandmother's rather explicit search history.* "Alice made herself a cup of coffee earlier. I haven't seen Nico or Lucy yet. It's Christmas. Time for everyone to relax." She had a feeling that it was the least relaxed anyone had ever been in their family.

She rescued the toast before it could burn and put it on a plate in the center of the table next to creamy butter and her homemade orange-and-ginger marmalade.

"You have no idea how good it is to have breakfast cooked for me." Fergus smiled at her. "I've been so busy lately breakfast has just been a quick bowl of cereal before I take Iona to school."

"What have you bought her for Christmas, Fergus?"

"I've bought her a telescope."

Clemmie smiled. "Iona's room is beautiful, Mum. Amazing."

Did the smile mean she was forgiven? She truly hoped so.

"You've seen it?"

"We went back to Fergus's house this morning. He was showing me the work he'd done."

So Clemmie hadn't been wandering, lost and miserable. She'd been with Fergus the whole time.

The relief was overwhelming.

"You've done a great job, Fergus."

"I'm getting there," Fergus said. "Not easy renovating a house with a daughter and a job, but it's coming along."

Clemmie glanced at him. "It looked finished to me."

"Then you obviously weren't looking too closely."

The conversation between them was easy and comfortable, an exchange between two people who knew each other well.

Glenda buttered a slice of toast for herself, which wasn't easy because her hand was shaking.

"Clemmie tells me she's going to be moving back here." Fergus helped himself to toast, relaxed and comfortable. "That's good news all round."

She felt a rush of gratitude. He'd bridged a potentially awkward moment.

"Yes, it is. It will be wonderful. I'm excited about it." She emphasized the words and Clemmie looked at her.

There was vulnerability in her eyes. "You are?"

"Yes." Glenda put the knife down. She had no idea how

much Clemmie had shared with Fergus, although she had a feeling it was a lot. She certainly seemed calmer. But Fergus had that effect on people. "Whatever decision you make, I'll be here ready to support you."

There was more she wanted to say, but that would have to be enough for now.

15

Alice

Alice took the stairs to the Loch Room, ignoring the growl of her stomach and trying not to think about the perfectly cooked bacon that was now no doubt being enjoyed by someone else. Part of her had wanted to stay and be there for her sister, but even she could see that a room full of people wasn't what Clemmie needed right now.

She didn't think she was capable of being shocked after so many years working in the emergency department and encountering just about every situation imaginable, but it turned out that she was. Maybe not *shocked* exactly, but certainly surprised. Not the fact that her sister wanted children, that wasn't a surprise at all. But the fact that she was willing to go it alone—that *was* a surprise.

Clemmie was the romantic among them. She'd played "weddings" as a child, a game both Alice and Ross had refused to take part in. It had never occurred to Alice that Clemmie might choose to stay single.

She wondered if the breakup with Liam had something to do with it, and thought back to Clemmie's words.

My dream is to be a mother. It's what I want more than anything. And my preference would have been to do it the traditional way, but life isn't always that neat and tidy. I don't want to date people knowing that all I really want from them is a baby. Equally I don't want to risk settling for a relationship that isn't right just so that I can have a child. I know I'm going to be a good mother, and I'm going to do it by myself. She'd paused at that point. *Using donated sperm.*

Alice had been as shocked as everyone else, not because of what Clemmie was suggesting, she knew plenty of people who had conceived using donor sperm for various reasons, but the fact that this was Clemmie. Ross had seemed equally surprised, if his expression had been anything to go by.

The irony didn't escape her. She had a man, but didn't want a baby. Clemmie wanted a baby, but not the man.

Why hadn't Clemmie said something before now? She must have been thinking about it for a while, and it wasn't as if there hadn't been opportunity. She could have said something that night when the three of them had shared dinner at Ross's apartment.

And then she remembered that she'd been talking about how she didn't want children.

She could see now how that might have made it hard for Clemmie to speak up.

Had Clemmie seemed upset that night? She thought back, trying to remember if there had been any signs that Clemmie wanted to talk but she came up blank and that shamed her.

She was a doctor, for goodness' sake, and she hadn't spotted that her own sister had something huge going on in her life.

Was she unapproachable? Did Clemmie think she wouldn't understand?

She'd let Clemmie down. She should have made it clear that she was always there to listen.

After Clemmie had rushed out of the room the night before, Alice had crept along to her sister's bedroom a few times in the night and tapped on the door, but Clemmie had refused to open it. She'd tried sending messages, but Clemmie had switched her phone off.

She discussed the option of breaking the door down with Ross, but he had rightly pointed out that destroying the house would attract further parental attention, which presumably Clemmie was keen to avoid given that she'd shut herself in the room in the first place.

Alice had intended to find time to talk to her this morning, but having been banished from the kitchen, that was going to have to wait until later.

She intended to make it clear to her sister that she was there for her, one hundred percent, but in the meantime she was going to focus on her own issues.

She'd stood there the evening before, listening as everyone had expressed their shock at Clemmie's plans, and been humbled by her sister's firm commitment to the path she'd chosen and her honesty. And it had made her think about her own situation. That night at Ross's apartment both Clemmie and Ross had urged her to have the conversation she needed to have. And they'd been right. She should have done exactly what Clemmie had done the night before, and been honest about her needs. She should have just said to Nico, *This is what I want*, and then dealt with the consequences, whatever those turned out to be. She would have saved herself weeks of anxiety and sleepless nights.

She'd always thought of herself as brave and fierce, but now she could see she was nowhere near as brave as her sister.

She hadn't tackled the difficult issues in her life, she'd avoided them. She'd taken the easy path, but that had led her nowhere.

But it was time to fix that.

Clemmie had shown real courage in going after what she wanted, and Alice was going to do the same.

She pushed open the door of the Loch Room and found Nico freshly showered, a towel knotted round his waist.

She closed the door behind her and took a deep breath. "I love you."

He narrowed his eyes. "Why are you telling me this now?"

"Because it's true. And it's important to me that you know it."

"Right." He swiped droplets of water from his face. "I admit I was beginning to wonder."

She felt a flash of guilt. "I know I've been difficult, but there have been some things I've been trying to get straight in my own mind."

"And now you have?"

"Yes. And I'm going to explain everything. But first—" she turned the key in the door, locking it "—I need you to know that I love you."

"Right. Good." He gestured to the towel. "If we're going to talk, I should probably get dressed."

"Later." She walked across to him and tugged at the towel. "Your family—"

"Don't worry about my family. They're all occupied with other things." She let go of the towel and it dropped to the floor. She loved him, she really did, and in the end that was all that mattered. She'd let all the other stuff come between them, but they'd figure a way through it.

"What has happened to you?"

"I don't know. I think I might finally have seen sense. Probably thanks to Clemmie. She had the courage to go after what she wanted. Which is pretty inspiring."

"And what is it you want, Alice?" He cupped her face in his hands. "Tell me."

"Right now?" She gave a saucy smile and slid her hands down his back. His skin was smooth and warm. "You. Also, if you could talk to me in Italian, that would be good. I love the way you sound when you're talking to your mother on the phone." She nudged him back toward the bed, easing her sweater off and then her jeans.

"You want me to talk to you as if you're my mother? Alice, that's weird." He tumbled onto his back on the bed and she came down on top of him.

"Not the words, just the language and the accent." She pressed her mouth to his throat and trailed kisses across his chest and lower.

She heard him groan and say something in Italian and she lifted her head.

"What does that mean? Would you say it to your mother?"

He gave her a wicked smile. "I most definitely would not." He flipped her onto her back and she felt the brush of his fingers on her thigh. His lips traced a line along her jaw, to her throat and then to her shoulder, the brush of his mouth sending a jolt of electricity through her body.

"Nico…" She slid her arms round his neck and brought his head down to hers, kissing him, wanting to show the depth of her love for him so that there could be no doubt. And he responded, kissing her back, his mouth searching and demanding, his hands sure and skilled as he touched her.

Her hunger matched his, the chemistry intensified by the emotion she was feeling, by her need to share and give all of herself. Later, they'd talk. But right now they had this, and this was the most perfect intimacy, a connection she'd never felt with anyone before.

He shifted over her, his gaze locked on hers, as if he was searching for something and she met his gaze without flinching, willing to give him anything, everything.

Never breaking eye contact, she curled her fingers into the hard muscle on his shoulders and they moved together, finding the perfect rhythm, and then there was only the heat of it, her heartbeat, his heartbeat, and the fiery intensity of the passion that consumed them both.

Afterward she lay against him, her limbs tangled with his, thinking that if marriage was coming home to this at the end of every day then she wanted it.

"So," he murmured, stroking his hand down her back. "You want to talk. You have something to tell me."

Her heart felt full. She had so much to tell him. Including the fact that she had the answer to the question he'd asked.

"Yes. But not here." She rested her head on his shoulder, feeling closer to him than she ever had before, and optimistic that they would work things out easily. Everything was going to be fine. "We're going out."

"Out?" He sat up and she decided that he was equally handsome rumpled and sweaty as he was when he was dressed for dinner.

"Yes, because I'm hungry and I want to spend time alone with you, which isn't possible in this house. Also, I want a plate of food that I don't have to share with my siblings." She slid out of bed and pulled on her jeans. "I'm going to take you to the best café in the whole of Scotland. You're going to thank me."

"Are the roads clear enough?"

"No. We're going to walk across the fields. You were raised in the Alps. Don't try and pretend you're afraid of snow."

"Not afraid, although I admit right now I'm warm, and comfortable, and you're half-naked—" He broke off as she reached for her sweater. "Do you have to put that on?"

"Yes, because I don't intend to cause a scandal in the village. Also, I'm starving." She freed her hair from the neck of the sweater and tied it up. "They serve the best ever French toast, with crunchy cinnamon and sugar, and very strong coffee. You'll like it."

"I only like Italian coffee."

"They serve great coffee. I don't know if it's Italian." She tugged him upright and kissed him again. He kissed her back and it was another half an hour before they finally made it out of the room.

The kitchen was empty but she could hear voices from the living room, also laughter which she hoped was a good sign.

Nico zipped up his coat and stamped his feet into boots. He wore black ski pants and a black jacket that he'd zipped up to the neck. Were there any situations where the man didn't look good? Winter clothing was generally so unflattering, but not on him it seemed.

They headed out across the snow, crunching their way toward the village.

"Is Clemmie all right?" He adjusted his stride to match hers. "Have you seen her this morning?"

"No. She went for an early walk and when she came back Mum threw us all out of the kitchen so she could talk to her." She linked her arm through his. "Is our family drama too much for you? Do you wish you'd never come?"

"I don't wish that. And every family has drama, Alice."

"Does yours?"

"Of course." He glanced at her. "You didn't know anything about your sister's plans?"

"No. She never mentioned it. Maybe she thought we'd try and talk her out of it. I suppose because she was afraid of being judged because what she's doing isn't exactly traditional, is it? I feel bad that I didn't know."

"If she'd wanted to talk to you about it, then she would have talked."

"Maybe. Or maybe I didn't give her the opportunity. It isn't always easy to find the right time for a difficult conversation." She knew that all too well. They'd arrived at the village and she headed to the café. "This place used to be a post office, but then it was converted into a café and it became everyone's favorite meeting place. I used to come here after school with my friends. The chocolate brownie is legendary." She pushed open the door and spied an empty table in the window. It was tucked away, which made it a safe place to have a private conversation without being overheard. She knew that for a fact because she'd always chosen that table when she was a teenager. How many crises had she and her friends discussed there? "Why don't you grab that table? I'll order for us."

She tugged off her gloves and checked the blackboard. She'd order a selection of things, and then Nico could choose what he wanted.

Their order arrived swiftly. Stacks of crispy bacon, cinnamon toast dusted with sugar and mugs of steaming coffee.

"I'm beginning to understand why you thought coming out for breakfast was a good idea." Nico unzipped his coat.

"This place has won so many awards." She helped herself to bacon, and pushed the rest across to him.

They both ate, and finally when the last of the toast was

finished and more coffee had been delivered to their table, Nico leaned forward and took her hand.

"So…" He spoke quietly. "What is it that you want to talk about? What was it about Clemmie's announcement that has changed things?"

She poked at the foam on her cappuccino. "She knew what she wanted and wasn't afraid to go for it, even though she knew her decision was probably going to be a bit controversial."

He sat back in his chair. "Are you telling me you've made a controversial decision?"

Her burst of courage and resolve dimmed. Now that the moment had come, she was nervous.

But this was Nico, and hopefully he would understand.

"Do you remember the night you proposed to me?"

He gave a faint smile. "You mean the night you didn't say yes? I remember. It isn't something a man is going to forget in a hurry."

"It wasn't our relationship that worried me, it was the whole idea of marriage." She stared at her coffee. It felt ridiculously hard to articulate her feelings. "I'm a perfectionist, you know that."

"I do know that."

"If I'm going to do something, then I always have to do it well. And I will study and keep trying until I'm really good."

"I know this about you, Alice. What I don't know is what this has to do with marriage."

She fiddled with the centerpiece on the table. "When you proposed I was shocked. I hadn't expected it. Hadn't thought about it. And in that moment I wasn't thinking about us, or our relationship, I was thinking that I'm not sure I'll be a good wife."

He frowned. "A good wife? What do you mean by that?"

"I don't know. And that's the point. I don't know what you expect."

"Expect?"

"Of me. Of us. Of marriage." Boiling hot, she unwrapped her scarf from her neck. "Obviously you want something different from what we have, or you'd just stick with what we have now and not rock the boat. What does having a wife mean to you? What does marriage mean to you?"

He looked bemused. "It means sharing my life with the woman I love. It's not complicated." He let go of her hand. "What does it mean to you?"

"That's just it—I don't know. Marriage wasn't something I'd thought about until you proposed that night. Growing up, I was never the sort of person who dreamed of getting married. I dreamed of being a doctor. That's what I wanted. Work was always more important than relationships."

"You're talking as if work and marriage aren't compatible."

"Every man I've dated before—and there weren't that many—hated the fact that I was so dedicated to my job. *Obsessed*, was the term they used, but I prefer *dedicated*." She paused. "I've always been like that. Whether it's an exam or a driving test or learning the piano—I've always worked and worked until I'm the best I can be. Marriage—I'm not sure how to be the best at that."

"The best?"

"Take my mother, for example. The home has always been her priority. She worked, too, but her focus was always the family. That was the part that really mattered to her. Caring for us. Making sure we were okay. She used to spend hours listening to us, talking to us." And she hadn't been the easiest of children to handle, she could see that now. As a teenager she'd been moody and uncommunicative. Not just as a teenager. She'd been the same since she arrived home. "No matter what was happening, Mum put us first. Dad worked very hard. The company was his main focus. He often wasn't home and it was our mother who carried the load of the family. Laundry, school runs, cooking, a listening ear—" Her mother, she decided, was a saint.

"She seems like a kind and special person," Nico said, "but I'm assuming you didn't bring me here to talk about your mother. So what are you saying, Alice?"

"I'm not like her. For my mother, home—us, her children—mattered more than anything. For me, it's work." There, she'd said it. And to be fair he didn't seem shocked.

"I know this about you. I know you love your work. And yet you are saying this as if it's a revelation."

"I'm not sure how to be a good wife, and good at my job. Marriage changes things."

He pushed his empty cup away. "How do you know? You've never been married." He sighed. "You're worried I'm expecting you to turn into your mother? You think you'll have to swap scrubs for an apron, is that it?"

"Well—"

"Please tell me that isn't what you think, because if you do then you don't know me at all."

She looked to see if he was laughing but there was no trace of humor in his face.

And that was before she reached the difficult part.

"I don't know. That's why we need to have this conversation. I need to know what you think. What you want. And maybe that seems unromantic, but I think it's important."

"Alice—"

"I don't want children." She said it fast, not allowing herself to think or pause, the same way she'd plunge into freezing water. "It wasn't something I'd thought about much, except occasionally when other people were cooing over babies and

I wasn't, and I realized I didn't have any maternal urges. But then you asked me to marry you, and all I could think when I was standing there by the river that night was that I didn't know what that would do to our lives. To my work. To the way we live our lives. The reason I didn't say yes wasn't because I don't love you, but because I didn't really know what I'd be saying yes to." There. She'd said it. Finally. And now it was up to him to respond.

She took a gulp of her coffee, now cold, and waited.

And waited.

Until eventually she couldn't wait any longer.

"Nico?"

He stirred. "That's why you didn't say yes to me? Because you weren't sure you wanted a family?"

"Yes. I—I wasn't sure what marriage meant to you."

"And you didn't think that maybe you could just ask me that question?" He wasn't being as sympathetic as she'd expected.

"It's not exactly easy to talk about."

"But it's been weeks, Alice. And all this time—" He let go of her hand. "It explains why you've been distracted. And not sleeping. You've had a lot on your mind."

"Yes." That was an understatement. Her tangled thoughts had invaded every waking moment, day and night. And she'd had more waking moments than she would have liked.

"And yet you didn't share any of it with me."

Every word he spoke made her feel worse. "I needed to figure out what I wanted."

He looked at her. "How about finding out what I wanted? It seems to me you've made a lot of assumptions. About what marriage means to me. About what my expectations would mean for you. Us. Our relationship. About whether that was something you wanted. You've been debating it with yourself, by yourself." He paused. "For the record, I don't think 'marriage' is a role you have to fit into. It's a partnership. A feeling and a promise. It's a promise that you're going to share your lives, that whatever comes you'll be in it together."

Her heart fluttered. "That's—beautifully put."

"The one thing marriage isn't, is making that promise and then going it alone. No collaboration. No discussion. We weren't in this together. You didn't share your thoughts with me. I didn't know what you were thinking. I couldn't contribute or offer my own opinion or thoughts on the subject, because you didn't ask me. I couldn't support you, because you didn't want my support. You didn't trust me with your thoughts and feelings. You didn't share your fears." He paused. "That's not a partnership, Alice."

The air left her lungs.

She couldn't breathe. The laughter and conversations going on around her retreated into the background.

"I wanted to—"

"You wanted to figure out what you wanted, but how could you do that without including me? You were figuring out your thoughts on marriage, but you were doing that without me."

Her throat felt dry. "You're making it sound bad—"

"It is bad, Alice. It's about as bad as it gets. Because if you won't talk about something as big as this—something that involves both of us, by the way—then what hope is there? I don't know if there's a definition of marriage, but if there is then there is probably an 'us' in there somewhere, and you're obviously still going with 'me.' And that's a problem."

"Nico—"

He reached for his coat. "For the record, I love how smart you are, and how dedicated you are to your work. I admire and respect your focus, and the fact that what you do is so important to you. I know how much you care. I know exactly who you are, Alice, and I knew all those things when I asked you to marry me. None of it was a problem to me. Far from it. I have never expected you to cook my dinner or clean the apartment, although if there are jobs that need doing it seems fair to split them depending on which of us is the busiest. Partnership again. I haven't given much thought to children, either, but I can see many compelling reasons to not have them—the most compelling the fact that you don't want them. If you'd shared that with me, we could have talked it through and worked it out together. We could have talked about whether it would be a problem or not. I don't think it would have been. What you want matters to me. What I wanted was you. The rest we could have figured out."

Why was he putting it in the past tense? Her sense of panic escalated as he rose to his feet and tugged on his coat.

"Nico, you have to understand that this was a big thing for me—"

"I do understand that." He tugged at the zip of his coat. "And that is the only part of all this that is a problem for me. It's the reason I'm concerned. In a marriage you have to be able to talk about the big issues as well as the small. I thought we did that. I thought we were a team, but it turns out we're not. You don't know what I want because you haven't once asked me. And you didn't turn to me when you were lying awake at night panicking."

She swallowed. "Nico—"

"Did you discuss it with anyone else? Ross? Clemmie? Your mother?"

"No, I haven't discussed it with my mother." But Ross and Clemmie—

She felt her face burn and his gaze met hers.

"Right. So you *do* talk about your worries, but not with me."

"Nico—"

"I need space. Don't follow me."

"But—" She stopped, because he'd already walked away. She heard the door open and felt a slap of ice-cold air before he closed it again, with himself on the other side.

He'd walked away.

He'd walked away from *her*.

For a moment she felt affronted, and then it occurred to her that she'd done the same thing, only less literally. She'd shut him out. And now she knew how horrid that felt. How frustrating and deeply uncomfortable to be excluded by the person you loved. And she *did* love him, she knew that. And she wanted to spend her life with him, except that option probably wasn't even on the table any longer.

The future she'd envisaged suddenly looked different.

A gaping hole opened up in front of her.

She'd totally messed things up. She could see now that by not sharing her thoughts with him she'd done irreparable damage to their relationship.

She'd handled it badly, which possibly proved that she was every bit as bad at relationships as she'd thought she was. This was why she hadn't thought about marriage. In the end, she wasn't good at being in a partnership. She did it all wrong, and she didn't even know she was doing it wrong until someone pointed it out.

Struggling to see past the mist in her eyes, she stood up and pulled on her own coat.

She had no idea where Nico had gone, and he clearly didn't want her to follow him, so she stumbled home across the snowy fields, feeling colder and colder and knowing that the ice spreading through her wasn't entirely due to the weather.

Now what?

She stumbled through the door to the boot room just as her mother was letting Hunter out for fresh air.

"Alice! I wondered where you both were. Did you have a nice walk? Where's Nico?" Her mother glanced over Alice's shoulder and then back at her daughter and Alice did something she hadn't done since she was twelve years old and failed a maths test that had been sprung on her unexpectedly.

She burst into tears.

There was a horrified pause and then she was being hugged tightly.

"Let's get you inside. You're freezing, you poor thing." Her mother tugged off her coat and her scarf as if she was a child, and bustled her into the chair closest to the warmth of the range cooker.

Alice put her head down on the kitchen table and sobbed. And sobbed.

She tried to stop. She wanted to stop, but the tears kept flowing until she couldn't breathe properly, until her head throbbed and her eyes were sore.

It felt as if a lifetime of carefully contained emotion had suddenly burst from her.

She felt her mother rubbing her back gently and heard her soothing, reassuring words, and was grateful for the comfort because right now it felt like the end of the world, as if something inside her had broken, and if there was one person she could always rely on in her life it was her mother. She'd always been there. Through the times when Alice had been moody, and stressed about exams and life generally, even when Alice had pushed her away and been difficult, she'd been there. And acknowledging how difficult she'd been on occasion, made Alice cry harder.

She was a difficult, horrible person. Her family only put up with her because they had to.

She tried to pull herself together, but she was flooded by tears and regret. "I'm s-sorry, Mum."

"Sorry? Whatever do you have to be sorry for?"

Alice scrubbed at her face with her sleeve. "Being me."

"Why would you say that? You're a very special person."

"You're only saying that because you're my mother."

"Well no, actually. I'm saying it because it's true." Her mother reached out and stroked damp strands of Alice's hair away from her face. "I don't know what's happened, and if you don't want to tell me that's fine. But I'm here if you want to talk."

It was unlike her mother not to probe, and she was grateful for it. At the same time she wished she'd just ask, because Alice did want to talk but didn't know where to start.

She'd never been the sort to dump her problems on someone. She'd never been the sort to ask for help. If she had a problem, she figured it out herself. If she fell, she found a way to get to her feet again. If she was bad at something, she practiced until she was good at it. She'd never really failed at anything before.

But she'd failed at this.

"I'm not good at relationships."

"Alice—"

"It's true." She took the tissue her mother offered her and blew her nose hard. "I'm a failure. A disaster. If you don't believe me, ask Nico. I don't know how to be good at it. I wish there was a manual or something." She tried to smile. "That's typical of me, isn't it? If in doubt, buy a textbook."

"You're not the first person to wish for a manual, I can tell you. I feel that way frequently."

"You do?" The news that her very competent mother sometimes struggled to understand people surprised her.

"Of course. But there never will be a manual, because relationships involve people and people are all different. And unpredictable. Even the people we think we know best can surprise us."

Alice wondered if her mother was talking about Clemmie. Or maybe she was talking about Alice, because when had Alice ever lost control like this before?

Her mother squeezed her shoulder. "Coffee?"

"Better not. I already drank two cups in the café. I'll be bouncing off the walls."

"Tea, then." Her mother stood up. "I'll make green tea. Soothing and healthy."

She bustled around the kitchen and by the time she placed two mugs on the table Alice was feeling calmer.

"Thanks, Mum. I'm sorry."

"What are you sorry for?" Her mother sat down next to her. "Being upset? It's allowed, Alice."

"I'm sorry for the way I've behaved since I arrived here. I've been rude and jumpy and thoughtless. I've messed everything up." And because her mother was so calm and kind, she told her everything. From the proposal, to all her doubts, to the conversation she'd just had with Nico. "And the ironic thing is that all the things that had worried me—my work habits, the fact that I don't want children—none of that seemed to bother him. The part that upset him was the fact that I hadn't told him. Hadn't shared how I was feeling." She blew her nose. "Are you shocked?"

Her mother handed her a fresh tissue.

"That you didn't talk to him?"

"No. That he proposed to me, and I didn't tell you. That I don't want children." She gave a watery smile. "Remember last year when you told me that by the time you were my age you already had two children?"

"Please don't remind me. I still regret it."

"Don't. Still, these are pretty big things for a parent to absorb."

"Alice," her mother said, reaching out and taking her hand. "You have no obligation to tell me anything. If Nico proposed, that's your business. You share what you want to share, when you're ready to share it. If you decided you didn't want to marry him, that's your business, too. And as for children— I want you to be happy. That's all I've ever wanted, for all of you. I want you to build a life that you find fulfilling. That life might not look like mine, but that's because we're back to that wild card again—people. We're all different. What matters is what you want. My feelings don't matter here, Alice."

But she did have feelings, Alice knew she did. She knew that deep down her mother was disappointed, adjusting her view of how the future might look, and the fact that she was burying her own feelings made Alice all the more grateful for the support.

"You want grandchildren," Alice sniffed, "and Nanna Jean wants great-grandchildren, but I guess Clemmie is going to give you those although not in a particularly conventional way. This hasn't exactly been the relaxed, traditional Christmas you were hoping for so far, has it? First Clemmie has a meltdown, and now me. And then there's Ross and Dad, and all the tension. You must be wondering why you had children at all, when we all cause you so much stress."

"I never wonder that. This is life, Alice. It is full of ups and downs, twists and turns. I wouldn't change a thing. And if you want proof that we all make mistakes, then just look at the way I handled your sister. I couldn't love her more, but I didn't say the things I should have said. I didn't react the way I should have done. I was surprised and unprepared and yes, I'm disappointed with myself."

"So I'm not the only person who beats myself up when I'm not perfect."

Her mother frowned. "I hadn't thought of it like that but yes, you're right. Being a good mother is important to me. When I fall short, I feel angry with myself." She paused, reflecting. "But the important thing is to learn from it, isn't it? If you feel you could have done something better, try and put it right. Which is what I intend to do with your sister."

"But that's exactly it. I try and be the best. I try and do the things I'm good at. But relationships—that's not on the list. Maybe I should just give up and accept that I'm probably going to be alone for the rest of my life. Listen to me—" Alice blew her nose again "—Miss Melodrama."

"There you go again, thinking you should give something up because you're not perfect at it. Maybe instead of having these unrealistic expectations, you should accept that relationships are complicated. They're probably the hardest thing in the world to get right because they involve people, and you can't control people. You can figure how to work things out yourself, but what you really have to learn is how to work things out with another person. And that's hard."

"Not always." Alice stood up and threw away the tissue. "Look at you and Dad. You've been together for decades."

"Yes. But it hasn't all been romance and roses." Her mother took a sip of tea. "There have been times when I could cheerfully have pushed your father out of the door and locked it behind him. And that's when he was here. Most of the time when you were little, he was working. But the one thing we always had, apart from love of course, was the ability to communicate. Your father has always been my best friend. When I'm uncertain about something, when I think I've made a mistake, when I don't know the answer to something—he's the one I talk to. I value his opinion, and I trust him. Trust is so important. And I know I have his support no matter what."

What had Nico said?

I couldn't support you, because you didn't want my support.

Alice felt the lump grow in her throat. "Dad is lucky to have you."

"I tell him so regularly. But I'm lucky to have him, too." Her mother pushed the mug toward Alice. "You and he are similar in so many ways. He has your work ethic, and your fierce determination to be the best. And when he feels he isn't doing his best, or 'failing' as you would call it, he gets frustrated just as you do."

"I never see that."

"Well, he doesn't often show it."

"Except to you."

"We've been together a long time," her mother said. "We know each other. Trust, again."

Alice slid her hands round her mug to warm them. "You're lucky."

"It's not luck, Alice. It's courage. Love, trust—they both take courage."

"Courage?"

"Yes. It takes courage to share your doubts and worries with another person. The side of you that you might see as less than perfect. That can be scary."

She hadn't thought of it like that. "That's true. I'm afraid to share all of me. I suppose I'm worried that if Nico really knew me, he wouldn't love me." She leaned on the table, absorbing the truth about herself. "How did I end up so insecure? It's pitiful."

"It's not pitiful. It's human to be confident in some areas, and underconfident in others. You are confident, and competent, in many areas of your life."

"But not relationships. I think, maybe, that one of the reasons I focus on work so much is because it's easy. Relationships are harder." And she could see now how that might have happened. She'd had some bad dating experiences, but instead of moving on she'd used them as evidence that she wasn't good at relationships.

"Nico proposed. You can't be that bad at relationships if a man wants to marry you."

Was that true?

"I don't really know how to share my thoughts and fears."

"You just do it. Talk, the way you're talking to me now."

"It's too late. He doesn't want to marry me anymore."

"Give him time and space. He's upset, too. Managing his feelings."

Feelings that he wasn't sharing with her. Feelings he was handling alone.

And she could see now, quite clearly, what needed to change.

"I *will* talk to him. Properly. If he comes back." And she was terrified, truly terrified, that he wouldn't.

"He has to come back. There is no way out of here, Alice." Her mother was ever practical. "His car is here. The trains aren't running. You're here."

"Maybe he doesn't care too much about that." And she didn't really want him coming back just because he was trapped. She wanted him to come back because he still loved her.

"Alice," her mother said, leaning forward. "You don't go from loving a person and proposing to them one minute, to cutting them out of your life the next. I'm pretty sure he will walk through that door any moment, and then the two of you will be able to talk."

"I'm afraid I'll say the wrong thing."

"You mean the way I said the wrong thing to your sister?" Her mother stood up and picked up the empty mugs. "You need to accept that however much you would like to be perfect, you are not going to go through life always saying the right thing. It's impossible. Don't let the fear of saying the wrong thing prevent you from saying anything. Say what's in your head. You don't have to have planned everything. Instead of trying to figure everything out yourself, see if you can figure it out together. Do you love him?"

"Yes. Very much."

"Then you need to do what you have always done when there is something you want. You go after it. Do what it takes. Try your hardest. If opening up to him feels hard, then keep doing it until you get better at it."

Her mother had a way of saying things that made sense.

"That manual on people—you should probably write it."

"I don't think so." Glenda slid the mugs into the dishwasher. "I should probably check on the others. Fergus went to talk to Douglas, I'm not sure where Clemmie went, and I haven't seen Ross since first thing this morning when we discovered Clemmie was missing. He disappeared."

"He probably went for a run. He runs every morning, whatever the weather. I hope he doesn't injure himself. And talking of injuries, I wonder how Lucy is doing?"

Her mother covered her mouth with her hand. "Lucy! How could I have forgotten about Lucy?"

"It's been a pretty busy few hours. There has been a lot going on." And she couldn't stop thinking about Nico. Where he was. What he was thinking.

Was it over?

The only thing keeping her calm was the knowledge that he had to come back at some point and then maybe, hopefully, they'd be able to talk and find a way through this.

"That's all true," her mother said, "but still—we have a guest in the house. What must she be thinking? I should have taken her breakfast. I should have checked on her."

"Why don't I do it?" Alice glanced at her phone, hoping for a message but there was nothing. "I need a distraction. And checking on Lucy's ankle will make me feel as if I'm not a disaster in every area of my life."

"You're not a disaster, but you definitely should check on her." Her mother gave her another quick hug. "I'll put together some breakfast for her. She's probably sitting in her room, not sure what she's supposed to be doing, feeling horribly out of place and alone."

16

Lucy

Lucy was sitting on the floor of the living room, next to the Christmas tree. Hunter was asleep on the floor next to her, and she was surrounded by pieces of paper covered in her neat handwriting.

"Short-form video is a really effective way of reaching and growing your audience. Take a look at that." She handed her phone to Douglas, who was sitting in the chair next to her.

After the drama of the evening before, it had been a relief to find him alone in the living room. Even more of a relief when he'd started to ask her questions about her work.

Better that than any more awkward conversations that made her horribly conscious that she was intruding on their private time.

He took the phone gingerly, as if it might explode. "It's a girl reading a book and crying. Is that good?"

"She has a huge audience and that particular video has gone

viral. That book is now on the bestseller lists and it's not even a new book. It was published eight years ago."

"Why is the video so short?"

"Because people have short attention spans." She thought for a moment. "Do you ever do TV advertising?"

"We have, in the past."

"And I'm sure your advert would have been around the thirty-second mark? This is the same kind of thing. It can be a powerful driver for sales."

He handed the phone back to her. "So we should be doing more of this?"

"I think you could certainly consider it. It's another way for people to discover your product. New people. Although it's always more effective if the people enjoying the product are the ones posting about it, rather than the company." She saw something change in his expression. "I've said something wrong."

"No. It's not you. This—" he waved his hand toward the sheets of paper covering the floor "—this is all good. Better than good. But do you know how it makes me feel? Tired. The weight of it all." He sat back in his chair and shook his head. "I'm too old for this, Lucy. If I had someone to hand the business over to, I'd be handing it over. It's time for younger brains to be in charge."

Was he thinking about Ross? Wishing he was involved?

His comment had to be about more than the challenges of adopting social media, surely?

And she'd thought this was going to be an easy conversation.

"I think you're underestimating the importance of wisdom and experience. You're the one who built the company."

"It was built by the generations that came before me. In some ways I've been the caretaker."

"Caretaker? Mr. Miller, you've grown the business 40 percent since you took over. That's hardly 'caretaking.'"

He raised an eyebrow. "Think you're smart now, do you?"

She grinned. "I am smart. And so are you. And you're not too old."

"Well if you're so smart, you'd know to call me Douglas. And you're right, I'm not too old to learn new ways of running the business. A few years ago, I would have embraced all this. But now? We're a small team and we're already stretched. Is that how I want to spend my time?" He seemed almost to be talking to himself and maybe he realized it because he shook his head and smiled. "Ignore me, Lucy. I'm rambling. Everything is fine. You've been helpful, and I appreciate it."

His words hovered in the air around them.

Everything is fine.

How often had she said those words herself, when things were far from fine, when she didn't want people to know how she really felt?

It was lonely, keeping those feelings inside, using a reassuring smile as a barrier to keep people from looking too closely.

Douglas had revealed a little of how he was feeling, and now he was hauling those feelings back inside away from public view.

She thought about Arnie, and the private pain he kept hidden behind a front of public optimism.

"It must feel like a big responsibility," she said carefully, "nurturing the business when it has been in the family for generations. It isn't just about you, is it? You have staff who have worked for the company since leaving school. And that makes things complicated because when you think about the future—*your* future—you're factoring in so much more than just what you want personally."

He stirred. For a moment she thought he might be about to tell her to mind her own business, but instead he nodded.

"That's true. And I shouldn't be burdening you with this."

"It's not a burden. I've seen my boss going through something similar. The circumstances are different—" this wasn't the time to remember the business they'd lost and her purpose in being here "—but his concerns are the same as yours. He feels responsible for the people working for him, and that brings its own pressures. Right now he's doing everything he can not to have to make staff redundant. And the truth is that he has been very successful over many years. He could probably take early retirement and sail around the world if he wanted to, but he doesn't want to, because he is responsible for so many people's jobs."

"And that's why you're here, a few days before Christmas? Because you were trying to do what you could to relieve that pressure on him?" Douglas bent to make a fuss of Hunter. "Your boss has good people working for him. He's lucky to have you."

"As it turns out, probably not, because I've messed things up." It was surprisingly easy to talk honestly with Douglas, perhaps because he'd been honest with her.

"I don't see you messing anything up."

She gestured to her leg, and then to the Christmas tree. "I'm pretty sure that having me here wasn't on Ross's Christmas list. I've brought chaos." That was true, but it was impossible to forget Ross's kindness the evening before. She'd lain awake thinking about it, the way he'd listened carefully while she'd told him about her grandmother. Moving the subject on when she'd found the conversation difficult.

And Douglas was dismissive of her concerns. "There is always chaos in this house. Your presence had nothing to do with it."

That wasn't quite true, but she was grateful to him for trying to make her feel better.

She wished she could help him.

"Is there anything I can do? I could talk to your team in the New Year if that would help." She felt herself blush. "No charge, obviously, just in case you think I'm taking advantage. But we could explore what you're doing already, and what you could perhaps consider moving forward. It would be a thank-you, for being so kind to me in my hour of need."

Douglas was thoughtful. "When you work with companies, you handle it all yourself?"

"The social media? It depends what the company wants. We can take on the whole thing. Sometimes we handle it in-house, but sometimes we work with them to develop a strategy that they implement themselves."

"Which is why you were up here taking photographs of reindeer."

"That's right. Connecting, collaborating, with influencers. Customers love user-generated content." She was in the middle of giving him a few examples when the door opened and Ross walked into the room. His hair was wet from the shower.

"This is where you are! We've been searching the house for you. Alice," he shouted back through the door, "she's in the living room with Dad." He glanced at the papers strewn across the floor and then at Lucy. "What is all this? What are you doing on the floor?"

"I'm comfortable here. Also, I like the way the Christmas tree smells." Her insides warmed. It felt awkward seeing him in the harsh light of day. They were strangers, and yet not strangers. He knew too much about her to be considered a stranger. The conversation last night had layered intimacy into a relationship that might otherwise have been superficial and brief.

"She's explaining social media to me," Douglas said. "Bringing me into the twenty-first century. I now understand all the different platforms."

Ross frowned. "I could have explained that to you, Dad. You didn't ask."

"Well you're busy and important running your empire, whereas Lucy here," he said, winking at her, "is trapped and helpless with a broken leg, so I'm taking advantage. Shameless, I know."

Lucy grinned back. She might be a little in love with Douglas, and not least because he was making an awkward situation much less awkward. Still, it was impossible not to be aware of the tension between father and son. She felt it in the atmosphere, a subtle shift, a wariness that settled over both of them. And part of her did wonder why Douglas hadn't discussed the business with his son. Miller Active was one of the fastest growing companies out there and Ross had a reputation for being an astute CEO, so presumably he could have made a valuable contribution to the family business if asked?

"She's a professional, Dad," Ross said. "She's not going to give you free advice."

He sounded irritated, and she wondered if she was the cause of that. Was he thinking that there was a catch? That she'd taken advantage of the situation to get business from his father? Maybe he thought she was suddenly going to present them with an invoice.

Or maybe, she thought, his father was the cause of the irritation. And maybe what she saw as irritation was in fact hurt, some manifestation of wounded pride because he knew the answers to the questions that his father was too stubborn to ask.

She reminded herself that none of this was her business. She wasn't here to fix tensions between father and son. She shouldn't be here at all.

But Douglas didn't seem in any hurry to hasten her departure.

She wondered if he was even a little relieved that she was here. She had a sense that the exchange between the two men might have been less polite had she not been present.

"Her advice isn't free. I'm going to pay her in shortbread. Call it a mutual exchange of assets. And you need to relax, son. You're altogether too uptight for your own good. Stress is bad for your arteries, and I can tell you that from experience. Carry on like this and before you know it you'll be chewing your way through oats and fruit instead of sinking your teeth into a strand of crispy bacon."

Ross didn't smile. "I rarely eat red meat."

"Well that explains why you're so tense. Occasionally it's good to let go a little bit. You're not a CEO now. You're a Miller, and your job today is to shovel the snow from the front steps so that your grandmother doesn't slip when she goes outside. And don't say she shouldn't be going outside in this weather." He lifted his hand. "That's a fight I've lost on too many occasions. I can't stop her, so the best I can do is make it safe. That's where you come in."

Was it a coincidence that he'd shifted the subject away from business?

There was no opportunity to find out what might have happened next because Alice appeared.

"Did you say Lucy was in here?" Her expression changed when she saw Lucy. "What are you doing on the floor? Did you fall?"

And just like that Lucy's quiet moment with Douglas was over.

She would have liked to finish the conversation and perhaps he felt the same way, because he sighed and exchanged
a glance with her.

"Of course she didn't fall. Why is my family so dramatic?
She has been devising a social media plan for me. She wanted
to spread it out to help me see how it all connected. The floor
seemed easier."

"But her leg—"

"Her leg is fine. She's resting it, isn't she? I didn't ask her
to run a marathon."

Alice shook her head and dropped to her knees next to
Lucy. "I should have come and found you sooner, but it's been
a bit of a morning. Have you been okay?"

"Completely fine. I woke up late." In fact she'd woken
fairly early, but she'd been conscious that the family drama of
the night might still be ongoing. She hadn't wanted to get in
the way, so she'd chosen to stay in bed, snuggled under clouds
of soft down while looking at the snowy peaks through the
window. Then she'd remembered that this wasn't a holiday
and she was, in fact, supposed to be working, so she'd grabbed
her phone and her laptop and spent a couple of hours working on the Fingersnug account.

She'd stayed in the room until she'd thought it was probably going to start looking strange if she didn't appear, and
that was when she'd hobbled downstairs and found Douglas
in the living room.

"How did you get down the stairs?" Alice was checking
Lucy's ankle.

"Carefully. On my bottom. Do you think I can walk
around a bit today?"

"I'd hold off weight bearing for one more day. After that,
we'll take it a day at a time and see how it feels." She looked
up as Glenda walked in.

"Nico just arrived back, Alice."

Lucy look more closely at Alice and she saw that her eyes looked a bit red, as if she'd been crying, and hadn't long ago stopped.

Was this to do with Clemmie? Something else?

She felt a pang of sympathy. Without Alice's calm kindness, yesterday would have been even more of a nightmare than it was.

Alice stood up. "I'll go and find him in a moment."

Glenda transferred her attention to Lucy. "Lucy, you must be starving. What sort of hosts are we? I can't imagine what you must think of us." She gave Douglas a reproving look. "You could at least have fed her before making her work."

"How?" He didn't flinch. "The kitchen has been a non-stop conveyor belt of emotion since I had my first coffee of the day. I don't know what Lucy eats for breakfast, but I assume it isn't drama."

Glenda ignored that remark. "I've made food. I'm not sure if it's late breakfast or early lunch. I've heated up some homemade soup, there's a loaf I baked yesterday and some strawberry jam that I made back in the summer. So why don't you all come through to the kitchen?"

Hunter stood up, lured by the smell of food but Glenda shooed him away.

"Not you. You *have* been fed, so you're not fooling any of us with those sad eyes of yours. Lucy, come through to the kitchen so that we can make up for our appalling lack of hospitality. I can't believe you missed breakfast."

Lucy tried to move but it turned out that standing up wasn't nearly as easy as sitting down had been. "You've been very kind. And I don't always eat breakfast anyway."

"Why not?" Alice reached down to help her. "Are you one of those people who practice time restricted eating?"

"No, I'm one of those people who don't always get up early enough in the morning."

Alice smiled and glanced across at her brother. "Hello? Help needed."

Ross crossed the room and Lucy promised herself that next time she was going to sit in a chair so that she could get up without help. As he lifted her, Maya's words rang in her head. *Ross Miller has a black belt in three different martial arts. He can ski. He's a killer in the boxing ring. He sailed across the Atlantic. He has muscles in all the right places.*

And didn't she know it.

He held on to her for a moment, checking that she was steady on her feet before he let her go.

She knew she was pink in the face. Hopefully no one would notice, but if they did then hopefully they would put it down to exertion.

Once she was back on her feet, Alice handed her the crutches.

"How does it feel?"

She almost said *unsettling*, and then realized Alice wasn't talking about the way she felt around Ross.

She tested her foot gingerly. "Not too bad, thank you. I'll research trains later. I'm sure I'll be able to get myself back to London."

"You won't be going anywhere for a few days," Ross said. "The bridge is impassable, and you can't exactly walk across the fields."

"That's awful." Lucy was appalled and embarrassed. "I can't possibly stay for a few days."

"Why not?" Nanna Jean had appeared in the doorway. "It will be fun having you. This afternoon we're making short-bread. It's a Christmas tradition. You can join in."

She'd made shortbread with her grandmother. It had been their Christmas tradition.

Grief hit her like a strong gust of wind, blowing her off her steady course. She was unbalanced by a sense of loss so powerful that she caught her breath.

Ross reached out and took her arm. "Are you all right?"

No, she wasn't all right. She knew from experience that grief had a nasty way of ambushing you when you least expected it, but the timing couldn't have been worse. She didn't want this to happen now. If she'd been on her own she would have just cried her way through it, but she wasn't on her own. She was with the Miller family, and she was the focus of their well-meaning attention at the worst possible moment.

This was why she was better off on her own at Christmas.

"I'm fine." But she wasn't fine. The tide of emotion was rising, beyond her control. Tears blurred her vision.

Keeping a firm grip on her arm, Ross stepped closer, blocking the family's view of her.

She was frozen to the spot, poised on the edge of an emotional precipice, afraid to move or breathe in case she lost her balance and fell.

She felt Ross's grip tighten on her arm and felt the gentle stroke of his thumb.

She probably should have pulled away, but his touch was the lifeline that was preventing her from falling, and the way he'd positioned himself gave her the privacy she so badly needed. She focused on the pressure of his fingers, the brush of his body close to hers, the connection with another human being and the terrifying flood of emotion started to recede.

Still she didn't move, swallowed up by that strangely intimate moment.

Glenda stepped forward.

"You're very pale, dear. Maybe Alice should take another look at you—"

"Don't fuss, Mum. What Lucy needs right now is space, not everyone crowding her." Alice's gaze was fixed on Ross, her expression curious.

"Alice is right." Ross didn't release his hold on her. "You should all go through to the kitchen and we will join you in a moment."

How did he know exactly what she needed? She wouldn't have expected him to be so sensitive to another person's distress.

And for some reason—maybe his tone—they all complied, even Nanna Jean, and she was left alone with Ross.

She expected him to immediately let her go, but he didn't. She felt his closeness and a punch of heat went to the core of her body. Her breathing was unsteady. Her feelings shifted from gratitude to something far less neutral and safe, and she wondered if maybe he felt it, too, because he finally let her go.

"Take your time." His voice was rough. "Do you want me to bring you something to eat here instead of joining us in the kitchen? My family can be overwhelming."

"They're wonderful." Her voice sounded almost normal, but apparently not normal enough to fool him.

"But…?"

"Just for a moment I missed my grandmother." She didn't know why she'd said it, except that she felt raw and vulnerable and he was standing right there, so close that she could feel the brush of his arm against hers.

She expected that to be the end of it. She expected him to back off, make his excuses and leave. Anything to avoid an emotional discussion with a woman he barely knew, but it was soon clear that she didn't know him, either, because he didn't move.

"What was the trigger?"

"Your grandmother inviting me to make shortbread. I used to make it with my grandmother. Funny, really, that we had the same tradition. It was one of my favorites. That, and decorating the tree together. And it wasn't really about the shortbread, it was about the closeness, the familiar routine of mixing all the ingredients, the way we talked while we did it." She swallowed. "I miss that. Those simple conversations. The companionship. Being with someone who loves you."

There was a pause.

"You must miss her very much."

"I do. Generally I do okay, but sometimes—well, it's hard." She looked at him, embarrassed, but she saw nothing but concern in his eyes. "Thank you. That was a very kind thing to do. If I'd broken down in front of your family I would have been mortified." She didn't ask how he'd known she was so close to the edge.

"So you're planning on spending Christmas alone in London?"

"That's right. It's not as bad as it sounds. And I have a ton of work to do, which will help." She didn't add that she needed to figure out how she was going to bring in new business now that she'd blown their chances with Miller Active. Arnie had messaged her that morning to congratulate her on her work on the Fingersnug campaign so far, and to let her know that the client was going to retain them for the following year. It was good news, but she knew it wasn't enough.

"Why alone? Why haven't any of your friends invited you to join them?"

"They have." How honest should she be? "I'm better off on my own. I used to love Christmas, but now it's something I dread. It's a tough time for me, and I don't trust myself to always be able to hide that."

"Why would you hide it?"

Wasn't it obvious?

"Because no one wants a guest dripping misery onto their Christmas table."

He considered that. "I think people want their guests to be themselves, to be comfortable. If they wanted nonstop cheer they'd hire an entertainer."

His words made her smile.

"Maybe, but I still think Christmas isn't the time to lean on friends."

"I would have said it is exactly the time." He spoke quietly. "What did you do last year?"

"I spent it on my own. I did all the things I would have done if my grandmother had been alive. All the things we did together."

"But you did them alone. That sounds brutal. Are you always this hard on yourself?"

"I don't expect you to understand." She glanced up at him, and because she saw that he was trying to do exactly that, she tried to explain. "You have a big, wonderful family. You can have highs and lows and there is always someone there to celebrate or commiserate. You're in it together. And you have two supportive sisters. There's always someone watching your back."

"Maybe. Sometimes trying to stab me in it." A smile touched his mouth. "I feel compelled to remind you that the reason my family thought you were my girlfriend is because both my 'supportive' sisters threw me to the wolves."

"That's true." It was a relief to laugh. "And it's possible that I romanticize families a little."

"We can cure that easily. A few days spent here with us should ensure an injection of reality. Not that I'm not grateful for my family," he added, "I am. But it does come with frustrations."

She wondered if he was thinking about his relationship with his father.

Having talked to Douglas, she felt ridiculously invested, even though she'd only just met the family.

"I appreciate the reality check."

"But you still intend to leave as soon as possible." He said it as a statement of fact. "Why? Because you're feeling unhappy and want to be on your own?"

"You're making it sound as if I'm an invited guest, and we both know I'm not that. This is your family Christmas and I'm a stranger."

He was about to respond, when Nanna Jean appeared in the doorway.

"You took so long I thought I'd check on you in case you'd tripped over Hunter or something."

Ross stepped away from her and just like that the mood was broken. She felt a stab of disappointment, although what she was disappointed about she didn't really know. What exactly had she expected?

"We were just coming," Ross said, and stood to one side so that Lucy could pass.

"And you're not a stranger." Nanna Jean had clearly overheard the last part of their conversation. "You're almost part of the family."

If only! What wouldn't she give to be part of a family like this one? She didn't care about the frustrations. She'd happily take the bad just to have the good.

Alice appeared. "You can't go anywhere even if you wanted to," she said, "because the trains are canceled again today. Roads are closed. Storm Scrooge is in charge, and nothing is moving or going anywhere. The good news is that we're off the hook for the dreaded family photo. I tried to wear my disappointed face when Dad told me. The bad news for you, Lucy, is that you're stuck with us. I promise we will try and behave ourselves."

"Speak for yourself," Nanna Jean said. "I'm too old to modify the way I behave. If I feel like being outrageous, I shall be outrageous. Now come and eat something, Lucy, and then we will make shortbread."

She felt Ross's gaze on her. She knew that if she made an excuse, he'd support her.

But she didn't want to make an excuse. Talking to him had made her feel calmer. She'd be able to get through a shortbread session without making a fool of herself.

"That sounds like fun."

They all headed back to the kitchen and Lucy followed, using the crutches carefully. She didn't want to knock something over and break it. Or accidentally spear Hunter, who seemed to have taken on the role of canine guardian.

She felt guilty for being here, but at the same time a little relieved. But she knew this couldn't last. If she really was unable to get back to London, then she needed to find other options. "I should try and find a hotel so that you can get back to your Christmas."

"We wouldn't be able to get you there with the snow as it is, and having you here is making our Christmas much more exciting. Don't you worry." Nanna Jean patted the chair next to her. "Anyway, you wanted to talk to Ross about his business and this gives you a chance to do so."

Business. A moment ago they'd been alone together, but had she seized the moment to talk about business? No.

Ross sighed. "Nanna Jean—"

"When you use that tone I know you're about to say something stuffy."

"You ought to listen to what Lucy has to say, son." Douglas was studying the notes Lucy had made, his glasses perched on the edge of his nose. "She's a genius. And if you're not going to take advantage of her expertise, then I certainly am. She's worked out a whole plan for Glen Shortbread." He waggled the papers in his hand. "Her ideas could transform the business. Hashtag tastechallenge. You should take a look. It's clever."

Ross ran his hand over the back of his neck. "Dad—"

"I know all about hashtags," Nanna Jean said. "Clemmie taught me. Where is Clemmie?"

"I believe she's upstairs making a phone call. Now enough work talk," Glenda said, stopping the conversation. "Time to eat. Lucy missed breakfast and she must be starving."

Lucy sat down in the chair next to Nanna Jean, grateful for the distraction. She didn't want Ross to feel pressured into talking to her about business. That felt too much like taking advantage. It had been different with Douglas because he'd asked her directly. He was clearly stressed about it.

She wondered if Ross knew that.

"If you're sure you're okay there, Lucy, I have things to do so I'll see you later." Alice absented herself and Nanna Jean frowned.

"Things to do? What does she have to do? She's on holiday. And why isn't she hungry?"

"She went to the café and had a lovely morning with Nico. You know how delicious their food is. I doubt she'll be able to eat a thing until tonight." Glenda put freshly baked bread on the table.

Lucy remembered Alice's red eyes and wondered if it had, in fact, been lovely.

After a meal punctuated by simultaneous and seemingly

unconnected conversations that appeared to be a hallmark of Miller family gatherings, Ross stood up.

"Right. I'm going to clear the snow."

"You're a good boy, doing that for your grandmother," Nanna Jean said. "You deserve to find a nice girl who appreciates you. A real one, I mean. I could make you a dating profile. Lucy could help. We just have to think of you as a product. Hashtag sexyCEO. What do you think?"

"Lucy thinks you're being intentionally provocative," Ross said, "and so do I. But I'm not going to be provoked. Sorry if that spoils your fun."

"It really does. You should be kind to me. I'm not going to be around forever, and you know you'll miss me when I'm gone."

Ross sighed. "Nanna Jean, that is a low blow. First you embarrass me, and then you smother me in guilt. What did I ever do to deserve a grandmother like you? And please don't reply to that by listing my failings. It would be good if you could try not to ruin my reputation while I'm out of the room." But he bent and gave her an affectionate kiss on the cheek.

Lucy melted. She no longer found him intimidating, but that probably had as much to do with everything she'd shared with him, as his obvious love for his grandmother.

Nanna Jean wasn't above taking advantage of that love. "When you're back, you're going to sit down with Lucy and listen to her plans for your company."

Lucy wanted to slide under the table. He'd already done more than enough for her, although his grandmother didn't know that. "Nanna Jean—"

"What? You need to go after what you want, and presumably you want to talk to Ross given that you came all the way here to deliver your proposal in person. You have to grab every opportunity that comes your way, Lucy, take it from me. And this is an opportunity."

"I didn't expect to actually see Ross himself—"

"Exactly my point. You got lucky. Or maybe not so lucky unless he stops frowning and looking so serious. Is this what you're like in the office, Ross? It's a wonder you can persuade anyone to work for you."

"What happened to the proposal Lucy brought with her?" Glenda put a fresh pot of tea on the table. "I don't remember seeing it."

"Hunter was chewing it," Nanna Jean said, "but I removed it from his jaws and put it out of reach on the table in the library. It definitely met with his approval, and I'm sure Ross is going to love it, too, if he can read through the teeth marks."

Ross exchanged an exasperated glance with Lucy, as if to emphasize that this exchange proved his earlier point about families.

"Nanna Jean—"

"You should sit down with Lucy, Ross." This time it was Douglas who spoke. "It will be less trouble than arguing with your grandmother."

And it seemed that sometimes Ross did take his father's advice, because he took a deep breath and chose the path of least resistance.

"Lucy—" he turned to her with a polite smile, spreading his hands in a gesture of surrender "—perhaps we can talk when I have finished shoveling snow. Would that be convenient?"

She was mortified. "It's your holiday. There's really no need to—"

"There's every need," Nanna Jean said. "Good decision, Ross. There's a lovely fire in the library and it will be completely private. In the meantime, Lucy is going to bake shortbread with me, which should hopefully sweeten you up. I'm going to give her some tips."

Ross's gaze met Lucy's. "If you'd rather not make shortbread, you could—"

"Of course she wants to make shortbread!" Nanna Jean shooed him toward the door and Lucy smiled her thanks.

"I'd love to make shortbread. I'm in the mood to make shortbread." Thanks to their conversation, she was feeling much steadier and perhaps he sensed it, because he gave a brief nod and walked out of the room.

Nanna Jean beamed. "That was a success."

Lucy felt more embarrassed than pleased. "This is awful. He's been forced into listening to me."

"Nonsense." Nanna Jean stood up and patted her on the shoulder. "I encouraged him to make the right decision, that's all. And you need to be a bit less sensitive about pushing yourself forward. I spent all that time talking him into it, and then you almost talked him out of it!"

"Nanna Jean!" Glenda raised her voice. "Lucy is a guest and you're scolding her—"

"She was a guest for the one night, but now she's a permanent fixture so I don't see why she should get special treatment. If I've got something to say, I'll say it." She looked at Lucy. "Do you, or do you not, have good ideas for Ross's business?"

"I think so, yes, but—"

"There you go. And you don't 'think' so. You *know*. Project confidence. Ross will like that."

Glenda sent Lucy a look of helpless apology. "I can't believe you're telling poor Lucy how to do her job."

"I'm not telling her how to do her job. I've created the opportunity for *her* to do her job, that's all. It's different."

"It's not that I lack confidence," Lucy said, "it's more that

I feel as if I'm taking advantage of the situation." She didn't just mean the fact that she was stranded here. Their relationship had shifted. He'd been kind, and she didn't want to take advantage of that kindness.

"What's wrong with taking advantage? That makes you smart. And because you're giving us the benefit of your expertise, I'm going to return the favor. We're going to make our special shortbread recipe, never before shared outside the family. You're to promise me that the recipe will remain forever secret, otherwise we won't be able to let you leave, isn't that right, Glenda?"

"Ignore her, Lucy," Glenda said. "Nanna Jean, if you don't start behaving Lucy will be escaping through the nearest open door regardless of snow and broken limbs."

"She wouldn't do that. She likes it here."

She did like it.

Poker, the cat, lay in the warmest spot, stretched out in front of the oven. Through the windows she could see the mountains, and the trees coated in snow.

She couldn't remember ever spending time in a more welcoming place.

She spent the next hour in the kitchen with Glenda and Nanna Jean, sifting flour, mixing in butter and sugar, and rolling out the mixture to the perfect thickness.

It wasn't long before they had her talking about her childhood and her grandmother.

Nanna Jean wiped her hands on her apron. "She sounds like a wonderful woman. And I'm sure she was very proud of you."

"She was. Sometimes she was quite tough, but that was good, too, because life is tough, isn't it? And I could talk to her about anything. Literally anything." And she missed that. She missed it so much.

Emotion rose from nowhere and this time, perhaps because

her defenses were already lowered after her conversation with
Ross, she wasn't able to contain it. With horror she felt her
eyes fill. She blinked hard, but the tears spilled, falling against
her will, resisting any attempts on her part to hold them back.

Nanna Jean was on her feet instantly and the next moment
Lucy was being held and rocked.

"There—you have a good cry. That's right. Let it out."
She murmured words of comfort against Lucy's hair. "You
must miss her very much."

"It's horrible." Lucy kept her face pressed against Nanna
Jean's apron. Now that she'd started crying, she couldn't stop.
"I'm sorry. So sorry." She gulped and choked on the tears.
"Ignore me. Please ignore me." She tried to pull away but
Nanna Jean held her tightly.

"Why would we ignore you?"

"Because you're having a lovely festive shortbread session—" she was still pressed against that apron "—and I'm
ruining it—"

"You're not ruining anything. You're sad. And why
wouldn't you be sad? You loved your grandmother. She was
special. Sometimes those memories are going to make you
happy, and sometimes they're going to make you sad. All those
emotions are equally valid. There's no need to hide them."

"I miss her so much…" Drowning in emotions that she'd
held back for far too long, Lucy clutched the front of that
apron as if it was the only thing holding her head above the
surface. "How can I possibly still miss her this much?"

"You loved her. Why wouldn't you miss her?"

"Because it has been two years. And mostly I'm fine. I
stay busy and I try not to think about it, but then sometimes
it hits me, wham, and I feel as if I haven't moved on at all. I
try and be cheerful and positive but it's exhausting." She felt
Nanna Jean's hand on her hair, stroking gently.

"Of course it is. Pretending not to be sad when you're feeling sad? That's far more stressful than being sad and accepting it."

Lucy's wet face was still pressed against that apron. Nanna Jean smelt of soap and warmth and comfort.

"She loved me unconditionally."

"Well of course she did."

"Even if I tried to hide how I felt, she always knew."

"Because she knew *you*." Nanna Jean held her tightly. "That's the greatest gift, isn't it? Having someone who knows who you are and loves who you are. But there are other people who will love you for who you are, too. You just have to let them."

Lucy scrubbed at her face again and pulled away. "Sorry."

"Stop apologizing. You're allowed to be sad, Lucy. You don't always have to be smiling." Nanna Jean sat down next to her and pulled her chair closer. "When I lost my Angus, I could have filled the loch twice over with my tears. When they wanted to come, I let them come. I didn't try and stop them. And neither should you."

Glenda passed her a tissue and sat down on the other side of her. "Nanna Jean is right."

"Of course I'm right." Nanna Jean took the tissue and gently wiped Lucy's face. "Now, this is what we're going to do. We're going to make shortbread, and you're going to tell us all about your grandmother. I'd like to know her a little better. I know Glenda would, too. We'd like to know you a little better, so that we know when that lovely smile of yours is real and when it's taking some effort on your part."

Lucy took the tissue from her and blew her nose hard. Her eyes stung and her cheeks were burning. "I might just splash some cold water…" She stood up and ran the tap until the water was freezing.

Glenda soaked a small towel and handed it to her. "Here."

She took it gratefully and pressed it to her face. "Thank you." She lowered the cloth, feeling calmer. "I think I'd been wanting to do that for a while, but—"

"It never felt like the right time, or the right place. But today was both." Nanna Jean had sprinkled flour on the surface and rolled out the mixture. "Come and choose a cutter. Usually we just make boring fingers of shortbread, but at Christmas we go all out. Christmas trees, robins, stars—take your pick. Once you've cut it into shapes, we're going to put it on the baking tray and pop it into the fridge."

Lucy washed her hands and then returned to the table.

Nanna Jean gestured to the cutters. "What do you think?"

Lucy chose the star and pressed it into the shortbread dough. And as she cut the shapes, she told them about her grandmother. She talked about her strength, and her sense of humor, and the way she never wasted a single thing. "All she really wanted was for me to be happy."

"Of course that was what she wanted. That's all any mother wants for their child, isn't that right, Glenda?" Nanna Jean pushed the baking sheet toward Lucy. "Pop those straight on there, pet."

"It is right." Glenda was staring blankly ahead of her. "Although I don't think I've done a good job of making that clear to mine this week."

Nanna Jean tutted. "There you go again, beating yourself up for trying your best. You're a wonderful mother, Glenda."

Lucy was about to agree, when Glenda blinked and turned to look at them both.

"I really don't think I am."

17

Glenda

Why had she said that? This wasn't about her, it was about Lucy. But somehow the conversation about unconditional love, and family, had started her thinking. Particularly about her own shortcomings.

Lucy had felt able to say anything to her grandmother.

Did her children feel that way about her? Alice had talked to her, eventually, but Clemmie had been making huge life-changing plans and hadn't once even hinted of those plans to Glenda.

"Do you think Clemmie didn't tell me her news sooner because she thought I'd disapprove?"

"No, I don't think that." Nanna Jean was brisk. "Clemmie has been living in London, and that isn't the sort of thing that you say to someone over the phone, isn't that right, Lucy?"

"There are definitely some conversations that are better had face-to-face," Lucy said. "A conversation is more than words, isn't it? It's helpful to be able to read someone's body language."

"But my body language was saying all the wrong things." Glenda rubbed her fingers across her forehead. "It's my turn to apologize. Ignore me, Lucy. We shouldn't be involving you in our family drama." She stood up and slid the baking tray covered in shortbread into the fridge. "It's not fair."

Lucy pressed the cutter down and produced a few more stars. "I've involved you in mine. And if you want my honest opinion, I think they're lucky to have you."

"That's kind of you, but I'm not sure they'd agree. I didn't say any of the right things to Clemmie, and I can't forgive myself for that."

Lucy put the cutter down. "No one can say the right thing all the time. And your feelings are valid, too, isn't that what you were just telling me?"

Nanna Jean looked smug. "She's got you there, Glenda."

"Maybe. Doesn't stop me feeling bad though. I've always told the children they can tell me anything—" she looked at Lucy "—like your grandmother. And then when Clemmie trusts us with her big news I didn't hide my shock."

"You were surprised, that's all. And why wouldn't you be?" Nanna Jean stood up and put another tray into the fridge. "You had a vision of what Clemmie's future was going to look like, and when you realized it wasn't going to look like that, you needed time to process it all. And now you're fine with it."

"I am." Was she? Yes, she was. "It isn't that I don't approve of her having a baby on her own. It's more that I'm already worrying about what that means for her. Being a mother is tough. And I know there are plenty of single mothers out there, and I know Clemmie will be brilliant at it, but it isn't an easy path."

"But no one is better placed to understand what she is taking on than our Clemmie." Nanna Jean pushed the last baking tray toward Lucy. "One more, and then we'll be done."

"But I remember when the children were young, and how anxious I felt, particularly with my first. Remember the time Ross had that high fever and we ended up in hospital? I was sure he was going to die, and Douglas was so calm and reassuring." She tried to imagine how she would have coped if she hadn't had someone to share that worry with. "I don't know what I would have done without him. Having him around made all the difference. He worked long hours even then, but he was always here when I needed moral support. Who will do that for Clemmie? Who will she turn to?"

"She'll turn to us," Nanna Jean said, "and we will be there for her. At least, you will. I don't mind being on day duty but I'm too old to be woken at two in the morning to deal with middle-of-the-night dramas, or help with a crying baby. You can tell me about it when I wake up and I will make you strong coffee and make encouraging noises."

Lucy smiled. "Nanna Jean is right. I don't think it matters where the support comes from. There are no guarantees that even if you have a partner, they'll be a tower of strength. One of my colleagues has just had his first—or rather, his wife has—and he's a nervous wreck most of the time. He's brilliant, and I love him, but calm and reassuring? I don't think so. I spoke to his wife when I was on the train coming here, and it seemed to me that she was the one calming *him* down, not the other way around. She told me that he'd spent the whole first night when they were home watching the baby breathing."

"Bless." Nanna Jean put the last tray in the fridge. "I hope you're listening, Glenda. Clemmie will be fine. And so will you."

"Maybe. But right now she probably feels as if she's on her own with it, and that her family is unsupportive." She was pleased that Clemmie seemed to at least have talked to Fergus, but it also made her feel as if she'd somehow failed her daughter.

"I doubt that she thinks that." Lucy fetched a cloth and started to wipe the table. "Just because someone doesn't say exactly the right thing, doesn't mean they don't care about you. You're human. I'm sure there are plenty of times when Clemmie gets things wrong, too. But that's the best thing about family, isn't it? You can mess up, knowing that you'll still be loved. Whatever happens, you know deep down that your family is in your corner." She walked to the sink and rinsed the cloth. "That's what I miss most. Having someone in your corner. Someone who loves you no matter what, even when life is tough. It's like falling onto a mattress, instead of concrete. Ross, Alice and Clemmie are lucky, but I'm sure they know that."

Glenda sat for a moment, digesting Lucy's words. And she was right, of course. Deep down her children knew that they were loved no matter what. Clemmie knew that.

She could make this right.

She would make this right.

Feeling better, she smiled and noticed that Nanna Jean was looking at Lucy.

"We're in your corner, pet. That's why I'm going to make sure Ross has that meeting with you." Nanna Jean stood up and transferred the baking trays from the fridge to the oven. "So you live in London, Lucy, just like Ross. That's convenient. Are you dating anyone?"

"That's enough." Glenda gave her mother-in-law a warning look but Nanna Jean wasn't paying attention. "Lucy might not want to discuss her love life with you."

"Why not? I'm in her corner, she knows that. Being in her corner means wanting what's best for her. And before I can want what's best for her, I need to know what she already has."

"I think Lucy can decide what's best for her." Glenda stood up and set a timer for the shortbread.

"I'm not dating," Lucy said.

Nanna Jean beamed. "Perfect."

Glenda sighed. "As you can see, she isn't subtle, Lucy."

"Subtle is overrated," Nanna Jean said. "Ross's favorite is the whiskey shortbread. Why don't we make a batch of that for your meeting? I'll fetch the bottle." She caught Glenda's eye. "What have I said now?"

"I just think you need to stop interfering, that's all. And Douglas won't be amused if you finish his single malt."

"There's plenty more where that came from."

Lucy smiled, and Glenda thought that she looked a lot happier than she had when she'd first walked into the kitchen. She didn't even seem to mind the blatant matchmaking. Which meant that either she recognized it as well-meaning, or she actually was interested.

The thought cheered Glenda up and by the time Ross reappeared in the kitchen, neat rows of shortbread lay cooling on a rack on the kitchen table.

"I've made tea." Glenda loaded mugs and a big teapot onto a tray. "You and Lucy can take this through to the library."

Ross took the tray from her and Nanna Jean added a plate piled high with shortbread.

"We made your favorite. If you need anything else—"

"We won't need anything else." His tone made it clear who was calling the shots on this one and for once Nanna Jean didn't argue.

"We won't be disturbing you, I assure you of that. We'll be very busy in here. We're overwhelmed with Christmas preparations. You'll have complete privacy." She gave Lucy a wink and Lucy grinned as she hobbled to the door on her crutches.

Ross closed it firmly behind her and Nanna Jean looked at Glenda.

"Well? What do you think?"

"We're not allowed to say what we think."

"Nonsense. We're on our own here. We can say what we like, and no one will ever know. Except the cat, and he is called Poker for a reason. Anyway, it's not good to bottle things up—wasn't that what we were telling Lucy earlier? Express your emotions. Let them out!"

Glenda laughed. "You're incorrigible. All right, I admit it, I like Lucy. I like her a lot."

"So do I. And, most importantly of all, so does Ross." Nanna Jean smiled. "I'd say that Christmas is looking more interesting by the minute."

18

Lucy

Lucy followed Ross into the library. She was gradually getting used to the crutches but still she was grateful when he pulled out a chair for her and took them from her.

"Thank you." She gazed around her. Floor-to-ceiling bookshelves lined the walls, and a huge window offered expansive views of snowy mountains. There was a window seat, piled with soft cushions. A book lay open, suggesting that someone had already been reading there that morning. "This room is incredible."

"We call it the library, but really it's our dining room although as you've discovered when it comes to family eating we rarely make it out of the kitchen."

"I have bookshelves on three walls of my flat. There's something comforting about being surrounded by books, isn't there? Some of them belonged to my grandmother. She could never throw a book away."

He sat down opposite her. Sunlight shafted through the window and slid over his dark hair. "How was the baking session? Not too stressful, I hope."

"It was fun." It had been so much more than that. It had been healing, but she didn't need to share that with him. Not right now. "You have a very special family."

"If you think that then that must mean you escaped without Nanna Jean signing you up to four dating agencies." He smiled at her and she felt the same punch of heat she'd felt earlier.

The intensity was disturbing, the attraction so powerful that it added yet more complication to a situation that was already complicated.

Their relationship had changed since that moment in the living room. She felt it. She was pretty sure he did, too.

But what did it matter?

She was going to be leaving soon. Returning to London, and if she'd dreaded the prospect of that before, it seemed even more of a bleak option now. Not just because she'd be returning to her empty flat, but because she'd be leaving this beautiful place.

Oh, who was she kidding? It wasn't really the place, although that was indeed beautiful, it was the people. The Millers.

She brought herself back to the conversation. "She did ask if I was single."

"Of course she did." He shook his head. "And for that, I apologize."

"Don't worry. I told her I had a boyfriend for every day of the week. Two on Saturdays, because they can't keep up."

There was a gleam of humor in his eyes. "Lucy, Lucy," he said, leaning forward, his expression serious, "you're not *inventing* boyfriends, are you?"

"Me?" She pressed her hand to her chest. "Now, why would I do a thing like that?"

"I can't imagine. Tea?" He waved his hand toward the tray and she helped herself.

"I haven't drunk this much tea since my grandmother was alive."

"Welcome to Miller Lodge, where tea is seen as the solution to all life's problems." He ate a biscuit and made an appreciative sound. "This is good. Did you make it?"

"Well technically I suppose I did, but it was under Nanna Jean's close direction." She bit into it and almost purred. "Oh that's good." The sweet, crumbly texture contrasted with the smoky hints of single malt.

"If she made whiskey shortbread with you, she must really like you."

She finished her piece of shortbread and slid her hands round her mug. "You're saying that because it's a recipe even more closely guarded than the butter shortbread?"

"No. Because it involves stealing Dad's treasured bottle of single malt, which always comes with a certain level of risk." He smiled at her and that smile sent a tiny thrill running through her body.

What would it have been like, she wondered, if they'd met in different circumstances? If she hadn't been trapped in his house, feeling like an uninvited guest, an interloper. If he'd been given a choice as to whether he wanted to seek out her company?

Would they have been drawn to each other? Would this dangerous, simmering chemistry have led to something more?

"I'm guessing Nanna Jean isn't afraid of much," she said. "Apart from you dying single, of course."

"Of course. Because that," he said, "would be a tragedy."

"Also, extremely unlikely, given that Nanna Jean seems to

have made your relationship status her priority." She loved his sense of humor. It had been evident in those first moments when he'd arrived, but then it had disappeared. But now it was back, and she wondered why everyone talked about Ross Miller's business acumen, and never mentioned his warmth and kindness. Or maybe he only revealed that side of himself when he was around his family. "Don't worry, you're rich and successful, so someone will have you. And rumor of your dad's single malt would probably clinch the deal."

"A fictitious girlfriend seems more appealing all the time. Right—" He pushed his plate to one side and picked up her proposal.

Instantly the atmosphere shifted. She went from feeling comfortable, to uncomfortable. The balance of power had shifted. She wondered if he could feel it, too.

"So," he said and leaned back in his chair. "I read your proposal."

"You did?"

"Of course. I'm far too afraid of my grandmother to do otherwise." He didn't look at all afraid. "I read it after I'd finished clearing the snow. It wasn't what I was expecting."

Her insides fluttered. "Right."

"I was expecting all the usual ideas, but there was nothing usual in this document. Your ideas were fresh and interesting."

Pride and excitement washed over her. "You liked it? You thought it was interesting?"

"Yes. Time and time again agencies pitch ideas for how we can expand our current market, but your proposal tapped into a whole new market. What made you think of it?"

"Fitness fanatics already buy your brand. But there are loads of people like me who aren't benching their body weight and pounding along the river for an hour before work every morning. People who are intimidated by gyms."

"You're intimidated by gyms?" He picked up a pen and scribbled in the margin of the document. "What intimidates you?"

"Er, the people and the equipment."

He glanced up. "That's basically everything."

"I know. I'm intimidated by basically everything, but if I'd said 'everything' you would have asked me to be more specific. But not all exercise has to happen in a gym or a yoga studio. And not all of the Miller Active range has to be specifically for exercise."

"None of the companies I've dealt with have ever suggested targeting people who aren't at all interested in exercise or the gym. It seems counterintuitive, although I admit it's a novel approach. The question is, would it work?" Was he talking to himself or to her? She wasn't sure.

"I am sure that it would." Behind him through the tall windows she could see the snowy mountains. "Think about it. You have a fan base among gym goers. My colleague Maya says that your yoga pants are the best. Apparently they don't shift when doing downward dog."

"So I'm told." There was a glimmer of a smile on his face. "But why would that quality interest the non–gym goer?"

"If you've read the proposal then you'll know that our strategy has two prongs. The first is to appeal to the mass of people who now work at home. They want clothes to be comfortable, but also stylish. Part of your range would fit that description. I'm suggesting that we curate a selection of clothes to appeal specifically to that market. The second part of the strategy is to encourage the nonexerciser to exercise."

"Something health officials and corporations have been trying to do for a long time. How do you propose to achieve what they haven't?"

"Use social media to connect people. Form a community.

Bring people together so that they can encourage each other. It's important that you're seen as more than a brand. You can actually drive change in people's lives."

He was silent for a moment. "And you'd head this up?"

Her pulse went into overdrive. He liked her ideas. Did that mean he was going to allow them to pitch? "We'd work as a team."

He made another couple of notes. "Does Arnie think it would work?"

"Arnie doesn't know about it yet." She paused. "He hasn't been well, and he needed time away from work."

He put his pen down. "I have a question. You went to my office to try and make an appointment—why didn't you just leave this with my secretary?"

"Because then it would have ended up at the bottom of your in tray, or maybe even in the bin."

"Are you this persistent with all your clients?"

"You're looking at a woman who stood on freezing moorland to get a good shot of a reindeer, so I think I can safely answer yes to that. I do what needs to be done."

"I used the Fingersnug when I went for my run this morning," Ross said. "It's good. I think we could sell them in our stores. Perhaps you could connect me to someone in the company."

She resisted the temptation to punch the air. "Of course. Would you consider posting a photograph of yourself using it on social media?"

He laughed. "Do you ever give up?"

"Not while I'm breathing. So will you?"

"I'll think about it. And now we'd better finish this tea, or we'll be lectured by Nanna Jean." He topped up her mug. "I'm sorry if my father took advantage, this morning."

"He didn't. I was pleased to help." She thought back to that conversation and the tension she'd sensed between the two of them. "Do you ever talk to your father about his business?"

"No." He pushed away his plate, as if the shift in conversation had removed all trace of appetite. "My father wouldn't want my help."

She was absolutely sure that wasn't the case. "Maybe he just doesn't want to bother you."

"Are you implying that I don't know my own father?"

For a brief moment she glimpsed the steel that had propelled him to the top and kept him there. The subtle shift in the atmosphere made her wish she hadn't said anything. The temperature cooled, and maybe that was her fault.

On the surface it was indeed presumptuous of her to suggest she had insight into his father's thinking that he himself didn't possess. But she knew she was right, and she couldn't forget how tired Douglas had looked. How eagerly he'd exploited her knowledge. And she suspected Ross had his own blind spot when it came to his father. Maybe that was inevitable, given the fact that Ross had chosen to take a different path. Maybe it wasn't.

Rebel Ross.

"I'm not implying you don't know your father, although if you think he doesn't want your help then maybe you don't know him as well as you think. Sometimes it's easier to have a clear view of a situation as an outsider."

"You think I don't understand him." He stood up abruptly, the scrape of the chair on the oak flooring an indication of his change in mood.

He strode to the window and stared out across the mountains, keeping his back to her.

And now she wished she'd kept her mouth shut.

Had she really thought that a few heated glances, a show of kindness on his part, and the sharing of confidences on hers, gave her the right to interfere with his family? He clearly didn't think so.

She felt regret, despair and more than a little confusion.

What happened now? Maybe this was her cue to leave, but how could she leave? She was snowed in, trapped here, and he was forced to endure her presence.

But she didn't have to stay in the same room.

Presumably he now considered the meeting to be over. The atmosphere, which only moments before had been warm and filled with delicious tension, was now as brittle as the icicles hanging from the eaves of the house.

She stared at his tall frame, at those broad shoulders filled with tension.

And then she stood up.

Bathed in regret, but at the same time knowing she would have done exactly the same thing again, she put the mugs and plates carefully back on the tray. "I'm sorry. You're right. It's not my business." She fumbled with her crutches, cautious and careful in the extreme because to fall now would make a bad situation worse.

She was about to leave the room when he turned.

"Wait." The winter sunlight and the shadows made it difficult for her to see his expression clearly. "I'm the one who is sorry. I was rude, and I regret that. The truth is, you touched a nerve. But I can tell you he definitely wouldn't want my help. He doesn't think I have anything to offer."

She could sense the complex emotions layered under that simple remark. And it made no sense. Surely he could see that?

"But you've turned Miller Active into—"

"It doesn't matter. Not to Dad." He thrust his hands into his pockets and turned back to the mountains. "When I chose not to join him in the business, to go my own way, I hurt his feelings. We don't talk about work. It's safer that way."

Was he serious? "You both run companies, and you never talk about work?"

"That's right."

"What, *never*?" It was hard to believe. Impossible to believe. "You must have at some point."

"No. It's the one topic we never discuss." He turned to look at her. "So you can see the problem."

"If you're talking about the fact that you're both as stubborn as each other then, yes, I can see the problem." The sharp intake of his breath made her realize what she'd said.

Oh, Lucy, Lucy. Whatever advantage she may have had, she'd blown it now with her honesty. She'd torn through the last of the fragile threads that had connected them.

Trying not to think about the personal price of that, she focused instead on work and sent silent apologies to Arnie.

She'd have to find another way to try and save the company. And she would. She'd leave Scotland and the Millers as soon as the bridge was cleared, and she'd spend the rest of the Christmas holidays researching companies. She'd pull together a plan. She'd work night and day to bring in new business. But it wasn't going to be Miller Active because there was no way of undoing what she'd just said.

And remembering Douglas's lost, tired expression, she didn't want to. This family had taken her in and welcomed her. They'd offered her sanctuary and kindness. They'd allowed her to be herself, to the point that her almost constant worry that she might lose control at the wrong moment had receded to nothing. So what if she did? She'd done exactly that earlier, and nothing bad had happened. On the contrary, her honest expression of emotion had drawn her closer to Glenda and Nanna Jean.

If only Douglas and Ross would do the same.

Douglas loved his son deeply, that was obvious. But his

pride wouldn't let him talk through his concerns. And Ross's pride was so wounded by the fact that his father had never acknowledged his success, that he wouldn't make the first move.

Both of them were afraid to talk honestly, at least to each other.

But it seemed Ross had no such reservations toward her.

"Stubborn?" His eyes narrowed. "That's what you think?"

It was too late to revert to tact. "Yes, that's what I think. Your dad runs a business, very successfully. You run a business, very successfully. And yet neither of you ever talk? Share ideas and experience? Don't tell me there aren't aspects of running a business that the two of you couldn't usefully discuss. But your dad is too stubborn to talk to you and you're too stubborn to talk to him."

"And how would I do that? What words would I use that wouldn't risk putting a dent in our relationship? *Hey, Dad, if there is ever anything you need help with let me know because I'm good at what I do, even though you haven't noticed*?"

"Of course he has noticed. And if that's the way you handle sensitive situations I'm surprised you have anyone working for you."

"I'll have you know," he said through his teeth, "that my team are happy and motivated. And I don't have trouble handling sensitive situations. This is different."

"How is it different?"

"Because in business," he said, "emotions aren't involved." She was silent for so long he frowned.

"What? No smart comeback? There's no point in holding back now. Tell me what you're thinking."

"I'm thinking that it's a good job you and your father didn't go into business together because you probably would have killed each other."

"That's the first thing you've said that we agree on." He

gave a faint smile and she was ridiculously relieved to see that smile. It was like seeing blue skies after relentless rain.

"So is that why?"

"Why I didn't go and work for Glen Shortbread?" He shrugged. "Partly. My father had very firm ideas about how things should be done. We were all involved in the business when we were growing up, and I spent summers working there when I was at college, so I had a pretty clear idea of how it would be. I knew I'd always be working for him, following his plan, unable to challenge anything and implement new ideas. I wanted to build something myself."

"Of course. You'd grown up watching him do it. He influenced you. In a way he's partly responsible for who you are. You probably learned a lot from him without even knowing it."

He gave her a curious look. "I hadn't thought of it like that but, yes, I suppose so. He was my inspiration."

"Have you ever told him that?"

"No."

She wanted to shake the pair of them. "So you moved away because you needed the distance."

"Yes, but it wasn't just that." He glanced out the window again. "I love it here. The mountains. The air. The people. It should be enough, but it isn't. It never was. I wanted the city. I wanted London. I love London. My father doesn't get that, either."

"I get that. I love London, too."

He turned to look at her. "You do?"

"Oh yes, and not just because I was raised there. I love it because—" She broke off, trying to articulate exactly why she loved it so much. "It's exciting, isn't it? You have a sense that anything is possible there. And even though I've lived there all my life I'm still in awe of the history. One minute you're walking past a futuristic glass building, and the next you're at the Tower of London."

"I can see the Tower of London from my apartment."

"Please don't tell me that or I'll have to hate you. I live in a dark basement flat, but I do have a brilliant view of people's feet as they walk past my window. It has made me an excellent judge of shoes."

"I work in one of those futuristic glass buildings."

"I know. I know where your offices are. I've been there." And she'd been impressed, and a little in awe, but she wasn't going to admit that. Her leg was aching, so she sat down on the window seat. "The problem with two stubborn people is that there is never progress unless one of them has the courage to make a move."

"Are you saying I'm a coward?"

"I don't know, Ross." She looked up at him and delivered a smile and a challenge. "Are you?"

19

Clemmie

"Clemmie?" There was a tap on the door and then the rattle of the handle turning. "Why have you locked the door? You never lock the door."

"I'm wrapping presents." Clemmie was on her back on the bed, staring up at the ceiling. Her presents were still in the suitcase she'd used to bring them home. Unwrapped. "You can't come in, Alice."

"Well could you wrap mine and put it under your bed or something? I need to talk to you."

The problem with being home, Clemmie thought, was that there was nowhere to escape for peace and quiet. Normally she loved that side of family life, but right now she was trying hard to pull herself together and didn't need witnesses.

She'd had it all planned out. Come home. Have a baby. Build a new life. Be friends with Fergus. She'd been excited. Positive about everything. She knew she'd be a good mother.

She still believed that, even in the face of her family's rather mixed reaction. She'd wanted this forever. The part she hadn't anticipated was that her feelings for Fergus would be as strong as ever. She'd spent years training herself to think of him as a friend. For the first six months after she'd moved to London she'd practiced saying those words to the mirror—*my friend Fergus*—in the hope that the more she said it, the more it might become a reality. She'd started writing a diary, instead of emailing him.

She'd thought she was doing well, until this morning when she'd realized that her feelings hadn't changed. All that had changed was the way she'd handled them. Turned out you couldn't switch love on and off. Which was a shame. Life might have been a lot easier if you could. Was she really going to be able to live here, see him all the time, and not die of agony?

And now she was being dramatic. Which was frankly pathetic.

"Clemmie." The door rattled again. "I've brought tea."

How was tea going to help? She didn't want tea, and she wasn't in the mood to talk to anyone, not even one of her siblings. "Give me an hour. I'll message you."

Or did Alice want to talk to her about Nico? Had something happened? Maybe she needed someone to talk to.

She slid off the bed. "I'm coming. Give me two seconds." She grabbed a sheet of wrapping paper and some tape and threw it on the floor. She dragged the suitcase next to it, evidence to support her claim that she was wrapping presents. Normally she would have had her wrapping done and all the presents under the tree, but for the first time in her life she hadn't felt like doing them. She didn't feel very Christmassy.

She smoothed her hair, not that it made any difference to her curls, and unlocked the door.

"Hi—is everything okay?"

"I don't know. You tell me." Alice walked into the room, balancing two brimming mugs of tea. She handed one to Clemmie and then glanced at the suitcase and the single roll of paper. "I thought you said you were wrapping."

"I was about to start when you knocked." She shifted the mug in her hands, trying not to scald herself. "Are you doing all right?"

"Not really, but it's you I want to talk about."

"Oh." Clemmie took a sip of tea to stop it spilling and then settled down on the floor. "I'm fine. And I don't really want to talk about it, if that's okay. I don't think it will help."

"I can see why you might feel that way, given everyone's less-than-tactful reaction to your news, but honestly we're all thrilled. Me in particular." Alice gave a wide grin. "It will take the heat off me if you produce a family grandchild. And I promise to be the best aunt on the planet."

Alice thought she was upset about the family reaction to her announcement. She didn't know about Fergus.

Her feelings for Fergus were so huge she thought they should be obvious, like some sort of emotional graffiti visible to all who looked at her. But no one knew. And that was a good thing, but also lonely.

"Thanks."

Alice sat cross-legged. "You haven't switched your Christmas tree lights on."

Clemmie glanced at the tree that her mother had positioned carefully by the window. "I forgot."

"You forget to turn them off, not switch them on." Alice frowned and lowered her mug to the floor. "This isn't like you. Is this all because Mum was tactless? Because she is beating herself up about that. She's pleased, you know. It just takes people a while to get their head around it."

"It's not about Mum. I mean, it's not about anything. I'm fine."

"I know you're not fine."

Clemmie rolled her eyes. "Could you stop being a doctor for five minutes?"

"I'm not being a doctor. I'm being a big sister. And I'm the first to admit that most of the time I'm a pretty rubbish sister."

Clemmie put her tea down. "That's not true."

"It is. I'm always busy, I'm totally focused on work, I'm obsessive and an annoying perfectionist—why do you think none of my relationships have lasted? But the great thing about having a sister, is that they have to forgive you. You're stuck with me, no matter what." Alice sipped her tea. "Have you decided on a birth partner?"

"Alice, I'm not even pregnant yet."

"I know, but it's never too early to start planning. Anyway, I'd like to volunteer. I'd love to be there for you. And before you answer, you should know that I'm always calm in clinical situations and I'm great in a crisis. Not that I'm anticipating a crisis." Alice flushed. "And if there's someone else you'd rather have, then I totally understand."

"Oh, Alice." Clemmie felt a rush of warmth. "That's a truly kind offer. And I can't think of anyone else I'd rather have next to me. If I actually get pregnant, of course."

"I'm sure you will. Have you talked to the doctors at the clinic? Yes, you must have done. And you did that on your own." Alice frowned. "I'll come with you next time if you like. I just want you to know you're supported. I'm here for you. No matter what."

"I appreciate that." Should she tell Alice about Fergus? No. Maybe she would one day, but right now it was all too raw. And, anyway, her sister was dealing with her own problems. "How about you? Have you talked to Nico?"

"Yes. And I have you to thank for that."

"Me?"

"Yes. You standing up there and making your announcement about what you wanted made me realize I'd been a total coward. You gave me courage."

"Oh." Clemmie couldn't imagine herself being a source of inspiration for anyone. "I'm glad you finally talked to him. How did it go?"

"Unbelievably badly."

"Oh, Alice…" Clemmie leaned forward and grabbed her sister's hand. "You should have come and found me."

"No need. I cried on Mum. Which was actually a bit embarrassing, but also good. Better than crying on Nico."

Clemmie had never actually seen her big sister cry. "So—what happened? He wants a big family? He doesn't think you want the same things?"

"That wasn't it. He's struggling with the fact that I didn't talk to him about it. What does that say about our relationship blah blah. He left me in the café. Not a bad place to be abandoned I suppose."

Clemmie wasn't fooled by her sister's flippant tone. "And? Where is he now?"

"Well given the choice I'm sure he'd be back in London, but one of the advantages of heavy snow and being trapped is that no one gets to escape." She gave a half shrug. "He's stuck here until they've cleared the roads and opened the bridge. So that isn't awkward at all. Let's just say, it's a bit frosty in the Loch Room even though there is a fire blazing. I'm sleeping in my old bedroom tonight."

Clemmie tightened her grip on her sister's hand. "I feel guilty. I was the one who encouraged you to talk to him."

"And you were right. I don't regret it, Clem. Avoiding something doesn't change the outcome, does it? I should have had the conversation the moment he proposed. I should have spelled out all my fears. Told him the truth. And maybe we could have figured out a way through."

"But if he loves you—"

"I'm sure he does. And I love him, but maybe that's not enough."

But if that wasn't enough, then what was? Clemmie couldn't bear it. She loved someone who didn't love her back. Her sister was in love with someone who *did* love her back, but still they couldn't figure it out.

"Talk to him again, Alice. Try again. Do you know how hard it is in this world to find someone you can be happy with? You and Nico are great together."

"Are you kidding? We've been exuding miserable tension since we arrived, although I admit that's mostly my fault."

"But I've seen you together in London. And I've seen the way you talk about him. Don't give up, Alice. Talk to him again."

"I intend to. And you need to answer a question for me— your determination to go it alone, is that because of the way Liam treated you?"

"No." Clemmie was able to answer that honestly. "It's nothing to do with him."

"Right. Just thought I'd check. So—" Alice glanced around. "Are we going to wrap these presents? I hope you got me something huge and amazing."

"I might have done." Clemmie gave her a push. "Now go away. Leave me to wrap them."

"I'll leave when you put your Christmas tree lights on. Only then will I believe you're okay." Alice stood up and picked up the empty mugs.

Clemmie switched on the lights and the tree glowed. "There. Done. Satisfied?"

"For now." Alice walked to the door. "Give me a shout if you fancy a walk later."

"Will do." Clemmie waited for the door to close and then lay back down on the bed. She'd barely stretched herself out when there was another knock on the door.

It seemed that no one was allowed peace and quiet to be miserable in this family.

Maybe it was Alice again.

But when she tugged open the door, it was her grandmother who stood there.

"Nanna Jean—"

"I have an emergency," Nanna Jean said. "I need your help."

"With what?"

"I made some gingerbread Christmas trees, but now I'm too tired to ice them. It's no fun getting old, I can tell you. Nothing works quite the way you want it to. Are you busy? You have a steady hand and you've always been good at icing." Nanna Jean peered into Clemmie's room. "What are you doing on your own in here?"

Trying to have a private moment, but that was an impossible goal in this house.

On the other hand lying on the bed staring at the ceiling hadn't exactly made her feel better.

"I was wrapping presents, but it can wait. I'll come and help you."

"You're a good girl." Nanna Jean patted her on the arm. "I should do it but I feel more like taking a nap to be honest."

Clemmie felt a flash of concern. "You go and lie down. I'll do the icing."

"I'm sure I'll be fine if I'm just sitting quietly at the table. That way I can order you around and tell you what to do. You know how much I enjoy that."

Clemmie laughed, and instantly felt better. "Come on, then. Let's do this." She took her grandmother's arm and together they headed down the wide curving staircase to the kitchen. "Where is everyone else?"

"Your parents have gone to the village to visit the Trents. Pauline Trent is only just out of hospital after breaking her hip. She needs cheering up, and your mother is the one to do that. Douglas is going to clear the paths for her so that she can have visitors more easily. Ross is in the library, frowning over that proposal document Lucy gave him, and last time I saw her Lucy had fallen asleep on the sofa in the living room. She had her laptop next to her so I moved it. She's obviously tired, poor thing. So it's just the two of us." Nanna Jean waved a hand toward the kitchen table which was covered in the evidence of her baking. "The two of us and about a hundred gingerbread Christmas trees."

"Then let's do this." Clemmie pulled on an apron. "This was one of my favorite Christmas traditions when I was little. That and making Rudolph cupcakes." She reached for the bowl of glossy icing and a knife.

"I remember." Nanna Jean settled herself in the chair next to her, "although if we're being precise, your favorite tradition was eating the icing from the bowl when you thought I wasn't looking."

Clemmie smoothed icing over the surface of the Christmas tree. "Nothing escapes you."

"That's right. My bones creak and my hearing isn't what it was, but there's nothing wrong with my eyes." Nanna Jean mixed a small amount of coloring into another bowl of icing. "The trees can be white and snowy, but we're going to add red candles."

Clemmie carefully iced each biscuit and with each sweep of the knife she felt herself growing calmer.

She placed a freshly iced "tree" down on the wire rack to dry. "Is Mum still very upset?"

"Yes. But with herself, not you. She thinks she said all the wrong things." Nanna Jean didn't pretend to misunderstand her. "Your mother sets a high standard for her parenting. I'm sure you will be the same."

Clemmie felt a lump form in her throat. "I didn't mean to blurt it out like that."

"I've always been of the opinion that if there's something to be said, it's best said as plainly as possible, and in as few words. Waffling doesn't change the meaning. Keep your eye on what you're doing—" Nanna Jean pushed the plate closer to her. "That looks more like a snowdrift than a tree."

"Sorry." Clemmie tried to concentrate. "You were the only one who didn't seem shocked."

"I wasn't shocked. I asked Santa to make me a great-grandmother. I didn't stipulate how. It doesn't pay to be too controlling in life, I find."

No matter how serious the topic, her grandmother always made her smile. "But what do you think of my plan, really?"

"You don't need my endorsement. You know what you're doing. You know what you want. But since you ask, I think that any child who has you as a mother will be lucky. Now concentrate. You're putting too much icing on your knife." Nanna Jean guided Clemmie's hand back to the bowl and let some of it slide off. "You've forgotten how to do this. You're going to need to get this right, if you're going to do this with your own child one day. Don't look at me—keep icing, or it's going to dry up in the bowl."

"You're probably wondering why I'm doing this. Having a baby on my own, I mean."

"I'm not wondering. I know." Nanna Jean pushed the rack closer to her. "You're doing it because of Fergus."

Clemmie couldn't breathe. She knew? She couldn't possibly know. Could she?

She felt the color rush into her cheeks.

"That's not—I mean, I don't know why you'd think for a moment—"

"With age, comes wisdom, haven't you ever heard that? You love him. You always have. That's not news, at least not to me. Put the knife down because at the moment you're icing the floor and it's slippery enough out there without making it lethal in here, too." She removed the knife gently from Clemmie's shaking fingers. "Why so shocked?"

"Does anyone else know?"

"That you're in love with Fergus? I don't know. It's been obvious to me for years, but it's funny what people miss when they're not looking. And not everyone is as sharp-eyed and emotionally intuitive as your grandmother." Nanna Jean gave the icing a stir to stop it setting. "I never understood why you chose to move away."

"I thought that if I moved away and dated other people, I might get over him. I was hoping I might fall in love with someone else. It didn't work."

"Well of course it didn't." Nanna Jean made a tutting sound. "How could it? You were already in love with him." She made it sound so obvious and normal that the initial shock faded.

And suddenly Clemmie felt relieved that Nanna Jean knew. She'd never been the sort of person who was comfortable keeping secrets. She was a natural sharer, but she'd never been able to share this before. It was too deeply personal. And she'd always been afraid that if she told someone, they might let it slip and Fergus would find out.

That, she thought, would have been mortifying.

"I should have talked to you years ago. You might have

saved me from wasting time on some really unfortunate dates."

"You should have talked to me, although I'm not always tactful as you know and it's possible I might have said something to Fergus if the moment presented itself. I assume you've considered that approach? Telling him how you feel?"

Clemmie shrank. "Tell him I love him?"

She couldn't think of anything more awkward.

"Why not? It's the truth. You've loved him forever."

"I know. It's horrible. And that's why I can't tell him." Surely her grandmother could see that? "He'd be embarrassed. I'd be embarrassed. It would be a nightmare."

"How did it feel to see him and spend time with him?"

Clemmie stared at the gingerbread shape in front of her. It no longer looked anything like a Christmas tree. Nanna Jean was right. She'd put too much icing on it. She picked up the knife and poked at it, trying to scoop some of it back up and rescue it, but it just made it look worse. "It was harder than I thought it would be. I thought I could handle it, but I didn't do so well. He's wonderful with Iona. He does her hair. Did you know he was taking piano lessons so that he can practice with her?"

"Yes. I was the one who arranged the lessons." Nanna Jean moved the tree onto a plate, away from Clemmie's tampering. "He asks after you, you know, all the time. Whenever your name comes up in conversation, he always listens."

"He's being polite."

"The occasional question is polite, more than that is interest."

Clemmie shrugged. "We're friends. Good friends."

"Exactly. And good friends should be able to tell each other anything." Nanna Jean passed her another Christmas tree. "If you're brave enough to uproot your life and move back here, brave enough to consider being a parent, then you're brave enough to tell Fergus how you feel about him."

"Not really. It means laying myself bare. Opening myself up to ridicule. What if he laughed?"

"He wouldn't laugh. That would be very cruel, and Fergus is anything but cruel."

"Okay, then, but I'd put him in a horrible position. He'd pity me. Every time we passed each other in the village it would be excruciatingly awful. I'd be too scared to go to the bakery or the café. And he'd hide every time he saw me coming. He'd be leaping over walls and cowering behind lampposts trying to avoid me."

"Goodness he'd have to be nimble to leap over walls. I do envy people with healthy joints who have all these athletic options at their disposal. And Fergus has never cowered in his life. Far from it. He stood up and took responsibility for his baby niece at a time when most of his friends were out getting drunk and partying." Nanna Jean was thoughtful. "I don't think he'd be embarrassed, and I don't think he'd want to hide, but if he did then that would be his problem. And you would hold your head up high when you met him in the bakery and bask in the satisfaction of knowing you'd done everything you could to make it happen. That you didn't settle for a second-best life because you were afraid to reach out for what you wanted."

A second-best life.

Was she settling? No, she wasn't. Well only if a life with Fergus was an option. And it wasn't.

Was it?

There had been that moment, all those years ago...

But she'd imagined it.

Hadn't she?

What if she hadn't? What if she hadn't imagined it and all this time Fergus had been feeling the same way she had?

No. She would have known.

But still…

Oh, this was torture!

Clemmie was starting to have some sympathy for Alice. It wasn't the conversation itself that was the problem, it was what happened afterward. "I'd die of mortification. I'm moving back here, and this is a small village. We'd have to avoid each other."

"No one ever dies of mortification. And are you sure that's what's going on here?"

"What do you mean?"

"You and Fergus have known each other forever," Nanna Jean said. "At least, it feels that way. The two of you were good friends. And now you're back, you'll be good friends again. I think you're afraid that if you're honest with him, you risk losing that friendship. And you'd rather have friendship, than nothing. You're afraid that by telling him you'd be risking it all."

"Yes," Clemmie said miserably. "That's it. Even a small part of Fergus is better than no Fergus. I miss his friendship. I want so much more than that, but I'd settle for friendship over nothing. You're very clever, Nanna Jean."

"I am. It's a curse, but one I've learned to live with." Nanna Jean patted her hand. "There's one thing you're not considering in all this. The fact that he has feelings for you, too."

Something stirred inside her. "Why would you say that? As you just pointed out, Fergus and I have known each other for most of our lives. If he had feelings for me, he would have said something."

Nanna Jean peered at her over the top of her glasses. "*You* haven't said anything."

"No. But that's different."

"Mmm." She pushed the icing bowl closer to Clemmie. "Finish this tree before the icing dries."

"What am I going to do, Nanna Jean?"

"That's up to you. But because you're a good girl and listen to your old, wise grandmother, you're probably going to talk to Fergus." Nanna Jean lifted the iced gingerbread trees that had dried and placed them carefully in the tin. "And then you're going to come back here and tell me all about it. And I am going to try very hard not to say, 'I told you so.'"

"If he runs screaming for the hills, I'll be the one saying, 'I told you so.'"

Nanna Jean put a Christmas tree on a plate and passed it to Clemmie. "There is another option, of course."

"Which is?"

"Write to Santa. I've always found him to be surprisingly receptive."

20

Glenda

Two days later Glenda stared through the kitchen window, watching as Ross and Clemmie cleared a path through to the woodshed. She could hear the rhythmic scrape of the shovel and Ross's deep voice as he talked to his sister. Occasionally one of them would pause to lob a snowball at the other, an activity accompanied by much laughter and loud shrieking on Clemmie's part.

The shrieking made her smile. Some things didn't change.

Growing up, Ross and Clemmie had always loved the snow. In the winter months they'd press their noses to chilly windows, watching the sky beyond, willing it to produce if not a blizzard, then at least a flurry sufficient to allow the creation of a modest snowman. If snow could have been produced by willpower alone, then the lodge would have been permanently cocooned by a layer of white. And when the snow finally fell, the two of them were always first out the door.

She remembered the Christmas when they'd given Clemmie a sledge. She'd been six years old and poor Ross had spent almost every moment of his holiday tugging his sister over the frosty lawn because there hadn't been a single flake of snow.

Now there was enough snow for them to open a ski resort. The snow had fallen on and off for almost three days, mocking those who had ever questioned the possibility of a white Christmas. She'd started to wonder if they'd be snowed in until New Year and been relieved when she'd woken that morning to bright blue skies and sunlight so brilliant and sharp that it hurt to look at it.

Beyond the lodge the trees were heavy with snow, droopy branches struggling to hold the weight of their burden.

Everyone was saying it was the heaviest snowfall recorded, and Glenda had no trouble believing them.

Outside the kitchen the snow Ross had cleared lay in soft mounds, twinkling under the bright sunshine. The intense light added dazzle and sparkle to the winter wonderland that surrounded them.

"What are you brooding about?" Douglas's voice came from behind her and she turned.

"Nothing. I'm watching Ross and Clemmie."

"Who is winning?" Douglas joined her at the window and looped his arm around her shoulders.

"It's a close run thing. Clemmie's aim is better, but Ross is ruthless. He keeps pelting her until she surrenders. She must have more snow down the neck of her jacket than is lying on the ground. They're having fun." And that was a relief because there had, in her opinion, been far too much stress punctuating the holidays up until this point.

"Where's Alice?"

"I don't know. I haven't seen her this morning." But she knew Alice had slept in her old room for the past two nights, and that wasn't a good sign. You couldn't mend a fight if you didn't talk, and Alice and Nico didn't seem to be talking. Each family meal had been a little strained but somehow, probably thanks to Nanna Jean, who refused to be daunted by atmospheres, they had struggled through. "Can you believe that tomorrow is Christmas Eve?"

"You love Christmas Eve. You always say it's the best day because Christmas is still to come."

"I know. Remember when the kids were little and we used to let them open one present, just because we couldn't handle their excitement a moment longer?"

"We did it on the condition they didn't wake us up until after six thirty."

"Ross and Alice used to have to sit on Clemmie to stop her racing into our room."

"I miss those days."

"I know. I do, too. But there are things we can do now that we couldn't do then."

"Like what?"

"I don't know." Douglas pulled her closer. "We could spend a month in the Caribbean, lying on a beach."

She felt a pang of yearning but managed to laugh. "We could, but we won't. And you, Douglas Miller, are a tease. There's nothing you'd hate more. You'd be bored in thirty seconds. What would you do when you arrived there?"

"I'd start by watching you enjoying yourself."

She reached up and kissed him. "If you just took a weekend off occasionally, that would be a start. We could spend a weekend in Edinburgh in a fancy hotel. Visit the children in London." The back door flew open and a flurry of freezing air flooded the room.

"I hate you, Ross Miller." But Clemmie was laughing as

she pulled off her snowy boots. Her jacket was covered and her hat was caked in snow.

"Bring it over here and I'll dry it." Glenda reached for her coat and hat. Once a mother, always a mother, she thought. It didn't matter how old they were, they were still her children.

"Your aim is shocking." Ross peeled off his coat, sending a flurry of snowflakes across the boot room.

"My aim is better than yours." Clemmie padded across to the range cooker in her socks and tried to warm herself. "What happened to the sledge, Mum? We could pull Lucy on it."

"Why? So that she can break the other leg?" Ross closed the door that separated the boot room from the kitchen.

"All I'm saying is that she hasn't been out for a few days and she's probably getting cabin fever. You're boring, that's your problem." Grinning, Clemmie hugged her arms round herself and headed out of the kitchen. "I'm going to have a shower and warm up, so that I'm ready for round two."

Ross sprawled in the chair. His hair curled damply over the collar of his outdoor fleece. "Talking of Lucy, where is she?"

"She had work to do, so I set her up at the table in the library. She wanted to stay in her room, out of the way, but I insisted." Glenda put a cup of strong coffee in front of him.

Douglas looked hopeful. "Is there one of those for me?"

"You're supposed to have one cup a day, and you've already had that."

"It's Christmas."

"You think your blood pressure takes a break over the holidays?" But she relented and poured him half a cup.

Ross was frowning. "Why would Lucy want to stay out of the way?"

"She's trying to keep a low profile and behave as if she isn't here."

"Well that's nonsense." Douglas took the cup from her gratefully. "We don't want her to keep a low profile. And she isn't in the way. She's probably feeling awkward about you, Ross. Give her your business. That might go some way to making this a happy Christmas for her." He waited. "Ross?"

"Giving her the business might make things…" Ross paused, searched for a word "…complicated."

Douglas made an impatient sound. "Why? Does it break one of your rules? Life is only complicated if you make it so. And by the way, a big tycoon like you should be able to handle complicated. You should eat complicated for breakfast, with a side of challenging."

Glenda rolled her eyes and gave up.

Ross, however, seemed surprisingly calm.

"It's not about rules," he said. "And you're right, I deal with complicated every day."

"Then what?"

Ross seemed about to say something but then thought better of it. "Nothing."

Douglas vibrated with exasperation. "Well I *will* be giving her business. In the New Year, I'm going to invite her up here to talk to the team. I know talent when I see it and I'm seeing it in Lucy. I need help, and I think she's the one to deliver it. So, if you change your mind down the road and ask her to work with you, don't be surprised if she's too damn busy to fit you in."

Ross put his cup down carefully. "You need help?"

"Not *help* exactly. Did I say help?" Douglas flushed. "I meant advice. From an expert. And unlike you I'm open-minded to good ideas. It's why we employ agencies, isn't it?"

"But you never have. You've always preferred to keep your business in-house. You have a marketing department."

"And they're good people. But that doesn't mean we can't be open-minded to new ways of doing things."

Ross leaned forward. "How's the business going, Dad?"

Glenda froze. She looked at Douglas, willing him not to rebuff what was so clearly an overture.

"Business is good. No problems."

Oh, for goodness' sake!

"Really? We've struggled with supply chain issues," Ross admitted. "Nightmare. We've virtually had to rethink the way we do business." He hesitated. "I'd love to talk it through with you, unless you'd rather not talk shop."

Douglas grunted. "What do I know?"

Glenda felt a rush of despair. She was ready to strangle the man with her bare hands. Bash him over the head with his own unyielding pride.

It was agony to witness so much tension between the two men she loved most in the world.

She expected Ross to give up and walk away, but he didn't. Instead he seemed to settle in.

"You've been running a successful business for your entire adult life, so I'd say you know a lot. It's just not easy to get you to share what you know."

"You've never been interested, at least not since you left home."

It took all Glenda's willpower to keep her mouth closed.

Ross took a breath. "Why do you think I wanted to set up my own business, Dad?"

"I don't know. Because you're stubborn and you didn't want to work with me?"

"Because you inspired me," Ross said quietly. "I saw you running this massively complicated operation, I saw the way you handled people, handled problems, the way you created something you could be proud of, and I wanted to be like you. Even as a child, when you used to take me into the office, I'd sit at your desk and I'd pretend to be you."

Douglas was silent for a moment. He cleared his throat and when he spoke his voice was rough.

"Then you grew up and decided you'd rather figure it out for yourself."

"In a way, yes, because it's not easy to persuade anyone to take you seriously when you're Douglas Miller's son. I wanted to prove to myself that I could do it. That I had as much of you in me as I thought I had. I couldn't have done that if I'd stayed here. And I knew that if I ended up even half as successful as you, then I'd be satisfied." Ross reached across the table and took his father's hand. "I went into business because I wanted to prove myself, that's true. But I also did it because I wanted to make you proud."

Glenda couldn't remember a moment in her life when her emotions had suffered such a dramatic swing. She'd gone from despair and frustration to pride and elation so quickly she had whiplash.

Her cheeks were wet. She tried to see if the words had touched Douglas, but she couldn't see through the mist in her eyes.

She'd never heard Ross talk like that before. Never seen him hold back the heat and show patience and vulnerability. It was as if he finally understood his father, although why he'd suddenly achieved that insight she had no idea.

Or maybe she did.

Lucy?

Maybe. But whatever was behind the change in attitude and the perfect choice of words, Ross had opened a door. It was right there, wide-open, just waiting for Douglas to walk through it.

If he chose to slam it in his son's face, she'd roast him alive.

She waited, holding her breath.

"I'm proud." Douglas sounded gruff. "How could I not be? You're a big shot. I read about you everywhere."

Ross gave a half smile. "You don't want to believe everything you read."

"Of course if you'd come and worked with me, I could have retired and taken your mother on a long holiday to the Caribbean."

Ross gave his father a long look. "Are you saying you want to retire? You don't need me running your business in order to retire, Dad."

"Well it's not going to run itself, is it? And who said anything about retiring? But maybe I'd take more time off if I had people around me I could trust."

"You're surrounded by good people, Dad. You just need to give them more responsibility. Trust them."

"You see?" Douglas looked at Glenda. "I give him one word of praise, and now he's telling me how to run my business."

"I'm not telling you how to run anything." Ross grinned. "All I'm telling you is that there are people out there who can help you run it. Smart people."

"People like Lucy you mean." But Douglas looked thoughtful. "If I reduced my hours, we could go away, Glenda."

She managed not to roll her eyes. "That's good thinking, Douglas."

He eyed her. "You're thinking that you've been telling me to do exactly that for ages, aren't you?"

She rubbed her hand over his shoulder. "I'm thinking that sometimes a person has to get around to something at his own pace."

"If you're going to travel then you could start by visiting

us in London," Ross said. "You can stay at the apartment. And I could show you round the office if you're interested."

Douglas scowled. "You think a fancy office is going to impress me?"

"I don't know. But we could find out."

"It's a good thing you didn't join me in the business. You're stubborn."

Ross smiled. "I wonder where I get that from?"

His father grunted. "We would have been fighting all the time."

"Probably. It would have been ugly because I would have been trying to prove myself."

"You've done that, Ross." Douglas squeezed his son's hand. "You've done that. And I should have said so before. But as your mother says, sometimes a person has to get round to something at their own pace. You've done a good job, and I'm proud."

Ross cleared his throat. "Thanks, Dad."

"Don't thank me." Douglas pulled his hand away. "You've got my genes, that's all it is. You're a grafter, like me. Lucy is the same."

Glenda sighed. "Douglas—"

"What? We've been talking frankly, haven't we? And I'm still talking frankly. I'm saying that Ross should be giving her the account, that's all. She's good. She knows what she's talking about. I like the way she thinks. And she has a strong work ethic," Douglas said. "She's a hard worker, a bit like you."

"Not really like Ross. She doesn't have much choice, does she?" Glenda poured a cup for herself. "Lucy has no family, no one to help her if she falls on hard times. No one to support her." It made her ache inside, thinking of it. Even when things were bumpy, there was nothing that mattered more to her than family. She couldn't imagine not having that.

Ross put his cup down. "That's emotional blackmail—" He stopped talking as the door opened and Alice walked in with Lucy.

Two streaks of color appeared on Ross's cheeks.

"Look at Lucy!" Glenda drew attention away from him. "She's walking fine without the crutches. Is that wise?"

Alice nodded. "As long as she doesn't overdo it, she should be able to do some weight on it now."

"That's great." Glenda waved them both into the kitchen, relieved that they hadn't arrived a few minutes earlier. "Come and sit down, Lucy. I was just about to start planning our Christmas Eve. I thought we could—" She broke off as Douglas's phone rang. "Well who on earth is that? Don't answer it. Oh, perhaps you'd better answer it, but if it's someone in the office, tell them it's Christmas and you're home with your family."

"It's that photographer who wanted a picture of the whole family." Douglas took the call and Glenda listened with relief as they made a new plan to profile the family in the summer instead.

"Good." She nodded approval as Douglas ended the call. "That's the last thing we need right now—" The phone rang again before she had even finished speaking and she looked at Douglas in despair. "Now what? If that's the office—"

"It's not the office. It's Fergus. Am I allowed to talk to him?" Douglas answered the call. "Fergus. Apologies for the delay in answering. Glenda is vetting my calls now, but you'll be relieved to hear you're on the auto approved list." He listened, then nodded. "Right. You're sure? Well that's good news. If I have to spend another day here trapped with my family without any respite, someone is going to die." He ended the call and glanced at them. "That was Fergus."

"We know that, Dad. And?" Alice looked at him expectantly. "What did he want?"

"He was calling to tell me that the lane has been cleared, as has the bridge. Access to Miller Lodge is restored and we are once again connected to civilization, such as it is in these rural parts." He gave his son a look. "People can come and go at will, which means that all those desperate to escape from the bosom of the family may do so now." He stood up. "That includes me. I still have a couple of Christmas gifts to pick up from the village, and if anyone wants to come with me there's room in the car."

His words were greeted by silence, as everyone around the table calculated what that meant to them.

Lucy was the first to speak. "Well that's great news. I'll be able to get home in time for Christmas." Her tone was so bright and cheerful that for a moment Glenda believed she actually did think it was great news. "I'll check the train times right now." She left the room as quickly as she could given the constraints of her injury.

Glenda glanced at Ross, but his expression revealed nothing.

Alice was pale. "I'll go and talk to Nico. See what he wants to do."

"Well if the two of you are planning a trip to the village," Douglas said, "let me know in the next five minutes."

He didn't know about Alice and Nico, because Glenda hadn't told him.

She hadn't trusted him not to be protective of his daughter, and Alice didn't need them interfering.

She'd held her daughter's secrets, but looking at her now she saw nothing but misery in her eyes. Alice had been hoping to fix things with Nico, and now it seemed that chance might be lost.

Glenda ached for her. Before having children she hadn't understood that seeing your child in pain was so much worse than being in pain yourself. She wanted to hug Alice and make everything better, but of course that wasn't an option.

Alice had to fix this herself.

Douglas picked up his mug and put it on top of the dishwasher. Then he looked at Glenda and changed his mind and put it inside. "You see how evolved I am?"

Nanna Jean appeared in the doorway. "Where is Lucy going? She rushed past me and almost tripped over Hunter."

"She's going home," Douglas said. "The roads have been cleared. Judging from some of the expressions round this table, that may or may not be good news."

Alice walked quietly from the room and Nanna Jean planted herself in front of Douglas.

"We are not allowing Lucy to leave."

He sighed. "I don't like the idea any more than you, but what's the alternative? Kidnap? I know you like Lucy—*I* like Lucy—but she has her own life to lead. You have to respect a person's wishes. She wants to go home for Christmas. She said so."

"And then rushed out of the room as fast as her leg would allow." Nanna Jean glared at Ross. "Do something."

"Me? What am I supposed to do?"

"She's leaving because she feels as if she's intruding on the family. She needs to know we want her to stay. How you do that is up to you, but there's mistletoe over the door in the library so I suggest a direct approach. You could grab her and kiss her."

Ross raised an eyebrow. "That's assault, Nanna Jean."

"I just thought—oh, it doesn't matter. What do I know about anything." Nanna Jean sat down on the nearest chair, looking tired and defeated.

Ross was on his feet and next to his grandmother in an instant. "What's wrong?" He crouched down next to her and took her hand.

"I'm feeling my age, that's all."

"You mean twenty-one?"

This was one of those rare occasions when Nanna Jean didn't respond to teasing.

"I'm too old for all this." She clung to Ross's hand. "Life is precious. Opportunities shouldn't be wasted. Lucy is exactly the sort of woman you should be dating. Warm. Genuine. Generous. Loves dogs. Enjoys her food."

"I know your intentions are good," Ross said, "but I can handle my own love life, Nanna Jean."

"Well forgive me for thinking otherwise. It could be because I've seen no evidence to support that."

There was a gleam in his eyes. "I do date, you know."

"Then why haven't you brought any of these women home to meet your grandmother? I'll tell you why. It's because you date the wrong type of woman. Women who don't want to meet your family. Women who are more interested in your bank balance than you."

"Thanks." Ross's tone was dry. "It's good to know you have such faith in my judgment."

"If you're going to let Lucy walk out of that door without at least trying to stop her, then I will have no faith in your judgment."

Ross stood up. He looked tired, and Glenda wondered in that moment if he wasn't as relaxed about the whole situation as he pretended to be.

"Lucy was here because of a twist of fate," he said. "She didn't choose to be here. When she found out that the roads were open and the trains running, she immediately left the room to pack. She couldn't get out of here fast enough." He glanced toward the door, as if going over it in his head, checking his recollection of events.

"And why do you think that was? I give up." Nanna Jean shook her head. "While you're opening your presents and laughing with your family, Lucy will be all alone, missing her grandmother, but don't you worry about that."

Glenda might have smiled at the blatant manipulation, but Ross and Lucy weren't her only worry.

She was also worried about Alice. Had anyone else noticed that Alice had left the room? Lucy wasn't the only one who had a decision to make now that the road had been cleared.

Nico did, too.

And what would that decision be?

21

Alice

Alice pushed open the door of the Loch Room. Sun streamed through the window and she wondered how she could ever have felt reluctant to use this room.

Nico was sitting at the table by the window, tapping keys on his laptop, working on his research paper.

Sunlight slanted across his hair as he stared at the screen, absorbed by what he was doing. He was, without doubt, the most striking man she'd ever seen and she felt a flutter of pure nerves. She wondered how she could ever have hesitated or had doubts. But her doubts had been about her, of course, not him. Whether she could be what he wanted. What he needed.

If she could have turned the clock back she would have snatched that ring out of his hand and jammed it onto her finger before he'd had a chance to ask the question that went with it.

But there was no turning time back. All she could do was move forward.

As she closed the door, he glanced up.

"Alice—" He was distant, as he'd been for the past couple of days. When she'd tried to talk he'd simply said *I need space*, so she'd given him space, even though it had half killed her to do it.

But now decisions needed to be made. She was scared of having the conversation, scared to hear his response, but this time she was determined to push past that. Whatever happened, she was going to do this. And afterward their relationship would either be stronger, or broken.

"You've been working hard, I thought you might like a break. The sun is shining and we could walk to the loch. If you wanted to. There's something I want to show you. But before you decide whether to come with me or not, there's something you should know." She'd briefly contemplated not telling him until after their conversation, but that would have felt dishonest. Also cowardly. If he was going to leave, then he'd leave. "The bridge is open. The road has been cleared. If you want to leave, then you can. You could be back in London in time for Christmas." She hesitated. "You could probably even make it back to Italy to your own family if that's what you want."

There was a long silence.

He stared at her for a moment and then at the lake. "When did you find out?"

"A few moments ago. I came straight up here to tell you. I didn't want to keep that from you, in case you wanted to leave. In case that was what you wanted. I hope it isn't." The words spilled out of her. "I hope you choose to stay. There are things I'd really like to say."

He closed the lid of his laptop.

"What do you want to show me?" The wariness in his eyes was painful to acknowledge but she pushed past that, too.

"Will you come?" She held out her hand and he gave a brief frown, waited just long enough for her to experience a serious explosion of nerves, and then stood up.

They dressed in warm layers and then went down to the boot room. There was no sign of her family anywhere, and for once she was grateful for that.

The moment they stepped outside she knew this had been a good decision. The frozen air blew away the strands of tiredness that had wrapped themselves around her brain after several sleepless nights, and the blue sky brightened her mood.

Nico paused, waiting for her direction. "We're going to the village?"

She shook her head. "Not this time." Instead of taking the route across the fields, she turned right and forged a path down the side of the snow-laden forest toward the loch. The snow had enveloped everything and lay deep on the ground, pristine and untouched, the surface sparkling under the dazzle of bright sunshine.

Once she stumbled and he reached out and grabbed her, steadying her before she could land on her face.

"Thanks." She gave him a brief smile but forged onward, determined to reach a place where they could both concentrate on the conversation and not on their own personal safety.

Finally the ground leveled out and they were right by the water.

Here the forest hugged the shoreline, and the loch was dull and glassy, the edges frozen over, the waters shielded by a thick crust of ice.

Nico pressed his foot onto it. "Solid. Did you ever skate?"

"No. It's frozen at the edges but not in the middle. It's too deep. One of our dogs fell in one winter. Dad managed to rescue it." And now they'd reached the part that had been her destination all along.

A cluster of large rocks that had been her chosen place to sit and reflect for all the years she'd lived here.

"This is where I used to come." She clambered up, brushing away snow as she found familiar handholds, careful not to slip. In three movements she was at the top, and she settled on the highest rock. "This was my place."

"I can see why." He stood at the bottom, legs planted firmly apart. "The view is incredible."

"It's peaceful. When the house was crowded and everyone was talking at once, I could always think here. It was where I came to sort out my problems. My thoughts." She swept some of the snow from the rock next to her and patted it with her glove. "Will you join me?"

He climbed up to her, athletic, lithe, and sat next to her on the rock.

"So what are we doing here?"

"I wanted us to talk." She picked up a stone and threw it, watching as it bounced and slid across the ice. "And I wanted to do it in a place where we're not going to be disturbed at an awkward moment. I love my family, but when everyone is home there is not a lot of privacy. It makes things complicated. I'm sure you've noticed."

"Families are always complicated, sometimes frustrating, but always important." He followed her lead and threw a pebble onto the ice. It went farther than hers, skidding and spinning across the frozen surface and eventually disappearing into the water beyond.

They were surrounded by a magical winter silence, and the stark, snowy isolation somehow made it easier to talk.

Here, they were away from their lives. Detached. Separate. Nature the only witness to their conversation.

"The thing about families," she said, "is that they know us. The good stuff. The bad stuff. All our weaknesses. They know it all, even when we try and hide it. And if we're lucky, really lucky, they love us anyway." She felt her eyes water and told herself it was the cold. "With family, we don't have to try and be perfect. There wouldn't be any point because they know who we really are."

"Are you trying to tell me you're not perfect, Alice?"

She tried to smile. "You already know that."

He adjusted his gloves. "So what do you want to talk about?"

"You said that if I had things on my mind, I should be open about it. I should share my thoughts with you. That's what I'm doing."

He turned his head to look at her, waiting.

She wrapped her arms around herself. It was bitterly cold. Too cold to be sitting, but she wanted all her attention to be on the conversation, not on staying upright.

"You're upset that I didn't share my thoughts with you. But the reason I didn't do that wasn't because I always have to figure things out by myself—it was because I was scared."

"Scared of seeming less than perfect?"

"No." She frowned. Did he really think that? "Scared of losing you. The problem with being open and honest is that there is nowhere to hide. It's all out there, visible. And I wasn't confident that you'd like the full undiluted version of me."

"You think I'm in love with half of you?"

He was talking in the present tense.

His words sent a dart of hope through her body. Did that mean they still had a future? That she hadn't blown everything?

"When you proposed, you took me by surprise. We'd never talked about what each of us wanted in the future. We'd never planned. We just lived day to day, enjoying our time together. We didn't really talk about tomorrow or the next day."

"Today is what we have, Alice. You know that. I know that. Today is what's important because it is real. We see every day that life can change in an instant, and without warning."

"I know." It was something she thought about often. It was impossible not to, confronted as she was by the evidence of that on a daily basis.

"So many people don't understand that. They believe they're in control. That if they do a certain thing, they'll be fine. We know that isn't true." He stared across the icy surface of the loch. "And I'm not sure if knowing that is a curse or a gift, but generally I prefer to think of it as a gift. It forces you to focus on the moment you're living now."

"That's true." She didn't know where this was going, but she understood what he was saying.

"You can worry about the future, you can talk about the future and plan, but no one knows what the future will bring. Plans can be derailed. Life is often cruel, and things happen that are outside our control. It is always humbling and a little inspiring to see what people can survive. How they can adapt in the face of the most challenging circumstances."

"Yes." She thought of what she saw almost daily in her work. The times she'd witnessed brutal change in a person's life. "I haven't heard you talk this way before."

He shrugged. "Usually I try and block it out and just do my job. As you do."

"We still care though."

"Of course." He leaned down and knocked snow from his boots. "But my way of caring is to do my best to fix whatever has gone wrong for the person. Even though that isn't always possible. I want to know there was nothing more I could do. Nothing anyone could have done. That's how I handle it. I do my best in the moment. And when we're together, I try and enjoy *that* moment. We can worry about the future, and we can plan, but the only thing we can ever really be sure of is now. The rest is just hope, dreams and chance. I always, always want to make the most of now."

She thought about that. "But when you proposed, you were thinking of the future."

"Maybe, indirectly, but mostly I was thinking that being with you makes my day—my life—better. You're the person I want to spend time with today, and tomorrow I will feel the same way. I suppose that what I was asking for was a lifetime of todays, however that might look. And I was assuming we'd figure that out together, as we went along."

She nodded, too emotional to speak.

No one had ever said anything like that to her before. It took a moment to let the words settle. To let her heart settle.

And then she looked at him. "And do you still feel that way?"

He reached across and took her hand, his glove settling over hers. "Do you have to ask?"

Relief flooded through her and only now did she realize how tense she'd been, how afraid she'd been that his answer might not have been what she wanted to hear.

"I thought I'd ruined everything. You were so upset. Angry. And you didn't raise it again. You said you needed space."

"I did need space." He increased the pressure on her hand. "Although I confess I didn't intend you to sleep in the spare room."

"It's not the spare room, it's my old room. We're staying in the love nest that my mother created for us." And now she saw the funny side. "It's a pretty room, isn't it?"

"Gorgeous."

He leaned toward her and she moved closer, narrowing the gap between them until they were pressed together, perched on the rock with the cold oozing through their clothes. She lifted her face to his as he lowered his head, and she felt his mouth on hers. His lips were ice-cold, but somehow his kiss was warm, and she felt a thrill of excitement mingle with the relief.

Yes, sometimes life went wrong, but sometimes it went right. Sometimes life was perfect, and this was one of those moments. And she held on to it, lingering on the special moment, until eventually she eased away just enough to speak.

"About that ring—"

"Which ring? I don't remember a ring." His eyes were alight with laughter. "Oh, you mean *that* ring. The one you gave back to me. What about it?"

"Do you still have it?"

"You think I threw it away?"

"I thought you might be saving it for another woman."

"No, but why are you so interested?" He zipped her coat a little higher to keep her warmer, the gesture both caring and intimate.

"I thought, maybe, that if you still had it, you might want to give it to me again."

He paused, his hands still locked on her coat. And then he released her and pulled off his glove.

"It's funny you should say that, because something has been digging into my ribs this whole time and I was wondering what it was. But now you've reminded me." He pulled out the box and opened it. "Is this what you were talking about?"

The diamond winked in the sunlight, its sparkle eclipsing even that of the pristine snow that surrounded them.

She tugged off her glove, too, and held out her hand. "My answer is yes."

He paused, eyebrow raised, the ring still nestled in its bed of midnight velvet. "I haven't asked the question yet."

"You already asked it. I didn't give you an answer. I'm giving it to you now."

"You don't want me on one knee?"

She eyed the slope of the rocks, and the ice and snow jammed in its uneven craggy surface. "You already did that once. I think I prefer it as we are, side by side." She thrust her hand toward him and he smiled and slid the ring onto her finger.

"Alice Miller," he said, his voice husky, "I don't know what's in our future, but whatever it is I want to share that future with you. I want to spend all my todays with you."

"I want that, too. And you probably already know that once I commit to something, I never give up on it. It's my worst and best trait." She kissed him, aware of the ring on her finger, heavy and symbolic.

She'd never felt so happy. She didn't know what lay in the future, no one ever did, but they had now, and they were making the most of it.

It was a while, quite some while, before she became aware that she was shivering.

He pulled away and rubbed her arms with his hands. "We should go back. You need to warm up."

"Yes." She waited while he slid down from the rock and then she did the same.

He took a last look at their snowy perch. "I'm glad you brought me here."

"Me, too."

He took her hand and together they trudged back through the snow, now dented with their footprints. "You said that the bridge is open. So does that mean Lucy is leaving?"

Lucy.

"I hope not." She thought back to that moment in the kitchen. She'd been too focused on herself to really notice anyone else. Lucy had said something about booking a train, and Ross—Ross had said nothing.

Why not?

Alice stopped walking. She'd been in the room when Ross had shielded Lucy. She'd noticed, even if others hadn't, that her brother had been unusually protective.

She was pretty sure he was interested. More than interested. So why hadn't he said anything?

She grinned. Because Ross wasn't used to feeling this way. He didn't know what to do. Her independent, confident, sure-of-himself big brother was feeling helpless.

If she'd had time, she might have enjoyed the moment a little longer, but she didn't have time. She just hoped she wasn't too late.

Nico was watching her, patient. "Is everything all right?"

"No, but I'm hoping it will be. There's something I need to do, if it's all right with you." She pulled out her phone and sent Clemmie and Ross a message.

Sibling summit.

She paused while she waited for them to reply. Clemmie was first.

Where shall we meet?

Alice thought about it and messaged back.

Library.

Ross's response was more flippant.

You're starting a sibling Book Group?

She ignored that. She'd picked the library because it was the room with a key, and she was going to have this conversation with her brother even if it meant locking him in.

Nico waited for her to put her phone back. "What are you doing?"

"Interfering with my brother's life." She zipped up her pocket.

"Is that a good idea?"

"I don't know. But this is what families do, isn't it? They help each other. And that's what I'm doing."

Nico gave a half smile. "Let's hope Ross sees it that way."

"He'll either thank me, or he'll never speak to me again." She put her arms round him and they kissed, gently at first and then with increasing passion. It was a kiss that brimmed with promise and she lost herself in the pleasure, lingering in the moment, slightly giddy at the thought of sharing her life with this man, before eventually pulling away. "After Clemmie and I have done this one little thing, you and I are going to celebrate."

He smoothed her hair away from her face. "Does that mean you're going to tell your parents?"

"Yes. And Nanna Jean." She grinned at the thought of it. "Brace yourself."

22

Lucy

Lucy pushed the last of her clothes into her bag and sat down on the bed.

Hunter had decided to keep her company and he sat next to her case, tongue lolling, apparently not quite understanding why she would want to leave.

She stroked his soft fur, wishing there was room for him in her overnight bag.

The truth was, she didn't want to leave.

She'd fallen in love with this magical place. With the Millers. They'd taken her in and welcomed her. They'd made her feel like part of their family.

But she wasn't part of their family.

No matter how much she loved it here, this wasn't her home, and this wasn't her Christmas. For a few astonishingly happy days she'd borrowed a Christmas that didn't belong to her, and now she had to give it back.

The thought of it made her wobble, but she set her jaw.

And she was going to be fine, of course she was. Christmas would be hard, but she'd get through it.

And who knew? Ross had seemed quite receptive to her ideas, so maybe he'd contact her, or Arnie, in the New Year and invite them to pitch. Her spirits lifted for a moment, buoyed up by the prospect of meeting Ross again in the future. Maybe this wasn't the end.

And then it occurred to her that working with him, if that happened, would be bittersweet because at some point over the past few days, her dream had changed. She'd arrived here desperately wanting the approval of Ross, the businessman.

And she could tell herself that it was still what she wanted, but she would have been lying to herself.

When she'd done her research on Ross, nothing had prepared her for the fact that she might actually like him. A lot. Not because he was smart, although he clearly was, but for so many other reasons. The kindness he'd shown to her, the way he teased his grandmother, looked out for his sisters, shoveled snow. The fact that he'd read her proposal and listened, despite the fact she'd forced him into a corner. The way he'd shielded her from scrutiny in that excruciating moment when she'd lost control. The way he'd encouraged her to open up and talk.

There were other things, of course. Things she wasn't allowing herself to think about, like the way it felt when he looked at her, when he smiled at her.

But she wasn't going to think about it again, because tomorrow was Christmas Eve and she'd already trespassed for long enough.

She'd done what she'd come here to do.

She stood up and finished packing her bag. She hadn't

forgotten a single item and yet she felt as if she was leaving a chunk of herself here at the lodge with the Miller family.

She imagined what the next few days would be like for them. Laughter. Games by the Christmas tree. Meals where they talked across each other and argued. It would be a noisy, chaotic nightmare and she wanted to be part of it more than she'd ever wanted to be part of anything in her life before.

Angry with herself, she leaned down and zipped up her case.

She was going to be fine. She'd say her goodbyes with a cheerful smile because they were kind people and she didn't want them feeling sorry for her. She wanted them to enjoy their Christmas, and their time together because spending time with family, she knew, was the most precious gift of all.

And she'd get back to her life and live it fully. No more hiding. No more pretending to be fine when she wasn't. She'd make it through Christmas, and next year if someone invited her as a guest then she was going to accept. If she lost her job, then she would get another one and although that wasn't her choice, she'd survive it.

Having given herself a pep talk, she checked her reflection in the mirror and was about to pick up her bag when there was a knock on the door.

Ross?

Hope soared, and she tugged open the door.

Not Ross, but Alice, who seemed flushed and happy for perhaps the first time since Lucy had met her.

"I thought you might need help. Unless you were planning on negotiating the stairs with your overnight bag. You don't need to use the crutches unless your ankle starts hurting, but it's probably not a great idea to start swinging heavy weights."

"Good thinking." Lucy pulled herself together. What had she been expecting? That Ross would turn up here and stop her leaving? It was definitely time she left. She was becoming delusional. "Another accident is the last thing any of us need right now. And this is great because it gives me a chance to thank you for everything. You've been so kind. And reassuring. I wish all doctors were like you."

"Well, thank you. And you're welcome." Alice reached for her bag and Lucy saw something sparkle on her finger.

"Alice?" She reached out and caught Alice's hand. The diamond solitaire gleamed in the bright sunlight and she stared at it, stunned. "Oh, Alice…"

"Yes. I'm going to marry Nico." Alice studied her hand as if she couldn't quite believe her luck. "I thought I'd blown it, but it turned out I hadn't."

"You must be thrilled. Your family must be thrilled."

"I haven't told them yet. Partly because I'm not sure I can tell them without getting all emotional, and partly because everyone is doing their own thing right now. I thought I'd break the news later, with champagne, although obviously Clemmie won't be drinking."

She could imagine the scenes. The joy. The excitement. The whole family would be pulsing with it, and she felt a pang of regret that she wouldn't be part of it but immediately squashed the feeling. It would be presumptuous of her to imagine that she could play a part in a celebration that didn't belong to her.

On impulse she hugged Alice.

"Congratulations. And what perfect timing."

"I know. Christmas is finally coming together." Alice peeled away from her and picked up her bag. "Is this it?"

"That's it. Fortunately. I should be able to manage one bag."

Alice carried it to the door and Lucy took a last look at the room that had been her home for the past few days.

At the bottom of the stairs she paused. She took a long last look at the Christmas tree and wondered if it would seem strange if she took a photo.

"I need to go and talk to Nico." Alice gave her another hug. "Ross will help you with your bag and things. Ross?"

Ross appeared from the library and Lucy was wondering what was going on when Nanna Jean appeared, closely followed by Glenda and then Clemmie.

Suddenly the hall was filled with people.

Alice glared at her sister in frustration. "Clem!"

"What was I supposed to do?" Clemmie gave her a look of desperate apology. "I did everything I could to distract them and keep them away, but privacy and this family don't go together. They're nosy and interfering."

"We prefer the term *caring*." Nanna Jean sniffed. "And if you were planning on putting Lucy in that cab without giving us the chance to say a proper goodbye then—"

"That wasn't what we were doing. We should give Ross some space to talk to Lucy." Alice tried to corral them back into the living room but it was like herding cats.

Nanna Jean waved her away. "If Ross has got something to say then I'd like to listen. To make sure that he's saying what he should be saying."

Lucy was bemused. She had no idea what was going on, or why Clemmie and Alice would try and stop Nanna Jean and Glenda from saying goodbye. And what Ross could possibly have to say to her. Presumably this was about work, but that conversation could easily wait until the New Year.

"I think I'm capable of saying what I'd like to say without additional family support." With a skill that clearly came from long experience, Ross gently urged his mother and grandmother back into the living room. He said something that

Lucy didn't catch, but whatever it was seemed to be enough to convince them to give him the privacy he requested.

Clemmie and Alice followed, and the door clicked shut behind them.

Lucy was left alone in the hall with Ross, trying to figure out what was going on.

In the time she'd been packing, he'd showered and shaved and now he was wearing black jeans, with a black shirt. He looked impossibly handsome and more than a little dangerous.

Or maybe he was just dangerous to her because he was making her want things she couldn't have.

"Before you leave, there are a few things I wanted to say." He was calm and confident and very much in business mode.

Which was good, she thought, because that enabled her to be the same. In a way it made things easier.

"There are things I want to say, too." She lifted her chin. "I shouldn't have said what I said. I shouldn't have interfered in your relationship with your father."

"I'm glad you did. And I owe you an apology for the way I handled that."

"No, you don't. It's a very sensitive issue and probably none of my business."

"I'm pleased you made it your business. You told me the truth and although it was difficult to hear, I needed to hear it. It…" He paused. "We talked. My father and I."

"I'm glad."

She really was. Also a little relieved. But if he didn't want to talk to her about that, then what was on his mind?

"If you have questions about the proposal, then—"

"You answered my questions."

"Right. In that case, do you think—" Normally she was articulate in business situations but right now her tongue was tying itself in knots. Something about the way he was look-

ing at her made it hard to concentrate. "If you'd consider giving us the opportunity to pitch in the New Year, then that
would be the best Christmas gift." She regretted the words
immediately. "Forget I said that."

"Why?"

"I shouldn't have mentioned Christmas gifts. I blurred the
lines between the professional and the personal, and that's
something I don't ever do. Let me start again. We'd be thrilled
if you'd give us an opportunity to pitch because we really believe we have a lot to offer your business."

"I believe that, too." He looked at her steadily. "Which
is why I'm not going to invite you to pitch. I'm giving you
the business."

It took a moment for his words to sink in, perhaps because
she hadn't expected to hear them.

"You're giving us the business?" She felt a flash of relief
and happiness. Arnie would be ecstatic. So would her colleagues. And as for her—well, she'd get to see Ross occasionally and the mere thought of that was enough to make her
smile. "You have no idea how pleased I am to hear that. You
won't regret it. Thank you."

"There is a condition," he said, "and you should probably
hear it before you thank me."

A condition? She didn't care. Whatever it was, they'd figure it out.

"Tell me."

"I don't want you heading up the account. In fact, I don't
want you working on the account at all."

The joy oozed out of her. Visions of seeing Ross again
faded. "You—don't?"

"No."

"Right." She felt as if he'd kicked her, but she absorbed
the blow and carried on. "Well Ted will probably manage

the account day to day, and he's excellent. He can arrange a meeting with you in January, along with Arnie. The two of them can address any other concerns you might have."

"Aren't you going to ask me why I don't want you on the account?"

She'd never felt more uncomfortable. "I assume it's because I'm not exactly a sporty person. You probably think—"

"That's not why. It's because, like you, I try never to blur the lines between the professional and the personal." He gave her a moment for the words to sink in. "Lucy?"

Her mind was racing. Her heart was racing. Was he saying what she thought he was saying? She *thought* she knew what he meant, but if she'd misunderstood it would be hideous. She was dizzy with hope and afraid to ask for clarification in case that delicious feeling vanished.

"Personal?" Somehow she managed to croak out the word.

"Yes, personal." The way he was looking at her made her light-headed.

"Ross?"

"I know you love Tower Bridge." He closed the distance between them. "And I have an incredible view of Tower Bridge from my apartment. I thought you might like to see it."

He was standing so close to her that she felt unbalanced. She put her hands on his chest to steady herself.

"I—I would. I'd love to see it."

"Good." His arms closed around her, holding her hard against him. "Then that's a date."

"A date?" She could feel the steady thud of his heart beneath her fingers. "I thought you were a workaholic, Ross Miller? Between that and running marathons, surely you don't have time for dating?"

"I'm going to make time. I'm going to be making time for

a lot of things. Unless, of course, you'd rather keep it professional and work on the Miller Active account." His voice was teasing and his mouth hovered dangerously close to hers. "Your choice, Lucy."

Choice? There was no choice to be made.

Still, she couldn't resist teasing him back.

"It's a difficult decision. For both of us. I am, after all, the face of modern marketing."

"You are, indeed. *Actual* Lucy." He said her name softly and brushed his fingers lightly across her cheek.

"Ted will be the perfect account handler."

"Good. Then that's sorted."

Was it? Really?

She tightened her grip on his shirt. "Are you sure about this? I arrived uninvited on your doorstep. I interrupted your Christmas."

"Lucky for me that you did. Lucky for both of us that you're so loyal to Arnie and so committed to your job." He lowered his head until he was almost close enough for her to taste his smile and then he was kissing her, his mouth slanting over hers, gentle and insistent, the intimate stroke of his tongue so sweetly seductive, so infinitely sexy, that the strength in her legs melted away.

She wrapped her arms round his neck and pressed closer, unsure that she could stay standing if he wasn't holding her. It was just a kiss, but it felt like so much more, and she kissed him back, consumed by the slow tide of excitement that rose inside her.

She had no idea how long the kiss would have lasted had they not heard the sound of a door opening behind them, whispering voices and then a cleared throat.

Both of them froze.

Ross muttered something that would no doubt have earned

him a serious scolding by his grandmother had she been close enough to hear it.

Mortified, Lucy tried to pull away but he kept his arms round her, holding her steady while their breathing slowed.

"I'm sorry," he murmured the words against her hair. "From the bottom of my heart, I apologize."

Lucy giggled, amused and embarrassed by equal degrees. "I love your family."

"You do? You're a strange girl, Actual Lucy." He placed a lingering kiss on her mouth and then gave a resigned sigh and turned his head.

Nanna Jean, Glenda, Alice and Clemmie stood in the doorway. Douglas was standing behind them. They were all grinning.

Ross gave Clemmie an incinerating glare. "You had one job—"

"To keep Nanna Jean behind this door, I know, but you know what she's like!" Clemmie had the widest grin of all. "She guessed what was going on and short of pressing her to the floor with my body weight, I didn't know what else to do. And, anyway, seeing you completely gone over a woman— a real woman I mean, not a made-up one—was something I wanted to witness. Otherwise I might not have believed it. For the first time in your life, Ross Miller, you're not an island."

"What's that?" Nanna Jean glanced at Glenda. "Has Ross bought an island? Why does he need an island?"

"He doesn't." Glenda was smiling at her son. "I think what he needs now is privacy."

Ross drew in a breath. "That would be appreciated."

"Privacy is overrated. We're all family here. We don't have secrets. Whatever you're feeling let it out, that's what I always say." Nanna Jean waved a hand in their direction. "Kiss her again, Ross. Pretend we're not here."

Lucy gave a gulp of laughter and buried her burning face in the front of his shirt.

"You see what I have to deal with? Is it any wonder my girlfriends are fictitious?" He kept a protective arm around her. "No real person could be expected to tolerate this level of scrutiny."

"Have you asked her about Christmas?" Nanna Jean was almost vibrating with impatience and Ross drew a long slow breath.

"Not yet. I was focusing on—other things."

"Well do it now! And hurry up."

Ross shared a look with Lucy. "I was getting there in my own time. I don't see a reason to rush."

"Try being eighty-six," Nanna Jean said. "Then you'll see a reason to rush. While you're dawdling there, I'm not getting any younger. And Lucy doesn't want you to take it slowly. She wants you to sweep her off her feet. Your problem is that you don't know anything about women."

"That's me," Ross said, his gaze lingering on Lucy's mouth. "Clueless."

She thought about the way he'd kissed her, the almost unbearable intimacy, the hard pressure of his body and the promise of more to come. "Clueless," she whispered. "Most definitely. But maybe you'll get better with practice."

"It's possible. So, you'll stick around so that I can try and get it right next time?"

She hadn't known it was possible to feel this happy. "I think I can manage that."

"Good. In which case…" he paused and gave Nanna Jean a look "…my family would like to invite you to spend Christmas with us. An invitation you are under no obligation to accept. In fact I'm half expecting you not to, because I can't imagine who would voluntarily spend Christmas with my family."

Christmas. Here?

Ross was watching her. "Lucy?"

"That's it, Ross? That's all you're saying? And he calls himself a salesman." Nanna Jean gave a tut of despair. "He couldn't sell ice to a penguin. It's lucky he has us to help. Here, Lucy. We have a gift for you." She walked over to them and pushed the soft parcel into Lucy's hands.

Lucy stared at it, confused. "Do I open it now?"

"Yes. Rip that paper right off."

She did as she was told and found herself holding a stocking. It was beautifully made, hand-knitted with meticulous care using a red wool shot through with silver. And there, embroidered at the top in bold letters, was her name. Lucy.

"Oh." She felt her eyes fill. "Oh. A stocking. For me."

"Well of course it's for you. It has your name on it. How else is Santa going to know where to leave your presents? He's not going to dump them on the floor, is he?" Nanna Jean gave Lucy the warmest, tightest hug anyone had given her in a long time. "Now go and unpack that bag and then come back down and have something to eat. You're about to be part of a Miller family Christmas and that requires significant energy. Also thanks to Clemmie's unsteady hand, we have about a million strange-looking gingerbread Christmas trees to eat, which couldn't possibly be served to anyone outside the family."

Ross bent and retrieved the wrapping paper Lucy had dropped. "She hasn't said she wants to stay yet."

Nanna Jean sighed. "Well of course she wants to stay. Tell him, Lucy."

She'd been dreading Christmas, but now that dread had

been washed away, replaced by something else. Something lighter and warmer.

The ache of grief was still there, of course, but it felt cushioned, less acute. She'd let people in. She'd let the Millers in. And only now did she truly understand the pressure she'd put on herself to present herself as "fine," when she wasn't fine at all. Only now was she able to acknowledge how exhausting it had been to hide her true feelings. When the pressure of holding in her emotions had proved too great and she'd lost control, she'd been mortified. But now she was grateful it had happened. Their acceptance and understanding, their reassurance that her feelings were normal, had relieved some of the terrible tension she'd been feeling. Sharing her struggle and sense of loss had made her feel less alone. It felt as if she'd made a step forward, and even if she stumbled again it didn't matter. What had Nanna Jean said? *It's okay to not be okay.* And the Miller family didn't expect her to be anything but who she was.

She dug her fingers into the soft wool of the stocking—*her own stocking*—and her body was flooded with an emotion she hadn't thought she'd feel again.

She'd thought that the magic of Christmas had gone forever, but maybe she'd been wrong about that. Maybe here, surrounded by the sparkle and warmth that was the Miller family, she might rediscover it. She could step into the future and take all those precious memories from the past with her.

"I want to stay." Somehow she managed to speak. "I can't think of anything I'd like more. Thank you."

"Great. You've got your answer." Ross waved his hand toward the door. "And now if you could all leave us so I can have five minutes alone with Lucy, I'd appreciate it."

This time they melted away with the minimum of protests

and she heard the click of a door closing before Ross drew her into his arms again.

"Where were we?"

Still clutching the stocking in her hand, Lucy slid her arms round his neck. "I think," she said, "that you wanted to practice kissing me."

23

Clemmie

Iona pressed handfuls of snow onto the snowman's body. The little girl's cheeks were pink, her hair escaping from under a cheery red-and-pink hat that had undoubtedly been knitted by her grandmother. There was no plait today, just a riot of blond curls. "Clemmie! We need more snow!"

"I think there might have been a 'please' missing from that sentence." Fergus's tone was mild, and Iona flashed him a smile.

"Please, please, please. He's not fat enough."

Clemmie obliged with more snow. Scooping it up from the deep drifts at the side of the village green and piling it next to Iona, who applied herself to the task with dedication and purpose.

"She's bossy," Fergus said. "In case you hadn't noticed."

"I'd noticed. I sense a future in management."

He laughed. "I'm glad you're here. I almost didn't message you. I thought you'd probably be too busy."

"It certainly is chaotic in our house at the moment. Alice and Nico announced that they're getting married, and I have a suspicion that my brother might actually be in love for the first time in his life."

He raised his eyebrows. "Really? That's great."

"It is. Of course, being my brother, he would strongly deny it, but I am pretty sure Lucy is about to become a permanent fixture in our lives." And she was pleased for him and pleased for Alice. But it had, inevitably, made her think about her own feelings for Fergus. Since her conversation with Nanna Jean, she'd thought about nothing else. And seeing both Ross and Alice going after what they wanted, had made her want to do the same. It was a risk, yes, but maybe the risk of not trying was greater. "I'm glad you messaged. You gave me a reason to escape. I can't think of a better thing to do on Christmas Eve than build a snowman. Also—I wanted to talk to you." She didn't confess to all the messages she'd typed to him and then deleted in the last twenty-four hours.

Hi Fergus, fancy a chat?

Hi Fergus, could we get together? There's something I need to tell you.

Hi Fergus. I love you. Clem.

When he'd messaged her she'd had a horrible moment where she thought maybe she'd made a mistake and actually sent one of those messages.

"What did you want to talk to me about?"

At that moment Iona reached a little too high and slipped on the icy surface.

Fergus responded instantly but Hunter got there first, nudging Iona, checking on her, allowing himself to be used as a frame so that she could scramble back to her feet.

The little girl put her arms round the dog and kissed him. "Daddy, can we have a dog?"

"Maybe. We'll think about it. Dogs need love and attention. All the time."

"I'd love him every minute of every day with my whole heart."

Hunter wagged his tail, smug.

Clemmie swallowed. "I swear that dog understands every word." She was relieved he couldn't speak, because she'd told Hunter everything.

"He's a good dog." Fergus gave Hunter's head a rub and then turned back to the snowman. "Right. It's getting cold out here. Let's finish this."

"There's Grandma and Grandpa!" Abandoning the snowman, Iona raced toward Fergus's parents, who were walking toward them.

Fergus's father scooped her up and carried her back to them. The affection between the two of them was plain to see.

"That is an excellent snowman." Rosa Maclennon admired her granddaughter's handiwork and then hugged Clemmie. "It's wonderful to have you home, dear."

"We're going to have a dog exactly like Hunter." Iona had her arms wrapped around her grandfather's neck.

Rosa glanced at her son, startled. "You are?"

"I said I'd think about it, but Iona took that to mean yes."

Rosa shook her head, but she was smiling. "That girl has you wound around her finger. I suppose if you had a dog, we could help out."

Fergus rubbed his hand across his jaw and thought about it. "Looks as if we might be getting a dog, then."

Iona whooped and Rosa glanced between Clemmie and Fergus.

"You two look cold. I think you've spent long enough building snowmen. Why don't you go inside and warm up? Your father and I will take Iona for a few hours. We have something secret to do, don't we?" She winked at her granddaughter, who winked back.

"It's about your present, Daddy. But it's a secret."

"That sounds exciting."

Iona glanced between her grandmother and Clemmie. "Can Hunter come with us?"

Clem smiled. "Of course he can." She checked with Fergus's parents. "If that's okay with you?"

"It would be a treat." Rosa bent to make a fuss of Hunter. "We'll drop him back later."

Fergus kissed Iona on the cheek. "Be good." He gave his mother a hug and then watched as they trudged their way back through the snow in the direction of their house.

Clemmie rescued the scarf and hat from the snowman. She was alone with Fergus and she still hadn't worked out what to say. "It must be great having them right here in the village."

"It is, for all sorts of reasons. Not least because it gives me the time to work and get things done." He frowned and took the snow-encrusted scarf from her. "You're shivering. We should go back to the house."

They walked the short distance and with every step she felt more nervous.

By the time they'd reached his door she'd decided that she wasn't going to tell him how she felt. What was the point? She could blow up a perfect friendship. And just because Nanna Jean thought he had feelings for her, didn't mean it was true.

He pulled a key out of his pocket. "You were going to tell me something, but we kept being interrupted."

"It's nothing. I can't even remember now." She stepped through the door and immediately tripped over one of Iona's toys. She would have fallen had he not grabbed her.

"Sorry—" He held her firmly, steadying her.

And in that single moment, pressed up against him, she knew. It was going to be now. Right now. And she wasn't going to tell him how she felt, she was going to show him.

Before she could change her mind, she lifted herself on her toes and kissed him.

She felt his shock, the moment when he registered that dramatic shift in their relationship, and then he was kissing her back, his mouth urgent, desperate, hungry. His hands were in her hair, holding her head, his body pressed hard against hers.

Joy exploded alongside passion because this was Fergus, *Fergus*, and he was kissing her as if this was their last moment on earth.

Without lifting his mouth from hers, he kicked the front door shut and found the zip of her coat with his hands. He yanked at it, and then at his own. They both staggered and his shoulders hit the wall, knocking a painting off its hook.

It crashed to the floor but neither of them paid any attention.

He pushed at her jeans and she felt her skin turn hot under the pressure of his fingers.

Half-naked, they ended up on the floor, next to the toy that had tripped her and the painting that had fallen.

She banged her elbow on the floor and he dragged his mouth from hers.

"Are you okay? We should go upstairs—"

"No." She tugged him back to her, wrapped her legs around him, not wanting anything to stop this. She'd wanted him for so long. Waited for so long. She didn't want to wait a moment longer. And he obviously felt the same way because he didn't argue with her, just shifted his weight, shifted *her* until they were intimately connected, until all she could do was arch against him, and urge him *please, please*, and then he eased into her and there was nothing but heat and excruciating pleasure.

She'd imagined how it might feel so many times, but not even her wildest imaginings had come close to the reality, because this was Fergus, and he knew her and she knew him and this was a whole new level of intimacy. The world around her blurred and there was nothing but the two of them, the hardness of his body, the words he murmured against her hair, her mouth, and then the excitement ripped through her, driving her over the edge, taking him with her.

She lay there, stunned and drained. Gradually she became aware of the floor pressing into her back, the wash of cool air on her naked limbs. And Fergus, holding her, unwilling to release her.

She smiled up at the ceiling. There were some things, she thought, that were better than conversation.

Fergus dropped his head against his forearm, trying to re-cover his breath.

Only when his breathing had slowed, did he speak.

"Are you still alive?" He kissed the corner of her mouth. "Say something."

Say something. What? She didn't know where to start.

"Hardwood floors might look good," she said, "but they're hell on the shoulders."

She felt his shoulders shake with laughter and then he was rolling onto his back, taking her with him.

He winced. "You're not wrong. Next time I'll opt for deep pile carpet. Or I could just put a mattress right here inside the door, in case this ever happens again."

"It's going to happen again." She lowered her mouth to his. "And again, and again, although maybe the hallway won't be the best place." She felt his hands slide into her hair and cup her face.

"You're not sorry?"

"Sorry? Why would I be sorry? I was the one who started it." She eased away slightly so that she could look at him properly. "Don't you dare say you regret it."

His eyes darkened. "Why would I say I regret it when I don't?"

His words filled her with a dizzying joy. "Good. The way I see it, your mother did tell you to warm me up. And now I'm warm." She watched, distracted by his smile, thinking that if she could spend the rest of her life waking up next to Fergus and his smile she'd never complain about anything again.

"That's true." He brushed her hair away from her face, his hand gentle. "So I have a question. Why haven't we done this before?"

"Because I didn't know you felt this way. I thought you wanted to be friends. I thought that was how you saw me."

"I thought the same thing about you. And I had reason. You moved to London."

"It was part of my Fergus Recovery Program."

He shifted so that he could look directly at her, his gaze incredulous. "You went to London to get away from me?"

"In a way, yes. It was just too hard being close to you, feeling the way I felt. And you didn't seem to be suffering. You dated Tina."

"I went on a few dates with her, that's all. For the record, Tina was no more interested in me than I was in her. She knew I was in love with you."

"She knew that? Why didn't I know that? Why didn't you mention that fact to me?"

"I was afraid of ruining our friendship. Of making things awkward. And then we lost Laura and I decided to take Iona—I was too busy handling that situation to even think about myself."

She swallowed. "And do you think it has ruined our friendship?"

He pondered, his fingers toying idly with her hair. "Not for me. How about you? Has anything changed?"

"Everything."

His fingers stilled. "Do you want to expand on that? On second thought, let's get off this hard floor and then you can tell me." He pulled her down to him and kissed her again and because both of them were desperate to make up for lost time, and desperate for each other, it was another half hour before they finally peeled themselves off the floor, tugged on their clothes and headed to the kitchen.

Fergus sat on one of the kitchen chairs and pulled her onto his lap. He seemed reluctant to let go of her, and she was more than happy with that because she didn't want to let go of him, either.

She leaned her head against his shoulder. "Did Tina really know you were in love with me."

"Yes."

"Do you think your parents know?"

"Yes, although they are far too tactful to say so."

She smiled to herself. "Nanna Jean knows, too. She was the one who encouraged me to be courageous and tell you how I feel."

He turned his head, his mouth a breath away from hers. "And how do you feel, Clem?"

"Happy." She couldn't stop smiling. If this was how it felt to go after what you wanted, she was going to keep doing it. She was going to keep telling the truth, starting right now.

"I love you, Fergus Maclennon. I love you with my whole heart and I am going to love you for the rest of our days, and the reason I know that is because I have tried my utmost to fall out of love with you and nothing I did worked."

"Thank goodness for that. I love you, too. I always have. And I'm going to love you for the rest of our days, too." His grip tightened. "There is one thing neither of us has mentioned."

"What's that?"

"I didn't use protection. First time in my adult life, by the way. It wasn't at the front of my mind."

It hadn't been at the front of her mind, either, but now it was. "If it happens, it happens. I can't think of anything I'd like more than to have your child." Maybe, she thought, if she got really lucky...

He kissed her again. "Will you marry me, Clem? I know it's quick, but it isn't really quick, is it?"

"No." Her eyes filled. "I've been in love with you forever. And yes, I'll marry you."

"Are you sure? I'm aware that I'm not exactly a straightforward proposition. I come with a child."

"Iona, and the way you are with her—that's just one of the many reasons I love you. Oh, Fergus!" She hugged him, her happiness spreading into every corner of her being. "We'll keep it a secret for now. It will give Iona time to get used to me being around. And I don't want to spoil Alice's celebrations."

"That is typically unselfish of you, and just one of the many reasons I love you." He stroked his hand down her back. "It will be difficult not telling people, but I agree it's the best plan. For now. We know, and that's the important thing."

"Come over tomorrow if you feel like it. Dad found our old toboggan. Iona might like it. Bring your parents."

"That sounds like a good idea. Do you want to stay tonight?"

It was impossibly tempting, but that would lead to questions neither of them wanted to answer yet. And there was an even bigger issue to consider. "Too soon for Iona," she said and he nodded.

"Probably true, although I feel obliged to point out that you are missing a sight very rarely seen. Me, dressed in a Santa suit."

"You're going to wear a Santa suit?"

"Of course. Just in case she wakes up and sees me."

Thinking about it made her smile. "It's so like you to protect the magic. Next year, if I get lucky, maybe I'll have an encounter with Santa myself."

"I'm sure that can be arranged. In the meantime, I hope he leaves lots of perfect gifts under your tree tomorrow." He pulled her toward him again and as they kissed she knew that there was nothing that Santa could bring her that would mean more than what she already had.

Fergus.

24

Glenda

G lenda put the finishing touches to the Christmas table. She'd twisted a garland along the length of the table and added candles and fresh greenery while Nanna Jean tied ribbon around the last of the napkins.

"There. We're ready for them all." She added the napkin to the final place setting and stood back to admire their handiwork. "It's a picture, Glenda. And the smells coming from the kitchen make me wish we were eating right now."

"Lunch is at two." Glenda checked her watch. "It's late, because I overslept."

And when had she last done that on Christmas Day? She'd woken in a panic and rushed downstairs, only to find that no one else was awake.

While Douglas had taken Hunter for a quick walk, Glenda had switched on the Christmas tree lights and lit a fire so that the room was welcoming.

By the time she'd headed to the kitchen to deal with the turkey, Nanna Jean was up and peeling potatoes.

Eventually the rest of the family had emerged, most of them bleary-eyed thanks to a late night celebrating Alice's news.

She'd thought, wondered, whether Lucy had spent the night in Ross's room, but she couldn't be sure and she had no intention of trying to find out.

After the traditional Miller Christmas breakfast gathering, they'd opened presents around the tree and then headed outside for a snowball fight while Glenda and Nanna Jean had finished their preparations for lunch.

"You'd think they were six years old again." Nanna Jean moved to the window to watch. "Alice's aim is good."

"Of course it is. Don't you remember the year she spent six hours a day throwing a ball so that she could perfect her technique?"

"Nico seems to be holding his own." Nanna Jean laughed as his perfectly aimed snowball exploded on Alice's shoulder. "I like him. If I'd been allowed to choose someone for her, then I would have chosen him, and not just because he has extraordinary eyelashes."

"He is handsome, that's true." But more than that, he understood Alice. He loved Alice. That was all that mattered to Glenda.

She watched now as her daughter tiptoed up behind her brother and pelted him with snow.

"Is it sensible for Lucy to be out there? If she slips she is going to break the other ankle."

"There was no stopping her and, anyway, look at Ross—" Nanna Jean nudged her "—he's hovering ready to catch her. He didn't even turn when Alice showered him in snow. I've never seen him like this."

"I haven't, either."

"They're going to see each other again."

"You don't know that."

"Yes, I do. I was listening at the door. Don't tell me off," Nanna Jean said, glancing at her. "I'm old. I have to take my pleasures where I can find them. And I was worried about Lucy. She's been stumbling through the last few years with no safety net. I'm glad she's here. Glad that we have managed to pull her into our family."

"Nanna Jean—"

"I know, I know, I'm leaping ahead but it's Christmas. I'm allowed to dream. And talking of dreams—there's Clemmie, with Fergus and Iona. She looks happy."

"She spent most of the day with them yesterday. She made reindeer cupcakes with Iona." Glenda stepped closer to the window, feeling a little guilty for watching. "Did you see the way Clemmie and Fergus just looked at each other? That smile they shared?"

"Yes."

"Do you think…" She hesitated. "I often wondered if there was something between those two, but nothing ever happened and Clemmie moved to the other side of the country so I assumed I was wrong."

"You weren't wrong. And I didn't wonder, I knew." Nanna Jean was smug and Glenda turned to her.

"You *knew*? Why didn't you say anything?"

"Because some relationships happen quickly—" Nanna Jean looked at Ross and Lucy, and then back at Clemmie "—and some take longer to develop. Look at Iona, putting her arms up to Clemmie to be lifted. She likes her."

"Well of course she does."

"And Iona had snow for Christmas. How magical is that?"

It was magical, but not as magical as seeing the smile on her daughter's face.

Clemmie and Fergus. After so many years. What would that mean for Clemmie's plans?

"Do you think—" But she didn't have time to finish her sentence because they all came tumbling in from the cold, bringing with them snow and freezing air, arguing, hanging up coats, hats, pulling off boots.

"I'm starving." Clemmie hugged her mother. "Can Fergus and Iona stay for lunch? We're going to eat lunch here, and then go to his parents' this evening, if that's okay."

"Of course! What a treat to have you." Glenda smiled at Iona. "Who would you like to sit next to at the table?"

Iona slid her hand into Clemmie's. "Clemmie. And Daddy."

"I've got this. Iona, come and help me, pet." Nanna Jean grabbed more cutlery and napkins and hurried through to the library to lay two extra places, Iona at her side.

The others followed, having simultaneous conversation.

"Your aim is terrible."

"My aim is perfect."

"Why Nico would want to marry you, I have no idea."

The conversation faded as they headed into the living room to play a game and warm up after their snowball fight.

Feeling content, Glenda tossed the parsnips in maple syrup and slid them into the oven.

You never knew how life was going to turn out, she thought. And you couldn't predict what would happen for your children. All you could do was offer support, and trust that they'd make the right choices. The right choices for them.

"Where is everyone?" Douglas appeared in the doorway, a parcel in his hands.

"Everyone is in the living room, apart from Nanna Jean." She straightened, her cheeks burning from the heat of the oven. "She is adding places to the table. Fergus and Iona are joining us for lunch."

"Good news." He accepted that without question and then closed the door behind him. "So you're all alone. Perfect." He crossed the room and handed her the parcel.

"I wrapped it myself, although Hunter helped. You can blame him for the crinkled paper."

She took it from him, intrigued. "You're giving me your gift now?"

"Yes. Because not every single thing that happens in this house has to be a whole family event. We deserve a quiet moment. Open it. Quickly. Before someone decides they need you for something."

She ripped off the paper and opened the box. "Oh—oh Douglas—"

"I wouldn't take you on a cruise," he said, "but how do you feel about Paris in the spring?"

"This spring?" She delved into the box. There was a guidebook, a map, a glossy brochure for a hotel and a novel set in Paris. She looked at him. "Are you telling me you're retiring?"

"No, but I am going to work on reducing my hours. And we're going to take holidays. Proper holidays. Starting with this one. I thought we could spend a few days in London first, visiting the children. I've been talking to Ross about it. He knows Paris. The hotel was his suggestion. And we're going to spend a few nights in London before we go, in his apartment."

He'd been talking to Ross. He was going to work on reducing his hours. Those two things made her almost as happy as the prospect of a trip to Paris.

She put the box down on the kitchen table. "Douglas Miller, are you seriously telling me that after all these years you're going to learn to delegate?"

"I am. Not that I can promise that I'll be any good at it." He kissed her. "And talking of delegating, tell me what I can do to help get this lunch on the table before we all die of hunger."

There was the usual last-minute flurry of activity in the kitchen, and a moment where Glenda thought it couldn't possibly come together on time, but everyone piled in and helped and soon they were all seated around the dining table, pulling crackers, reading terrible jokes and eating a delicious meal.

And they drank multiple toasts to each other, and also to Lucy's grandmother, and Glenda thought that all the work, the anxiety, the preparation was all worth it because this day brought the whole family together in one place and that was something to be treasured.

Through the windows she could see pale winter sky and snow-coated trees and she wondered if, despite the complications it had caused, the weather had helped make this Christmas special.

Would Lucy even have stayed if the snowfall hadn't been so heavy?

Would Nico have left when he and Alice had fallen out?

And when they all glanced expectantly in her direction she knew exactly what her toast should be.

"To family and to friends—" she smiled at Lucy as she said it "—and to being snowed in for Christmas."

They all raised their glasses one more time.

"Snowed in for Christmas!"

★ ★ ★ ★ ★

ACKNOWLEDGMENTS

Writing a Christmas book every year has become one of my own Christmas traditions and I'm lucky to be supported in this fun and festive endeavor by many excellent people, not least my family who are patient and accepting of this strange job of mine and never complain when I put the Christmas decorations up early to create the right mood.

My thanks to my publishers, in particular the teams at HQ in the UK and HQN Books in the US. Your continued support and belief in my stories means so much to me. It has been a challenging time for publishing, but still you have managed to get my books into the hands of readers and for that I am deeply grateful (also impressed!).

I'm hugely grateful to my wonderful editor, Flo Nicoll, who patiently reads multiple drafts and provides endless insight and encouragement. We've been on quite a journey together over the last ten years, and I wouldn't have wanted to make that journey with anyone else. We've shared so many laughs (and excellent pizza) and I treasure the memories of so many fun times.

My agent, Susan Ginsburg, is nothing short of brilliant. I'm endlessly grateful for all her support, wisdom and humor, and also the support of the excellent Catherine Bradshaw and the rest of the team at Writers House.

Big thanks to my readers, many of whom have been with me from the beginning. Thank you for choosing to read my books, and for all the messages, gorgeous book photos and emails you send. Hearing from readers across the world is a joy and I value that connection. And to all the wonderful book bloggers who review, share recommendations with friends and spread the word—thank you. The book community is truly special and I'm grateful to be part of it.